THE DARLINGTON SERIES

IF THIS IS

Love

NAOMI FINLEY

Cover designer: Victoria Cooper Art
Website: www.facebook.com/VictoriaCooperArt

Editor: Scripta Word Services
Website: scripta-word-services.com

Other Books

Prologue

Provincia of Barcelona, 1850

N IGHTFALL HAD SETTLED OVER THE COUNTRYSIDE WHEN HER mistress's labor pains commenced. The chambermaid hastened to fetch the midwife, then snuck the woman into the villa through the back entrance, using the night's shadows to her advantage. A quiet had descended over the estate, with the servants retired to their quarters for the evening. The chambermaid feared the clacking of their shoes against the travertine floor as they raced toward the back staircase would surely give them away, but the wrath of her mistress compelled her onward.

Light poured from the kitchen at the far end of the corridor, casting shadows that stretched across the floor. Scullery maids left tidying the kitchen chattered, and the maid gripped the midwife's arm and steered her around the corner to the bottom of the steep, spiraling staircase. She halted so they could catch their breath and coughed at the potent scent of herbs and spices wafting from the woman.

"We'll take the servant stairs," she whispered, peering into the darkness above. "Can you make it?" She eyed the weathered face of the woman draped in a tattered, gray woolen cloak.

The midwife's brow furrowed. "What do they call you?"

"Marta."

"Don't let my appearance of deteriorating health fool you. I am stronger than one may think." She grasped the rail and mounted the stairs, her bones crackling their protest.

When they reached the upper floor, Marta signaled for the woman to wait with a tug on her elbow. Stepping past her, she peered into the dimly lit corridor. Discovering it devoid of prying eyes, she gestured for the midwife to follow, and as swiftly as the woman's legs could move, they dashed toward her mistress's chamber. But as they turned the corner, Marta froze and yanked the woman out of sight. A servant stood outside the mistress's chamber with his ear pressed against the door.

Marta signaled the woman to stay hidden before reaching for a lantern on a nearby table. Then she turned on her heel and strode down the corridor.

The servant jumped at the sound of her purposely heavy footsteps. He spun and held a lantern high, squinting in her direction. "Who goes there?"

"It is Marta." She stopped before him. "Why do you linger outside our mistress's chamber? You know what she does to those she catches eavesdropping. She will be most displeased if I am to inform her." She struck an authoritative stance foreign to her.

The lantern in his hand rattled. "Please, that is not necessary, I assure you. I heard cries from within and grew concerned over the mistress's welfare." He swallowed hard, shifting from one foot to the other.

Marta glanced at the door, feigning concern. "Her nights have been disturbed with nightmares, of late. I assume this evening will not differ."

"I see," he said. "I will let you tend to her needs." He bolted past her and scurried down the corridor.

She held her breath as he strode by the midwife, who appeared to have made herself scarce. After he disappeared, a door to another chamber opened, and her wiry gray head poked out. Marta waved her forward.

They entered her mistress's chamber to find her on her knees by the bedside. Her hands gripped the bed linens, and she fought to muffle her cries. A look of relief mixed with pain shone in her dark eyes, but no gratitude fell from her lips. "You fool, I thought you'd run off."

She glared at Marta before eyeing the midwife. "Get this child out of me." Pearls of sweat beaded her brow and pasted tendrils of dark hair against her cheeks and neck.

Her mistress's husband had left on crusade, and soon after, she'd discovered she was with child. It was undoubtedly a blessing of the Mother Mary, but her mistress hadn't seen it so. Instead, she had become consumed with trepidation, a result of the duke's persistent threat to put her aside and take her youngest sister to bear him a son. The duchess had borne him three daughters, one of whom had not survived beyond the first night. When the duchess discovered she was with child again, she retired to their estate in the countryside to conceal her pregnancy.

Marta hastened to her mistress's side and helped her to bed, propping her against the headboard so the midwife could assess her progress. Marta dipped a cloth into a basin of tepid water beside the bed and mopped her mistress's brow and throat.

The midwife instructed the duchess to relax so she might check her.

"There's no need. I can feel the head. I would've delivered it myself if I had to wait much longer." She clenched her teeth to get through another contraction. The agony seizing her face never softened when the contraction passed. For a fleeting moment, Marta's heart went out to her mistress. She had experienced the fight to bring life into the world herself with the birth of her son, who resided with her sister in the village.

However, the sentiment vanished with the sting of her mistress's slap. "Enough, you imbecile. Stop hovering over me and help get this over with before the child rips my insides from my body. It has to be a male, to cause so much havoc." Hope hung in her words.

"I will go and fetch cloths and hot water," Marta said.

"There is no time." The midwife rolled back the mistress's shift. She removed a blade from the twine tied around her narrow waist. "Hold this blade to the flames." She nudged her head at the hearth. "And make it quick. The babe comes."

Marta scrambled to do her bidding and returned as the head of the baby crowned. Her mistress moaned but kept from screaming. Then as the baby plunged into the world with one last effort from her mistress, she released an excruciating cry before collapsing against the pillows.

The midwife cleaned the birth matter from the infant, and it let out a healthy howl. Her skilled hands checked it over as she worked. "This one is a fighter indeed," she said with satisfaction and handed it to Marta before turning her attention to its mother.

"Show me my son." Anticipation softened her mistress's usual harshness.

Marta peered at the child, and her breath caught.

"Don't dally. Bring me the child," her mistress said, agitated.

Despite her urging, Marta swaddled the infant in a blanket with care. The baby lay peacefully, staring up at her. A heaviness settled in her heart, and she turned and walked to the bedside.

Her mistress took the child and regarded it with awe. "The saints be praised. He will be a handsome man, making my husband and our household proud."

She unwrapped the babe, and her hand froze. "No!" she shrieked before catching herself and lowering her voice. "I am cursed." Misery contorted what one would consider a beautiful face, though the malice in her heart had extinguished all beauty. She pushed the child at Marta. "Discard it in the sea."

Clutching the babe in her arms, Marta stumbled under the weight of her words.

The midwife paused in her movements. "But Duchess, you've been blessed with a healthy daughter."

"Silence." The duchess's eyes flashed, and she looked at Marta. "Take the back stairs. Be discreet. No one must find out."

"But the servants. They'll wonder what happened to the child," Marta said.

"We will tell them the child died and the midwife discarded it. No one will know of my failure here today. I forewarn you all: if my husband finds out I was with child, you will all pay with your lives."

"Yes, Mistress." Marta's concern for her own young son growing up without a mother silenced any protest.

"Take my cloak." Her mistress pointed to a dark blue cloak spread over a chair next to the fire. "Ensure the child doesn't cry out. Now go. I grow weary of the sight of you."

Marta moved to the chair and tenderly set the bundle down. She swung the cloak around her shoulders, then pulled up the hood. Gathering up the babe, she tucked it beneath the fabric of the cape. She took one last look at her mistress, who had closed her eyes, appearing to block out everything around her.

"May you and your household know everlasting pain for what you do here today," Marta said under her breath before walking to the door. She opened it and peeked into the corridor to ensure her safe escape. Finding it clear, she stepped into the hallway and closed the door behind her.

She made it to the stables undetected, saddled a mare, and rode out of the estate with the moonlight at her back, never stopping until she reached the cliff.

Her heart pounded faster as she approached the cliff's edge. Tears welled, blotting out the view of the raging sea lapping against the rocks below.

"May God forgive me for what I'm about to do." She removed the babe from her cloak and, aided by the moonlight, examined the raven curls and the perfect pout of the innocent child nestled in her arms. "I am sorry about the mother who bore you. May heaven bring you peace…" Anguish robbed her of words. Holding the babe high above the sea, she told herself the child would not suffer. She'd ensure her aim was precise. The ocean would swallow the child and end its existence, and she and her son would live another day. She squeezed her eyes tight, willing herself to drop the baby. Several moments passed before she stepped back, lowering the mewling infant to her bosom. "There, there, little one."

She paced, pondering what to do next. The glow of a distant villa captured her attention. It was the Darlington hacienda. Her mind raced. At the market earlier that day, her friend, Dorotea, who worked for Señora Darlington, had informed her the family had sold their estate and were to set sail for the Americas at dawn. The British family had two young daughters of their own, and from what Dorotea had said, Señor Darlington's love for his family knew no bounds. The thrashing of her heart eased, and hope rose. Perhaps she had found the solution to her dilemma.

She nestled the baby closer and kissed its velvet cheek. "No harm will come to you." She concealed the infant under her cloak, mounted the horse, and rode toward the villa.

The Darlington hacienda sat well-lit and tucked into the hillside, surrounded by meticulously manicured, gray-leafed cistus and citrus trees heavy with fruit. Outbuildings echoed the villa's white stucco walls, red clay roof tiles, and exquisite wrought iron railings and balconies; all conveyed the family's wealth.

Marta dismounted, her senses tuned to her surroundings and the soft breathing of the sleeping infant. She looked for anyone who would try to stop her before dashing across the yard to climb the curved, clay-tiled staircase leading to the carved wooden double doors.

Pausing to catch her breath, she glanced back in the direction she had come, then to her right. Suddenly hearing whistling, she ducked behind one of the columns on either side of the grand entrance. Above her, near the left wing of the house, she spotted a servant as he strode across the terrace, pausing now and then to refill low-burning lanterns. She waited until he moved out of sight before stepping to the door, lifting the wrought iron knocker, and tapping it three times.

Voices rose inside, and when the door swung open, a fair-haired gentleman stood before her. "Hola, señorita." His deep voice hinted at friendliness.

She swallowed back the nerves building in her throat. "Hola, señor."

"How can I help you?" he said in English.

"Ayuda," she said.

"Help. You need help?" He looked past her for those who might pursue her.

She couldn't understand what he said, and although everything in her screamed *run*, she remained steadfast. There was no turning back now. She removed the infant from beneath her cape and held it to him.

His gaze slipped from her to the babe, and he took a step back. "What is the meaning of this?" His eyes widened.

She read the surprise in his eyes. "Ayuda." Tears welled. "Por favor." She thrust the babe at him with growing urgency.

He shrugged while appearing to search for words she'd understand. "No entiendo."

"Ah," Marta said, realizing he didn't understand what she wanted.

"Phillip, darling, who is it?" The soft voice of a woman came from behind him.

"A woman," the man said over his shoulder, never taking his eyes off Marta.

A petite woman she recognized as Señora Darlington joined him, dressed in white flowing evening attire. Her jaw unhinged when she glanced from the baby to Marta.

"Come inside," she said in Marta's native tongue.

Marta hesitated, but Señora Darlington bestowed upon her a warm smile. "You are safe here."

"Gracias." Marta settled the baby against herself, and stepped inside.

"Marta?" someone called as Señor Darlington closed the door behind her.

"Dorotea!" Marta burst into tears when her friend entered the foyer holding a lantern.

"What are you doing here?" She strode forward, worry gripping her pretty face.

"Perdón." Marta inclined her head at the Darlingtons, side-stepped them, and hurried to her friend.

Dorotea gripped Marta's arm. "What has happened? Whose child is this?"

Marta stood trembling. "The duchess's," she whispered.

"What?" Dorotea mimicked Marta's hushed tone. "I was unaware she was with child. The infant appears only hours old."

Marta turned to the Darlingtons, who stood studying them with blank expressions, and nudged her head at the couple. "Can you trust them?"

Dorotea pressed slender fingers to her forehead.

"Well, can you?" Marta urgently shook Dorotea's arm. Maybe she was wrong in believing the Darlingtons could help her. She should never have come here. Her heart sped up, and she looked at the door.

Dorotea touched her arm, reassuring. "You are safe here. But you must see how you appear, showing up here at this hour, claiming that infant is your mistress's."

Marta hurried to explain her predicament. "…you see, if I do not dispose of the baby, I fear what she will do to my family and me. She has threatened to harm anyone who breathes a word."

"She wouldn't."

"She would." Marta clutched Dorotea's arm, tears pooling in her eyes. "I saw her throw a scullery maid down the stairs when she caught her gossiping about the family to a delivery man."

"And what do you expect by coming here?"

Marta glanced back at the Darlingtons. "You said they were a good family with children of their own."

"This is so."

Marta adjusted the baby in her arms, gathered all the courage she could muster, and on trembling legs, approached the Darlingtons. She held a hand up in peace.

Dorotea took a position at Marta's side.

"Do either of you want to explain what is going on?" Señora Darlington said, appearing more fluent in Spanish than her husband.

"This must be confusing, but I plead with you to hear me out," Marta said.

"You have given us quite a start," Señora Darlington said.

Dorotea hastened to fill the couple in on what Marta had told her. Señor Darlington gasped. "How could a mother consider such an act?"

The tension pinging through Marta's body eased. "Please. Take my mistress's child to America so that she may live. You can provide her with a good life."

The couple exchanged a weighted look.

"See." Marta stepped closer, thrusting out the baby for their inspection. "She is a beautiful child."

Señor Darlington placed an arm around his wife's shoulders.

"Dorotea," Señora Darlington said.

"Señora?"

Señora Darlington eyed her with keen respect. "I trust you like my own kin. Could there be any truth to the atrocities your friend speaks of?"

"Si, señora. Marta is an honest and hardworking woman. A mother. She would not risk her family's lives if it were not so."

Her mistress's complexion paled, and she turned troubled eyes on her husband. "What are we to do?"

He rubbed the sides of his temples and shook his head. "I've heard stories of the duke. If his wife bears any similarity, the child is in danger."

"Oh, Phillip. We must intercede." She placed her hands on his chest.

Conflicting emotions crossed his face. "But darling, we can't just steal away with someone's child and claim it as our own."

"What does she say?" Marta whispered to Dorotea.

Her friend translated under her breath.

"The child is without a family. Didn't you hear the girl? The dreadful woman sentenced her own child to death upon the rocks." Determination had hardened the señora's soft voice. "We will raise the child with our daughters. No one will be the wiser."

Señor Darlington's shoulders slumped, and he pressed his lips into a fine line before shaking his head in surrender.

Señora Darlington smiled and patted his cheek before spinning to hold her hands out for the baby. Marta handed her the child, and she took the infant and cradled it to her bosom. Her slender shoulders curved ever so slightly, as if seeking to protect.

Señor Darlington peered down at the bundle in his wife's arms, and the corners of his mouth softened.

Gratitude swelled in Marta's heart, and she whispered a prayer. "I must get back before my mistress becomes suspicious." She half-curtsied and hurried to the door. As her hand circled the knob, she spun back to them. "May the Lord be with you."

"And you." Señora Darlington's face looked overwhelmed, but her words soothed Marta's apprehensions.

Marta disappeared into the night, returned to her mistress, and related the story she had concocted of how she had disposed of the child.

The following day, before the household rose, she saddled the mare and rode to the docks to await the Darlingtons' boarding. From a distance, she observed the family when they disembarked from the carriage. Señor Darlington walked with a golden-haired girl of two or three years at his side, hand clasped in his, and a small child in his arms. Señora Darlington walked behind, carrying a satchel and nothing more.

"No!" Marta gasped and quickly covered her mouth. Betrayal washed over her. But then she spotted Dorotea a few steps behind, carrying an infant swaddled in a white blanket.

She could not hold back the tears, and only after the family and Dorotea vanished into the crowd of passengers on the ship's deck did she melt into the bustle of the wharf.

Braxton Hall, Manhattan, New York, 1862

I BOUNDED DOWN THE GRAND CURVED STAIRCASE OF OUR COUNTRY estate, fleeing the surge of memories chasing at my back.

"Kat!" My oldest sister, Evelyn, peered up at me from the entrance hall, displeasure reflecting in her cornflower-blue eyes. She balanced our one-year-old sister, Grace, on her hip.

Ignoring her, I continued down the steps two at a time, my favorite honey-yellow muslin frock billowing behind me. Age had deteriorated the material, making it thin but less restricting and more to my liking. I'd spurned gowns made of silks and taffeta for softer fabrics without all the flounces and fuss.

My baby sister regarded me with a drooling grin while gnawing on her chubby fist. I paused to caress her cheek.

"With Mama gone, the responsibility for this household and the rearing of you girls falls on me." Evelyn's scowl deepened.

"Oh, flummadiddle," I said with a snort. "You are hardly in charge." I had no patience for her usual parading about and acting much older than her fourteen years.

I glanced at our governess, Dorotea, standing behind her, one brow arched in warning, and I bit my tongue. She was more like a family member than an employee, and we loved her dearly. My chest tightened at her disapproval.

"Señorita Evelyn means well," she said with a tender smile.

I shrugged. The need to escape to the one place I could think of where I'd be alone felt like life or death.

"How are we ever to make a lady out of her?" Evelyn said with exasperation, looking from me to Dorotea.

"We aren't," I said before bolting past her and charging down the corridor.

"Must you run?" Evelyn called after me.

I waved a hand in dismissal, ducked by our butler, and dashed out the salon door. I gasped as the fresh air hit me and the impending tears were unleashed. Rarely in my eleven years had I succumbed to tears—until Mama had fallen ill. Even then, I only permitted them to fall when I had escaped high into my tree and shut out the world's chatter.

I raced through the courtyard, slipped out the side gate, and charged down the lane in search of the solitude of the ancient red oak tree at its end. Blinded by tears, I climbed the tree. A branch caught my stocking, and I felt the sting of its bite, but it did not stop my ascent. Warmth trickled down my leg but any pain was dulled by the grief wedged deep in my heart. Using the back of my hand, I brushed away hot tears and leaned back to examine the moving clouds overhead through a small gap in the tree's canopy.

Mama was gone, and no amount of crying would bring her back. And each day I awakened with an unshakable emptiness upon realizing it hadn't been a nightmare. I missed the tenderness of her embrace. The assurance of her smile. When my soul was troubled, she'd draw me into her embrace and say, "Oh, my sweet Kat. What troubles you so?" I'd unburden my troubles, and soon she'd have me laughing and acknowledging the humor in my view of the matter.

Mama and Papa had five daughters, and I considered life good until the war changed everything. Papa was a colonel in the Union army, and we hadn't seen him since he'd left. He wrote when he could, but his letters never arrived until the news had become dusty. After Mama fell ill, we sent word, but her death came swiftly.

Granted a short leave to care for matters at home, Papa had returned yesterday to discover Mama's body had lain cold in the ground for weeks. At the news, he'd crumpled to the entrance hall floor in a heap of uncontrollable sobs. I'd never witnessed him in such a state. He'd always been strong, and I aspired to be like him, and not succumb to the whining and whims of other girls. Yet, his vulnerability in that uncanny moment swayed my existence. If he crumpled, what would happen to us all?

Dorotea had ushered my sisters and me away before returning to his side. I witnessed her surprise when he clung to her in search of comfort, as I'd often observed Mama do in times of despair.

Last night Papa had sat on the settee holding Grace on his lap. Alice nestled into his side while Evelyn and my second oldest sister, Adelaide, sat at his feet. My sisters posed like meek little kittens in need of comfort. I stood in the doorway of the parlor, eyeing them and fighting an inner battle of yearning.

Papa looked at me and offered a small smile. "Come, Kat. Sit with us awhile." He patted the empty spot on his right.

I shook my head and retreated into the shadows to regard my family before withdrawing to the room I shared with Adelaide.

While my sisters still slept that morning, I'd awakened to the sound of voices outside. I hurried to the window to observe Papa and Dorotea beside a readied two passenger open carriage.

"Señor, are you sure this isn't too soon?" There was concern in Dorotea's voice as she pulled her shawl closer.

He touched her arm. "I have no choice. I'll be back by midmorning." He climbed into the carriage and headed down the lane toward town.

Dorotea had stood peering after him until his carriage disappeared, before wandering back inside.

My mind segued from my sorrow to Papa's early departure.

What had called him away before the birds had scarcely risen for the day? But as the thought occurred, the creaking of approaching carriage wheels drew my attention, and I cocked my head to get a glimpse of the roadway.

"Papa?" I squinted to get a better look. It was him all right, but who was the woman adorned in feathers and silks perched next to him? And for heaven's sake, why was her hand tucked into the curve of his arm? I bristled. As they turned down the lane toward our home, I scrambled down the tree, my feet hitting the ground with a thud. I winced at the reminder of my injury.

The woman squealed, and clung tighter to Papa. "What creature is this?"

I scowled at her dramatics.

Papa's warm brown eyes widened at my sudden appearance before them. My gaze drifted from him to the impostor claiming his arm. As they drew closer, I got a better look at her. She was an attractive woman, I suppose. She wore the modern designs Evelyn and Adelaide cooed over in the catalogs they collected; however, I concluded that is where it ended. In the brief glimpse I got before Papa urged the team onward, I noted her pinched face and how she jutted her nose upward, dismissing me to instead consider our estate.

"Phillip, darling, your estate is marvelous…." Her words faded with the racket from the carriage.

Darling? Who does she think she is, calling Papa darling? I hobbled after the carriage. "Phillip, darling, your estate is marvelous," I mimicked.

What did that woman want? And what was Papa doing with her? Furthermore, why had he brought her here? A dreadful thought occurred to me. What if he had enlisted her to be our guardian, like a nursemaid of sorts? But we had Dorotea, and she was irreplaceable. Then I recalled how a girl had shared with my older sisters and me at a recent social gathering how her father had shown up with a new mother for them after her mother had passed.

No, that couldn't be it. But if Papa had got some fool-hearted notion in his head, I had to warn the others.

I limped faster, baring my teeth to withstand the pain of my injured leg.

When Papa reined the team to a stop at the carriage stone, I darted around the back of the house.

"Dorotea. Evelyn. You aren't going to believe this," I called as I raced down the corridor.

Evelyn poked her head out from the parlor, followed by Dorotea and Adelaide.

"Where have you been…" Evelyn's words faded into a scowl. "You're bleeding."

I glanced down and noticed the tear in my dress and the crimson stain. "That doesn't matter now," I said, pausing to catch my breath. "P-Papa is back. And he has bought a woman with him."

Dorotea walked to the window and looked out. She spied on them a moment before turning away. The apprehension I'd witnessed on her face earlier had returned.

"What is it, Dorotea? Did you know Papa was returning with this woman?" Evelyn asked.

"All will be well, girls." Dorotea's smile never reached her eyes, and the churning in my belly persisted.

Adelaide exited the parlor, joining the rest of us. "Who is she?"

"I don't know, but they look mighty cozy." I had barely got the words out of my mouth before voices sounded at the front door.

We all spun toward the entrance hall, and the heaviness in my gut was reflected on everyone else's face.

"Good day, Mr. Darlington," Our butler said outside the front door.

Evelyn strode toward the front door, but I darted down the corridor and beat her to it, pulling the door open before the butler could.

His hand hung in midair. He blinked and lowered his hand. "Ah, Miss Katherine."

"Mr. Dalton." I nodded, looking beyond him to Papa as he reached the top step. Evelyn and Adelaide stepped up beside me.

Papa presented a weary smile. "Hello, my girls."

"Who is this?" I folded my arms across my chest, nudging my chin at the woman standing behind him, giving her my best "I have no use for you" look.

"Kat," Evelyn said under her breath, jabbing me in the back.

I kicked out my heel and got her on the shin. She winced but quickly suppressed it—for the sake of our guest, I assumed.

Papa cleared his throat and regarded me with hooded eyes. I swallowed hard. I had done it now, but I cared not. That woman was up to no good. I could sense it.

Papa half turned, pulling the woman forward. "This is Miss Audrey Boseman. I expect you to offer her a proper greeting." He focused his gaze on me.

"How do you do, Miss Boseman?" Evelyn stepped around me and offered a low curtsy.

Fearing a reprimand from Papa, I quelled the urge to roll my eyes and offered a small curtsy before stepping aside to allow them entry.

Papa ushered Miss Boseman inside.

"May I take your hat, Papa?" freckle-faced Adelaide said. She always appeared eager to please.

Evelyn and Adelaide were quite boring, with their need to follow societal rules and conditioning, never seeking disapproval. It was exhausting, watching them carry on so. It made my blood boil as the two traitors regarded Miss Boseman with admiration, even when she returned her hand to the crook of Papa's arm.

I pressed my lips together and strode after them into the salon, never allowing my eyes to leave the woman. On closer inspection, I reconsidered my early analysis of her apparel. Her attire had once been of quality, but showed wear. However, not a strand of her auburn hair was out of place. She wore it in a fashionable style under a lavish plum velvet hat adorned with feathers and ribbons.

Alice entered the room. She had an unusual way of walking, as though she stepped on her tiptoes. "Papa." She launched herself at him.

He laughed and embraced her before planting a kiss on the top of her head. She pulled back and smiled up at him. He affectionately brushed her cheek.

Papa had never seemed to yearn for a boy, appearing quite content with daughters. Many nights I had dreamed that if I'd been born a boy, life would have been more enjoyable, but instead, it consisted of "Kat, you can't be climbing trees," or "Miss Katherine, what have you gotten yourself into now?" The servants and my sisters' nagging never ceased. But Mama, although a genteel English lady, had accepted me as I was—dirt, stains, untied hair and all. She'd grip my chin and wipe my dirtied cheeks with her handkerchief. There was no judgment or scorn in her devoted approach. The ache of what I'd lost was too great.

My mind turned to Jude, my dearest friend. He understood me like no one else could. He was a few years older than me and from North Carolina. My mother had been friends with his mother, Mrs. Williams, a white Southern lady, and his father, a free Black doctor who had stitched me up on more than one occasion. Neighbors had scorned my parents for permitting a Black doctor to tend to our family. The Williams family had lived in Seneca Village, a settlement in the borough of Manhattan where mostly Blacks and some Irish and German immigrants lived. However, when the vision for Central Park unfolded, the city forced citizens from their homes and tore the settlement down.

"I reckon you're more boy than a girl," he'd said with a chuckle as we'd sprawled in a sun-drenched meadow, studying the clouds one day.

"Why can't I just be me?" I said, feeling the need to defend myself.

"That's what I'm saying. I like you the way you are."

My peevishness eased, and I snuck a look at him to discover

him regarding me with a strange expression. My heart skipped a beat. "What are you looking at?"

He'd laughed and returned his attention to the sky.

To my dismay, the Williams family moved to an elite Black community in Brooklyn after the demolition of Seneca Village, and I rarely saw him. On the odd occasion Papa had business in Brooklyn, I'd pester him until he consented to take me with him.

I snapped from my reminiscing at the sound of Papa's voice.

"Girls." There was a squeak in his tone.

We all stood gawking at him, waiting for what he was about to say. Nausea roiled in my stomach, and that funny feeling washed over me again.

He swept a hand through his wavy blond hair and glanced at Dorotea, where she stood just inside the threshold with her hands clasped tightly in front of her. They exchanged a look, and Papa swallowed hard. There was dread in his eyes as he returned his gaze to us. Clearing his throat, he said, "Miss Boseman and I are now married."

Gasps echoed throughout the room. My jaw unhinged, and I glanced at Evelyn and Adelaide. All admiration for the woman had fled, and their brows were pleated.

"That's right, ladies. I am to be your new mother."

"But we don't want a new mother," Alice said meekly before dissolving into soft sobs. She had never liked change, something I could relate to wholeheartedly. I yearned for consistency, for things to stay as they were. But lately, that hadn't worked in my favor.

Dorotea moved in to comfort Alice, and Miss Boseman's jaw set at the maternal display.

My head spun. Then heels clicking across the parquet floor registered, and I realized Miss Boseman was striding toward me. I took a step back, my heart pounding faster.

"Do close your mouth, dear," she said in her nauseating, honey-sweet voice. She stopped before me, and her piercing green eyes cut through me. She gripped my chin, not with the gentleness Mama had, but with a need to command.

I glowered at her, removing myself from her clasp.

"I see we have a tiger in need of taming," she said in a low voice, for my ears and perhaps those of Adelaide, who stood next to me.

She fixed a smile and swung to take a good look at the room before marching to the mantel and running her gloved finger over it. "Despite there being no shortage of staff, I see the home needs a good cleaning. But," she brightened and returned to Papa's side, "worry not, my darling. It's nothing I can't handle. With my guidance, the home will shine. I'll see that your daughters," she leveled a stern look on me, "will be ladies you'll take pride in upon your return."

All eyes turned to Papa. He stood silent, looking preoccupied. His new bride's expression darkened. "Phillip, darling." She nudged him.

"Where were we?" He shook his head to dislodge whatever thoughts had occupied him. "She will care for you while I am away." He strode forward, opening his arms, and my sisters and I dashed forward.

"Please, Papa," I breathed into the fabric of his coat. "Don't leave us with her."

"Yes, Papa, please don't go," Adelaide said.

"Now, now, my loves. We'll get through this." His voice cracked. "All will be well. I hate to leave you, but I must catch the afternoon train."

"So soon?" Evelyn pulled back.

Adelaide appeared on the verge of tears. Alice openly wept.

I brushed off the arm he placed around my shoulders and stepped away.

"Kat…" Hurt shone in his eyes.

I looked away, the burn of his betrayal too fresh to

comprehend. How dare he take a new wife! Mama had only been gone a few weeks.

"I'm relying on you," Papa said, resting a hand on Evelyn's shoulder.

Evelyn slumped with the burden he absent-mindedly placed on her. "Yes, Papa." She bowed her head.

Less than an hour later, a groomsman took Papa's trunk out to the waiting carriage and strapped it down. Our new mother dabbed her eyes with a handkerchief as she stood in the doorway. Her performance fanned the fire that had been stirring in my gut since she'd arrived. As Papa bent to hug my sisters in farewell, I darted down the corridor and out a side door and escaped into the security of my tree's canopy.

"Kat." Papa's call drifted on the light afternoon breeze.

I stayed hidden, nestled in the curve of a limb and the trunk. I pulled my knees to my chest as Papa's call came again. I lay my cheek against my knees and imagined how I could make the intruder disappear. The thoughts brought me comfort. I never moved from my position until the carriage faded from sight.

"Papa…" Tears cracked my voice as agony rooted in my soul.

What was to become of us?

# Chapter 2

Braxton Hall, 1870

THE WAR HAD ENDED, AND WITH PAPA'S RETURN, I'D HOPED THE happiness we'd experienced when our mother was alive would return to Braxton Hall. But it was not so.

When the stifling heat arrived in the summer, our family retired to our estate in the country. However, Papa spent most of his time at our townhouse in Manhattan, burying himself in managing his manufacturing company. The man I once viewed as steadfast and unbreakable had vanished, and I became indifferent toward him. Adelaide and Evelyn claimed that I'd become problematic in my view of Papa, and accused me of lacking empathy and compassion.

Papa had abandoned us seven years ago when he replaced Mama with Audrey and marched off to the battlefields to drown his sorrows. I'd never forgive him for the hardship we endured under her care. My refusal to bend to my stepmother's whims and demands had put me at a disadvantage and made me her target.

After Papa had left us in Audrey's charge and in her hunger to transform our home and remove Mama's essence, she had taken it upon herself to remodel our estate—an undertaking taking almost the entire span of the war. She adjusted our sleeping arrangements, moving me to the west wing and far from the comfort of my sisters. At first the loneliness was almost too much to bear, and I yearned for the nights we'd talk until dawn.

One evening shortly after Papa returned, I snuck into Grace's room to read to her, as I often did when Audrey retired to the parlor to sip on brandy until late into the evening. Grace had fallen asleep, and I closed the book and slipped off of the bed.

Lantern in hand, I tiptoed from the bedchamber to the main wing. I hurried across the mezzanine between the split staircases leading to the entrance hall, hoping to return to my room undiscovered. I halted as I heard voices raised in heated discussion. The mezzanine provided an open view of the entrance hall, and I noticed light seeping from the open double doors of the library.

I crouched down, peering through the railing, and observed Papa pacing the floor.

"You dishonor the memory of my wife," he said.

I tiptoed down the steps to get a better view into the library.

"Surely you didn't expect me to live in a home with her touches all over."

"She is my wife!"

"Was. Or have you forgotten she is dead?" Despite my awareness of her indifference to my sisters and me, the harshness of her remark jolted me.

Taken off guard by her unmasked disregard, Papa strode forward and seized her arm. She winced. "You will watch your tongue."

"Release me." Audrey yanked her arm free. "What would people think if they were to find out the noble Mr. Darlington mistreats his wife?" Her threat rang loud and clear.

"I will not permit you to speak of her with disrespect."

"Need I remind you that you came calling for *me*? Our marriage was an arrangement and nothing more. You required a mother for your brood of children."

"And you were on the verge of ruin and in need of my money.

In my grief, I made the error of permitting you full reign of Braxton Hall and its affairs in my absence. But heed me when I say it will not be so from here on out."

The conversation gave me insight into Papa's mindset all those years ago and shed light on Audrey's motive in agreeing to take on my sisters and me in his absence when she possessed not a maternal bone in her body.

I shook off the memory and regarded the open journal before me and the splat of ink marring the page. I leaned back in the carved Italian Piedmontese chair Audrey had shipped from Europe, drumming my fingers on the sculpted arm glazed with gold to accentuate the details. She had spared no expense in her remodeling: gold and navy damask wallcoverings, dramatic ceiling mural, gilt window treatments, lavish gilded plaster crown molding. To the left of my dressing room sat an oversized carved marble fireplace.

My gaze rested on the painting hanging over the mantel of a woman dressed in a pale pink frock, standing at a window overlooking a courtyard. Wildflowers were woven through her golden hair, pinned into a crown atop her head. She held a letter in the hand hanging loosely at her side, and I'd often wondered about her melancholy expression. Evelyn, the romantic, imagined the woman waiting for her lover's return. But I envisioned the woman as a spy of royal descent and imagined the exciting life she lived as a free spirit who fought against societal constraints.

"Good morning, señorita." Dorotea strode into my bed chamber with a tray containing my breakfast, but the ribbon-wrapped box tucked under her arm drew my eye.

I closed my journal as she set the tray down before me. "What is that?" I gestured at the box under her arm.

"Señor Williams delivered it."

"Jude was here and didn't come to see me?" I leapt to my feet.

Jude attended Howard Law School in Washington, DC, and I missed him terribly, but he was set to graduate in the spring.

"I'm afraid so. But it wasn't his choice. Señora Darlington

wouldn't permit him to see you. You know how she feels about you being seen with him."

"Oh, how I loathe that woman! She can't keep me in my chamber forever." I dashed to the window and pressed my face against the glass, attempting to see the lane. "I can't see anything from this room." Many times, I'd cursed Audrey's calculated choice for my chamber.

"Aren't you going to open what he left you?" Dorotea said.

I turned and took the box she offered. I yanked the light blue ribbon off and removed the lid. Inside, on a velvet bed, lay two feathers, one black and one white.

"Feathers?" Dorotea's brow furrowed. "Why would Señor Williams give you feathers?"

My heart swelled at the gift, and I gathered my journal and the feathers and walked to the locked wooden box I kept tucked away from the prying head housekeeper, Mrs. Cox. I never trusted Audrey or the house staff she'd hired to replace those loyal to our mother who had been in service to our family for years. When Papa had returned, he'd been outraged to discover she'd dismissed them. Several days later, he arrived home from town with Dorotea, who'd taken a position as housemaid to Mrs. Brown and her family, and Mr. Kelly, our coachman. The others had left town, obtained other employment, or refused to work under Audrey's dictatorship.

I removed the key I hid under my bodice and locked journal and feathers inside the box, then returned it to its hiding place. Then I returned to Dorotea and kissed her soft cheek, giving her a tight squeeze. She smelled of bergamot and lemon oil, a scent that reminded me of my mother. "I will be back. Cover for me, won't you?" I said, stepping back to regard her beloved face.

"Señora Darlington will be most displeased. She has forbidden your leaving this chamber until Sunday."

"Her reasoning is madness." I balled a hand on my hip. "And for what did I receive this punishment? For telling the dressmaker that Papa refused to fund any more of her extravagant spending and she has no access to my family's wealth without his consent," I said with a snort. I smiled, recalling the temper tantrum that had occurred after the snitching Mrs. Cox informed her why the dressmaker had departed soon after her arrival at Braxton Hall. "She's determined to fill the opulent new closet she had constructed next to her bedchamber. No one can ever wear that much clothing in a lifetime."

"There is truth in your words. However, if she catches you, you will find yourself locked away for more than a few days."

"As long as she allows you to come to my chamber, I will have a way out."

"Which can be taken away at any moment. On a whim, she could stop me from visiting you."

"And that will be the day I leave Braxton Hall forever." I clasped her in a fierce embrace. "I will never let that happen."

Dorotea gently stroked my back. "You are a willful young woman, and I admire your spirit." There was a hint of amusement in her tone.

"Now, I must be going." I pulled away and raced for the door.

"Be careful." Her voice trailed after me as I fled the chamber.

Staff bustled along the corridors, going about their daily duties. Prestige was everything in New York society, and a staff of forty-five or more was required to run a well-ordered estate of Braxton's size. Mama had come from a prominent family in England and had been properly schooled on how to run and maintain such a household. Unfortunately Audrey could not run the estate like Mama, and the previous staff had complained about her deficiency. I suppose it also sealed their fate and discharge.

With all the eyes, I knew my chances of getting outside unnoticed were impossible, so I never slowed my pace. Reaching the mezzanine, I descended the right set of marble stairs while keeping my eyes open for Audrey and Mrs. Cox.

Exiting through the glass doors, I leaned on the marble balustrade outside and looked over the retaining walls at the pathways around our expansive property, lined with manicured hedges. In the center stood a granite fountain, its water splashing to spritz the footpath around it. The rolling hills in the distance were painted with gold, crimson, and orange, winter's promise of its approach. I raced down the sweeping stairs and under the marble portico, which extended as a colonnade over a walkway to a black wrought iron gate framed by vines. I lifted the latch, stepped through, and bounded for the tree line and the meadow beyond, savoring the taste of freedom.

I halted when I broke through the trees and observed my surroundings, exhilaration pounding in my chest. After a moment, my heart plunged. Had I been wrong in my assumption?

"Good day, my lady!" The cheerful call came from my left.

I spun to discover him striding toward me, his hand gliding over the blades of high grass under the midmorning sun. I took in his dark locks and dusky complexion and my heart leapt. "Jude. You're back. I received your message."

His hazel eyes glittered with merriment as he stopped in front of me. "Indeed." He swept a hand toward the landscape. "This has become our place if I am ever to catch sight of you. I've come to feel as though we are entangled in some kind of scandal."

"I am sorry our meetings have to be so clandestine. I wish it weren't so. You are my oldest and dearest friend. I long for the days when we were children, before Audrey entered my life. Life was less complicated then."

"It is not only Mrs. Darlington who adds complexity to our relationship, although she is indeed a significant hindrance. We are no longer children, and our lineage plays a role."

I hung my head.

His strong but gentle fingers lifted my chin, and he looked deep into my eyes. Conflict flickered in his, followed by the peculiar stare he gave me from time to time. Then, as quickly as it surfaced, it vanished, and he returned to the carefree individual I knew.

"If I am to reiterate the words of Katherine Darlington, 'You and I are the clever sorts. We will not conform to what society dictates,'" he said.

I lifted a hand to shield my eyes from the sun. "I must say, the feathers were quite witty."

He released my chin and stepped back. Inclining his head, he placed a hand at his waist and executed an exaggerated bow. "You always underestimate my wit and charm."

"And you, my friend, minimize my need to be free," I said, tilting my chin.

"A tiger can't be caged forever." His eyes danced.

"How did you know?"

"I have my sources."

"Is that so?" I said, smiling up at him. "Keeping an eye on me, are you?"

"Always," he said with a devilish smile.

"This source wouldn't happen to be about this high," I held out a hand at waist height, "fair-haired and doe-eyed, would she?" My littlest sister was infatuated with Jude.

His fetching smile widened. "One never reveals their source, for fear of jeopardizing the relationship."

"Relationship?" I said with amusement. "Is that what you are calling the arrangement you have with Grace?"

"One could hardly call Miss Grace's aid an arrangement."

I laughed and looped my arm through his, enjoying the comfort his presence brought. "What brings you to Braxton Hall?"

"What always brings me?" His hand covered my hand in the crook of his arm, and we strolled the meadow.

I inwardly smiled at his insinuation. "And you thought my stepmother would let you waltz in?"

"No, I am well aware of her opinion of me, but I had faith in your ability to find a way out."

I winced at his reference to Audrey's insults and her refusal to allow him anywhere near Braxton Hall. However, when Jude returned home from school to visit his family, he would send word.

Grace and, on occasion, Alice and Dorotea had been my eyes in getting past Mrs. Cox and Audrey to spend time strolling the meadow with Jude. Evelyn called the encounters indecent and inappropriate for a lady without a chaperone. But Jude and I were friends, and undoubtedly there was no sin in spending time in each other's company.

"As I've told you, don't pay her any mind. Her ignorance may affect the faint of heart, but we are—"

"Ah yes, the clever sorts," he finished for me.

"She can't force anyone to drink her poison unless we conform."

"Conforming is one characteristic I do not possess. Besides, Mrs. Darlington's insults aren't the first or the last time I'll face contempt for a reality I have no authority over."

As his friend, I'd witnessed the inequities he continued to endure. North or South. Union or Confederate. Ill-mannered people existed, and no war could change the deep-rooted conditioning in America.

"But let's speak about more pleasant matters, shall we?" he said, his serious expression softening as he shuffled away internal pain. He turned the irritation and pain on and off to exist, and it pulled at my heart.

"My sisters and I are to attend the upcoming Goddard Banquet. I wish you were coming. It will be a bore without you."

"I would have found amusement in seeing you squirm in your evening attire," he said with a chuckle.

I paused and turned to observe him. "I prefer to forgo the event altogether. An evening spent with pretentious people, their judgment, and tedious conversations about politics, religious matters, and gossip holds no appeal. Moreover, unlike Evelyn, Adelaide, and their friends, I find no satisfaction in being the object of gentlemen's scrutiny, hoping they can win a dance or corner me and pressure me to become a wife. I'd much rather spend my time with the horses and groomsmen than be confined to the conventions deemed fitting for a woman for an entire evening."

"Leave it to Kat Darlington to defy all essence of femininity and grace." He took in my plain green dress and the ivory ribbon securing my hair at the nape of my neck.

"Do I displease you, Mr. Williams?" I said with a smirk, immensely enjoying our usual friendly banter.

Solemnity shone in his eyes. "You could never."

I frowned at his expression but brushed it away. "I can't wait to see Birdie." I turned and continued on, picking a blade of grass and dissecting it with my fingernail. My thoughts turned heavy at the news Birdie had shared last week. "She is to marry in the spring."

"And do I sense that troubles you?"

"How could it not? It changes everything. What am I to do with a married friend? I shall never marry." I jutted out my chin.

"Never is a long time," Jude said.

"Too soon, in my opinion. Evelyn has her sights set on Mr. Peyton from Charleston, South Carolina. Can you believe the nerve? Seeking to marry a Southerner," I said with a snort. "It's as though she cares little for what the North fought for. Not to mention the years Papa spent away from us in the service of the Union army."

"Is it the years your father spent away or what you and your sisters suffered under the supervision of his new wife, or the injustices the enslaved encountered that weigh on your mind?"

His words sliced through my heart. I halted and spun to face him. "You'd best mind your words, Jude Williams. You know I am not one to agree with the antics of the South or anyone seeking to belittle and mistreat another. The audacity of you, to pose such a question."

"Forgive me." He gripped my forearms. "I know your heart more than anyone."

"Do you?" I shook free and jabbed a finger at his chest. "If you did, you wouldn't say such a thing."

"Kat."

"No." I spun and marched back the way we had come.

"Kat," he called after me.

I waved a hand in dismissal and suppressed the tears clogging my throat. "Good day, Mr. Williams."

After all our years of friendship, did he not know me at all? The tall grass beat against the fabric of my skirt and nipped at my hands, swinging wildly at my sides in my need to put distance between him and me.

Chapter 3

I STORMED ACROSS THE COURTYARD AND ALONG THE COLONNADE BACK the way I had come, forgetting I'd been confined to my chamber before I'd slipped from Braxton Hall. Jude had gone too far with his insinuation that I condoned slavery and what the Blacks faced in our country.

I entered the house through a side door, and as my foot touched the first step in returning to my chamber, Audrey's curt voice rang out. I froze.

"Where have you been?"

Chastising myself for my recklessness, I braced myself and turned to face her.

Garbed in a green-gold satin gown with ivory rosettes, she stood on the threshold between the main wing and the entrance hall. Mrs. Cox stood to her left with a smug look on her pinched face. I detested the woman as much as I did my stepmother. Her black eyes reflected the rot in her soul. Only last week, while Audrey was in the city, Dorotea had witnessed Mrs. Cox striking Grace and reported it to my stepmother on her return, but she'd dismissed by remarking that if Dorotea wasn't fit to keep her stepdaughters in line in her absence, Mrs. Cox would.

"Enjoying the morning air, were we?"

I straightened to my full height as she strode toward me wearing a murderous expression.

"You have forgotten your place, my dear," she said, her demeanor devoid of any affection. "I restricted you to your chamber." She halted, towering over me by several inches.

"Not now." I turned back to the stairs, all logic leaving me.

She grabbed the fabric of my sleeve to prevent me from leaving, and the seam tore. All obedience and common sense vanished; I spun back around and moved to stand nose to nose with her. Challenge flashed in her eyes.

"I am not a child anymore, that you can lock away without a fight. It stops here and now."

"I will remind you who you are talking to."

Her breath smelled of brandy, and her nauseating Otto of Roses perfume made my nostrils rebel. My lip curled. "I am aware of your shenanigans. You came into our home and took advantage of my grieving father and his preoccupation with the war. Must I remind you, dear stepmother, that the war is over? Papa is back."

"Is he?" She arched an auburn brow. "Where is he?" She swiped a hand around the room. "He hides away in the city to avoid the responsibility of you all."

Her words were like a stab to the heart and spoke to the belief I harbored. But I would not back down to her, or all foothold I may have gained would be lost.

"Is that so?" I leveled a stony glare at her. Perhaps he was revolted by the sight of her. Had she ever considered that? But I dared not breathe the words aloud. "Mrs. Ainsworth says it's only a matter of time before he divorces you." I lifted my chin, recalling Mrs. Ainsworth gossiping about Audrey with the other ladies at a summer social.

Audrey's cunning laugh reverberated, and she placed a hand on her bosom. "Gets rid of me?" She glanced at Mrs. Cox, who had moved closer as though seeking a front row seat for what transpired between us. "What do you think of that, Mrs. Cox?"

The head housekeeper's voice maintained its usual oily tone. "That old sow has nothing better to do than gossip."

"Yes, or I will see to her ruin." Audrey's eyes gleamed, and her peachy complexion flushed. "Besides, dear one" —she gripped my chin and squeezed— "the likelihood of your father putting me away is…well, never." Certainty radiated from her. "It would do Mrs. Ainsworth well to keep my name and that of this family out of her mouth, or she will live to regret it."

Despite Audrey marrying into the Darlington family, Mrs. Ainsworth's social standing was far more influential than Audrey could ever dream of attaining. However, the confidence in Audrey's eyes left me spinning. How could she be so sure? Was there more to Papa's and her arrangement than I had overheard?

"And it is only a matter of time before you hang yourself," I said, my assurance wavering.

I stepped back. My legs trembled as I understood the line I had drawn between the two of us. I had opposed her before, but now I had sealed my fate. I could only imagine the tyranny she'd unleash on me. I suppressed a shiver, never wanting to give her the satisfaction of knowing she had gotten to me.

I spun on my heel and ascended the stairs, and to my relief, Audrey said no more.

At the landing, I paused to watch her stalk from the room, and the smug-faced Mrs. Cox followed like an obedient dog at her heels.

"Kat," Evelyn said through gritted teeth, and I turned as she marched toward me from wherever she'd been hiding. "Do you seek to be locked away for the remainder of your existence?"

At that moment, I questioned my wisdom before my annoyance at Jude returned. It was his fault. He had caused me to lose my discretion. I pushed him from my mind and focused my attention on my sister. "I am no longer a fearful child, uncertain of the world. You may yield to her demands, but I will no longer be subjected to her cruelty and oppression." I noted her bonnet and cashmere paletot. "Where are you off to?"

"Mr. Peyton is taking me for an outing." She wriggled her fingers into wrist-length white gloves.

My indignation flared. Was the man daft? The audacity, courting my sister without Papa's permission. Evelyn had assured me that Mr. Peyton would ask, upon Papa's return from the city, but still. "Why is Mr. Peyton coming calling again? He was here only yesterday."

Her face glowed. I had observed the same lovestruck look on the faces of courting couples. "First Birdie's engagement to that obnoxious Zane Goddard with his family's need to monopolize every business from here to the West Coast, and now you," I said with disgust before claiming her arm and leading her down the corridor toward the west wing.

"Need I remind you, we are to attend the Goddard Banquet, and you must be on your best behavior. New Yorkers don't look fondly upon untamed women like you. You will never fit into society and you will bring shame to the Darlington name."

"And our dear stepmother does not?"

"I can't reason with you about this."

"You are complacent and turn a blind eye to the harm she brings to this household. Do you not care at all what some of us suffer?" My fingernails bit into my palms. What couldn't she see? Why didn't she care? I forced back tears as conviction surged within me.

"Kat, I must go. He will be here soon, and Adelaide is waiting in the entrance hall to accompany me."

I shook off her words as though I'd never heard them. "Do you seek to marry out of convenience?" I said, and as the insight hit me, I halted. "That's it, isn't it? You want to be away from Braxton Hall too." I continued tugging her along with me. "Of course, one can't blame you, with the yapping dog and taskmaster who patrol this place. Damn Papa and his neglect of his family."

"Let me go!" She planted her feet firmly, refusing to move farther. "Take care of that tongue. You mustn't use such vulgarity. A lady—"

"Oh, flummadiddle." I folded my arms across my chest. "The infamous words I've heard all my life."

"Perhaps it's about time you abide by them."

I threw my hands in the air. "Do you ever grow tired of toeing the line? Do you ever think of what it'd feel like to race through the meadows with the wind blowing in your hair?"

She stepped back in horror. "I wouldn't."

"Then you have not yet lived, dear sister."

Our differences as sisters were vast. As children, my goldened-haired sisters' flesh turned bright pink, even red, as though slapped by the sun. Mine, on the other hand, darkened to a warm tan under its kiss. Evelyn and Adelaide bore Mama's pale blue eyes and carried themselves with the same sophistication. Alice, Grace, and I had brown eyes like Papa. Whereas Adelaide and Evelyn had inherited Papa's height, I had taken after Mama. But our dissimilarities went beyond the physical.

"You are impossible, Katherine Darlington," she said in exasperation. "Merely impossible."

"Because why? Because I won't be cornered and mistreated? You keep bowing to the lion and see whose head ends up in her jaw."

"Listen." Her voice softened as she touched my elbow. "All I mean is, you don't need to struggle so. You make it harder on yourself with your defiance. I'm afraid of what will happen to you now." She lowered her voice and glanced over her shoulder. "I suggest you find yourself a husband and rid yourself of Audrey."

"Is that it? You plan to abandon us all by marrying the dashing Mr. Peyton?"

"That is not my reasoning," she said. "But if he were to ask for my hand in marriage, I would certainly consider."

I glared at her. "You would, wouldn't you? Always thinking about yourself over the rest of the family."

Her gloved hand went to her slender throat, hurt shining in her eyes. "Kat."

"Don't you Kat me. You are a traitor and no better than Papa." I turned and marched down the corridor.

My sour mood hung like a storm that never passed as I wandered through the corridors. I took in the frescoed ceilings, gold leafing, and ornate moldings throughout our home, all installed by the French designer Audrey had hired for the remodel. The estate had become my prison and held no sense of home. I often roamed the corridors in search of some essence of the woman who had loved me unconditionally, trying to find purpose in a family and society where I didn't know where I fit. Evelyn and Adelaide had each other. Alice and Grace were closer in age, and then there was me, the outsider looking in. Mama, why? Why did you have to leave us?

I walked into my chamber and discovered one of Audrey's chambermaids tidying the room. "Out! Now." The maid scurried from the room without protesting, and I slammed the door behind her.

I paced the floor until I came to the painting of the woman, and I paused to study it once more. "Why must all women have a husband in order to find purpose in the world?" I said to it as though expecting her to answer.

I had daydreamed of many happy situations in life, but marriage was not one of them. Instead, I envisioned myself as a pirate, voyaging across the Mediterranean Sea, searching for treasure. A notion Jude and I had shared when we were children. During the war, I imagined what it would be like to be a spy for the Union, advancing into the enemy's territory. Oh, the exhilaration it had brought me.

My thoughts turned to Jude's and my disagreement in the meadow. Regret plagued me. His companionship had brought me much joy, and he didn't deserve to be the target of the discontent souring me. I retrieved the locked wooden box and took it over to the desk. Sitting down, I unlocked the box and withdrew the feathers. As I held them, a memory of Jude and me as children surfaced.

When Mama lived, Mrs. Williams visited Braxton Hall occasionally, bringing Jude with her. On this particular day, as we often did, we strolled the meadow and skipped rocks on the pond. Then we sat on the bank and regarded the single black swan amongst the flock of white ones floating on the pond.

"That bird is like me," Jude said.

"Which one?"

"That one there." He pointed at the dark swan.

"Because he is beautiful?" I asked, admiring the creature.

"No." His voice hitched. "I wasn't thinking that."

I cocked my head to look at him and noticed his wrinkled brow. "Then what were you thinking?"

"Although he is the same, he is not. He is one black swan amongst many whites. You see how he circles the pond alone?"

"Yes, but maybe he was meant to stand out."

He looked at me with confusion in his eyes. "What do you mean?"

I returned my gaze to the pond and studied the black swan. "If he was the same as the white swans, we wouldn't notice his beauty. He would be just another white bird, and the view of the pond would not be as lovely."

He gasped, and I looked back at him to discover the tears in his eyes before he lowered his head.

I hadn't understood what Jude referred to that day in the meadow until I'd gotten older. We had just been children then, but my love and admiration for my friend remained unchanged.

Opening the drawer, I withdrew stationery, then dipped a pen in the inkwell. I gazed out the window and heaved a sigh before scribing the words in my heart.

My dearest Jude,

Remorse weighs my heart at the outcome of our recent encounter. Please forgive me for behaving rudely and lacking the wisdom to conduct myself more suitably, regardless of how I felt at the moment. I did not seek to offend or hurt you. I am not your adversary—a fact of which I know you are aware.

Until we meet again, my friend.

My deepest respect,

Kat

I folded the letter and sealed it in an envelope before the sound of footfalls in the corridor drew me to my feet. I raced to my bed, concealed the envelope beneath the bed linens, and spun back as I felt her approaching presence.

"Why do you look so flustered, daughter?" Audrey asked as she strode into my chamber.

I cringed at her reference but bit my tongue. "What do you want?"

"Did you think I was going to allow that escapade and your blatant disregard of my orders?"

"I am not a child—"

"So you keep saying, but you carry yourself as such. You will learn your place in this family if I have to lock you in this chamber for the remainder of your days."

"You wouldn't dare. Papa wouldn't allow it."

"If he ever cares to show his face here, then we will discuss the behavior of his daughter. You have lost your mother. Do you want to send your father to his grave too?" She walked around my chamber, trailing her fingers over the furniture. "Can you imagine the disgrace he will feel once word gets out that you were found bedded by a Negro. You will be ruined, and no gentleman will ever want you."

My heart leaped into my throat. "That is a lie!" The vulgarity of her words burned my flesh.

"Is it?" She spun, and her eyes narrowed. "A trusted staff member witnessed it herself. Isn't that so, Mrs. Cox?"

I turned as the head housekeeper walked into the room. I could only assume she'd been lurking in the corridor.

"I saw Miss Katherine racing toward the meadow and followed her. Then, as I watched from the trees, I saw the Negro overpower her and throw her to the ground. I knew I couldn't overwhelm him, so I came back for help. But you returned distraught and wouldn't speak on the matter."

"Lies. All lies!" Tears burned my eyes, and I wanted to rip the bloody woman's throat from her neck.

"One can only imagine what the fine citizens of New York will do when they find out that Negro forced himself upon the esteemed Mr. Darlington's daughter. They will hang him from High Bridge before disposing of him in Harlem River."

"You wouldn't dare."

"I would!"

I lunged at her. "I will kill you!"

She stepped aside and stuck out her foot, tripping me. I grabbed the footboard to steady myself. I saw a flash in the corner of my eye, then her hand connected with my cheek. I cried out and cradled my cheek with my hand.

Face twisted with hatred, she adjusted her clothing before squaring her shoulders. "You have no one to blame but yourself for your suffering. Perhaps this time you will finally know your place. I told you I'd tame the tiger within you." Elation flashed in her eyes, and she turned and walked toward the door before swinging back to face me. "I will be gone for a few days, but in my absence, Mrs. Cox will keep an eye on you to guarantee you remain here until my return. And don't expect that fool governess to come to your rescue. I will see she is kept far from your chamber. After she facilitated your escape today, I will see her permanently removed from this household."

"Papa wouldn't allow it," I said.

She charged forward, and I shrank back, but she stopped and came no closer. "Where is this hero of yours?" She threw her hands in the air.

I remained silent.

"Well, girl, where is he?"

I hid my trembling hands in the fabric of my dress, willing my tears back.

"What? Have you nothing to say?"

Still I didn't speak.

She spun and stormed from the room, and Mrs. Cox shut the door after them, but not before I witnessed a cynical smile creep onto a face that had never brightened in her lifetime. The key turned in the lock, and I crumpled to the floor by the bed, buried my face in my hands, and wept.

Eventually I fell asleep on the bed. Hours passed before the key turned in the lock, and I scrambled to my feet. The door swung open wide, and Mrs. Cox stepped aside to permit my chambermaid, Colleen, entrance.

"Make it quick. I will be down the hall," Mrs. Cox said to Colleen. "And for your sake, Miss Katherine, I wouldn't try anything."

I kept my gaze lowered, not wanting her to recognize the defiance that simmered within me. Audrey and Satan himself would not keep me prisoner. I had fashioned a strategy and intended to see it to completion.

Mrs. Cox closed the door behind Colleen, and I waited until her footfalls disappeared down the corridor.

"Come, set that down." I gestured at the tray of food she held.

"Ye all right, Miss Katherine? Yeer sisters and Miss Ruiz are terribly concerned, but Mrs. Darlington said no one is authorized in or out of yeer chamber except for me, Mrs. Cox, and Mrs. Darlington," she said in a low voice.

I regarded the door and kept my voice down. "Has Evelyn returned?"

"Not yet."

"Good. We must make sure she doesn't find out, or I'm afraid she will try and stop me for what I'm about to do."

Colleen set the tray of food down, and I studied her. A light breeze could blow the gangly girl over, but she had a calmness about her I appreciated. I had learned to become an observer in life, reading the emotions of others in an attempt to see what could occur next, in hopes of protecting myself. I had a keen respect for the girl, above all Audrey's replacements. She was not to be disregarded; I'd noted the quiet fierceness that flitted in her eyes from time to time.

I had witnessed Audrey's mistreatment of the girl, and she was no stranger to my stepmother's abhorrence of me. I would not let Audrey win. She would not break me. I withdrew a letter from beneath a pillow. "Please see that Alice gets this. I require her help tomorrow. Can you do that for me?"

"Yes, Miss Katherine. Ye can trust me."

"Good. Mind that you are careful. I will not see harm come to you or Alice."

Colleen helped me out of my clothing, and I slipped into my nightgown and robe. I seated myself at the desk by the window as Mrs. Cox returned and stood on the threshold.

"Are you finished in here?" She directed her question to Colleen.

"Yes, Mrs. Cox."

Colleen hurried to her side, and they were gone without another word.

Chapter 4

S LEEP EVADED ME THAT NIGHT, AND BY THE TIME THE KEY TURNED IN the lock the following morning, I had paced the floor until my feet hurt. I held my breath, waiting to see if I would be greeted by friend or foe.

"Kat!" Alice burst through the door with Colleen close behind. She raced across the room and threw herself at me. I embraced her, and her small hands pressed into my back. "I was so worried. I feared what Mother had done to you now."

No matter how often I heard the reference Audrey had forced on my little sisters, I flinched. I pulled back and cupped my eleven-year-old sister's face.

"You blessed girl. I'm so happy to see you."

"Colleen gave me your letter. I waited until Mr. Kelly drove away with Mother before taking it to Dorotea. Mother has forbidden her from seeing you."

"Do you know where she is going?"

"She appears to be going for a few days, as I saw Mr. Kelly strap a small trunk to the carriage."

"Let's hope she is off on one of her extended excursions," I said.

I often contemplated what so frequently called her away.

However, I cherished her stretches away because I felt safe and almost content during these times. The farther she was from Braxton Hall, the better for us all.

I covered Alice's ears and whispered to Colleen, "Did you mix the potion and give it to Mrs. Cox?"

"As ye instructed. She will be out for hours. Dorotea instructed the cook to inform the others that Mrs. Cox had fallen ill and wouldn't be makin' her rounds today. And that Mrs. Cox isn't to be disturbed."

"Well done. We could all use a day around here where we can breathe a little lighter."

"Kat, is everything all right?" Alice's big brown eyes searched mine when I released her.

"You mustn't worry about anything. If everything works out the way I intend, I may have a gift for you."

"Truly?" Her face lit up.

I bobbed my head.

She squealed and hugged me around the middle before stepping back and considering me with building anxiety. "But what if—"

"No what ifs." I dabbed a finger on her upturned nose. "All will be well. Now, you run along and ask Mr. Kelly to prepare a carriage and meet Dorotea and me at the east entrance. Be discreet. And remember, you can't tell Evelyn and Adelaide."

"Is the gift for all of us?" She frowned.

"Indeed. The fewer people involved, the better. We don't want people to find out about the surprise and ruin it, do we?"

She shook her head, beaming with anticipation.

"I knew I could count on you. I will be back before nightfall. Now, remember…" I placed a finger to my lips.

"I won't say a word," she said with a smile before skipping from the room. I decided, for Alice's sake, keeping her in the dark about what I was up to would save her from Audrey's ire if she found out about her involvement.

Colleen closed the door behind Alice and followed me to my

dressing room. I sat at the vanity and regarded the dark-haired chambermaid through the looking glass. She had brown eyes that penetrated the soul and a jagged scar that ran from her chin and disappeared into the hairline by her ear. I pressed fingers to my temple and took a weighted breath.

"Ye all right, miss?"

"I will be once I'm on the road and heading to the city to speak with my father. Let's just hope that dreadful woman doesn't wake up before I can get out of here."

"Mrs. Cox is…"

"An overlord," I said. "She forgets her place, and with that fool stepmother of mine enforcing her behavior, no one is safe. Didn't her husband pass last year?"

"He did."

"She was probably the death of the poor soul, no doubt."

She stifled a giggle. I took a second look at her, and my jaw relaxed. "We better make haste," she said. "Is there a suitable frock ye've got in mind?"

"Something cheery, but ensure the material and trimmings aren't stiff or itchy."

A small smile played on her lips as she turned and walked into the adorning closet to return moments later with a ruby satin day frock trimmed with black lace and cording. She held it out for my inspection. I recognized the dress as one Papa had purchased for me last Christmas for Mrs. Ainsworth's charity bazaar I never attended. I ran my fingers along the inside lining and seams of the bodice and sleeves.

"I believe that will do. The shade is quite fetching."

"It will complement yeer dark features." She laid it across the cream-colored chaise next to the window in my dressing room. "And…" she disappeared back into the closet and shuffled around before returning with a ruby-colored velvet hat embellished with black netting, a touch of ribbon, and a small, glimmering white gem.

"It isn't too much?" I looked to her for guidance. "I don't want to look like an overstuffed turkey on Christmas morning."

"Extravagance is lost on ye, miss."

I arched a brow.

"It is what I quite admire about ye." Shifting her stance, she rubbed a hand on the fabric of her dress before placing the hat next to the ruby gown. "Forgive me. Sometimes my words come out wrong." She took a step closer, extending her hands as she spoke. "What I mean to say is, ye ain't one for the pretentious things in life, so the fear of appearin' excessive is not a concern."

I smiled at her. "Good." I patted her arm. "Come now, let's see what can be done with my hair."

"Do ye want yeer hair swept into a chignon like I do for Miss Evelyn and Adelaide? Tortoiseshell hairpins with rhinestones would be lovely." She lifted one of the shoulder-length ringlets framing my face.

I shook my head and regarded her in the mirror. "To spend the next hours feeling as though my scalp is being tugged from my skull would be dreadful. But you know I prefer my hair down, so my mother's hair combs will suffice, don't you think?"

Her eyes flickered with amusement. "As ye say, miss." She lifted the pewter brush and glided it through my hair.

I watched her skilled hands working; for some unknown reason, she piqued my interest. "How did you come by that scar?"

Her hands stilled. "Da says it's best we don't talk about unpleasant matters and not to be troublin' ye all with me problems."

"Let me be the judge of what I consider problems."

She quickly looked at me in the mirror before lowering her eyes. Uncertainty wrinkled her freckled brow.

"Please, if it isn't prying, I would like to know."

Without looking at me, she said matter-of-factly, "It happened the night me mam was murdered in the Five Points."

I swallowed hard. "I-I didn't know. If I had, I would never have broached the subject."

She shook her head. "It is quite all right. I don't recall the night."

"No?" I wondered how such a tragic event could be suppressed.

"I was a babe."

"Colleen." I twisted on the stool and gathered her hands in mine. "You don't have to speak about it."

"I like to speak about Mam." Tears glistened in her eyes.

"Tell me about her." I gave her hands a gentle squeeze before turning back to face the mirror. The eternal ache for my own mother created an invisible connection with Colleen.

"Me da's parents arrived in America as indentured servants. And like most immigrants, their life wasn't one of privilege. Da met Mam at a saloon in the Bowery where she was a woman of the night."

She glanced at me, and I did my best to conceal my shock. If she noticed, the need to speak of her mother displaced all fear of judgment.

A tender smile curved her lips. "Da said she was a singer and a pianist, too. The first night he saw her, she was 'a vision of blue silk.' He was smitten with her, but she dismissed him every time he sought to court her."

I frowned, and she rushed to explain. "Although she had lain with several men, she never did with Da."

I wasn't accustomed to intimate relationships between women and men, but my friend Birdie had found amusement in educating her naïve friend. I had left appalled at what I'd learned.

"She wasn't the courting type, she told him. But he never gave up. He won her heart, and they married. A year later, I was born. Then, one night as they strolled through Five Points on their way home, me parents were robbed and left for dead. Da says somewhere in the struggle, I must have been injured." She shrugged the injury off.

"I'm sorry for your loss."

"A loss we both share," she said softly, placing the last pin and stepping back.

I lowered my head. "Indeed. Not a day goes by that I don't miss her."

"Do ye care to speak about her?"

I lifted my gaze to eye her. "You seek to defy my stepmother?"

She grinned.

"Very well," I said, returning her grin. "As you may know, my parents are from England. They came over to America when I was an infant. Papa was five years older than my mother, and his family arranged a marriage between him and a Miss Phoebe Birdwhistle."

"Birdwhistle?" Colleen said with a giggle.

"That's right." I stood and faced her. I had broken into a fit of laughter over the name myself when Mama told me the story. "Papa never had an eye for the woman." I removed my frock and kicked it aside with the toe of my shoe. "My grandparents were displeased when he rejected their attempt to match him with Miss Birdwhistle, but they were more than pleased when he told them he had met a woman he intended to marry. Until, of course, he informed them that Mama did not yet know that he had set his eyes on her."

Awe shone in Colleen's face. "A romantic Mr. Darlington, like Miss Evelyn."

"Perhaps." My voice was muffled as I put my head into the ruby gown she held out.

"Tell me more." She pulled the dress down over my hips before circling me to fasten the fabric-covered buttons.

"I daresay you too are a romantic." I glanced at her over my shoulder. "And am I to believe you may have a beau?"

Her cheeks reddened. "Ain't got no feller. That is, he doesn't know I exist."

"Do enlighten me who this young man is."

She hesitated.

"Go on, now. You must tell me."

"Alfred."

"One of our groomsmen?"

She nodded, nervousness flickering in her eyes.

I envisioned the straw-haired man with a slight limp, caused when a horse had thrown him last summer. She finished the last button, and I turned to face her. "He appears to be a considerate man," I said.

She brightened. "He is. He helped Da repair the roof when our landlord refused to have it fixed. Alfred used his own wages and told Da that Mr. Darlington had been pleased with my services to his family and contributed to the repair."

Considerate, indeed.

"Then you must tell him that you return his affection."

She shook her head. "I couldn't. I'm sure he doesn't see me the way I do him."

"Not that I'm well versed in the relations between a man and woman—courtship and matters of the heart are more Evelyn's expertise—but perhaps I could help."

"What do ye suggest?"

"Let me ponder on it," I said with a pat on her arm.

"Thank ye, miss."

"If I am to survive another day and be of aid to you, I require my father's help. Now getting out of here undiscovered will be the problem."

"I will be yeer eyes," she said and darted for the door. I followed suit, and with her help, I made it outside and across the courtyard to the east entrance with the lowest level of engagement possible.

Chapter 5

M R. KELLY STOOD WAITING, CLOAKED IN A TAN CARRICK COAT with our family crest stitched onto the breast. He removed his silk top hat, revealing a full mane of silver, and bowed at the waist. "Good day, Miss Katherine," he said in a heavy Irish accent. "Miss Ruiz awaits inside."

"How do you fare today, Mr. Kelly?"

"I am good, miss." He tilted his head to gaze at the overcast sky. "Don't care too much for the look of those clouds." He didn't question why I had requested that he bring the carriage around to the east entrance, but I could tell he was puzzled.

"How's the family?" I asked, avoiding divulging any information.

"The missus is visitin' our daughter in Charlottesville."

"How lovely. And how is the new grandbaby?"

He opened the door, and I regarded Dorotea, garbed in a chestnut two-piece wool walking dress, seated inside. She appeared beside herself with nerves. I took the hand Mr. Kelly offered.

His weathered face lit up at my question. "He is growin' fast. A real fine lad."

I stepped into the enclosed carriage and settled across from Dorotea, leaning back against the whiskey-brown leather seat.

"Thank ye, miss," Mr. Kelly said.

I looked back to him and frowned. "For what, may I ask?"

"For always askin' about the family."

I inclined my head in acknowledgment. "Of course—you may work at Braxton Hall, but you are very much part of this family." I smiled, recollecting his son's impish face. "I recall that rascal son of yours." Mother had encouraged Mr. Kelly to bring his boy to the estate to play with us.

He laughed, his blue eyes sparkling beneath unruly gray brows. "I recall the squeals as he chased ye girls with snakes and spiders. A devil of a lad, he was."

"He was marvelous," I said. "I do miss those years."

Dorotea squirmed in her seat, and I sensed her building tension.

He chuckled, shaking his head. "I remember the time I spotted ye deliverin' a garter snake to my lad so that he could chase yeer sisters."

"I was simply aiding his cause," I replied with mock innocence, delighted by the memories of a carefree time in our lives.

"Or the time ye marched around the gardens with the critters inside Miss Alice's baby buggy."

I belted out a laugh, which erupted as more of a snort, surprising us all. I placed a gloved hand to my mouth in a fleeting attempt to retract it.

Mr. Kelly's grin widened.

"Señorita Katherine, we must be on our way." Dorotea's patience had run out.

"Dorotea is right. But it is always a pleasure to reminisce and hear about your family," I said.

"Much appreciated, miss. Where are ye ladies headed today?"

"To see Papa in the city." I opened the black brocade reticule dangling from my wrist and retrieved the letter I'd written to Jude. "Can you see this is mailed?"

He took the letter. "Very well." He tipped his top hat, closed the door, and took his position on the driver's seat.

The carriage lurched forward, and we were off.

"Why delay our departure?" Dorotea leaned forward and looked out the window for observers before settling back against the seat with her hands clasped tightly in her lap.

I pondered her question, then said with a shrug, "Loneliness, I suppose."

"I am sorry for what you endure at that woman's hands, but what do you suppose will change with this visit to the city to see your father that your letters haven't already communicated?"

"I will make him face me," I said with determination. "I will inform him of Audrey's shenanigans and demand he do something once and for all." I weighed Audrey's threat to spread falsehoods about my virtue and the danger inflicted on Jude if she was allowed to cultivate them. I wouldn't let any harm come to him. I'd fall on the mercy of my father. His return to his family was the only way I could think of to save us all.

"Tread lightly," Dorotea said.

"Treading lightly will no longer suffice. It's a dire matter. Life and death, frankly." I picked at the seam of my gloved finger. My head throbbed from a sleepless night.

"If we are to speak frankly, what has Señora Darlington done differently this time that has you so distressed?"

"I can't speak of it. Let's hope that Papa is available and we don't have to pursue him all over Manhattan."

As we rode past the lane leading to our estate, I regarded the ancient red oak, and it brought me solace. It had been years since I'd climbed into the sanctuary of its canopy. Audrey had threatened to have the tree cut down if she found me in it again. And at my age, I suppose it would be entertaining to catch a grown woman scaling the tree. I smiled at the notion.

Dorotea and I sat in silence during the ride. Her tension never eased, and my determination rose. Last night I had banished all worries of what would happen if my mission failed, and Audrey found out I had escaped my chamber and ventured into the city, but when the brownstone buildings and factories of Manhattan appeared, my own tension rose. I readied myself to face what lay ahead.

Trams, carriages, and wagons congested the streets, while steamships, schooners, and paddle-wheelers crammed the river. In growing excitement, I regarded the humming boardwalks. Women strolled in bright day frocks, hats, and paletots and other outwear. Gentlemen paraded in dark three-piece suits, felted bowler hats, morning coats, and walking sticks, their more subtle hues melding with the abundance of color. A frenzy of voices rose from workers and patrons ambling in and out of tailor and hat shops, dry goods and department stores, and paint and wallpaper shops. The full-length windows of restaurants and cafés revealed tables crammed with diners.

Some time.

later, Mr. Kelly reined the team to a halt outside our townhome, and before he could open the door, I flung it open. He gasped and stumbled back.

"Señorita Katherine," Dorotea scolded.

"My apologies," I said. "But I must make haste." I took the hand Mr. Kelly offered and disembarked. A light mist dampened my face.

Dorotea stepped from the carriage and stood at my side.

Mr. Kelly shut the door and swerved back to face us. "I will be at the carriage house. Send word when ye are ready. Hopefully the rain holds off until we reach Braxton Hall. Please send my best regards to yeer father."

"I will." I patted his arm and gathered the sides of my gown to ascend the stone steps.

The door swung open, and Mr. Holmes, the butler, stepped out. "Miss Katherine, Miss Ruiz, we weren't expecting you."

"Good afternoon, Mr. Holmes. Is my father in?"

As I stopped on the landing, he looked beyond me to Dorotea, who followed on my heels. "He is. However, he is pre-disposed at the moment—a business engagement."

"We will wait until he is finished."

I marched inside and spun to take in the carved mahogany panels and marble columns of the hall entrance. A lavish crystal chandelier hung front and center, and a single curving staircase rose to the mezzanine brightened with large stained-glass windows. Giant ferns and palms towered in corners, and extravagant flower arrangements accented stands and hall tables. I heard the quiet movements and voices of staff in the corridors and floors above. The townhouse was smaller than our estate in the country but held an exquisite charm and warmth unmolested by Audrey. The feeling of being home summoned tears, and I blinked them away.

"If you care to wait in the salon, I will ask Mrs. Dixon to fix you some tea and refreshments."

I inclined my head and followed him to the salon. A fire burned in the carved marble fireplace, radiating warmth throughout the room. The fire's glow and the glittering light from the chandelier danced off the velvet green walls and gilded moldings. Rich ivory drapes trimmed with gold cording framed the window overlooking the street.

"If you will excuse me." Mr. Holmes bowed and went in search of Mrs. Dixon.

I settled on the medallion back sofa and removed my gloves and the hat pins, then placed my hat and gloves on the sofa and rose to stroll to the fireplace and warm my hands. The cooler weather was upon us, and most families returned to the city until the stifling warmer months, but since his return, Papa had not arranged for us to join him.

I stood gazing into the flames, contemplating Papa's disconnect from his daughters, and the pain and misery it caused—even more so when Audrey sought to punish me for every move I did or didn't make. I turned from the fire and returned to the settee. Dorotea continued to pace. The clicking of her shoes grated on my nerves.

"Please, won't you take a seat?" I gestured at the chair across from me.

A memory flashed into my mind: my mother sitting there, doing needlework, while we older girls sprawled on our bellies before the fire with boxes of watercolors, paintbrushes, and paper. I thought of how Mama had cooed over each of our creations and whispered in my ear so my sisters wouldn't notice, "You, my love, will be an artist one day." My heart had expanded with pride. Now, the memory warmed my heart.

"Miss Katherine, Miss Ruiz, what a lovely surprise." Mrs. Dixon ambled into the room with a tray of tea cakes and a teapot.

"Mrs. Dixon. Always a pleasure," I said.

"How do you fare, dear?" She regarded me tenderly.

"I will be better once I speak to Papa."

"Unrest at Braxton Hall, I see." She set down the tray and poured the steaming tea into a royal blue, fluted porcelain cup.

I lifted the sugar nippers and dropped two sugar loaves into the amber liquid. "You could say that." I added a splash of milk.

"I'm sorry to hear that, dear." She straightened her full figure and regarded me with concern. "It is not my place to say more, but your father loves and misses you and your sisters."

"He has a shoddy way of showing it," I said, speaking more candidly than appropriate. Evelyn's lecture on suitable relations between staff and family members replayed in my head and my mood soured. Mrs. Dixon had served our family for years, and she was openly devoted to my sisters and me, with a particular fondness for Alice. Surely it was safe to speak to her.

"What does he do with no one to fill this home?" I asked, looking around.

"When he isn't preoccupied with work and colleagues, he takes long carriage rides and strolls in Central Park."

I added another sugar log. "With whom?"

"By himself." Her brow furrowed, and she moved the sugar bowl beyond my reach.

"How can you be certain?"

"Your father is an honorable man, Señorita Katherine. He would not bring scandal upon your family," Dorotea said.

"Yet he married…her." I took a sip of the tea, and my tastebuds rebelled against the sweetness.

"Thank you, Señora Dixon," Dorotea said. "We will manage until Señor Darlington is free."

Mrs. Dixon nodded and dismissed herself.

After she left, Dorotea regarded me. "You must tread lightly and not converse so openly with the staff, especially regarding the family," she said, keeping her voice low.

"I understand, but how am I to know about Papa unless I ask? You know as well as I how he's neglecting his family."

"Although your hurt and displeasure with your father are warranted, you mustn't speak so candidly with those outside your trusted circle."

"Mrs. Dixon can be trusted, can't she?"

She gathered my hand in hers. "You're young and know not the ways of the world."

"How can I learn if I'm never permitted to leave the confines of my bedchamber?" My shoulders slumped. "There is a rage inside me. An unrest." I looked deep into her eyes. This woman had soothed my soul with her devotion and love. I had sensed her fondness for me, and my older sisters claimed she indulged my insubordinate behaviors and ideals. I trusted her like no other.

Concern flickered in her dark eyes, and for a moment she seemed far away.

I continued to express what was on my heart but realized she hadn't heard a word I'd said. "Dorotea?" I waved a hand in front of her face.

She started and lightly shook her head. "I'm sorry, señorita. I suppose my mind drifted for a moment."

"Care to divulge what occupied your thoughts?" I asked.

"It is nothing." She offered me a smile, and I sensed she did not wish to discuss whatever memory had stolen her attention, and I didn't press her.

"It was a pleasure, Mr. Huntington." Papa's deep voice echoed in the corridor, followed by advancing footsteps.

I rose, the matter I had come to discuss with Papa ever pressing, and strode to the threshold of the salon. I tipped my head into the entrance hall.

"Thank you for agreeing to see me. My mother insisted I approach you after we learned of Hamilton's disregard for our previous agreement by endeavoring to market Stockwell Industries to you at a higher price."

I lingered in the doorway until Papa and a younger gentleman with wavy brown hair and a short-cropped beard strode into view. The man's blue eyes locked on me, and he halted.

Papa stopped and considered him before looking for what had captured his attention. "Kat." Papa's face brightened before his brow puckered.

"Hello, Papa," I said, acknowledging the gentleman beside him with a brief nod.

Mr. Holmes entered the entrance hall from a nearby room. "I was going to tell you that you had company, Mr. Darlington."

"Yes, thank you, Mr. Holmes, but my daughter is hardly company." He swung back to face me, and Mr. Holmes retreated. "How are you, my darling?" Papa extended his arms.

I walked forward, embraced him, and planted a peck on his cheek before taking a step back.

He held my elbows and regarded me at arm's length. "Is everyone well?"

"We are fine, Papa." I glanced at the dapper man in the dark three-piece silk suit.

His shoulders relaxed, and he stepped aside and encircled my shoulders with an arm before addressing the gentleman. "Katherine, I would like to introduce you to an acquaintance of mine, Mr. Merritt Huntington."

I held out a hand. "How do you do, sir?"

He offered a mysterious smile but stepped forward and clasped both of his hands around mine. "I am well. It's nice to meet you, Miss Darlington…or is it Mrs.?"

Papa chuckled softly and said, "It'd take a man with impeccable patience to tame my daughter."

Amusement flashed in Mr. Huntington's eyes and he regarded me with an intrigued expression. "Is that so?"

"My daughter prefers her independence."

"You speak as though I'm not here." Heat rushed over my cheeks, and I stepped from the protection of his arm.

Mr. Huntington's look of intrigue deepened, and my distaste for the exchange and the gentleman magnified. I supposed he was used to ladies flocking to him, swept away by his good looks, but I was not such a lady.

"If you will excuse me." I turned to Dorotea, standing in the salon doorway. "Dorotea and I will wait in your study while you show Mr. Huntington out."

Dorotea walked over to join us, and I observed how Papa regarded her with deep affection, and his body relaxed in her presence. "Miss Ruiz, I didn't see you there."

Dorotea considered him with respect and admiration. "Señor Darlington, it has been too long."

"Indeed."

I looked to Papa's colleague. "Good day, Mr. Huntington."

He dipped his head. "And to you."

"T-thank you," I stammered, unnerved by his intense gaze. I whirled and marched off toward Papa's study, sensing him watching me.

The study bore the same mahogany paneling as the entrance hall. I paced its carpet, pausing to study a painting of Mama hanging above the mantel. She wore a yellow gown, and an exquisite emerald and diamond necklace hung around her slender neck. Her eyes were as blue as sapphires plucked from the sky. Traces of Mama lingered in every room of the townhome, and I knew why Audrey rarely visited. The thought brought satisfaction.

I strolled to the window, which overlooked the courtyard and carriage house, and observed Mr. Kelly sitting outside, smoking a cigar and conversing with Papa's coachman.

Papa walked into the room with a broad smile. "All right, ladies, to what do I owe the honor of this visit?"

I bristled at his cheerfulness. Had he not missed us at all? "I have come to fetch you home," I said, stepping away from the window.

"Have you now?" He lifted a brow. "That is presumptuous of you, to think I can just up and leave when I have a business to attend to."

"Is it business that keeps you away?" I delivered a hard stare.

His smile faded. "Of course."

"You may fool Evelyn and the others, but not me." I closed the distance between us and stood on the Persian carpet Mama had shipped across the ocean for this room.

He stiffened. "Why do you arrive here with so much hostility, daughter?" He looked from me to Dorotea.

"What Señorita Katherine means to say is, your presence is missed at Braxton Hall," Dorotea said.

The tension in his brow eased at her reply, and I realized I needed to reconsidered my approach, if I wanted to accomplish what I had come there to achieve. I softened my tone. "You must return. It's been almost a year since your last visit. Grace is growing so fast."

"Yes, my Grace." Affection eased the weariness on his face. Years had created fine lines and etched his brow, but Papa's attractiveness had always been the gentleness in his eyes. "What is she, seven now?"

"She is nine, Papa," I said with exasperation.

He lowered his head. "Forgive me. Most of my days meld together."

"You must return to Braxton Hall and set things right again. Or that woman will be our downfall," I said. "You dropped her into our laps and fled off to war, never giving us a choice in the matter."

He lifted his gaze, and his gentle demeanor faded, as it often did when he felt coerced. "I am your father, and you will speak to me as such. And you will mind how you speak of your stepmother." He walked around his desk and sat down.

I swung to face him. "You must listen, Papa." Dorotea reached for me, but I sidestepped her grip, strode to the desk, and rested my hands firmly on it. "Why, just the other day, Dorotea witnessed Mrs. Cox striking Grace, and when she reported it to Audrey upon her return from wherever she gallivants off to, she dismissed it."

He flinched and looked over my shoulder at Dorotea. "Tell me this isn't true."

"I'm afraid it is true," she said, her voice heavy.

His hand balled into a fist on the desk. "Has Grace turned into a mischievous girl in my absence?"

"No!" I slammed an open palm on the desk, succumbing to my concern over Audrey's threat to Jude. Her aggressiveness toward me the previous night, and endless days spent locked in my chamber and humiliated by her drove me to continue. "Grace is tender and kind. She is a meek child, Papa. You would know this, if you hadn't abandoned your family."

Dorotea gasped.

"Katherine Darlington, I warn you to watch your tongue." His eyes flashed.

I straightened and took a step back. "Forgive me, but how can I make you hear me if I don't defy the respectable approach? I become a child without a voice, easily disregarded despite my years." Tears clotted my throat, and my voice shook. "Audrey leaves for days at a time, never saying where she's going. I fear she will make a mockery of our family."

He leaned forward. "What do you speak of?"

"Just as I said." My need to make him come home overwhelmed me, and my body trembled. I swept a hand around the room. "You keep this place like a museum in your desire to keep Mama alive. But nothing you do will bring her back. She is gone. You must accept that and move on. *We* have had no choice but to." I clasped my hands tightly in front of me to still their trembling.

Tears glistened in his eyes, and his jaw quivered as he looked away to gaze out the window at nothingness. The bitterness I felt toward him fractured, permitting me to see his loneliness and pain.

I circled the desk and rested a hand on his shoulder. "I don't mean to cause you more pain." He nodded, never looking at me, but lifting a hand to rest it over mine. "Mama is gone, and we are very much alive. We need you…" My voice hitched. "I-I need you to want us. We lost her too. We hurt too." Tears burned my eyes.

He gulped and turned to face me, guilt reflected in his eyes. "I'm sorry, Kat."

I nodded my acceptance. "I know you don't mean to hurt us and that you miss her terribly."

"The pain never fades," he said and cleared his throat. Then he rose and embraced me. "I will endeavor to do better."

I need you to do better than try, my heart screamed, but I remained silent and lay my cheek on his chest, soaking in all the love and comfort the safety of his arms brought. The tension that never left my body lifted for a fleeting moment. "I love you, Papa," I said softly.

"And I, you." He held me out to study my face.

I searched his eyes and saw resolve there. "Audrey is no mother. Alice and Grace are young and impressionable and lack the love and devotion Mama would have given them."

He cupped my cheek. "I will heed your advice. Your sisters are blessed for the fierce champion who defends their cause."

My heart swelled.

"What a gift you have been to this family." He stared through me as though captured in time, the same far-off look I'd seen on Dorotea earlier.

We left him with the promise that he'd come to Braxton Hall by the end of the week and gather his family to bring us to the city.

Chapter 6

RAIN WAS PELTING OFF THE CARRIAGE AND RUNNING DOWN THE windowpanes by the time we reached the city outskirts. Dorotea and I grasped the sides of the carriage as rutted roads, now slick and treacherous, tossed us to and fro. Nevertheless, the discomfort of the ride couldn't displace the hope buoying me at Papa's promise to bring my sisters and me to live with him in the city.

"The road is sure to be flooded by the Doyles' place," Dorotea said.

"Mr. Kelly is a skilled driver. He will get us home." I rubbed the ache in the back of my neck caused by the bouncing. My thoughts turned to Braxton Hall. I'd return to my chamber before Mrs. Cox awakened from her induced slumber. Tomorrow Papa would come to fetch us, and all would be well.

"We are sure to have headaches by the time we reach Braxton Hall." Dorotea closed her eyes, attempting the impossible task of resting.

I thought of Mr. Kelly, exposed to the storm's fury, but the need to get to Papa kept me from feeling guilty for long.

We continued for about a mile before coming to the Doyle place, and Mr. Kelly slowed the carriage and moved forward cautiously. My view out the window was limited, but I saw the water flooding the road. The carriage convulsed and groaned as Mr. Kelly urged the team onward. My fingers dug into the upholstery of the carriage wall as I fought to steady myself.

Dorotea removed her glove, and the small cross of the Rosary she clasped flashed. Then she quietly began to pray the Rosary in Spanish. I gritted my teeth, trying to stop the jostling of my brain. We lurched forward as the carriage gained ground and broke free of the steady stream of water deteriorating the roadway.

We had scarcely left the city and our journey back to Braxton Hall had been too adventurous for Dorotea's liking. She held a white cotton handkerchief to her mouth and appeared paler.

"How do you fare?" I leaned forward and touched her knee.

"I have never been one for too much tossing around. I don't have the stomach for it. After sailing with your family to come to America, I never had much liking for storms. I thought it would be the death of us all. The ocean waves were so high at times, it was as if the hand of God sought to strike us down for what we..." Her voice trailed off.

"For what?" I frowned.

She continued as though I hadn't spoken. "I was deathly sick throughout the voyage. You were an infant, and I was of no use to your mother in caring for you. I could barely lift my head."

Thunder rumbled overhead, and I drew back the chestnut velvet curtain to observe the sky. "This storm doesn't intend to let up. At this pace, we won't reach Braxton Hall until nightfall, and Mrs. Cox will be on to me. So I may not live to see Papa's arrival tomorrow."

"Don't despair, señorita. Without Señora Darlington home, Mrs. Cox wouldn't dare harm you. Confine you, yes. But you will see your father tomorrow. I only hope he sees my services warranted in the city."

"Why wouldn't he?"

Her words jerked out as she was jostled by the movements

of the carriage. "A-as you girls get older, the need for a governess is waning."

"You mustn't say such things. Grace and Alice require a governess. You're my confidant and my greatest supporter. Without you, we'd never have survived these last years."

"It is troubling to stand by, powerless, and that is what my position has come to."

I had witnessed Dorotea's struggle in her expression and body language when she was silenced or forced to stand aside while Audrey took the rearing of my sisters and me into her own hands.

"May Papa's return bring us all peace," I said.

She offered a small smile. "Si, señorita."

I peeked out the gap in the curtain at the horizon. "Mr. Kelly must be miserable out there."

"A hot bath and a hot toddy should fix him right up," Dorotea said, trying to alleviate my remorse.

"Let us—"

The carriage wheel hit a rut and lurched sharply to the left. Dorotea squealed and clung to the side of the carriage. The pounding of my heart punctuated the panic in her eyes as Mr. Kelly shouted at the team and fought to regain control of the carriage.

With a sharp crack, the left front side of the carriage plunged down to grind across the ground. I screamed as the carriage overbalanced and tipped. The carriage rolled, tossing us around like we were weightless, slamming our bodies into each other before plowing us into the roof. My cheekbone smacked the corner of the window frame, and pain radiated. Then as the carriage stopped moving, my head smashed against a hard surface, and my world went black.

When I came to, I struggled to recall what had happened. I lay in a heap, wedged into the corner of the carriage. Pain throbbed throughout my body, and I groaned, lifting fingers to touch the warmth trickling down my cheek. I blinked, trying to gather my senses, then recollected the accident.

"Dorotea!" I scrambled to get up, suppressing the pain. Daylight was fading, and I wondered how long I had been unconscious. I scanned the darkness for Dorotea and my eyes stopped on a crumpled form to my left. I called for her again, but she remained motionless. *No, no, no.* I reached for her, blinded by welling tears. "Please be all right." I cradled her head, and blood from her brow oozed through my glove. I checked her pulse. She yet breathed! I hugged her close and took in my surroundings. I had to get us out of here.

Dorotea stirred, moaning as she came to before releasing a wail. "Ay!" She rambled on in Spanish.

"Can you move?"

"My ankle," she said, and I regarded the ankle visible below the hem of her dress.

"Is it broken?" I leaned forward to examine it. I recalled the time Adelaide had fallen down the stairs and the strange way her foot had looked. "It doesn't appear so. Perhaps you sprained it. What about the rest of you?"

"Bruised and battered," she said as I attempted to help her to sit up.

"Ay!" She slumped back against the carriage floor. "My ribs." I heard the pain in her voice. Dorotea pushed me away. "Leave me, and go check on Mr. Kelly."

My chest tightened. In my concern over her, I had forgotten about him. "I'll be back. Everything will be all right."

The carriage had come to a rest on its side. I reached over my head and tried to open the door, but it wouldn't budge. The door was too damaged to open, but to my astonishment, the window remained intact. "Cover your eyes. I will get us out of here." I leaned back on the seat and kicked at the window, shattering the glass. I regarded the size of the window, then the circumference of the bottom of my dress. I removed my paletot and hat. "You must unbutton me." I angled my body into an awkward position so that she could reach the back of my dress.

She fumbled with the buttons and said through chattering teeth, "My fingers are chilled to the bone." Several minutes passed before she released the last button.

I hurried to shuffle out of the gown then half stood, wearing nothing but my camisole, petticoat, and black lace-up boots. Using the fabric of my dress, I removed shards of glass and splinters from the opening before hoisting myself up.

"Be careful, dear," Dorotea called up at me.

I poked my head outside, looked around for Mr. Kelly, and spotted his body sprawled in the ditch. I wiggled through the window, grateful for my petite figure, and landed with a splash on my backside on the ground. Mud seeped through my undergarments, filling every crevice. I pushed my palms into the earth, feeling the bite of pebbles and the mud oozing between my fingers.

Gaining my feet, I raced to Mr. Kelly and dropped to my knees beside him. He lay unmoving, and one glance at the odd angle of his right foot made my chest constrict. "Mr. Kelly?" I squeezed his hand and gave him a gentle shake. My panic heightened, but logic set in, and I resisted the impulse to shake him, recalling Mama saying once that you should never move a person without first examining their injuries. "Mr. Kelly." I gently slapped his face, looking for a response, but he remained motionless. "This is all my fault." The rain weighing my lashes mixed with tears, and my body quivered. Audrey's relentless words, repeated throughout the years, echoed in my head: *"Foolish, foolish, girl. You lack all sense and purpose."*

Think, Kat, think. I glanced around, my attention turning to the horses. One appeared to have broken its neck in the accident, and the other struggled to stand but was snarled in the driving reins. I trudged through the puddles to help the beast. My fingers numb and shaking, I fought with the bridle. My wet undergarments hung like heavy, dirty linens and clung to my body.

The horse kicked at the ground, its eyes wide with panic. Using the back of my hand, I wiped the water from my eyes and concentrated on unfastening the buckle. Then, as the bridle and tackle fell away, I moved to release his hind leg, wrapped in the driver's reins. "Easy boy," I said, struggling with the reins. But they were wound too tight.

"Miss," a voice called above the storm, and I froze and scanned my surroundings. I jumped when my gaze landed on a carriage stopped in the middle of the road and a man walking toward me.

I pushed to my feet and inched back, becoming aware of my vulnerability. He put out a hand to show he meant no harm. As he drew near, I recognized him. He was none other than the gentleman who had been doing business with Papa in the city. Mr. Huntington, I recalled.

"Let me help." He brushed by me and bent over the horse. He worked swiftly, and the horse thrashed and kicked to rise as the reins fell away.

"Whoa, boy. Steady," Mr. Huntington said, but the horse took off and stopped several yards down the road. He turned to me. "Are you all right?"

"I believe so. It's Mr. Kelly," I said through chattering teeth, and pointed to where he lay. "And Dorotea."

"Here." He pulled off his overcoat and threw it around my shoulders. "You get into my carriage, and my driver and I will see to your friends."

"No, I will stay with you."

The concern on his face shifted to determination. "You will do no one any good if you catch your death. Now go." He gave me a gentle nudge.

Cold, miserable, and gravely concerned for Mr. Kelly and Dorotea's well-being, I nodded and turned toward his carriage. I noticed another man kneeling beside Mr. Kelly, assessing his injuries.

I opened the carriage door and stumbled inside. I sat down, shaking, and tried to see what was happening outside. Minutes passed, then the door opened, and Mr. Huntington stood there, drenched, holding Dorotea in his arms.

"Dorotea," I gasped.

She offered me a weary smile before her face tightened in pain.

"Grab the blankets stored under the seat there." Mr. Huntington nodded toward the seat opposite me.

I scrambled to do as he asked, and once I retrieved a bundle of blankets, he placed Dorotea on the seat next to me.

She suppressed a wince, and I fought back tears.

"Don't worry, señorita. I will be fine," she said as I wrapped a blanket around her shoulders.

"I fear we can't say the same for your driver." Mr. Huntington glanced over his shoulder before regarding me. Suddenly aware of my near nakedness, I drew his coat tighter around myself. "He is conscious now but in a great deal of pain. Your friend here says your place is another ten miles from here. My family's country estate is less than a mile back the way you came. May I suggest we take you there, and I'll send my driver for the doctor?"

"Yes. Please, hurry," I said.

He closed the door and was gone, only to return minutes later with his driver, with Mr. Kelly suspended between them. Mr. Kelly cried out in pain as they loaded him into the carriage and settled him across from us. I covered him with a blanket.

"I'm sorry, Mr. Kelly. I wish—"

"Don't be sorry, lass," he said through gritted teeth. "The accident wasn't your fault."

Mr. Huntington climbed in and sat beside him. "Get us to Rosehill Manor," he said to the driver.

"Straightaway, Mr. Huntington." He shut the door, and soon the carriage lurched forward. The driver headed back in the direction of the city.

"Would it not have been best to stay in the city with your father?" Mr. Huntington said.

"If only it were that simple," I said as Dorotea slumped against my shoulder, and I wrapped an arm around her.

"Most have returned to the city from their Newport cottages

and country estates. So why does your father leave you to reside in the country?"

I regarded him in the last rays of daylight, meeting the intense gaze I had noted in our previous encounter. "If you don't mind, I don't feel much like idle chitchat."

"Have it your way." He inclined his head, not appearing the least bit offended.

I looked away and eyed Mr. Kelly, who appeared to have passed out again. I closed my eyes, determined not to break down.

We sat in silence, except for the occasional whimper from Dorotea, and in no time, the carriage veered to the left, and I leaned forward to look out the window.

"We have arrived," Mr. Huntington said. "Soon we will have you all as comfortable as possible to wait until this storm passes."

I welcomed the smoother ride down the lane, which curved around a hillside, concealing the estate from the roadway. We rode along for a bit longer before the lights of a house appeared. I had never noticed the estate before, probably because of its discreet location.

The carriage pulled to a stop, and Mr. Huntington opened the door before his driver could and stepped out.

"Mr. Huntington, sir, we weren't expecting the family until the spring. Is everything all right?" a man said.

"All is well, Mr. Robinson. I need you to send a rider to fetch the doctor."

"But sir, you said everything—"

"My family is safe in the city. On our way back to the city from visiting the Hamilton estate, we encountered an accident on the roadway. I've brought the injured to shelter from the storm and provide aid. Please, make haste. And send out Mr. Lewis and Mrs. Quinn to assist."

"Yes, sir."

Mr. Huntington poked his head inside. "Come, Miss

Darlington. Let's get you out of those wet undergarments and into a warm bath and fresh clothing."

I drew his coat tighter and took the hand he offered. And as the warmth of his hand engulfed mine, a charge ran through me. I disembarked the carriage and quickly removed my hand from his.

"If you head inside, Mrs. Quinn will attend to your needs."

"I will stay with Dorotea and Mr. Kelly," I said.

"You will do no one any good standing out here in the rain."

I tilted my chin. "I will see they are cared for first."

He stepped toward me and I stepped back, but not before he gripped my chin in his hand. "You need to get your cheek tended to." He placed a thumb on my cheekbone, and I winced. "I have no time for a spoiled child," he said, releasing me. "Go into the house."

I bristled at his treatment of me but noticed the firm set of his jaw. Realizing I would not win with him, I cast aside my stubbornness for the sake of Dorotea and Mr. Kelly. "Very well, Mr. Huntington. We will accept your help, but heed me when I say that as soon as the sun comes up, we will get out of your way and back to Braxton Hall." I spun around and strode across the cobblestones to the house. I was halfway to the broad marble staircase when a plump woman with flaming red hair waddled toward me with an umbrella.

"Are ye one of Mr. Huntington's charges, lass?" She sheltered us both under the umbrella and looked me up and down.

"Hardly one of his charges," I said.

"Yes, well, whatever ye want to call it. We bes' get ye inside and out of the cold and this rain before ye catch yeer death."

I followed her into the house and welcomed the warmth.

Inside, the lanterns were turned down low, and the entrance chandelier sat unlit. Mrs. Quinn placed the umbrella upside down in the corner while I stood dripping water over the marble tiles. I looked to the adjacent rooms, noticing the drawn drapes and white sheets covering the furniture.

"We are operating at quarter staff with the family's return to

the city, but we will see yeer taken care of, don't ye worry none."
She favored me with a warm smile and gestured for me to follow
her to the staircase on the right. She collected a lantern on a nearby
stand and turned it up before mounting the first step. "Let's get ye
upstairs and into something dry. We will have a bath drawn and
have ye warmed up in no time."

I halted on the steps to observe the portraits in the low glow
of the wall sconces. The first was of a silver-haired, middle-aged
woman with a prudish countenance with a younger, timid-looking
woman stationed at her side. Next was a portrait of Mr. Huntington
and a hunting dog. I glanced back at the previous one and noted
his similarity to the silver-haired woman.

"Hurry up, now. Ye're dripping water all over the runner." The
woman stood on the upper landing, waiting for me to catch up.

I glanced at the stair runner and mumbled an apology before
hastening my ascent.

"We will see what Miss Josie may have that would fit." She
took a second look at me as we walked down the corridor. "Ye appear to be about her size."

"Thank you…"

"They call me Mrs. Quinn. And who may ye be?"

I smiled at her and said, "Katherine, but I prefer Kat."

"Miss Kat it is." She nodded. "What are ye doing out and about
on a day like this, and what happened to yeer clothing? If you don't
mind me asking," she added.

"I went to visit my father in the city. My sisters and I require
his attention at home."

"I see, and the storm caught ye."

"Yes."

We walked in silence and turned a corner or two, and I regarded the skylights in the high, domed, frescoed ceilings. The dim
corridor provided little insight into the Huntingtons. Nevertheless,
the family's name was familiar, and I was sure I had heard it before
but had paid it no mind.

"As you can see, we weren't expecting anyone." She stopped outside a door and turned the knob.

"I will change and see to my friends," I said, following her into the room.

"As ye wish." She walked around the room, lighting extra lanterns.

I turned to observe the chamber, decorated in dusty rose and gold leafing, a feminine touch, but a child's toys and other items were placed here and there.

"This is Miss Josie's chamber. I'll remove the dust coverings and change the linens. Ye'll sleep here tonight." She disappeared into an adjoining room, which appeared to be a dressing room. If Miss Josie were a child, how could I possibly fit into her clothing?

"Are ye coming?" Mrs. Quinn said from inside.

I entered the dressing room and found her standing in front of a wardrobe, sorting through a drawer. She removed a white garment and held it out.

"This shift will have to do." She retrieved another item and handed it to me. "Let me get ye a towel to dry off, and ye can change over there." She pointed to the privacy screen.

Eager to be out of my wet garments, I stepped behind the screen and slipped them off and removed my muddied boots. I stood naked until Mrs. Quinn thrust a hand behind the screen.

"Here."

I took the towel she offered.

I dried my body and patted my hair before pulling the night-shift over my head. Mrs. Quinn had been right in her assumption that Miss Josie's clothing would fit. I fastened the buttons and slipped on the night-robe.

I stepped from behind the screen, and Mrs. Quinn marched past me to gather the towel and my wet garments. "If ye head back down the way we came, ye should find Mr. Huntington and yeer friends."

I wondered if I would find my way back, but didn't want to inconvenience her any more than I already had.

"When yeer bath is prepared, I will come and fetch ye. Then get the chamber aired out and add fresh linens."

"Thank you." I hurried by her and exited the chamber.

As I padded down the corridor in my bare feet, my thoughts turned to Evelyn and Adelaide. They'd scold me for sure when they learned of the predicament I found myself in. Stranded and barely clothed on the roadway…perhaps I'd leave that part out. When I didn't return home, they'd be beside themselves with worry. And Mrs. Cox…my stomach plunged; she would've gathered her senses and sought to expose my escape to Audrey. But Papa would stop the conspiring sows and keep me from their grasp.

Everything depended on his arrival at Braxton Hall the following day.

Chapter 7

Merritt—Rosehill Manor

I STOOD OUTSIDE MY FAMILY'S ESTATE, OBSERVING MISS DARLINGTON clad in only her undergarments and draped in my overcoat as she walked toward the front steps. The outdoor lanterns elongated her petite shadow across the cobblestones. I considered the condition I'd discovered her in on the road: half naked, covered in mud, her dark brown hair pasted to her face. Her panic had turned to relief before she replaced it with defiance.

Earlier in the day, at her family's townhouse in the city, she'd been a vision in red satin and black lace, but the fire in her dark eyes captured my attention. She seemed to hold the world at arm's length, and her dismissive disposition intrigued me. She never gravitated toward me, like the pretentious ladies from affluent families my mother wanted me to wed. I spent my time investing and expanding the Huntington wealth to avoid enduring another one of her insufferable assignations.

I took one last look at Miss Darlington before she disappeared inside. "That one is not a woman to be ignored," I declared, and turned back to the carriage.

"Sir?"

The butler's voice alerted me to his presence, and I noticed him standing to my left for the first time. "Mr. Lewis, please help me get the passengers inside."

We got Miss Darlington's driver inside before I returned for the woman. She put her arms around my neck, and I gently hoisted her into my arms. She winced from the pain.

"Gracias, señor," she whispered into my neck as I walked toward the house.

"You have more gratitude than your charge," I said under my breath.

"She is more delicate than she seems."

I regarded her upturned face as I climbed the steps. The pain had drained her of color, and her full lips were purple from the cold.

"I detect Miss Darlington is fond of you, and you, her."

"She is special," she said as I reached the landing.

Mr. Lewis stood at the open double doors, looking like a drenched rat, and one could assume I appeared no better. Adjusting the woman in my arms, I walked past him and into the drawing room. Mr. Lewis set to lighting lanterns in the darkened room as I lay the woman on the settee, still draped with a white dust cover. I straightened as the room brightened with lamplight and wiped a hand over my face and hair to skim off the moisture. I whirled at the sound of Miss Darlington's voice.

"Dorotea." Now wrapped in a night-robe, she darted across the room to the woman's side and dropped to her knees.

The woman cupped Miss Darlington's cheek. "I will be all right, señorita." Her eyelids closed.

"We need to get you out of these wet clothes." Miss Darlington rose and turned to me. "Where is Mr. Kelly?"

"We have settled him upstairs until the doctor arrives." I regarded the woman before me.

She pulled her night-robe closer over the nightshift brushing her delicate ankles, and lowered her eyes. "Forgive me for my indecency."

"You are more clothed than you were a short time ago. I am not here as your judge or jury but as a Samaritan wanting to help."

She looked up at me and said with a small smile, "Thank you."

I nodded. "I will locate something for you to change her into."

I left her and climbed the stairs to my mother's room, where I gathered woolen stockings, a nightshift, and a robe before rejoining Miss Darlington in the drawing room.

Mr. Lewis knelt by the open fireplace, stoking a recently started fire. A stack of blankets lay next to the sofa.

Miss Darlington took the items from me and voiced her gratitude.

"If you will excuse us, Mr. Lewis and I will be nearby if you require anything."

She nodded before returning to the settee to perch on its edge. She leaned forward and stroked the woman's hair. Her dainty feet peeked from beneath her shift and her long dark hair hung damp down her back.

I turned and left the room. In the hallway, I paused. "Mr. Lewis, I will be in my chamber. See to it that my bath is prepared, and bring me something to quench my thirst."

"Right away, Mr. Huntington."

Later, fully immersed in the copper bathtub, I let my head sink below the water and savored the heat extracting the chill from my bones. I remained so until my lungs screamed for air before I sat up and leaned back against the cool metal.

Mr. Lewis stood nearby with a tray holding a glass snifter and a bottle of cognac. "As requested, sir, I've brought you a Maison Rouge Grand Reserve Vintage Fine Champagne Cognac—1840 vintage." He held out the bottle for my inspection.

"Splendid."

He opened the bottle, poured some into the snifter, and passed it to me.

"Thank you, Mr. Lewis," I said before taking a mouthful and swirling it around on my tongue. "Leave it here."

He placed the tray on a stand next to the tub. "Will that be all, sir?"

I nodded, and he left me. I held the glass out in front of me and swirled the amber liquid around, watching it chase the diameter.

I reflected on my previous visit to the countryside. After learning of Mr. Hamilton's attempt to sell Stockwell Industries to Mr. Darlington despite his prior agreement to sell to me, I'd paid him a visit to discuss the matter.

Unfortunately, Mr. Hamilton had gotten in over his head and had been forced to sell his Manhattan townhouse last year. His reign as one of New York's most successful businessmen was ending. When I learned he was selling off Stockwell Industries, I sought to buy him out. I recalled the desperation on his face the day I had walked into his office, weeks prior, and presented him with an offer he couldn't refuse, given his predicament. His recent change of heart had not come as a shock to me, as he was reputed to be corrupt. My father had tried to take over Stockwell Industries for years, and the bad blood between him and my father had trumped his hunger to sell—he had tried to sell Stockwell Industries out from under me.

I lifted the bottle and refilled my glass before my thoughts returned to Miss Darlington, and what people would say if they learned of the predicament we found ourselves in. I couldn't have left her by the roadside, nor could I have forced the injured to make the journey to her country estate.

I exited my chamber just as the doctor finished with Miss Darlington's driver, and she and he stepped into the corridor.

"He hit his head hard, and unfortunately, that leg will take a while to mend. He won't be fit to drive a carriage for some time."

Miss Darlington's face tightened, and she stood wringing her hands in front of her. "Thank you for coming out here on a night like this. What about my governess?"

"Those ribs will also take time to heal. I'm afraid they will both require time away from their responsibilities while they mend."

"Again, I thank you. Let me show you out."

"May I suggest we take care of that wound on your cheek first?"

"Oh," she said, lifting fingers to touch her cheek. "I had forgotten."

I cleared my throat before sauntering down the corridor, and they glanced in my direction.

"Ah, Mr. Huntington." The doctor held out a hand, and I clasped it.

"Thank you for coming," I said. "Why don't we go downstairs, and you can tend to Miss Darlington?" I gestured for them to go ahead.

Downstairs, I led them to the parlor to discover it empty. "Where is the woman?" I asked Miss Darlington.

"Mr. Lewis and Mrs. Quinn helped her into the bed in one of the upper chambers." Fatigue haloed her face, and a stiffness governed her movements. "We must be gone at first light. I have to get home. My sisters will be terribly worried when I don't return."

"You need not worry, Miss Darlington. I will see to your safe return first thing in the morning. Now, sit and allow the doctor to tend to your cheek." I eyed the wound and considered the scar it would leave, but it seemed to be the last concern on her mind.

She seated herself on the settee, and while the doctor worked, she never let out a wince. Rather, she looked past me, a troubled look on her face.

What caused the woman so much anguish?

Chapter 8

Kat—1870

MRS. QUINN MARCHED INTO MY CHAMBER THE FOLLOWING DAY and tugged open the dusty rose brocade drapes. The sun poured over the dark hardwood floors. Its golden threads illuminated dust particles floating in the air.

I sat up, recalling where I was, and threw back the blankets.

"Good morning, Miss Kat." Mrs. Quinn raised a beefy hand and tucked a stray curl beneath her white maid's cap. "Mr. Huntington awaits ye in the dining room. He has requested ye join him for breakfast."

"What time is it?" I asked as I swung my feet to the floor.

"Half past nine."

I leaped to my feet. "Why didn't someone wake me? I have to get home."

"No need to worry, miss. Mr. Huntington had yeer carriage wheel fixed and brought here this morning. He retrieved yeer gown, and I had it pressed and hung in the dressing room." She pointed to the door to the left of the fireplace.

I retrieved the night-robe I had discarded on the end of the four-poster bed and slipped it on.

"Let's get ye dressed. It's bes' not to keep Mr. Huntington waiting. He must return to the city and requests yeer company."

"Is Mr. Huntington always so demanding to his guests?" I said.

Her eyes widened. "Mr. Huntington isn't one to be persuaded. He doesn't take kindly to insubordination."

I bit my tongue, not wishing to dismiss Mr. Huntington's help, but the sooner I was away from Rosehill Manor, the better.

I followed her into the dressing room and permitted her to help me with my dress. While she pinned my hair, I regarded the stitches on my cheek in the looking glass and the bruise haloing my eye. Evelyn would indeed have a lot to say when I returned home.

"A pretty little thing ye are. Ye clean up real well, miss," Mrs. Quinn said with satisfaction. The woman had a pleasant face and maintained an eagerness to help. "Now, let's get ye downstairs." She turned and waved a hand for me to follow.

Downstairs she led me to the dining room, which had sheets covering the furniture as in the rest of the home, and only a large table and chairs sat uncovered. The table held a spread fit to feed five people. I regarded the textured ceiling, then the ivory velvet walls and long golden drapes accenting windows with a view of a lush courtyard. There was no sign of Mr. Huntington.

While dressing, I had envisioned him sitting at the table, drumming his fingers impatiently. "Where is Mr. Huntington? You insisted we not keep him waiting, but now he keeps me waiting."

Mrs. Quinn gawked at me as though I had said something inappropriate before merriment glimmered in her eyes. "Ye can take a seat there." She gestured at a chair next to the chair at the head of the table. "I will go and fetch Mr. Huntington."

I nodded, and after she departed, I strolled to the window and looked over the property to the pastures beyond, where horses grazed in green fields. I thought of the portraits I had gained a better view of in the daylight on my way downstairs. At social gatherings, I had heard the name Huntington but had paid no heed; now, as I stood in their home, I imagined the place alive with activity.

However, I wondered if the empty feeling wasn't only because of the family and staff's absence.

I moved away from the window and paced the floor while watching the doorway for Mr. Huntington. What was taking him so long? He was aware of my need to get home.

I exited the dining room in search of him, or anyone I could question about his whereabouts. Low voices, accentuated by the house's emptiness, drew me to a closed door. I placed my ear to the door.

"The young woman seems on edge. I suggest ye make haste. Miss Kat has a strange urgency to get home." Mrs. Quinn's voice. "Perhaps the lass fears the rebuke of her stepmother. Rumor has it she is a bit hard on the Darlington sisters. Ye'd think with the new Mrs. Darlington not coming from an affluent family and nothing more than a chambermaid, she'd be mighty grateful for the Darlingtons and the life Mr. Darlington gave her."

Chambermaid? I frowned. My heart thumped faster.

"With all due respect, Mrs. Quinn, I don't heed whisperings," Mr. Huntington said gruffly.

"Forgive my intrusion in affairs not of my concern, sir. I suppose the young woman's distress got my mind rambling," Mrs. Quinn said with a hint of remorse.

No, please don't stop, my mind screamed. I wanted to throw the door open and barge in, but my desire to know more about what Mrs. Quinn referred to concerning Audrey held less importance than succumbing to such impropriety.

"If we were to believe every rumor we heard, we'd be leery of everyone," Mr. Huntington said. "Speaking of such matters, my mother is not to find out about our guests. I don't need her meddling, nor wagging tongues bringing reproach on Miss Darlington."

"Yes, Mr. Huntington," Mr. Lewis and Mrs. Quinn said in unison.

"Good. Now I must attend to my guest."

I pulled my head away from the door and darted back the

way I had come. Reaching the dining room, I rushed to the chair where Mrs. Quinn had told me to sit and sat down. I tried to catch my breath and calm my nerves.

"Good morning, Miss Darlington."

I jumped at the sound of his voice behind me.

"Don't worry, I don't bite." He strode into the room and seated himself at my left. The alluring scent of bergamot, orange blossoms, and a hint of rosemary wafted after him.

I considered his three-piece navy suit and neatly pomaded wavy brown hair while he adjusted his cutlery and place setting to his satisfaction. Then his blue-green gaze captured mine. I hesitated, enthralled by the ribbons of various colors in his irises, before dropping my gaze.

"I trust that you slept well." His voice held amusement—at my staring, I assumed.

"When sleep came, yes." Avoiding eye contact, I spread the white linen napkin over my lap. Anticipation filled me. I had never been alone with a man before, outside of Jude and Papa. "I must get home. My sisters are probably beside themselves with worry."

"They were," he said.

My head snapped up, and again his intense gaze captured mine.

"Miss Ruiz and I rode to Braxton Hall this morning."

"Dorotea went with you?"

"Yes, she was concerned about your sisters, and you were still sleeping. Due to Miss Ruiz's injury, I thought it best if she remained at Braxton Hall instead of returning here. Your driver is welcome here for a week before making the short journey home."

Papa's return to Braxton Hall stood paramount because if he didn't show…I shivered. Audrey would see my end. "I suppose I am left with no choice."

With tongs, Mr. Huntington lifted a soft-boiled egg in a crystal bowl in the middle of the table and placed it on a pewter egg cradle in front of me. "It's best your driver isn't bounced around in a carriage even for a short distance, until he has some time to heal. Your father is known to be a fair man with high esteem for his family; I do not understand the cause of your worry. Surely he can obtain another driver until Mr. Kelly recovers."

I nodded, and cracked the top of the egg before retrieving a fingerling of toasted bread to dip in the yolk.

"I've never been out of the city that far. I was impressed with your estate. I spoke to a Miss Evelyn when I was informed that Mrs. Darlington wasn't at home. She is your sister, am I correct?"

"She is," I said.

"She was relieved to hear you were safe, but none too pleased with your decision to go into the city. She said—and I believe her exact words were, 'Leave it to my sister. She listens to no one.'"

"Did she, now?" I said. There was no pleasing Evelyn. Unless, of course, I was an entirely different person. But I refused to give him insight into our sisterly quarrels.

Sensing my reluctance to discuss my sister, he moved on with his next question in what appeared to be a growing list.

"You referenced Miss Ruiz as your governess last night."

"That is correct," I said between mouthfuls.

He studied me. "You are hardly a child, Miss Darlington, that you would require a governess."

"I no longer require a governess. Her duty remains to my younger sisters. However, that doesn't exclude her from being my confidant and an important person in my life. You may not be aware, but my mother passed some years ago, and if it weren't for Miss Ruiz, we wouldn't have made it through the hard times."

"And what about your father's second wife?" He lifted his cup of coffee and took a sip.

"What about her?" I stabbed a piece of ham and added it to my plate before glancing at the gilded clock on a walnut stand behind him. The sooner we finished, the sooner I could return to Braxton Hall and face what awaited me.

"From what I gather from my mother, your stepmother doesn't have the best standing amongst the ladies."

I stiffened. "I am not one for gossip, Mr. Huntington."

"And I do not seek to obtain any, but the urgency to return home leaves one to wonder what you are afraid of."

I considered Mrs. Quinn's revelation but, not wishing to divulge to him anything about our life and what happened at Braxton Hall, I addressed the other concern that had weighed on my mind since my arrival at Rosehill Manor.

"I wish to avoid others finding out I stayed here, alone…with you."

"It is not as though you shared my bed."

Heat rushed to my cheeks at his candidness. "To spend the night alone in a gentleman's home is improper, and I fear what others will say if they learn of my stay at Rosehill."

"One isn't always in control of one's circumstances, Miss Darlington. An accident happened, and Rosehill provided needed shelter."

"Even so, I don't seek to bring scandal upon my family."

"I didn't peg you as the sort to give much consideration to what others say or think."

"That is presumptuous of you," I said curtly.

He arched a brow. "Indeed. Are you always so hostile?"

Maybe Evelyn was right; I lacked in social etiquette and didn't know how to conduct myself in mixed company. In fairness, Mr. Huntington had been most helpful, but his intensity unnerved me more than I cared to admit.

"Please accept my apologies. I would like to return to Braxton Hall without delay, if you don't mind."

"As you wish. Your carriage is ready, and I will accompany you to Braxton Hall."

I placed my napkin beside my plate, scraped back my chair, and rose. "No need. You have been most hospitable. I'm afraid I've been a lousy guest."

He stood and looked down at me, and our gazes locked. My breath caught before I took a step back. "That you have," he said bluntly. "If you don't allow me to accompany you home, you will at least permit me to accompany you to your carriage." He lifted a hand toward the corridor. I gathered that he wasn't easily swayed.

I walked into the entrance hall with him close behind me. At the main doors, he stepped around me and opened the door. I stepped outside, welcoming the warmth of the sunshine.

"Miss Darlington," Mrs. Quinn called after me.

I turned on the marble landing as she bustled outside.

"Yeer hat, miss."

"Oh, thank you, Miss Quinn." I accepted the outstretched hat.

"Would ye like me to pin it on for ye?" She revealed the pins in her open palm.

"No, that is quite all right. No need to endure the discomfort. The ride home isn't far."

She curtsied. "It was a pleasure to meet ye."

I expressed my appreciation for her kindness, and she stepped back inside. Then, sensing Mr. Huntington's gaze, I avoided looking at him and turned my focus to my carriage and a driver waiting at the bottom of the staircase.

"I am glad to see my staff's assistance didn't go unnoticed by you." I detected humor in his tone, but his stoic expression didn't waver.

I considered his concerns I'd overheard about his mother's meddling and wondered how mothered he still was at his age. Or if women routinely paraded themselves at him. Perhaps he'd become accustomed to women bending to his every whim. "Do you require women to mollycoddle you?" I said.

His breath caught at my bluntness. "On the contrary."

"Should I consider you a philanderer?"

"Now who is the presumptuous one?" His curtness matched mine.

Although it pained me to offer another apology yet again, I apologized, to which he obliged me with a nod.

At the carriage, he held out a hand, and I placed mine in his and regarded him. "Despite whatever impression you may have gathered about me, I appreciate your hospitality. You have been most hospitable."

"At last, behavior befitting a lady of the Darlington name," he said, rewarding me with a benevolent smile.

I admitted how women might deem Mr. Huntington attractive when he smiled, which hadn't proven to be often. But then again, with my nervousness of what awaited me at home, I admitted I wasn't the most reasonable guest.

"Good day, sir." I entered the carriage, and without another word, he closed the door behind me.

Chapter 9

T HE DRIVER TURNED THE CARRIAGE DOWN THE LANE TOWARD Braxton Hall, and my nerves thrummed. What if Audrey had returned early and Papa hadn't arrived to fetch us? I fumbled with my hat where it lay in my lap.

The carriage stopped in front of the mansion. The driver scrambled down from his seat and opened the door.

"Miss Darlington." He held out a gloved hand.

"Thank you." I exited the carriage. Peering up at the house, I closed my eyes and inhaled deeply, summoning the courage to face what lay ahead. I cracked my neck, attempting to release the tension.

"Where do you wish me to leave the carriage?" the driver asked.

I opened my eyes. "Here is fine. Someone will be around to fetch it."

"Miss Darlington." Alfred, a stable boy, darted toward us.

"And here he is now." I said as the lanky young man took hold of the team's reins. "Thank you for bringing me home. I will let you get back to your duties."

The driver tipped his hat, untied the horse from the back of the carriage, and mounted. He inclined his head. "Miss." He heeled his horse's flanks and rode back toward Rosehill Manor.

Alfred led the team and carriage away, and I stood alone on the cobblestone drive. I looked down the lane at the red oak and longed for days of old. If I could be a child again…

"Katherine!" Evelyn called out, and I turned to see her descending the stairs with Adelaide, Alice, and Grace behind her.

I gathered the sides of my gown and climbed to meet my sisters. I met a scowling Evelyn halfway but didn't pause to engage with her.

"I've had it with you and your need to antagonize our stepmother. You endangered Dorotea and Mr. Kelly's lives with your antics. Not to mention your nerve in concocting a sleeping potion for Mrs. Cox and risking Colleen's position in doing so. Do you think Mrs. Cox will not tell Mother what you've done?"

I kept walking. "It's good to see you too, dear sister. I see my welfare is of no concern. And you would rather conform to the evils that woman bestows upon this family than stand up for what is right."

"Oh, save me the martyr act, Kat."

Alice and Grace stopped on either side of me. Grace slipped her hand in mine, and Alice looped her arm through mine. I smiled at them, drawing comfort from their unconditional love, and continued toward the landing.

"Are you all right?" Grace looked up at me with large, fawn-colored eyes. "I was worried."

"No need to worry, little one." I squeezed her hand. "There is nothing I can't handle."

"I feared what I had helped you do," Alice said. "I didn't want whatever happened to be my fault."

"It could never be your fault." I freed my arm from hers and encircled her narrow shoulders. "Has our stepmother returned?"

Alice shook her head.

"Good," I said.

"The surprise you mentioned. Where is it?" Alice asked when I stopped on the landing.

Evelyn stood to my left, looking none too pleased. And here I thought it was Audrey and Mrs. Cox I'd battle, I grumbled mentally.

"Alice told me you coerced her into aiding you with the promise of a surprise. Honestly, Kat?" Evelyn said.

"I never said it like that," Alice said. "I helped Kat because she is my sister, not a prisoner."

I tightened my arm around Alice's shoulders. "You could learn from our sister what side you stand on."

Evelyn threw her hands in the air. "There are no sides to take. Enough with the dramatics."

"So keep quiet is what you are suggesting? That is the problem with you. You're afraid to speak for fear of offending."

"Offending who?" she said with exasperation.

"Well, I'll be damned. How can you possibly be so dense?" The familiar restlessness stirred in my belly.

"Kat!"

"Don't you Kat me." I stomped my foot. "If I step out of line here, I'm chastised. If I breathe the wrong way, I'm ridiculed. If I choose the wrong word, I'm disparaged." I heaved a sigh as the fight in me wavered. "Why can't I just…be?" My shoulders slumped.

Evelyn gulped, and her expression softened.

"Come now, ladies. You mustn't fuss amongst yourselves. Not everyone can say they are blessed with the sisterhood you could embrace if you all would stop bickering." Dorotea stopped a few steps up with her hand cradling her side. A night's rest had done little to ease the weariness in her face, and I contemplated the pain she still endured.

"Dorotea is right," Adelaide said. "Evelyn, you worry too much about what others think and lack empathy for what Kat endures from Mother."

Although I would never grow used to the misuse of the word "mother," my heart softened at Adelaide's defense of me.

She turned her sights on me. "And Kat…"

I tensed. Had I been too quick to assume I'd gained her support?

"…you need to consider the adversity you bring upon yourself, this household, and your sisters. You are not alone on the cliff. We are your family." Never one to mince words, Adelaide displayed wisdom beyond her years. When she spoke, others listened. "Alice and Grace, you go inside and prepare for your studies. Mr. Taylor will be here soon."

They scampered into the house, and Dorotea limped after them. We watched them go before returning to our conversation.

"But I'm the one she has targeted. She devotes her days to making my life unbearable." I yearned to confide in them about Audrey's threat in my chamber the other evening, and the fear it had elicited in me. It was the reason I defied all to guarantee Papa's protection.

"How does a bird survive without a mother to mother it?" Adelaide said.

I frowned. "What does that have to do with our circumstances?"

She looked at me tenderly, wanting me to comprehend. "A father bird provides enough food in the absence of the mother. The father won't take on the task of keeping the brood warm. The fledglings provide warmth until the baby bird is old enough to care for itself.

"When father brought Audrey here, we had just lost our mother. We were vulnerable and scared. But we survived. Our father provides for us but avoids this place and, in doing so, withholds the love and warmth he once gave so freely. It is up to us to fill the void so we have the strength to fly when we leave Braxton Hall behind."

Evelyn and I exchanged a look, and I lowered my gaze. Adelaide was right. My sisters were not the antagonists.

"I'm sorry," I said. "There are situations I can't discuss."

Alice touched my arm. "You can tell us anything."

"This I cannot. Not until I'm sure the plan I put in motion works in our favor. But please know, in my leaving, I didn't seek to harm you or anyone in this household."

"You may be brazen and direct, but you are not malicious." Evelyn squeezed my hand where it hung at my side. "We are sisters, and I will do better at championing you."

I raised my head to regard her and found a renewed conviction there. But I remained reserved and uncertain about her sworn commitment.

"I promise, Kat." She tugged at my hand "When Mr...." She glanced at Adelaide.

"Huntington."

"Yes, when Mr. Huntington rode here and informed us you all had been injured, I was beside myself with worry about you all. But I thought of our last dispute in the corridor before my outing with Mr. Peyton and didn't want it to be the last thing on your mind if…well, you didn't make it."

"Now who is the dramatic one?" I said with a laugh. "I was hardly on my deathbed." My amusement faded. "Dorotea and Mr. Kelly's injuries are far worse than this." I pointed at the stitches and bruise under my eye.

Evelyn rolled her eyes in the most unladylike manner, and I grinned. "Leave it to you to show up to the Goddard ball looking like a ghastly pirate," she said, but as swiftly as her nonchalance emerged, it retreated, superseded by her need for perfection. Her habitually rigid demeanor returned. "We must find some way to hide the blemish before the ball."

My hope in our newfound comradeship faded, and my heart plunged. "The banquet is more than a month away. I'm sure my face will meet your approval by then."

Adelaide narrowed her eyes at our oldest sister.

Evelyn cringed and said with an awkward smile, "Habits aren't broken overnight." She turned my cheek to inspect the injury. "It is the least of our concerns. Audrey and Mrs. Cox are the ones we need to concern ourselves with." She looped arms with Adelaide and me, and we walked toward the door.

We had barely stepped inside before Mrs. Cox strode toward us. Her usually stringent and callous expression provided no insight into the severity of her anger.

Arms still looped with my sisters', I felt Evelyn's body tense. The walls of my fortress dropped into position. I held my breath and planted my feet.

"You wait until Mrs. Darlington hears about this." Mrs. Cox stopped before us and balled her hands on her hips.

"Stand down, Señora Cox."

We all turned to Dorotea, exiting the library, and beyond her I saw my sisters seated at the table with their books in front of them, awaiting Mr. Taylor's arrival. Dorotea closed the door behind her and straightened to her full but diminutive height. She winced and placed a hand to her ribs before suppressing the pain and walking to join us in the entrance hall.

"And you!" Mrs. Cox's lip curled with disgust. "You will be out on your backside as soon as she returns."

"You're no longer in charge of matters here," I said, slipping away from my sisters to station myself at Dorotea's side. "Papa returns today to take us to the city, and I will see to it that you're dismissed from your duties."

Mrs. Cox's mouth unhinged before she snapped it closed.

"Is it true?" Evelyn said, tears in her voice.

"Señorita Darlington speaks the truth." Dorotea encircled my shoulders with her arm. "We visited Señor Darlington in the city, and he assured us he'd come and take you all to spend the colder months with him."

Adelaide and Evelyn squealed and embraced each other before parting and moving to stand next to me.

"Is that where you were?" Evelyn asked.

I nodded. "He is the gift I promised Alice." I regarded the key ring hanging from Mrs. Cox's waist. "I will take those." I pointed at the ring, and she grudgingly handed them to me. "That will be all, Mrs. Cox."

She pursed her lips, mumbled under her breath, and marched off.

After she disappeared, I turned back to my sisters. "I had to reason with Papa without Audrey dictating from the sidelines. Dorotea helped me convince Papa that we needed him."

"But why now? We have voiced our need before." Adelaide's brow pleated.

I shrank under their gaze. "Well...I may not have employed empathy or tenderness in my urgency to force his hand, but my attempt was successful."

"If you were successful, and Papa shows up, we all will be indebted to you." Adelaide glowed with hope.

"In the meantime, we should pack," Evelyn said. "To be in the city again will be marvelous. The shopping and luncheons with friends will make me feel alive again. And we will be able to attend every social event." She clapped her hands, her eyes shining with excitement.

"Lovely," I said sarcastically. "Exactly the way I want to spend my days."

Adelaide and Evelyn laughed, and I found myself smiling.

"But I will enjoy visiting with Birdie more." It had been far too long since we had seen each other, and I suppose the one good thing that could come out of the Goddard ball would be spending time in her company.

"More time in the city will give me ample time to get to know Mr. Peyton," Evelyn said with a dreamy look.

I cringed at the thought. Why couldn't it be my sisters, Papa, and me? We had let one outsider into our family, and the auburn-haired Lucifer had proven catastrophic.

I signaled to the laundress passing by under a load of dirty linen.

"Yes, Miss Katherine?" She craned her neck to look beyond her armload.

"Please ask Miss Alice and Grace's chambermaid to pack their trunks. We leave for the city today. And if you see Miss Colleen, please have her sent up to my chamber."

She looked past me to my sisters, and looked nervous.

"What is it?" I frowned, glancing from her to them.

Adelaide shuffled from one foot to the other.

"Out with it."

"Mrs. Cox locked her in her chamber until Mother's return. She said no one but she would bring her food and water," Adelaide said.

"The madness in this house." My chest tightened with accumulating displeasure. "She has become the warden and Mrs. Cox, her deputy. Together they have converted Braxton Hall, once a magical place overflowing with laughter and love, into Camp Alcatraz itself. But it imprisons women and children instead of Confederate prisoners and sympathizers. A disgrace to the Darlington name and the memory of our mother." I looked from Dorotea to my sisters. "Can you all not see, we stand a house divided?"

Dorotea's dark eyes revealed her agreement, but she remained silent. I guessed because she didn't think her opinion carried value.

I rubbed the nape of my neck to ease the tension. "I'm going to free Colleen and prepare for our departure."

I left them and strode down the corridor to the staff quarters.

"Which room is Miss Colleen's?" I asked the butler as he exited the staff dining room, next to the kitchen.

"At the end of the corridor, the room on the right. But I must warn you, Mrs. Cox has given clear instruction—"

"So I hear. But Mrs. Cox will be dismissed from her duties when my father gets here."

He raised his brow. "Mr. Darlington is coming to Braxton Hall?"

"Indeed. He comes today to take his family to the city. You can inform the staff to prepare for Braxton Hall's closure until spring."

The butler hesitated.

"Do as I say."

"B-but Mrs. Darlington…"

"Is not here, and my father is about to arrive. When I inform him that you disregarded an order from the family, you will find yourself looking for employment elsewhere. Do I make myself clear?"

He bowed. "As you request." He pivoted and walked off.

"Incompetent. The whole lot of them," I grumbled and continued down the corridor. I would see the staff in Audrey's pocket were dismissed and replaced.

I paused to unlock the door at the end of the corridor, and walked inside.

"Miss Katherine." Colleen scrambled to her feet from one of the four beds in the room. "I was worried when ye didn't come back. After Mrs. Cox locked me in here, I heard whisperings in the corridor that ye had been in an accident. Ye all right?"

"I'm fine." I gripped her hands. "But how are you?"

The scar on her face reddened. "There ain't nothin' that old sow can do to me that I haven't experienced before."

I grinned at the feistiness I was coming to recognize as normal for her. "Come, let's get you out of here. My sisters and I are moving to the city."

Her eyes twinkled. "Ye've enlisted yeer father's help?"

I nodded.

"I am happy." Then the sparkle in her eyes disappeared.

"What is it?"

"If ye succeeded in earnin' yeer father's ear, what does that mean for the servants here? Da ain't farin' well and relies on my income."

"You needn't worry. When Papa gets here, I will speak with him about bringing you to the city with us."

"Truly?"

"Indeed," I said with a smile. "I require a chambermaid. And I have taken a liking to you."

She clasped her hands together under her chin, and tears welled. "Ye renew my faith in humanity, miss."

My smile faded at her statement, and I thought for a moment, then said, "I suppose it is the little reminders of the good in the world that bear the most weight. It inspires in the moment and provides hope for the day's outcome. Not a day ago, I was bound in misery and feeling defeated, but now, thanks to your aid, I have secured my father's help to end all our misery. There's good in our world if we have an open heart and mind to behold it. I suppose it all comes down to perspective, doesn't it?"

"Yes, miss."

"Now let's get my trunks ready. Papa will be here soon."

Chapter 10

MORNING FADED INTO THE AFTERNOON, AND EVENING WOULD soon settle over the countryside, and still there was no sign of Papa. I paced the entrance hall, circling the trunks readied for our departure for the city. At every little sound outside, I raced to the window to peer at the lane, my heart thudding with anticipation before my spirits dropped. As the hours ticked by, I fought back tears of frustration and disappointment.

"Have these trunks returned to our chambers," Evelyn said to the butler.

"No!" I said. "He is coming."

Evelyn walked up to me and placed a hand on my arm. Empathy shone in her cornflower-blue eyes. "I don't believe he is. We all share your disappointment."

"But he promised. I told him of our need here." My lip quivered.

Evelyn embraced me. "Oh, dear sister." Her voice was thick with her own dismay. "I fear if we keep holding onto hope that the father we once knew will return, we will face a lifetime of heartache and disappointment."

I lay my head in the curve of her neck, letting my silent tears soak into the fabric of her dress. Why, Papa? Why? I had spent the last years clinging to a kernel of hope that he would care enough about my sisters and me to become present in our lives, but I'd ended up disappointed and angry. Why had I been such a fool to believe this time would be any different?

"Kat, is everything all right?" Alice's sweet voice rose from behind Evelyn.

I released my sister and quickly wiped the dampness from my eyes. "Yes." I forced a smile.

Alice regarded the trunks with puzzlement. "Are we going somewhere?"

We had decided against telling Grace and Alice of Papa's expected arrival in case he didn't show.

Her face brightened, dispelling her usual apprehension. "You promised you would return with a gift. Is this the gift? We are going on one of the adventures you tell Grace and me about." She clasped her hands together under her chin before her eagerness faded. "Wait. But what if we don't like where we are going? What if we are cold and scared." Alice's dislike of change and the persistent worry no child should feel at her tender age robbed her of the joy of being a child.

"Do not fret so, Alice," Evelyn said. "Come, you must prepare for the evening meal."

"Miss." The butler stood waiting for instructions. "Am I to have the trunks returned to the chambers?"

"Yes…" Evelyn's voice faded as, like me, she perked up at the sound of a carriage approaching.

"Wait!" I dashed to the window. Evelyn and Alice gathered around me, and we waited for the carriage to rein to a stop out front. My heart pounded in my throat as the driver jumped down, and when he looked toward the house, I let out a squeal. "It's Papa's coachman."

I raced to the door, and in Evelyn's excitement, she abandoned her nagging and ran to keep up. Throwing open the door, I dashed out onto the landing to wait for the coachman to open the carriage door. Evelyn and Alice came to stand beside me, and I clasped their hands. My chest felt like it would burst with anticipation while my mind and heart screamed, *Please be him.*

The carriage door swung aside, and Papa stepped out.

"Papa!" Alice burst into tears and darted down the stairs as Adelaide and Grace raced out. My sisters hurried to greet our father, but my feet remained rooted.

He had come. I rubbed my arms to control the chill. He had indeed come.

"My girls." Papa's grin widened as he held out his arms, and my sisters ran into them. He kissed each of them before looking up at me. Then, before breaking the embrace, he mumbled something to them and climbed up the stairs. Concern diluted the happiness on his face. "I'm sorry I'm late. I had business—"

"Oh, Papa. I care not." I threw myself at him. "You came, and that is all that matters."

The warmth of his embrace healed my aching soul. He stroked my head before planting a kiss on my forehead. "My darling girl. I appreciate your grace." He stepped back. "What happened here?" He tilted my chin to inspect my cheek. "Have you been climbing trees again?" His voice was teasing, but his eyes narrowed with concern.

"No, but you mustn't worry about that now. I will tell you all about it later," I said as my sisters came to stand behind him, eagerness to be in his company shining on their faces.

"Mr. Wood." Papa turned to peer down at his coachman.

"Yes, sir?"

"Go to the carriage house and have Mr. Kelly prepare a carriage."

"But Mr. Kelly isn't here," Grace said.

"What do you mean, he isn't here?"

"That is what I was going to tell you later." I took his arm and led him inside. "There was an accident on the way back from the city. The carriage wheel broke, and Mr. Kelly was thrown. Dorotea and I were injured, but Mr. Kelly took the brunt of it."

The staff gathered in the entrance hall to greet Papa, and I eyed Mrs. Cox, standing toward the back with her head down. I narrowed my eyes. I would see the woman gone tonight.

"Are you telling me Mr. Kelly was killed?" Papa's face paled.

"No. He is at Rosehill Manor. It was thought best that he recover for a few days before making the short journey to Braxton Hall," Adelaide said.

"Rosehill Manor." Papa rolled the name over his tongue. "Do you refer to the Huntingtons' country estate?"

Evelyn took his coat and hat. "Mr. Huntington was most kind when he came upon them on the road. I fear Mr. Kelly's fate would be much worse if it hadn't been for him."

Papa gaped, overwhelmed by the news.

Adelaide signaled to the butler. "Please prepare Papa a drink."

"That isn't necessary. I must get back to the city."

"So soon?" Grace said with a pout. "But you only just arrived."

Alice dropped her head, and her shoulders curled forward.

Papa bent and swooped Grace up into his arms, and she giggled. She appeared so small in his arms, and my heart melted as she gently stroked his day-old beard, as though touching to see if he was real.

He looked at me and winked. "I have come to take you to our home in the city. I have decided that I simply can't survive another day without my girls at my side."

Alice inched cautiously forward. "Truly?"

"Indeed," he said with a broad smile. "It saddens me to admit that I have wronged you all. I have been absent for too long and will do my utmost to ensure it never happens again. I will not be far from your sides, unless business calls me away."

Grace squeezed his neck with all the fierceness her little body could muster.

Alice broke into tears, and Papa moved closer and wrapped

an arm around her. She calmed, and peered up at him. "Where will we sleep?"

"At the mansion, in your chamber."

"But I don't recall my chamber."

"Not to worry, you will."

"But how far is it from my sisters? I don't like to sleep alone."

Papa regarded her, perplexed.

"Come now, Alice, save your questions," I said as Papa gawked at his children with overwhelming uncertainty. My heart galloped. I wouldn't allow him to abandon us. I held out a hand, and she walked over to me, and I encircled her shoulders with my arm. "All will be better now. You will see."

"Promise?"

"Yes, my love."

She appeared to draw security from my words.

Papa set Grace on the floor. "If you younger girls will go play in your chambers, I have matters to discuss with the staff."

"Yes, Papa." My younger sisters curtsied, then crossed to the staircase.

Papa observed the girls' retreat, and when they disappeared, he turned his attention to the staff, who stood silently waiting.

I looked over the sea of faces, some familiar and others strangers. With the continuous turnover of servants and people not wanting to work as domestic servants, the staff problem had become a continual complaint at social gatherings. In addition, Audrey's reputation as an unfair and unsympathetic tyrant made it much more challenging for us to obtain good staff.

"Good evening, everyone." Papa squared his shoulders.

A mumbled greeting rippled through the ranks.

"Some years ago, I returned to find my wife deceased, and in need of a mother to care for my children, I married the present Mrs. Darlington. It is no secret that she has abused her position in my family in my absence. She dismissed the staff who helped my wife and daughters run our household. It pains me to do this, but

I am hereby relieving you all of your duties." A wave of disgruntled whispers filled the entrance hall. "I will see you are compensated for three months' wages."

My mouth unhinged at the announcement, and Adelaide and Evelyn gasped. I gawked from them to the stunned faces of our staff. I had expected him to thin out the bad seeds, but not to dismiss them all. How could we possibly run a household with the scarcity of good help? I decided against questioning his logic in the matter.

"You can leave in the morning. I will see carriages are prepared to take you into the city." He turned to me and held out a hand for me to join him. "Miss Katherine will remain to see to it. Tomorrow new staff will arrive to take care of the home during the winter months. At half past four, I require you to line up outside the library, and I will see you are given your wages and gratitude for services rendered. You are dismissed."

They turned to leave, and Papa's voice lifted. "Mrs. Cox, you are to remain."

I regarded Mrs. Cox, who stood with her back to us in her eagerness to flee, and she braced herself before turning and walking to stand a few feet from Papa.

"It has been brought to my attention that you abused your position and laid hands on my youngest daughter."

"I-I—it was under Mrs. Darlington's orders."

Papa stiffened beside me. "You will see yourself removed this evening. You will not be compensated for your immediate dismissal. I have half a mind to make you walk to the city. But I could not in good conscience allow a woman to travel the roads alone, and surely not with evening approaching. Nor will I allow you to remain here without my supervision. So you will join me in my carriage, and I will see you to the city's outskirts, where you will find yourself on foot. Do I make myself clear?"

Mrs. Cox pursed her lips and exaggerated a curtsy.

"Off with you, before I change my mind."

She rolled her shoulders back and marched off.

Exhilaration chased up and down my body. On his return, life had already taken a turn for the better.

"Kat." Papa turned to regard me earnestly. I looked up at him as he placed his hands on my shoulders. "I am sorry to leave you here, but I trust you to apply a firm hand in seeing this place is attended to, and the new staff knows their tasks. Mr. Holmes, my butler, is to arrive first thing in the morning to assist you."

I nodded, and my stomach plunged. I wanted to be as far from Braxton Hall as possible, but the need to please him took precedence. "As you say, Papa."

"Good." The tension gripping his face eased. "Where is Dorotea? You said she was injured."

"I am here, señor," Dorotea said from the doorway of the salon.

"Come."

She obeyed and stopped before him.

"You have been loyal and trustworthy. I hope you will consider coming to the city."

"There is no place I'd rather be, señor. I love your daughters as though they were my own. My hands have been tied these last few years, but I hope I can once again give my undevoted attention to their care and rearing."

Papa looked down at her, his expression tender. Her cheeks grew rosy under his stare, and she looked away.

"I'd like you to stay with Kat and accompany her into the city tomorrow."

Dorotea inclined her head in agreement.

"Very well. I will pay the Huntington estate a visit on the way back to the city and check on Mr. Kelly, and hope he will honor me with his continued service," he said. "Now, if you all will excuse me, I have matters to attend to in the library. Evelyn, you see that these trunks are loaded, and Adelaide, you ready your sisters."

A chorus of "Yes, Papa" rose before they hurried off.

"Papa." I touched his arm. "May I speak to you for a moment, in private?"

"What is it?"

"Not here," I said, eyeing staff lingering in the corridors. I took his arm and guided him toward the library. Inside, I closed the door and moved away from anyone seeking to eavesdrop before releasing my burden.

"You are aware of my previous complaints about the times I've been locked in my chamber."

A muscle twitched at the corner of his eye. "Yes. I thought little of it, deeming it my wife's inability to handle my free-spirited daughter. Am I to believe the situation holds more weight?"

"I can hardly spend the rest of my days locked away because she dislikes me and seeks to break my spirit."

"I concur. I understand your distress."

"May I be frank?"

He gestured for me to continue.

"I mean no disrespect, but you barely know your wife. She is not a woman of quality."

"You have informed me of her disappearances, and it is obvious she still hasn't returned home from her recent venture."

"She hasn't. But what I want to discuss with you is of the utmost importance." I looked to the door, half expecting Audrey to barge in and stop me.

"Go on, daughter."

"She does not permit Jude anywhere near the estate, or me. She has insulted him in our home."

"You refer to Thomas Williams's son?"

I nodded.

"Despite the narrative the North speaks, it is not only the South that holds no care for the mistreatment of the Blacks. The North may not have been built on the backs of slaves, but the imbalance between the Blacks and whites did not differ, certainly not then and not now. I expect my wife is no different. She and most

New Yorkers will not speak kindly of your involvement with the Williams boy."

"He is hardly a boy. He is set to become a lawyer." I crossed my arms.

"Brilliant." His face radiated delight. "Thomas and Ellen must be proud."

"I expect so, but it is not Jude's accomplishments that I wish to speak about. Jude is my dearest friend and has recently attempted to visit me, only to be turned away."

"Can this discussion not wait for another time? I have business to conduct and we need to be on our way back to the city before it becomes too dark to travel."

"This will only take a moment, and I need your help."

"For what cause?"

"The day he came to Braxton Hall, she had me locked in my chamber, but with Dorotea's help, I escaped and met Jude in the meadow."

His face hardened with disapproval. "It is hardly fitting for a woman to roam the woods unchaperoned."

"But he is my friend."

"And he is a man, and you are no longer a child. You wish to be seen as a woman, yet conduct yourself as though you and he are still children. I won't permit it to happen again."

"I heed you."

"Then that settles it." He looked about the room as though it was foreign territory and he a stranger in his own home.

"It isn't quite that simple," I said.

He stiffened and leveled a sharp look at me. "What is your meaning?"

"That day, she was informed of my escape for a stroll in the meadow with Jude. She locked me in my chamber again."

"And rightfully so. Do you understand the harm that could come if people witnessed your disregard for social decorum?" He shook his head before circling behind the mahogany desk to face me.

I strode forward. "It's more complex than that, I'm afraid." I stared at my hands and the cuticle I had picked almost raw since we had walked into the library.

He pressed his hands onto the desk and looked across at me. "Explain yourself."

"She struck me and threatened to spread the rumor that Mrs. Cox had witnessed Jude r-rape me." A bitter taste soured my mouth. "She said she'd see him hung from High Bridge and disposed of in Harlem River. She threatened to ruin my reputation so no honorable gentleman would look upon me."

He stumbled back under the weight of my words before slamming a fist on the desk. "Damn that woman. How dare she concoct such a plot against my daughter."

"Can't you see the harm she brings to our family? She is dangerous. Why can't you put her away?"

"Put her away?" he scoffed, his expression darkening.

"Divorce her. Birdie says people are turning to divorce when marriages aren't working. The courts are honoring them."

"Birdie? I hope you aren't sharing the happenings within this household with the Vello woman."

I shook my head, too frightened to tell him I had indeed turned to Jude and her for comfort.

"Besides, it isn't that simple," he said. "For a husband to divorce his wife, there must be evidence of infidelity."

"Can't we concoct something like the outlandish stories she seeks to spread against me? After all, she is always off on these adventures, informing no one of where she disappears to—not even her own husband."

His eyes narrowed, warning me that I spoke too candidly. "I will not drop to her level. But if it is as you say, I will discover where my wife disappears and bring it to an end."

My indignation flared. "I hope she has a lover, and you will do what you must and pluck her from our lives for the betterment of us all."

"I will take care of my wife. Now, I must proceed with matters here so your sisters and I can be on our way."

"I have one more matter I wish to discuss with you."

His jaw tightened. "Out with it, and make it quick."

"I wish to speak to you on behalf of Colleen, my chambermaid, and perhaps Alfred, the stable boy."

He studied me. "What about them?"

"I request that Colleen come with me to the city and serve me as she does here."

"You trust this maid?"

"I do, and I'm indebted to her."

"How so?"

"She aided in my escape from my bedchamber and took care of Mrs. Cox so I could go to the city to see you," I said sheepishly.

"Took care of her how?" his eyes narrowed, his interest piqued.

I lowered my gaze to pick at my finger again. "Providing her with a potion to keep her sleeping most of the day."

He belted out a laugh, and I lifted my head. He shook his head and regarded me. "And you wonder why you always find yourself in trouble." He composed himself, sat at the desk, and clasped his hands in front of him. "Very well. The maid can come."

"And Alfred."

"What is your need for him?"

"It's not me. It's Colleen."

He frowned, and I rushed to explain my position. "Alfred is a nice boy, and he and Colleen hold affection for each other. If they are to be separated, I fear they will not see each other again, and I promised to help Colleen in a courtship with him."

"Courtship? You?" A smile tugged at the corners of his mouth. "You hardly know the first thing about courtship."

Heat touched my ears. "There is truth in your words."

"Am I to believe there is hope that you won't end up a spinster?" he said in jest.

"There is always hope," I said.

"Very well, have it your way. The stable boy and the chambermaid come. But that is all."

"Thank you, Papa," I said with a curtsy.

"Now off with you. And send the first person in." He gestured at the door and the hum of gathering voices beyond it.

I scurried to the door and opened it to discover the cook standing at the head of the line. "He will see you now," I said before hurrying past.

I eyed Colleen, standing some way back. She stood wringing her hands, her eyes pinned on the library door. I walked up to her, plucked her from the line, and led her away.

"Miss Katherine, what is it?"

I stopped when we were out of earshot of the others. "I spoke to my father, and if you are willing, you are to have a position as my chambermaid in the city."

Tears welled in her eyes and overcome, she bobbed her head.

"Is that a yes?"

She nodded.

I turned as the front door opened, and various yard and stable hands entered with drawn faces, their hats clasped in their hands. They joined the line waiting to speak to Papa.

"You go and inform Alfred he is to stay on with our family in the city, if he chooses. I will see you later."

She dashed off, and I left the main floor and climbed to Audrey's chamber. I opened the door, strode inside, and stood on the edge of the oversized Persian Serapi rug. The scent of Otto of Roses lingered in the air as though it bled from the drapes, rug, and furniture. Despite the physical distance from my stepmother, a simple whiff of the fragrance in public places halted me in my tracks and made my heart race. The smell would haunt me forever.

Papa said he would see to Audrey, and I'd allow him to do so. But if he delayed, I'd take the matter into my own hands.

I crossed the room and knelt before the embossed zinc trunk at the foot of the bed. Unbuckling the strap securing the lid, I pushed it up and dug through the contents until I found what I'd hoped she had hidden inside. "Fool woman. She really should be more resourceful." I retrieved my japanned tin box of watercolors and the walnut paintbox containing my tubes of oil paint, brushes, palette, and woven paper.

A shiver ran over me, and I glanced over my shoulder as though expecting to discover Audrey or Mrs. Cox standing behind me before closing the lid, securing the buckle, and gathering my belongings.

I recalled days before when I'd dismissed the dressmaker and how Audrey had made me stand by while she ordered a groom to burn my artwork. Why she had not burned my paints, I didn't know. Perhaps she planned to amuse herself by inflicting future heartache. Understanding the woman had never been my primary concern, as my survival bore more weight. I could never comprehend her motives. I suppose some people drew pleasure from others' discomfort as a way of making themselves feel superior. But there was only one true sufferer in the end: the perpetrator, the one consumed with hate and misery.

What must it be like to live in her skin?

Chapter 11

THE NEXT DAY, AS PAPA HAD STATED, SIX NEW EMPLOYEES ARRIVED at Braxton Hall. Dorotea and I directed them around the mansion and communicated what would be required in the family's absence.

As I finished packing a small trunk with my paint supplies, a new groom readied a carriage for Dorotea and me. The excitement of moving to the city and Papa's pledge to make his daughters a priority in his life had kept me awake well into the night. I daydreamed of painting in the gardens at our city home and leaned into my future and what life with Papa would bring.

Downstairs, I asked the butler to have someone bring down my trunk, and after he hurried off and I stood waiting, someone knocked on the door. I opened it to the postman, standing winded from his race up the expanse of stairs to the front door. I'd often observed him take the fifty-five stairs two at a time when he arrived with our mail, and marveled at the fellow's infinite supply of energy. Over the years, I had joked that he seemed to have ants in his pants because he could never stay still.

"Good day, miss."

"Good day."

He looked past me for my stepmother or the butler Papa had dismissed. "Is the lady of the house home?"

"I am." It pleased me no end to say the words. Soon after arriving at Braxton Hall, my stepmother had instructed that all mail must pass through her hands first.

The postman's brow wrinkled. "I refer to her ladyship."

"Her ladyship?" I scoffed.

"Yes, that is how she wished to be addressed."

"Did she now?" I said with a cheeky grin. Audrey's infatuation with herself made her look like a fool. She bore no title; from what I understood, she'd never come from a prominent family. "Her ladyship is no more."

"I do hope she fares well." His good wishes fell flat, and a nervous twitch moved the sparse golden mustache lining his upper lip.

"Oh, she is fine, I assure you. She has been stripped of her farce of a title and demoted to kitchen wench."

His eyes grew round. "I was informed some years ago that no mail is to be left unless delivered directly to her lady…her hand."

I held out my hand for the bundle of mail. "You can disregard that order, as Mrs. Darlington will no longer be abiding here. The family has moved to the city, and the staff will collect any mail that comes to the estate."

Hesitantly, he handed me the mail.

"Good day, sir."

"Miss." He inclined his head, dashed down the stairs, and slung his leg over his mount. He sent one last nervous look up at me and directed his horse down the lane.

After he was gone, I closed the door, flipped through the mail, and noticed a letter addressed to Dorotea.

"See this mail is packed in my satchel," I said to the new head housekeeper, who had a pleasant face and was much more appealing than Mrs. Cox. The ambiance of the mansion had magically transformed, and the walls themselves breathed a sigh of relief at the departed villain. Only the red-haired, two-headed dragon remained. Under the protection of Papa's household, I would see her removed too. I relished the thought of seeing Audrey's face when she returned to Braxton Hall to discover she no longer had dominion over us.

I handed the head housekeeper all but the letter for Dorotea.

"Is there anything else?"

"That will be all. Thank you," I said with a smile.

"Are you ready, señorita?" Dorotea walked into the entrance hall carrying a brown leather satchel.

"Indeed. I long to be away from this place and to spend time with Papa." I held out the letter. "Mail with no return address arrived for you."

Panic swept over her face, and she darted forward and grabbed the letter from me. I frowned. I hadn't mentioned who the letter was from. Why did she seem so distressed?

"Thank you, señorita," she said when she caught me scrutinizing her. "My apologies. I told my sister not to write because Señora Darlington controls the mail."

I had heard her speak of a brother—a mason who lived in the country outside of Madrid, Spain—but she'd made no mention of other family.

"My stepmother's reign is over," I said confidently. "You should welcome your sister's letters."

"Let's hope you are right," she said, favoring me with a smile of affection. "Why don't you go and get in the carriage? I have one last matter to attend to, and I will join you." She looked at me, but her gaze drifted as if something had seized her thoughts.

"All right."

She patted my arm like I was an obedient child who had won favor, pivoted, and walked toward the open door of the library.

I shook my head and moved to the front door, but paused and glanced back. Tiptoeing to the library door, I peeked into the room and saw Dorotea reading the letter. After finishing it, she held it to her bosom as though relieved, and my confusion deepened as she turned and threw the letter into the fireplace. She stood as if in a daze, watching the letter burn. I thought of the notes I had received from Birdie and Jude and how I'd kept them and savored each word. Why had Dorotea been so quick to destroy her sister's?

I tiptoed back to the door, opened it, and stepped outside, closing it silently after me. Darting down the stairs, anticipating her catching me spying, I arrived at the carriage stone winded.

"Good day, miss," the new groom said. "With your coachman on the mend, I will see to your journey to the city."

"Thank you." I clasped his gloved hand and stepped into the carriage.

Several minutes ticked by before Dorotea climbed into the carriage and settled across from me. It appeared her earlier panic had disappeared entirely. She leaned back against the seat as though about to embark on a delightful ride, something impossible to look forward to with broken ribs. She raised a petite hand and tucked a gray-threaded black tendril beneath her bonnet. Then her dark eyes locked onto mine, and I recognized the laudanum glaze in her eyes. Mr. Huntington's doctor had given her a tincture of opium to ease the pain.

I had witnessed the same look in men who returned from war, addicted to opium pills. I'd seen them stumbling down the streets in a drugged stupor. But the drug hadn't only created addicts in the wounded and pained veterans; middle-class and upper-class women had also succumbed. Audrey too had become a partaker. The easy obtainability of opiates had orchestrated an epidemic. Dorotea's intoxication concerned me.

I looked out the gap in the curtain as the carriage took off down the lane.

Dorotea rested throughout the journey to the city, and I was grateful. However, the letter she'd felt the need to destroy occupied my thoughts, and I decided I would approach her on the subject when she felt better.

Chapter 12

Merritt—Manhattan, NY

IN THE STUDY, I PORED OVER THE ACCOUNTS OF A COMPANY SEEKING my investment. As I thumbed through the records, he again shifted in his seat, and I looked across the desk at the company's owner. "Is something troubling you?" I asked.

"No, sir." Tiny pearls of sweat glistened on a high forehead.

"Your company appears to be struggling."

"That is why I seek an investor of sorts. We have a buyable product but need the finances to extend it across the ocean."

"Which will include the additional cost of tariffs."

"It's my belief that in expanding our market, we will increase our profit margins."

I lowered my eyes and continued to study the annual reports. Then, returning to the previous page, I studied the information that had captured my attention earlier and pressed my lips together. After my final analysis, my decision made, I pushed the documents toward the man.

"Your business is failing and failing for one significant reason."

"Why?" The man gawked at me.

"Do not patronize me by acting as though you don't understand my meaning."

"I assure you, I do not."

I clenched my jaw, having no use for men like this one. My father had been such a man. "I do not play games, Mr. Peterson. I know you are a man who puts his needs ahead of his family. The type of man who will cut down the one next to him to win. Men like you may feel you are winning, but in the end, you lose." I tapped my fingers on the documents. "You take advantage of a person's need to provide for their family. Each day more immigrants arrive in New York and flood the docks and streets, looking for work. Most are unskilled and will take unfair wages and work long hours to make a go of it in a foreign country. There are capitalists like you throughout New York and the world. You consider those in their situation the ideal candidates to work in your sweatshops. This leads me to believe you also provide a dangerous working environment with few benefits for them. Your records show that for months, you have cut their wages to feed your expenses."

The man gulped and pulled a hand down over his mouth. The sun streaming in from the window overlooking the street gleamed on the sweat beading his prematurely receding hairline.

I continued. "Like many men driven by greed, you have undercut your business's greatest asset, your staff. Employees are not mules to be put to the field and worked until they drop from exhaustion. A wagon cannot haul without wheels, and wheels will not function properly if not sufficiently greased. You may be the owner of your company, but without your staff, you have nothing. Loyalty and dedication are won by showing your employees that you appreciate their commitment, and to do so, you pay them a fair wage and allow them time to recuperate, so they can work at their best capacity the next day and the day after. As a result, your profit margins will go up. This is the way you succeed."

He pulled a handkerchief from inside his coat and removed his spectacles to wipe them. The vein on the side of his temple pulsed as he concentrated, and after he replaced his spectacles, he looked at me. "So you aren't interested in investing in the product?"

I grimaced, realizing the insight I'd shared to aid in the betterment of his company had flown over him like the pesky housefly he'd swatted at off and on since he sat down.

"You have a product worth investing in. But I am not so driven to prosper that I could in good conscience invest. You will again sit in the same position a year from now. You must be willing to see your errors and apply the change I've suggested to change the outcome. Are you willing to do that, Mr. Peterson?" I leaned back in my chair and steepled my fingers at my lips, observing how the corner of his eye twitched and his face reddened.

"I will do as you say if you invest 20 percent." A flicker in his eyes warned me of the falsity he sought to sell me.

I dropped my hands, gathered the documents, and stood. My Redbone Coonhound, Winston, who had lazed by the fireplace, whimpering and chasing rabbits in his dreams, rose and moved to my side. I stroked his head before calling my butler, standing outside the study. "Mr. Murphy."

"Yes, Mr. Huntington?" He entered the room.

"See Mr. Peterson out, will you? Our business is concluded."

Mr. Peterson scrambled to stand. "B-but we haven't come to an agreement."

"Because there will be none. I decline your offer and choose to invest my money in a business that is not only sure to succeed but exhibits morals I can stand behind."

"B-but…" He searched for a defense that would persuade me.

I held out the documents, and he took them.

"Come, sir. I will show you out," Mr. Murphy said.

After they left, I returned to my seat and looked out the window. I had a clear view of the street and Mr. Peterson's waiting carriage. I watched him reach the boardwalk, look at the study window, shake his head, and climb into his carriage.

I sat there staring blankly out the window until her calculated footsteps echoed in the corridor. I glanced toward the doorway as Mother entered the study.

"What is it, Mother?" I regarded her pursed lips and her usual rigid posture. I saw neither tenderness nor warmth.

She marched across the room and halted in front of the desk. "You never came home the other night. Where were you? I hope you weren't spending time in the company of that Densmore woman again. She is beneath your social class."

I narrowed my eyes at her. "If I was, that is no concern of yours. Besides, many of the people you surround yourself with have far more scandalous secrets than my choosing to spend a night in the company of a woman. New York's society is filled with those who condemn others from behind a façade of propriety."

"Everything that happens in this family is of my concern." She squared her broad shoulders and eyed me with contempt. "You may be the man of this family, but I am still your—"

"Yes, Mother. So you remind me each waking hour." I leaned back in the chair.

"I won't have you tarnishing your name or that of the family by mingling with the likes of that harlot."

"You and Father did a fine job of that on your own," I said. "You needn't worry, Mother. Miss Densmore is a friend and nothing more."

She stood even straighter, attempting to use every bit of her height to intimidate me. It may have served her well with others, but the tactic was wasted on me. "So you say. But I know she sees you as more. She is looking to get her hands on our money."

I pressed two fingers to the bridge of my nose and closed my eyes, trying to block out her nagging.

"You have a duty to this family. You need to find a woman worthy of the Huntington name and one who comes with a substantial fortune."

I stood and walked toward the door. After thirty years, I realized I could not win against her persistence. "Yes, Mother." I left the room, but she followed on my heels.

"Your sister has agreed to receive and wed Mr. Flint."

I halted and spun to face her. "A man three times her age? I think not."

"He wasn't my first choice, but that Spanish woman got her hooks in Zane Goddard before I could convince his mother that my daughter would be a wiser choice."

"You are hardly the expert on love, Mother."

"What does love have to do with it? Your father and I had an arrangement that worked well until his death."

"Yes, and it worked nicely for the pair of you because you were cut from the same cloth. You see your children as objects."

She didn't even flinch at my remark, and a familiar ache tightened my chest.

"It is a business arrangement for the betterment of this family. I have arranged for him to visit today. They should get to know each other better if they are to wed."

"I won't allow it," I said. "You need to stop with your meddling. The patriarchal relationship between parents and children is a condition of the past. A colonist ideal fading in its appeal. Josie is capable of finding her own suitors."

She dabbed her mouth and cheeks with a handkerchief, feigning weakness. "Unlike you, she looks to please her dying mother."

My hand knotted at my side. I turned and continued down the hall. "You've been dying since Josie breathed life. You will withdraw the invitation."

"It is too late. He will be here within the hour," she called after me.

I waved a hand of dismissal, veered to the right, opposite the direction I had been headed, and went in search of my sister.

I turned down another corridor, and the rich sound of her voice accompanying the piano pulled me toward the music room.

Many evenings when I was troubled, she would urge me to accompany her to the music room, where I would sit with a brandy snifter in hand, and the day's tension would evaporate as I became mesmerized by the soulfulness of her voice. If I were a church-going man, I'd say the angels danced when she sang.

I stood on the threshold and observed her sitting at the Brahms Streicher piano I had surprised her with last Christmas. She sat with her back to me. The flounces of her Prussian blue satin gown poured over the stool, and her petite frame swayed ever so slightly. Skilled fingers moved along the ivory keys, and she tilted her head back as though she sang for heaven's entertainment. I leaned a shoulder against the doorframe, clapping when the melody ended.

She looked over her shoulder, and a broad smile revealed the single dimple on her left cheek.

I strolled into the room and stopped beside her. "Mother says you are to entertain Mr. Flint this afternoon."

Her eyes flitted away. "Yes, Mother sees him as a fitting suitor for me." She pushed back the stool and stood.

I gripped her elbow and forced her to look at me. "But how do you feel?"

She shrugged as though complacent to the manipulations of our mother.

My body tensed. "Josie, you don't have to marry to help Mother climb this unattainable ladder she has been on all our lives. Can't you see it will never be enough? You marry Mr. Flint and his money, and then there will be something else. We are not her puppets to be molded and used to give her some sense of security that will never be. I am your brother. I am also the man of this family. I will see you are well cared for."

"But Mother..." Her eyes welled up with tears. "I don't want to anger her."

"I won't let you be a pawn in Mother's game. We are her children, but we aren't items to be owned and manipulated in ways that suit her."

"But..." She wrung her hands. "I don't want to disappoint her, and she becomes so upset."

"You leave Mother to me. Entertain Mr. Flint today, and let me take care of the rest."

She nodded, a spark of hope glimmering in her fog-blue eyes.

I embraced her and planted a kiss on the top of her head. She clung to me a moment before I released her and smiled down at her upturned face. Naivety and the desire to do good were at my sister's core. She was the best of us, and I would not see her poisoned.

Before returning to the study, I found Mr. Murphy, the butler. "You are to inform me if Mr. Flint steps out of line while he is here, and when he is ready to leave."

He inclined his head. "Yes, Mr. Huntington."

I returned to the study, and hours later, there came a light rap on the door before it opened, and Mr. Murphy stuck his head inside. "You asked me to inform you when Mr. Flint was leaving."

"Yes, thank you." I gathered the documents I had analyzed for the last hours and placed them inside the desk drawer. I stood and rubbed the ache in my lower back before circling the desk and marching out into the corridor.

I strode to the entrance hall where Mother and Josie stood saying farewells. Mr. Flint, a burly man with a wavy silver mane, regarded my sister as one would a trophy they sought to obtain. She appeared no bigger than a child next to him. His large hand reached for my sister's, and I cringed when he pressed his lips against it. Of the many eligible women in New York, the man had always pursued the most timid, the youngest, the innocent—young women like my sister.

They looked in my direction as I strode toward them.

"Ah, Mr. Huntington," Mr. Flint said, shifting to observe me. "These lovely women informed me you were home but preoccupied with business matters. I appreciate your family's hospitality." He glanced at Josie like a cat who had caught the mouse and now held it with its paw, razor-sharp claws sheathed but poised to descend. Assurance glinted in his gray eyes.

Josie's shoulders were curled forward, her eyes lowered.

"Mother, Josie. If you will please excuse us, I would like to speak with Mr. Flint."

Mother's eyes narrowed with warning, but she said, "Certainly. Farewell, Mr. Flint. Until next time." Looking at me, she said, "Come, Josie." Gripping Josie's elbow, she steered them across the entrance hall toward the library.

"What is it you wish to speak about?" Mr. Flint said after they had gone. The charm he had displayed in the company of the women retreated, and he regarded me coldly.

I stood at eye level with him, noting the twitch of his jaw and how he postured before me. We were in a silent standoff, both seeking to defend our claim. He had no heirs, and Mother wagered my sister's happiness on the hope that a wife would inherit his wealth on his death, or she would see it was arranged so. My parents had stopped at nothing to obtain wealth, with no thought for those they trampled to reach the top. But Josie's happiness was worth more than any additional wealth their union could bring.

"I have another gentleman in mind for my sister," I said.

He rolled back his shoulders, his chest expanding. "And who might this be?"

"You will know him when you see them happily together." I considered the tension drawing at his hairline. "And if not him, my sister will pick a husband of her own choosing, or none. I won't subject her to a loveless marriage, and I certainly won't sanction a union with a man who has one foot in the grave and lusts for women much too young for him."

"I do admire youth," he said, unflinching, but his eyes narrowed as he observed me. "Your protectiveness makes me wonder if you have an infatuation with your sister."

His remark took me off guard, but I remained composed. "Only a vile man would consider such perversion. If I were a brawling man, I would drop you where you stand, but I am not. You have confirmed my conviction that you are unworthy of my sister. Therefore, I advise you to take your leave before I throw you out on your backside." Everything in me wanted to raise my fist against the man, but I rejected the impulses of my belated father, who had used violence to control. I had rejected every trait of the man since I'd been a small boy, and understood the man who had sired me. "Don't ever let me catch you near this house or my sister, or you will come to learn my hold in this city." A sour taste instantly burned my throat. In a moment of weakness, I had allowed the man to unnerve me, resorting to Mother and Father's tactics of using influential power.

"I am not one to be deterred or scared off, Mr. Huntington," Mr. Flint warned as he gripped the doorknob.

The cold glint in his gray eyes might cause a less confident man to waver, but I had encountered many men like him, and I, too, wasn't easily frightened. The war had seen to that. Before, I had been a peaceable man, and my father had endeavored to harden me, to make me more in his image. *"I need a man, not a woman, to run this family when I'm gone. You're too soft,"* he'd say. The blow that would follow had been a daily occurrence.

When the war came, I enlisted. For years I had watched men young and old, brothers and enemies, gutted and decapitated on a battlefield bathed in crimson. War does something to a man. My former self died on the battlefield and I returned home a hardened version of myself. War taught me there was nothing I couldn't face that life hadn't already served me. Father's death in the war had been a gift to our family, though Mother saw it differently.

"Nor am I," I said to the imbecile still standing before me. "Good day, Mr. Flint." I gripped the door he had opened and waited for him to exit before slamming the door shut.

"How dare you insult our guest." Mother strode toward me from wherever she had been, most likely waiting in the wings, eavesdropping.

"I told you, I won't allow you to marry my sister off to an imp. She is not a prize cow to be sold to the highest bidder. He unclothes her with his eyes."

"And you have never looked at a woman so?" Challenge flashed in her eyes.

"Not one I seek to marry."

"Your lust is no different from any other man's. I learned long ago that a woman's power lies in wealth and status, nothing more."

"Are you trying to fool me into believing that you do this for the good of Josie? That with her gaining wealth, she'll become more powerful as a woman?"

"Yes, that is precisely what I'm saying."

I threw back my head and laughed.

"You mock me, but know this: I won't rest until Josie is wed to Mr. Flint."

I eyed her with unmasked pity. "You have never done anything for the well-being of your children. Instead, you seek power for yourself, but it is an illusion. No power or wealth will ever quieten the frightened child inside you. You married Father, a man of influence and wealth, in hopes it would bring you protection, but that didn't bring you any solace. Instead, you suffered at his hand, as we all did. But rather than seeing the wrong in his ways, you adopted his warped notion that people are to be ruled by an iron fist."

She stumbled under my words before catching herself and regaining her stiff posture, masking any vulnerability. Face weathered with deep lines, the map of a miserable life, she regarded me with eyes empty of emotion. All decency, if she had ever possessed any, had died in her years ago. She unleashed her razor-sharp tongue. "If you had died on the battlefield with your father, I would not have to endure your presence."

Her verbal knife sliced open my heart, and I flinched. I read the satisfaction in the small smile that lifted her thin lips before she pivoted and marched across the entrance hall and down the corridor without another word.

I stood in the aftermath of her contempt for men and life, a victim to her poison. Unnerved and floundering in emotion I had so skillfully learned to block, I stared at the fern in the corner and it grew smaller and smaller in my mind's eye.

"Merritt." Josie's soft voice, in front of me.

In my daze, I hadn't heard her walk up. I fought to shake off the emotional wound, and as my vision recovered, I floated back into the room.

Josie touched my arm and looked up at me with concern. "Are you all right?"

I forced a smile. "Yes, quite." I put an arm around her shoulders.

"I'm sorry," she said.

"For what?" I looked down at her.

"For Mother. I heard you defend me against her trying to marry me off to that dreadful man. And what she said about wishing you had died." Her voice cracked, and she began to sob.

I drew her into an embrace, and my eyes burned. "Don't weep. Mother's contempt can't hurt me anymore."

Josie only wept harder and clung to me. When she calmed, I held her at arm's length and used a thumb to dry her tears. "You will marry a man of your choosing. Your happiness is my goal in this life. I will give my life for it."

"I am unworthy of your love," she said with conviction.

"Is that what Mother has you believing?" I lifted her chin and held it gently, staring into eyes with more beauty and heart than the world merited. I feared the person who could rob my sister of her purity. "You are worth so much more."

"Your love brings me peace," she said with a soft smile.

I released her. "Maybe at the Goddard ball, you will find a suitable gentleman who holds your interest and doesn't have one foot in the grave."

"But I heard you tell Mr. Flint that you had found me a gentleman suitor."

"That was to push him off."

"I would have married him for you."

"Your loyalty disarms you," I said. "You can bend to everyone's wishes and do all you can to please, but loyalty is fleeting. Remember that."

"I want to be happy. I do."

"What is happiness?" I stared at her blankly, hardly recalling a time when I had felt truly happy.

"Happiness comes when I sing and play the piano. When I see Winston's smiling face." She held out a hand as my dog sauntered into the entrance hall. "Come here, boy."

I thought of the comfort I found in her company and that of my dog and realized, indeed, I had experienced forms of happiness.

"Will you honor me with an afternoon carriage ride?" I asked.

She nestled Winston's head into the skirt of her gown, and he leaned into her with a lopsided grin of pleasure. I smiled at the pair, my heart softening.

"I would be delighted," she said.

Sometime later, we rode through the streets of Manhattan in an open carriage with my driver given the instructions that we had no destination in mind. As we turned a corner, squeals of happiness drew my attention to the boardwalk, where a group of young women embraced and conversed. A coachman unloaded trunks while another man perched one on his shoulder and climbed the stairs to the townhouse. I got a clear view of the young brunette amongst the golden-haired womenfolk and my breath stopped, and Josie's cheerful rambling faded as recognition struck. Katherine Darlington. The others turned their attention to the middle-aged brunette, Miss Darlington's family's governess. The woman embraced them warmly, as a loving mother would her daughters.

The womenfolk almost bounced in glee at what appeared to be a reunion of sorts. Katherine smiled at the youngest girl and interacted with her playfully, as I had with Josie when she was younger. A smile formed on my lips as I witnessed their exchange.

Josie shouldered me. "Do you know them?"

"Who?" I said, unable to draw my gaze away.

"Them?" She pointed, and I quickly looked away and pushed her hand down. Josie gave me a cheeky smile. "You do know them. Does one hold your fancy?"

"Those are the Darlington sisters. And no, I don't fancy them. However, I provided aid to Miss Katherine when I found her and her coachman stranded on the roadside."

"Oh, the Darlingtons. I've heard of them but have yet to make their acquaintance."

I looked at the group as Katherine put her arm around the youngest girl's narrow shoulders. Again, my face softened. As though sensing me, Katherine twisted and looked in my direction. Our eyes locked, and before I could look away, feeling exposed over my pleasure in the union, I saw her expression grow guarded.

As we rode by, I focused on the street ahead while Josie squirmed in her seat to glance back at the sisters.

"Do you have to make it obvious?" I said.

"Me?" She settled back in her seat and adjusted the furs covering our laps to ward off the chill. "I believe it was you who was doing all the staring. As though you were a groom catching a glimpse of his bride for the first time."

I laughed. Josie had a way of bringing out the best in me. In her presence I felt human, not numbed by the harshness of life.

Chapter 13

Jude—Brooklyn, NY

OUTSIDE THE COFFEE HOUSE, OUR DRIVER REINED THE CARRIAGE to a stop. The brisk midmorning air captured my breath as I opened the door and stepped outside, then turned back to assist my mother.

She placed her delicate gloved hand in mine and exited the carriage. "Thank you, my darling."

I placed her hand in the crook of my elbow and strode toward the coffee house. I sensed Mother's tension and patted her hand to reassure her. We stepped inside, and the aroma of freshly brewed coffee delighted my senses. The conversations of patrons hummed like busy bees.

Heads turned in our direction as we stood in line to place our orders.

"What is he doing here with a white woman?" a lady whispered.

My mother maintained a pleasant smile, but I sensed her curve into herself.

"Next," Mr. King, the owner, said.

I strode forward, and he displayed an inviting smile. "How are you today, Mr. Williams? It's been a while." He glanced at Mother as she positioned herself to my right. "Ma'am."

"Mr. King, always a pleasure," she said.

"Your Pa was here yesterday and mentioned you were home for a short visit. So proud of you he is."

Heat touched my ears. Where many young men sought their father's approval, receiving my father's had come without conditions. Father boasted shamelessly of my accomplishments as a law student. He was a proud Black man and a pillar of success in the community. My parents had taught me that it didn't matter what I chose to do with my life, but that life was a privilege, so make it count. I heeded their wisdom. I strove to make them proud and aspired to positively change the world, especially in my community.

"You have some shoes to fill, son," Mr. King said. "It's no secret, what he has done for his assistant, that Scott girl, paying for her to attend New York Medical College and Hospital for Women. Now, I disagree with this modern sentiment that women should work outside the home. But I suppose if she became a certified physician like that McKinney-Steward, graduating as valedictorian and the first black woman to be a certified physician, it can't harm nothing."

"Indeed." I glanced back at the impatient customers stirring behind us.

"What can I get you?" Mr. King said.

"Two coffees, tea biscuits, and preserves will do." I withdrew my pocketbook.

Mr. King gave me my total, and I paid the man before guiding Mother to an available table by the full-length windows overlooking the street. I pulled out her chair, and she removed her hat and took a seat. I followed suit and placed my hat on my knee under the table while Mother removed her gloves and tucked them in her reticule. She regarded me uneasily as stares and whispers continued around us, and smoothed back wisp of brunette hair peppered with gray.

"It's been lovely to have you home, son." She gently covered my hand where it lay on the table. "I shall miss you terribly. But in the spring you will graduate, and your father and I will be happy to have you closer. It pained me to let you go."

"I know, Mother," I said with a laugh. "I recall the endless tears for a month leading up to my departure."

"One can hardly fault a mother for her bond with her child. However, letting your child go out on their own in the world is difficult after spending your life trying to protect them from the world's harshness. It's as though you are being asked to cut off your right arm." She spread her napkin over her lap.

"And to think you considered uprooting Father and his practice to be closer to me."

"A moment of despondency, I reckon." She blushed. "I remember the day your father graduated medical school. I was so proud of him. The adversities he has overcome. He allowed nothing to stand in his way of achieving what he set out to do." Pride gleamed in her gray-blue eyes, then it faded. "When we lost your brother, I thought I'd never be whole again. Then life blessed us with you."

My brother had been born six years before me and had drowned in the Harlem River. My parents had never gotten over his loss, and I suppose a parent never could. I wondered if that was why my mother clung to me to the point of making herself sick with worry over my well-being.

I attended a colored school in Brooklyn, founded by Blacks aimed primarily for Black students, although white students also attended. The school mainly employed Black principals and teachers, but also whites.

I'd suffered at the hands of my fellow students. I was too dark to the whites, and to the Blacks, I was too fair. So I learned to fight my way through school. The day I returned home from school with my clothes dirtied and torn and a blackened eye, my mother, wanting to shield me from the cruelty of my reality, beseeched my father to hire a schoolteacher to instruct me at home.

My father had refused, telling her they couldn't coddle me and I'd learn to deal with life.

"Not a day goes by that I don't think of my brother and what he was like. Or what it would've been like to have a brother, and an older one, at that. I used to dream of how he and I would've taken on the world together. How he would've protected me against the prejudice amongst my classmates."

I looked up as a man stopped at our table with a tray holding our order. He set the items down. Mother offered her thanks, and the man nodded, but the glint in his eye spoke of his bias. Mother looked at me as he turned and strode off, ignoring the censure in the man's eyes.

"When you were younger, I carried a lot of guilt and shame over the love I had for your father because, from that love, I birthed a son who'd be judged and ridiculed from the start. I felt selfish and questioned my cruelty."

I gawked at her in disbelief. "Mother…"

She lifted a hand to halt my reply and then dropped a sugar nugget into her coffee. "When you came to us and told us you wanted to pursue a career in law with the intent of fighting for the injustices for all with no barrier to wealth or race, I knew God had blessed your birth and us with a son who'd make a footprint in the world for the better." Her eyes pooled as she looked at me. "For out of pain, heroes are born. If we cultivate from our adversities, we learn empathy and mercy for all of life. Our power lies in listening and observing others. We can hear the cry within when we are silent and truly listen. Love and understanding will free us from the fear, hate, and greed of scared men and women. We can claw and scrape to pile over each other, or we can choose to see there is more than enough for all of us."

"I know it hasn't always been easy for you." I looked from her to the women adorned in gem-toned gowns and feather hats, sipping tea and conversing with friends. Refined businessmen sat conducting business arrangements, and other men chatted about the upturn in the economy and the corruption in politics.

"No, it hasn't," Mother said with a soft smile. "But to win your father's love and to have you for a son, I'd walk through the fires again."

I looked back at her, and a smile formed on my lips. I admired the love between my parents and hoped I'd share the same passion one day.

My mother had come from nothing. She had been an illiterate farm girl and fortune smiled on my parents when an aristocratic white family, the Davenports, hired my mother as a chambermaid and my father as a groomsman. Eventually, Mother moved up to head housekeeper and my father a coachman. The fondness and respect between the family and my parents became the catalyst that altered my folks' lives forever. Mrs. Davenport taught Mother to speak as a woman with a proper education would. In the evenings, Father taught her to read and write. The family paid for my father to attend Rush Medical College in Chicago, where he earned his medical degree. Then, when war came, he served in the Fifty-Fourth Massachusetts Regiment.

"Father aids all with kindness and compassion, and I hope I can one day bring pride to the family name."

She regarded me tenderly. "There is no fear of that, son. Our pride in you is infinite."

"I hope I can live up to your expectations."

"There are no expectations. Every parent wishes for more for their children than what we have. But your life is yours, not ours, to dictate what you should or shouldn't do."

"Your and Father's support means everything to me," I said. "I will need that support more than ever as I advance with my desire to aid in the movement for equal rights."

She gripped my hand where it lay on the table and gave it a passionate squeeze. "More like-minded people banding together will bring the change we need. Dwelling in the past will keep us trapped. The power lies in each new day. If we seek a better to-morrow, we must make today count."

I took encouragement and inspiration from her wisdom.

"You are a decent and kind man. Never lose focus on that."

"Thank you, Mother."

She had pushed me to achieve greatness, and I'd be forever grateful to the parents who'd sacrificed so much to put me through law school. And for a mother who had wanted the best for me, so much so that she moved into the elite Black neighborhood. She endured ridicule and hostility because she wanted me to have dignity and pride in my father's heritage. She wanted me to sense what a Black man in America could achieve and to fight the bar-riers of oppression.

"Now, you mentioned that you were paying Miss Kat a visit. How did that go? And do tell me about the Darlingtons. How do they fare?"

"As well as can be expected. The new Mrs. Darlington—not so new anymore, I suppose—had me turned away at the door."

The crease between Mother's brows deepened. "The nerve of that woman."

"However, I did enlist Miss Grace's aid in getting word to Kat that I had come," I said with a smirk. "We met in the meadow we used to visit as children. Our conversation was pleasant…at first."

"What do you mean, 'at first'?"

"I upset her."

"How so?"

"By questioning where she stood on the politics between the South and North."

"I believe the young woman has made it very clear where she stands. Why would you question any differently?"

I picked at the handle of my mug and gazed into the dark liq-uid in search of an answer. The conversation between Kat and I had bothered me ever since. "I was a fool, I guess." I looked at my mother, the lifetime ache in me surfacing. "I suppose I allowed suppressed demons to rear themselves. I made her the reason for my suffering. But, of course, I was wrong in my treatment of her."

Mother grimaced. "I hope you plan to make it right."

"The first chance I get," I said.

"I would hope so. The Darlingtons have been our friends for years, although we've lost touch since this Boseman woman came into the Darlington family. However, that does not alter the respect and friendship I had for Victoria Darlington."

"I'd rather speak to Kat in person, but I don't want to cause her more trouble by revisiting the estate, and I am set to return to DC tomorrow. So I will write to her and hope she receives my letter."

"And why wouldn't she?"

"Because Mrs. Darlington controls all the mail coming in and out of the estate. In Kat's letters to me, she mentions she never receives my correspondence."

Mother's mouth twitched, and conviction hardened her face. "Phillip has a responsibility to his daughters. He must run his household as though he is the man."

"Kat says Mr. Darlington rarely visits the estate."

Mother gasped and blinked rapidly. She dropped her head, retrieved a lace handkerchief from her reticule, and dabbed the corners of her eyes. "Victoria would be so heartbroken at his disregard for the girls."

"It seems as though Kat gets the brunt of Mrs. Darlington's contempt. She shuts Kat away in her chamber when she doesn't conform to her demands and absurdities."

"Katherine has always had a fire in her. She comes by it honestly, I suppose." She glanced out the window as though lost in thought.

"To what do you refer?" I asked, trying to pull her back to the room.

She shuddered, then shook her head to dislodge whatever had captured her thoughts. "Just that the young woman is a fighter, and some of us have had no choice but to be. Her spirit will serve her well."

Later, as we returned home to our townhouse, our neighbors, Mrs. Abraham and her daughter Mercy, were ascending their front stairs. My mother had spent many days helping Mrs. Abraham and her daughter in the slums of Five Points, and they had become steadfast friends.

Mrs. Abraham had been a slave as a child in the South but had escaped on a ship to New York. Her husband Saul worked as an editor at the *Manhattan Observer*, once a penny newspaper with a strong focus on its motto: Freedom for All. After the war, the paper's focus had turned to the fight against the racial imbalance in America.

"Ruby." Mother strode forward and embraced the woman.

"Ellen, how lovely to see you." Mrs. Abraham eyed me with a smile over my mother's shoulder before they parted and she straightened her lavish hat and rust-colored paletot. "Mr. Williams, it is nice to see you."

"Ma'am." I tilted my hat and returned her smile. "How are you today, Miss Mercy?" I regarded the girl who would overtake her mother's height any day now.

She dipped her head. "I'm well." Her brooding demeanor suggested her answer was false. Mrs. Abraham's face tensed, and I sensed turmoil between mother and daughter.

"How are the wee ones faring?" Mother eyed the basket Mrs. Abraham held containing food and bandages.

Mrs. Abraham adjusted the basket in her hands. "Better each day. I have tracked down a relative who has agreed to take them in."

"Such a shame. They're so young to be orphaned." Mother grimaced.

"I've never become accustomed to the suffering and poverty in the Points. But every day, I am reminded of the resilience of humanity."

"The place has a way of making you see your hardships as minor in the face of what others endure," Mother said.

Mrs. Abraham nodded in agreement and looked at me; her expression softened. "Your mother says you are set to graduate in the spring."

"I am," I said.

"We are all proud of you. You prove to other Black men what they, too, can achieve. Perhaps this imbalance plaguing our country will be behind us when I am blessed with grandchildren."

At her mother's side, Mercy narrowed her eyes.

"Let us hope," I said. "But I fear the scars of slavery and the injustices will last for generations to come."

Mrs. Abraham's bright countenance dulled. "I fear you are right. Humanity has much work to do to heal the sins we have forced upon each other."

"Why must we talk about such things?" Mercy lifted her chin, indignation flaring. "I, for one, don't care to talk about the past. Our people are no longer enslaved, so we should forget and move on."

"A past not so long ago," her mother said with a look of dismay. "Your ancestors have suffered to make America great. It is not something one can so easily forget, or wish to."

"Why can't we move away from this place? Somewhere where…"

"You can fade into the crowd and disown your Blackness?" Mrs. Abraham glared at her daughter. "No, daughter. We are a proud people. But, unfortunately, life has taught us to carry shame for a fact we can't change. You can try to reject your ancestors, but all you will ever do is keep running from yourself. It's time you embrace the power of who you are and fight for your right to exist in a just world. It is your duty to all those who died at the hands of slavery."

Mercy's eyes welled as she fought an all too familiar battle within herself. "Why couldn't I have been born anything other than Black? Then life wouldn't be so cruel. I could walk the streets, shop in the finest stores in New York, and hold my head up with pride."

Weariness slumped Mrs. Abraham's shoulders, and she touched Mercy's arm. "Please, daughter, let us keep our quarrels to our household. Neither the Williams nor the neighborhood want to hear them."

Mercy pulled away, and pain shone on her mother's face. I recognized the misery within Mercy, and my heart went out to her. As a girl barely old enough to comprehend most facets of life, she faced the bigotry we did. She sought to be accepted and belong in a world that had not made room for us. A world untethered in the appetite for power and in their smallness, they sought to break and oppress. The ache and fire in the girl's disposition bolstered my desire to do my part to ensure equality and a promising future for all.

"If you ladies will excuse me," I said.

"Certainly," Mrs. Abraham said. "My apologies."

"There is none needed," I said with a smile. "We all can understand Miss Mercy's disheartenment."

Mrs. Abraham dipped her head in gratitude, and Mercy avoided eye contact, appearing to want to be anywhere but where she was.

I left my mother to speak with the ladies further and climbed the front steps to our brownstone home.

Mr. Washington, our butler, opened the door. "Welcome back, Mr. Williams, sir." He placed a white-gloved hand to his middle and bowed before stepping aside to allow me entrance.

I recalled the day my father hired Mr. Washington and his wife, our housekeeper. His face had gleamed with pride. My parents had built a prosperous life together, despite their struggles as a biracial couple. I never met my mother's family because they disowned her after finding out about her marriage to my father. The state of North Carolina didn't condone interracial marriages, so my parents left the state to legally wed before returning to their home state. Mother returned to her family home alone, fearing what they'd do to my father, to tell them of her marriage. My grandfather spat on her and told her she was a disgrace, stating he'd not accept any mulatto children as his grandchildren. Nor would he accept a whore of a daughter who'd willingly lie with a Negro. I abhorred a man I'd never known for mistreating my mother, a good and righteous woman who'd chosen to love without prejudice.

The door opened behind me, and Mother entered.

"A letter came for you, Mr. Williams." Mr. Washington retrieved a letter from a hallway stand.

"Thank you." I took the letter. Recognizing the handwriting, I felt my heart beat faster. Kat.

"Who is it from?" Mother said, removing her hat and cashmere paletot.

"Kat."

"Splendid. Leave it to a woman to set everything straight." She offered me a wink and handed her outerwear to Mr. Washington. "I suppose the girls have all grown and become sophisticated ladies like their mother." Her expression grew reflective, with a trace of sadness. "Victoria was a woman of candor and compassion. She used to host grand charity bazaars. But I've only heard stories because, sadly, I never got to attend."

My chest tightened at the remark. I'd spent my life trying to protect her from the pain of prejudice I knew all too well. After Mother befriended Kat's mother, Mrs. Darlington invited her to a charity event. Barely an hour had passed before she returned home, her face puffy from crying, and retreated to her chamber to spare me from witnessing the heartache she had faced when she showed up at a white charity event as a white woman who had married a Black man. She had remained in her bedroom until Father returned home later that evening from tending to patients.

I had placed my ear to the door at the sound of their hushed voices.

"Please don't weep, my love," Father said.

"The audacity of those women, to speak to me in such a manner. As though I had not been invited by the hostess herself. They had me so upset, I fled without thanking Mrs. Darlington for the invitation."

"Jude, are you listening?" Mother said, and I blinked the memory away.

"The Darlington women are faring well, but the void left by their mother's passing has divided the family."

Mother nodded. "In recent years, when I've paid Braxton Hall a visit, I've been turned away by the staff and told Mrs. Darlington was indisposed or the family was away. Perhaps I should speak to Phillip on the matter. Victoria was my friend. I have just cause to be concerned for the welfare of her children."

"Do as you see fit." I glanced at the letter in my hand.

"Please don't let me keep you. Go and see what Katherine has to say."

I inclined my head, turned, and walked down the corridor to the study. Inside, I seated myself at the desk and tore open the letter. I lifted the paper to my nose, hoping to catch a whiff of her scent.

I winced when I recalled how she'd substituted "Mr. Williams" for my first name, and the blaze in her soulful, whiskey-hued eyes before she pivoted and stormed across the meadow, her arms swinging angrily at her sides. I unfolded the letter, fearful of what lay inside. The end of our friendship, or the loss of all hope of winning her favor…her heart.

I suppose I had loved Kat all my life, but she had never shown she saw me as anything more than a childhood friend. I guess I was foolish to aspire one day to win the heart of a white, affluent woman. Nevertheless, I allowed myself to be caught up in the enchantment of my parents' love story and lay awake, envisioning the same could happen to Kat and me.

I read the words she'd written.

My dearest Jude,

Remorse weighs my heart at the outcome of our recent encounter. Please forgive me for behaving rudely and lacking the wisdom to conduct myself more suitably, regardless of how I felt at the moment. I did not seek to offend or hurt you. I am not your adversary—a fact I know you are aware of.

Until we meet again, my friend.

My deepest respect,

Kat

Again I felt the ache that snatched my heart each time she closed her letters with "friend." But to accept the title was better than not having Kat in my life at all. I had retreated many times from telling her my true feelings because I understood she was not like most women. She pursued independence and adventure, not a husband—or children, for that matter.

I dipped my pen into the inkwell and composed a letter to her with the intention of paying her friend Birdie a visit and requesting she personally deliver the letter. I hoped Birdie's regard for me would aid her in breaking down the barriers of our obstinate friend.

After I sealed my reply in an envelope, I leaned back in the chair and peered out the window overlooking the street.

One day I would muster the courage to tell her the truth in my heart.

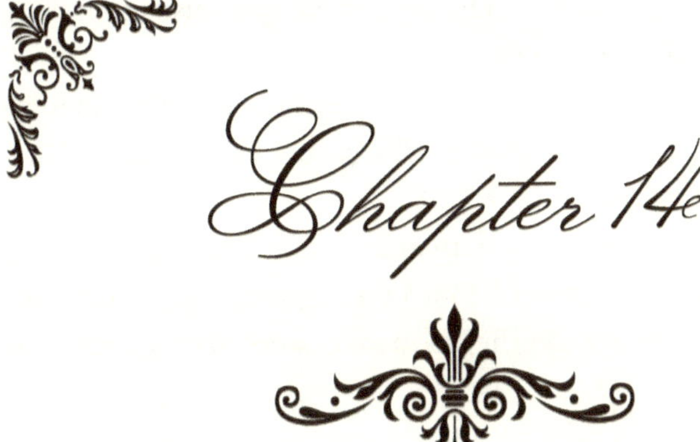

Chapter 14

BLISS FILLED THE CORRIDORS OF OUR FAMILY'S TOWNHOUSE. HAPPINESS radiated from my sisters' faces and sang in my heart for the first time in years. Papa devoted his days to his business and the evenings to reacquainting himself with his daughters. The heaviness surrounding him days prior faded, and merriment shone on his face. Sometimes I caught him smiling at my sisters; other times, he stared with a yearning look before dabbing away tears. I suppose he glimpsed bits of Mama in them.

Life had become livable again in the days since our return, and hope for the future filled us all. I was grateful for the gift of family and their love, and I never wanted to wake from the dream. In the warmth of the afternoons, I spent hours painting in the courtyard, lost in the ecstasy of liberation and creativity.

Audrey's whereabouts were still unknown, and I didn't care because I worried about what would happen when she finally showed up.

One morning while we sat at the dining table for the morning meal, my sisters started talking about the Goddard Banquet.

"Mrs. Goddard knows how to host a banquet," Evelyn said, her face alight with eagerness. "I cannot wait to show everyone my dress. It is simply divine. The dressmaker promised to have it to me by the end of the week."

Between mouthfuls of crumpet, Adelaide said, "She does indeed. The food will be delightful." She covered her mouth with a hand while she talked.

Evelyn's lightheartedness withered, and she looked at Adelaide with contempt. "You won't fit into your gown if you keep eating those crumpets. And for heaven's sake, stop talking with your mouth full."

Adelaide's face reddened, and she returned the last bite in her hand to her plate.

"Must you always be so rude?" Alice glowered at Evelyn.

Evelyn's mouth dropped open, but she quickly gathered her composure and said, "I don't mean to be. I'm merely stating the obvious."

"Observations best left unstated," I said.

"Like you would know the first thing about fashion," Evelyn said with an unbecoming pout before rubbing the nape of her neck. "You must understand, it is like we are making our grand entrance with our return to the city. People will be observing us, and we must make Papa proud."

"This ball is sounding more dreadful by the moment," I said.

"Of course, you'd turn a promising night filled with grandeur and excitement into a chore." Evelyn's pout returned.

Dorotea entered the room carrying a graniteware and pewter teapot. "Must you fuss so?"

"It is Evelyn's doing," I said. "Her fear of what others think is exhausting. I'm not sure how she won Mr. Peyton's affections. She is quite a bore." I scraped back my chair and threw my napkin on the table. "I am going out."

"And to where, pray tell?"

"To visit Birdie, if you must know."

Evelyn lifted a brow. "Did she invite you?"

"No."

"Honestly, Kat." She shook her head with exasperation. "You can't merely show up at people's houses without a proper invitation."

"And why not? I want to see her, and waiting for an invite could take weeks."

"But you haven't finished your breakfast." Evelyn scrambled to find a reason to snare me into the confines of her cocoon.

"I've lost my appetite," I flung over my shoulder.

"Ensure you are escorted and don't venture out alone," Evelyn called after me. "We are in the city, after all, and you can't get away with indecency as you did in the country. Everyone is always watching, and I won't have you disgracing our family by conducting yourself as a trollop."

"Evelyn! Must you?" I halted and spun back to face her.

"What?" She looked at me with an innocent look on her face.

Not seeking to quarrel with her, I gestured a hand at Alice. "Very well. Have it your way. Alice, will you accompany me?"

Alice opened her mouth to reply, but Evelyn gasped and said, "She is a child and won't suit."

Adelaide stood and took another bite of her eggs before pushing back her chair. She swallowed a half-chewed bite and said, "I will accompany her."

I waved a hand in the air. "There you have it. Mind your affairs, and I will see to mine."

Evelyn's squeal of frustration trailed after me.

Adelaide accompanied me into the entrance hall.

"Thank you," I said. "Must she always be so overbearing?"

"She can be a bit demanding, but she means well."

"Why do you defend her?"

"It's not defending, but more understanding. You see, when Mama died, Evelyn, being the eldest, took it upon herself to be responsible for us."

"In my recollection, that is also a burden Papa laid on her shoulders the day he brought home our darling stepmother."

Sarcasm and bitterness soured my tongue as we strode toward the staircase. "I grow weary of Evelyn's nagging. Perhaps marrying her off to that Mr. Peyton will provide peace of mind. She has always been a pest, but it has become more apparent as I grow older."

Adelaide's solemnness rarely faltered, but consideration pulled at her forehead. "They say there is a time when birds should fly the coop."

The analogy did not surprise me. Adelaide's love of nature and birds had her poring over books for hours. I couldn't comprehend how a book could captivate the mind so. She had once sauntered into the dining room with her nose buried in a book and seated herself at the table. An encyclopedia engrossed her as though it exploded with captivating adventure. Although she was the most intelligent person I knew, I thought spending a day in her mind must be tedious. How could one person hold so much knowledge?

Since our return, I'd accompanied her to one of the many New York libraries. The building had previously been a personal residence. It wasn't the books lining the floor-to-ceiling shelving that covered two floors but the architect's brilliance and vision that enchanted me: the ornate glass dome ceiling with fleur-de-lis design; the mahogany-paneled walls; the magnificent staircase. However, after Adelaide had acquired a subscription, we arrived home buried under a stack of books.

"Colleen." I brightened when my chambermaid walked toward me carrying a watering can, leaving a trail of dribbled water behind her. "When you've finished watering the plants, please come to my chamber and help me prepare to go out, won't you?"

"Yes, miss." She curtsied.

Later, after donning a coral-colored day dress with a ruffled hem and burgundy velvet trimmings, I put on my outerwear and exited the house.

The buzz of the city excited me. Carriages congested the streets. Neighbors conversed on landings and boardwalks. Coachmen and groomsmen clad in Velour Russe uniforms in rich hues of ruby, blue, and brown trimmed in gold cording and brass buttons awaited ladies and gentlemen across the street and to my left and right.

I regarded my readied carriage from the landing as I slipped on my gloves. Alfred and the coachman stood waiting at the bottom of the stairs. Colleen stepped out after me and stood to my right with her hands folded in front of her. "Isn't it swell to be back in the city?" I lifted my nose as though I could inhale the intoxicating excitement.

"Ye wouldn't be doin' that in the Points," Colleen said. "The mornin' air oozes with the stench of shite from the privy runoff."

I lowered my head and glanced at her. "I can't say I've been to the Points. I've only heard stories of it."

"Not even passin' through?"

"No. Papa and Mama said the place is filled with thieves and murderers and is no place for a lady. Although I never prided myself on being a proper lady. I have always wondered what the place is like."

"Yeer parents are right. The Points is no place for a lady like yeerself, and it's best ye steer clear of it."

"It can't be all bad. Look at you. You are a person of quality."

She beamed. "Some would say that's a matter of opinion."

"But why should one care what others think?" I squared my shoulders. "I believe it should be what the heart thinks that guides us. And I like you."

She dipped her head and toed the marble landing with the tip of her scuffed black shoe. "Thank ye kindly, miss."

Adelaide exited the house with a book tucked under her arm. "What?" she said when I glanced at the book. "You don't expect me to sit and wait with nothing to occupy my mind."

"Of course not. Let us go." I turned and took the first step before remembering Alfred stood below. Recalling my promise to Colleen in my chamber at Braxton Hall about helping her with Alfred, I said over my shoulder, "Come, Colleen."

"Miss?"

I glanced back at her. Confusion sparked in her dark eyes. I kept my voice low. "Adelaide and I may need your assistance at the carriage."

"Somethin' the coachman can see to, ain't it?" She wiped her palms on the front of her white pinafore. Her gaze flitted to Alfred and the coachman below.

I cocked my head, pondering my reasoning. "From what I've gathered from women about courtships, women will do whatever they can to get a glimpse of the gentleman who has won their favor. It is ghastly, I know. But Evelyn will go to great lengths to get a mere glance from Mr. Peyton. I suppose I will never understand such infatuation."

Adelaide, who had stopped beside me, stifled a laugh.

"Come now. I told you I would help you with Alfred."

"You?" Adelaide's eyes twinkled. "I wouldn't say you are qualified."

I shrugged. "Perhaps not, but when I make a promise, I keep it." I continued down the stairs.

Colleen hurried to keep up. "I appreciate yeer willingness to help, but maybe—"

"Good day, Miss Katherine, Miss Adelaide," Alfred said in a cheery voice as he strode to the bottom step to await our descent.

Colleen tucked herself behind me as though wanting to make herself small, but her height was greater than mine, making me an unlikely candidate to aid in her desire for concealment.

"Colleen," Alfred said, his lopsided smile broadening, revealing a gap between rather good teeth. But as he regarded the girl, it vanished. "Are you well?"

"Yes," she squeaked from behind me.

I pulled the girl from my shadow and noted how her complexion had blanched in his presence. She appeared ready to faint. I studied her, brow puckered in puzzlement. The love between a woman and a man was a peculiar thing. It robbed a person of their abilities and clouded all senses, leaving a fragile flower, vulnerable against a strong wind. I encircled her waist with an arm to keep the fool girl upright. I, for one, would never allow myself to succumb to such foolishness. It boggled my mind to think that throughout time, women voluntarily surrendered their minds and their will to men and became advocates for man's dictatorship.

"Miss Colleen's under the weather today. Isn't that right?" I tightened my hold on her waist.

"Yes, Miss Katherine. I believe I am comin' down with some-thin'." A tinge of color touched her cheeks.

And there we had it; love would not claim another victim for the time being.

"Please see the drapes in my room are taken down and aired out." I directed my attention to Colleen and conjured an excuse for my lame attempt at playing matchmaker. "And if your illness does not pass, you are permitted to rest a while in your chamber."

"Yes, Miss Katherine." She bobbed her head like a gobbling turkey in her eagerness to disappear. "Will that be all?"

"That will be all," I said.

She curtsied, turned, and climbed the steps more vigorously than she had descended.

I regarded the lanky stable boy gazing longingly after Colleen. "I've witnessed that look before."

"Pardon, miss?" He broke his nauseating trance and returned his gaze to me.

"You hold affection for my chambermaid. Do you think your continued employment came from our desire to keep anyone my stepmother hired? I assure you it wasn't."

He gawked at me, appearing uncertain about what to say.

I continued with my mind's ramblings as the coachman extended a gloved hand to help me into the carriage. "If you have feelings for the girl, why don't you plan a romantic outing to win her heart? In doing so, you'd put us all out of the misery of the long faces and observations from afar."

His face turned crimson.

"Kat." Adelaide's warning came out like a hiss between clenched teeth.

I regretted my forwardness. "Forgive me; I don't intend to be brash, but sometimes I cannot diplomatically articulate what I honestly think, or so I'm told." I glowered at Adelaide before returning my gaze to the stable boy. "From what I gather, women seek to be swept off their feet."

He frowned, seeming as ignorant in the understanding of courtship as I.

I recalled Evelyn recently crowing over how Mr. Peyton had taken her for a carriage ride. He'd brought a blanket and a picnic basket, and they dined in a meadow next to the creek before they were chased off by ants.

"Perhaps you could take her for a walk next to the river. The view and the soothing sound of the water is an assured way to win a girl's heart."

He brightened at the idea. "That is a right splendid idea. On my day off, I will ask her. Many thanks, miss."

I delivered a smug look to Adelaide, who smiled and shook her head in disbelief. I lifted my chin and took the coachman's outstretched hand. "Good day, Alfred," I said and stepped into the carriage.

He mumbled his thanks.

Adelaide climbed in beside me, and soon we were off.

Chapter 15

ADELAIDE LIFTED THE BRONZE DOOR KNOCKER AND TAPPED IT twice, then stood back to wait. I fidgeted on the step and looked at the street traffic and the boardwalk in front of us as a crew of street sweepers cleared debris and gathered piles of fallen scarlet and gold leaves. A lady who greatly resembled her King Charles spaniel walked by at a brisk pace while the dog half dragged her down the boardwalk.

"Tippet, you must slow down," she cooed in a high-pitched voice, expecting the dog to understand her. I smirked at the pair before turning back to Adelaide.

"What is taking so long? Perhaps they never heard you." I stepped forward to rap the knocker again.

Adelaide grabbed my arm before I could. "Patience, dear sister." Her eyes held no criticism, only amusement at my impatience.

"It's been far too long since I've seen Birdie, or anyone, for that matter. I miss the camaraderie of my friends. Wouldn't you?"

She eyed her book in her grasp as though it held an incredible secret she must discover before it vanished.

"There are more compelling things in life than to have your nose stuck in books for days on end." I glanced at the door. What in heaven's name was taking so long?

Adelaide flipped the book pages and skimmed the words while we waited.

I compressed my lips. Adelaide leaned toward friendships with those much older than her. And I hadn't missed how middle-aged and more refined gentlemen captured my sister's attention—not just any sophisticated gentleman, but those with a passion for literature and the brilliance of the mind. I understood the latter, but a woman could achieve that alone if set free to pursue the life she wanted.

The door swung open, and the Vello butler gawked at us. "Miss Katherine?"

"We apologize for showing up without an invitation, but is Birdie home?" I rooted my feet to avoid barging in and humiliating Adelaide and myself.

"Yes, Miss Vello is here, but she's busy with the dressmaker."

"Who is it, Mr. Marino?" a woman said from inside.

"It's Signorina Katherine and…" He stared blankly at Adelaide.

"Adelaide," I said.

"Signorina Adelaide," he said over his shoulder.

"Well, do let them in." I recognized the voice of Mrs. Vello.

The butler half bowed and stepped aside to allow us entry. Inside, Birdie's mother, a regal woman in her mid-forties, strode toward us, her ageless skin glowing in the sunlight pouring through an overhead skylight open to the outdoors. Four men stood on ladders, balancing a large glass replacement panel over their heads.

"Kat, darling, how lovely to see you." She hugged me.

"Good day, Mrs. Vello," I muffled into the warmth of her embrace.

She pulled back and extended an embrace to Adelaide before releasing her. Laugh lines creased the corners of her eyes, and affection shone on her face as she looked at me. "Birdie is in the parlor with the dressmaker. I fear this wedding gown will take years to create, with my daughter's minute attention to detail."

My friend's admiration for high fashion bore no resemblance

to my tastes. We were gravely different, but Birdie's heart and zest for life endeared her to me. She spent her free time writing short stories, and many had reached publication. She spun gold from everything she touched, and her cleverness fascinated me. Her love for food kept her locked away in the kitchen for hours, concocting new recipes for her latest venture, a recipe book.

Activity buzzed from every corner of the mansion. Painters applied a pale blue to the entrance hall walls, and carpenters secured painted gold trim, wall sconces, and crown molding. The earthy, nutty scent of linseed oil hung in the air.

"Do excuse the disarray. As you can see, we are under a remodel." Mrs. Vello gestured at the tradesmen. "We are on the cusp of a new age. Not only are political views changing, but fashion and interior design as well."

"It is exquisite," Adelaide said with a smile.

"Thank you, my dear."

"Yes, it's quite lovely," I said, although I didn't particularly like the shade of blue, as it reminded me of a color Audrey had chosen at Braxton Hall.

"Shall we go and inform Birdie you are here?"

I bobbed my head.

She gestured for us to follow her across the yellow marble of the hall entrance to the salon. Opening a meticulously etched golden door, Mrs. Vello swept into the room, the fabric of her magenta pinstriped day dress swishing around her. Like her daughter, she defined elegance.

"Birdie, my dear, look who came calling."

Adelaide and I stepped into the room. Birdie sat on the settee with a woman I recognized as the dressmaker I had sent away from Braxton Hall.

Birdie's face brightened at the sight of me. "Kat." She jumped to her feet, closed the distance between us, and crushed me in an embrace. "I'm delighted to see you."

"And I, you," I said when she released me and I could breathe.

She had inherited her mother's loveliness, and it wasn't a wonder Zane Goddard sought to steal her from me. Politeness and grace came effortlessly to her, and she maintained a gentleness I didn't possess.

"Adelaide, you are looking fashionable, as always," she said.

Adelaide, not one easily swayed with compliments, mumbled a thank you.

"I sent word asking you to come for afternoon tea the other day, but the coachman returned saying Braxton Hall had closed for the cold months. Is it true?" Birdie gripped my arm in anticipation.

"Kat convinced Papa to let us come to the city with him." Adelaide gave me a keen look of gratitude.

"You don't say." Birdie looked at me with admiration, and my cheeks heated under the attention. "Kat can be most persistent when she sets her mind to a matter."

"Indeed," Adelaide said with a laugh. "Us arriving uninvited is no different. Kat was insistent we visit you today."

"I'm delighted," she said sincerely. "Madame DeRose and I were just finishing up." She turned back to the dressmaker. "Thank you, Madame DeRose, for your input. I look forward to seeing the creation you come up with after our adjustments to your vision."

The dressmaker stood and gathered her sketchbook and pencil. "It's a pleasure, Mademoiselle Vello." She walked over to stand before us, and recognition gleamed in her eyes when she regarded me, but she made no remark about our previous encounter. "Madame Goddard insists her son's bride must impress all of New York on her wedding day. Your wedding to Monsieur Goddard will be the wedding everyone will talk about for years to come. Madame Goddard claims they will spare no expense to make her son's wedding that of the century. Her expectations are lofty, but I believe the bride has the final say. Your insight is most valued."

"Greatly appreciated," Birdie said, followed by a fetching smile.

"Until next time, mon chéri. Au revoir." She leaned in and kissed one of Birdie's cheeks, then the other.

"Let me show you out." Mrs. Vello indicated the doorway.

"Merci."

After they'd gone, Birdie enthusiastically approached Adelaide and me, clasping her hands under her chin. "Let's catch up, shall we?"

"I will stay here, if you don't mind. I wish to finish this book, so I may return it for another I have my eye on." Adelaide sat down on the settee.

"If you keep up that pace, you will have every book in New York read by spring. Massachusetts and Connecticut's citizens will close their borders and libraries to you, to avoid a shortage of books," I said.

"And you consider that offensive?" Adelaide's eyes gleamed. She unpinned her hat and laid it beside her before removing her paletot.

"If you questioned her on the Amazon rainforests, she'd know every species—their habits, life expectancy, and characteristics."

"It'll take a confident man with appreciation for an intellectual woman to convince you to marry," Birdie said with awe.

I threw my hands in the air. "Must all conversations turn to marriage? Women are such predictable creatures."

Birdie laughed and twirled around the room on her tiptoes in exaggerated elegance. She was a vision with her crown of brunette hair neatly pinned in the latest fashion, and her lavender silk day dress. The skirt of her gown barely missed the glass ornaments on a nearby table, and she stopped to steady the items. The affliction of love had clearly stolen her senses.

"I rest my case." I waved a hand at her antics.

"You are as much a woman as we are." She straightened and stood breathless, gripping an invisible stitch in her side.

"That may be true, but unlike you, my senses are still intact."

Birdie laughed, and I smiled at the lighthearted atmosphere in the room.

"Forgive me, Adelaide, but your sister has a way of bringing out the worst in me."

"Your behavior is yours and yours alone," I said. The sight of her was salve for my soul.

"It is good to hear my sister laugh. I never realized how long it's been since last I heard her laughter." Adelaide regarded me fondly.

"It appears we all could use some lightheartedness," Birdie said. "The pressure of this wedding has been trying. It's a beautiful day, and with winter approaching, I'm unsure how many more we will get. So why don't we go outside and sit in the summer house?"

"You two go along. I will be here when you are finished," Adelaide said as Mrs. Vello returned.

"Can I get you ladies some refreshments?" Mrs. Vello said.

"No, thank you," I said as Birdie took my arm and steered me from the room.

"Perhaps some tea will do. I can see you're busy. I am eager to devour this book, so there is no need to entertain me," Adelaide said.

Birdie and I sauntered down the corridor to the glass-paned double doors opening onto the exquisite gardens.

Outside, I marveled at the splashes of green, crimson, and orange foliage filling the gardens. When in full bloom, Mrs. Vello's sanctuary took your breath away. But even now, while the city's greenery had faded to sepia and naked tree branches, Mrs. Vello's garden still held enchantment. She found fulfillment in the gardens and preferred to do the labor herself, ignoring the criticism of ladies at socials for not employing a gardener and not taking the proper care to protect her skin from the sun.

When Audrey permitted me to leave Braxton Hall, I visited the Vellos, and some of my best memories derived from the times Mrs. Vello asked Birdie and I to help her in the garden. I considered it a privilege and relished the time spent with Mrs. Vello and her daughter. Birdie's mother possessed a warmth I clung to, a kindness that filled a void in my heart for a fleeting moment.

The tension clawing at the walls of Braxton Hall didn't appear to exist in the Vello household. Birdie and I had spent many days in the kitchen, where she insisted I try her newest recipes before we would retire to the gardens and avoid the heat or rain in the summer house, which lay open to the expansive gardens. We'd daydream about life and what it held for us. I dreamed of seeing the world, starting with visiting the pyramids in Egypt and Rome's Colosseum. Thanks to Adelaide, I became an expert on the many historical sites worldwide and envisioned capturing them on my canvas. Birdie dreamed of traveling to France and learning under the tutelage of Chef Auguste Escoffier. But her inspiration was the famous French chef Marie-Antonin Carême. In his time, he'd served royalty, becoming renowned for his pastry sculptures dubbed pièces montées.

"To what do I owe the pleasure of your visit today? It's been far too long," Birdie said as we strolled along the stone path.

"Do I need a reason to see my friend?" I said with a laugh.

"Of course not. It's good to see you are feeling better."

I halted and frowned at her. "To what do you refer?"

"Do you not recall? You invited me some weeks back."

"Yes, and you didn't come. I had refreshments prepared that would've impressed you. I waited for hours."

"But I did come." Her warm chocolate eyes regarded me earnestly. "When the butler answered the door, Mrs. Darlington arrived shortly after and said that you had gone to bed with a headache and couldn't receive me."

My hands balled at my sides. "Why does that not surprise me?"

"Are you saying that you weren't sick?"

"No, I wasn't sick. However, the woman makes my life miserable at every turn. I don't understand why she detests me so."

"Perhaps because you never adjusted to her arrival in your life."

"No, she was hostile from the day she marched into Braxton Hall. She wanted to break my spirit."

"So there is no truth in what Madame DeRose says?" Birdie's eyes gleamed.

I blushed. "There may be."

She tilted her head and examined me, appearing to be awaiting an explanation.

I continued walking, and she fell into step. "Papa is beyond himself with Audrey's uncontrolled spending and has limited her access to funding. So when Madame DeRose arrived at Braxton Hall, arms loaded with bolts of fabric, I greeted her and informed her my stepmother no longer required her services."

Birdie gasped. "Did you tell her of your father's restrictions?"

"No, of course not. I don't seek to provide gossip for all the chinwags. I merely turned her away, and when my stepmother found out, she confined me to my room for days."

"Without food and water?" An impish grin brightened her pretty face.

"You make light of my plight."

"I aim to return a smile to your face," she said, then her brow furrowed. "If your father limited her access to money, it leaves one wondering how she finances her travels."

"Or how she travels without a passport," I said.

I contemplated how married women remained anonymous on their husbands' passports. I recalled Papa's passport stating *Mr. Phillip Darlington and wife.* I often considered the strength of women in the act of childbirth alone. A woman's body created life and could carry that life inside her for nine months. Yet men had deemed us the weaker sex? And over time, women surrendered to the belief. Had we not become a society conditioned?

"How did you escape Braxton Hall to come here?"

I informed her of Audrey's disappearance, the escape from my chamber, and how I made it to the city to implore my father to step in. I finished with the accident, and the intense Mr. Huntington. "So you see, now my sisters and I live here in the city."

"And Mrs. Darlington?"

"She has yet to appear, but she will." I paused to brush my hand over the top of a fern and studied the water droplets on its fronds. I clenched my jaw, and a familiar ache radiated through my neck and head. "I used to hope when she disappeared that she'd never return. Or that her carriage would turn over, and she'd be tossed out like poor Mr. Kelly, only not to rise. Or that she would be trampled in the streets."

Birdie inhaled sharply, and I looked at her to find her standing with her mouth agape.

"Do you think me a monster for my vivid thoughts?" My heart raced, and I feared her judgment.

"It's shocking. But I've been raised in a loving home."

"I once had such a home," I said with longing. My eyes misted, but I blinked to ward off the weakness. Then I shared how Audrey threatened to circulate falsehoods about Jude and me.

Birdie gasped, and her hand went to her throat. "What a vicious woman. Does she have no scruples at all?"

I shrugged, numbed by the whole conversation.

"Perhaps this time she won't return." Birdie smiled for my sake.

"But she always does." I turned away from her and closed my eyes, fighting to suppress the pain and feelings of vulnerability.

"It's the strangest thing. People know nothing of her family, the Bosemans. It's as though the woman appeared out of nowhere." I recalled Mr. Huntington's servant, Mrs. Quinn, and what she said about Audrey's past, something that had troubled me yet I'd never divulged it to anyone. "But somehow, my father found her. Their marriage was one of convenience and nothing more.

"The mystery of Audrey Boseman will have to wait for another day," I finished briskly. "Let's not waste our time discussing her. She consumes too much of my life." I decided against sharing with Birdie what I'd overheard.

"Very well," she said. "I almost forgot. Jude stopped by on his way to the train station the other day."

I gulped, and my heart galloped. "What did he want?"

"He wanted me to give you a letter."

I swallowed hard, and her brow furrowed.

"Am I to assume matters with him are also awry?"

"I fear I've offended him somehow, but I don't understand how—perhaps I failed to understand what I said to offend out of ignorance."

"Tell me what happened."

I told her about Jude's and my conversation in the meadow. When I had finished, she shook her head. "I believe you experienced Jude's internal battle. This upset between you will all blow over. Jude holds deep affection for you. He is in love with you and has been for years."

I jabbed her in the side with my elbow. "It isn't true. He cares for me as a friend and nothing more."

She arched a brow as if to say *If you say so*, but remained quiet.

"I'm being serious, Birdie." Despondency overwhelmed me. "I can't have him complicating our friendship with such absurdity."

"Only a few years ago, your refusal to marry would've been frowned upon, but times are changing, and the modern-day woman appears to find appeal in spinsterhood and working outside the home, and men aren't too accepting of it."

"If we keep advancing, the past will have no hold on us. Despite my dislike for change, I relish a progressive world. We can accept the good humanity has created and learn from the errors."

"You may be right," she said. "But what about this Mr. Huntington? I couldn't help but see a flash of interest in your eyes when you mentioned him."

"You imagine things." An image of Mr. Huntington standing

in the dark, drenched in the glow of Rosehill Manor's lamps, came to mind.

"I certainly did not. See? There is that look again."

I pushed away the memory. "Whatever you caught was my annoyance at his assertiveness."

"You mark him for his candor? He would be you in the flesh if you were a man."

"We are hardly comparable. He is dapper and experienced in the ways of women."

"And how do you know, after your brief encounter?"

"I saw it in the intensity of his eyes and the way he speaks. It's uncanny. There is a smoothness about him I don't trust."

"Perhaps he has fallen under your spell?" She found amusement in my discomfort.

"I would have to have a spell to start with," I said. "And I concoct none. I simply don't trust him; that is all I will say on the matter."

"Who do you trust?"

"Plenty of people." I started counting them on my fingers. "Jude, you, Evelyn—"

"You mustn't look at every person as though they are your stepmother," she said. "Perhaps I will meet this Mr. Huntington at Zane's family's ball, if an invitation was extended."

"How dreadful that would be." Seeking to change the subject, I asked, "How does your betrothed fare?" In all honesty, I cared little if he fared well or not. On the list of humans I did not like, he ranked next to my stepmother.

"He is well." The nauseating, doe-eyed look of a smitten woman swept over her. "I have delightful news. After our wedding, we are to sail to Paris for our honeymoon."

"Splendid news indeed. Then good *will* come with you marrying the man. Your dream of visiting Paris will come true." My heart swelled for that reason and that alone.

Her eyes hooded. "Why can't you be happy about my

engagement to Zane? He comes from a good family with enough wealth to rival the Vanderbilts."

"But wealth doesn't warm the heart," I said. "It may bring comfort, but it doesn't make one happy. My family's wealth has never brought me happiness. Surely you hold more value for yourself than thinking that marrying into the Goddard family and the power and financial guarantee it will bring will provide you with some sort of protection or contentment."

She looked around as though to ensure no one eavesdropped and pulled me close. "You know his family would reject me if the truth about my heritage got out. Maybe even Zane himself would refuse to marry me."

I reflected on the secret Birdie had shared with me soon after discovering the truth herself, when we were twelve years old. Her parents had told her she could never reveal the truth to anyone, which confused her, and that was why she had confided in me. Her maternal grandmother was from the Mohican tribe, and her grandfather was a Spanish shipmaster. Only in recent years, when Birdie coaxed the information from Mrs. Vello, did she learn her grandfather had raped her grandmother, and Mrs. Vello had been the outcome of that rape.

"The constitutional amendment may have ended the enslavement of the Blacks, but my grandmother's people and tribes across America are still enslaved and are not considered citizens of the United States. New Yorkers would not accept my mother or me if they were to find out we bore Indian blood."

"But to hide your heritage seems wrong," I said.

"Forgive me. I mean this with the utmost respect, but that is easily said by a person who hasn't faced the prejudices in the world."

"I do not intend to insult." Our conversation felt all too similar to the one I had with Jude, and I felt uneasy, filled with a sense of shame I couldn't shake.

"I know you don't," she said with a gentle smile before looping her arm with mine. We continued along the path. "I can't help but be angry at the Spanish explorers—my father and grandfather's ancestors—and their European abettors. To deny their wrongs would be a crime upon humanity." She lowered her gaze and heaved a sigh. "But my heart is heavy with shame and guilt."

"You are hardly at fault for your ancestors' evil. You did not have a hand in their decisions."

"But do we not bear our ancestors' scars?" she said.

Her comment highlighted a matter I had never considered. "I suppose in many ways we do."

"I feel I dishonor my grandmother and ancestors by denying our heritage. I am silent to protect myself. As a child, I abided by my parents' belief that it was for the best. However, now that I'm older, I question society's hold over them, primarily my mother, that she'd seek to abandon a part of herself. I am no different.

"The government strives to control the tribes, and the swarm of white settlers in need of more land combined with Congress talking of invoking an Indian Appropriations Act has caused distress amongst the tribes. They fear extinction and that their culture and spiritual practices will vanish. But their voices go unheard. It is as though the world does not consider the injustices against them of any importance. I can't help but feel, in my family's silence, that we are cowards and no better than the government. Are we, too, facilitating a world that silences their rights?"

The torment in her eyes squeezed at my heart. Bereft of the right words to say, I listened.

She rubbed her temples. "I lie awake at night, distraught. Or sit up in a cold sweat after nightmares of Zane's wrath upon his discovery. Other nights I dream of a crying child in a cradle cloaked in tribal garb. Sometimes a little girl in a meadow with beautiful raven braids and haunting black eyes holds her hand out as though summoning me, but I turn and run."

I gripped her arm. "Maybe it is your ancestors guiding you," I said sincerely, my motive concern rather than my desire for our friendship to stay the same, without the hindrance of a husband. "Like an omen to reject Zane's proposal and find a man who would embrace all the attributes that define you. To deny a part of oneself is like a phantom limb. If Zane's love for you is honorable and steadfast, surely he would not seek to harm you. Maybe he will surprise even me and honor you in your entirety. Maybe he would go so far as to hide the truth of your heritage from his family."

"Maybe." Hope flickered in her eyes. "But I know without a doubt his parents would end the engagement and expose my mother and me if they got the slightest inkling."

"I have witnessed and heard of Jude's parents' fight against the bigotry of a biracial marriage."

"A fact they can't easily hide. I want to believe Zane's love for me would surpass all prejudice." She hugged herself, appearing more miserable by the moment. "I love him, and life without him seems unbearable."

"For your sake, I hope his love is as steadfast," I said with a shake of my head. "And I suppose if I can't keep our relationship untainted by you acquiring a husband, then all I can do is support your decision."

She leaned in and embraced me. "Thank you. Your friendship brings comfort." She released me. "And who says our relationship will change because I'm married?"

"Oh, it will," I assured her. "Mark my words." I encircled her waist with an arm, and we turned back toward the house. "Now, give me this letter, and let me see if Jude has forgiven me."

Chapter 16

"K AT!"

I jumped at Alice's cry, and my paintbrush bounced across the canvas.

I tipped my head to look around the canvas to Alice, who raced across the courtyard toward me. She arrived breathless, her brown eyes round with panic. She glanced back at the house.

"For heaven's sake, what is it?" I scowled at her disruption.

She trembled. "It's Mother. She has arrived."

"Jupiter's thunder!" I stood, knocking over my stool in my haste to throw a drape over the canvas.

"It will take more than Jupiter or Dorotea's God to help you now. And Papa is not expected back home for some time. What are we to do?"

Papa had left early that morning, informing Dorotea that he wouldn't be back until late.

I put a hand on her shoulder. "You make yourself scarce, and let me deal with her. Go to the stables. I'm sure you can find someone to pester in there," I said with a fixed smile.

She searched my face. "Will you be all right?"

"Most certainly. Now off with you." I shooed her with a hand. She waited a moment longer, then raced off. I stood observing her before turning to regard the house. As the days had turned into weeks, I had hoped Audrey wouldn't return, but she had, and again with Papa gone, I stood unprotected against my enemy. My heart pounded in my ears, but I squared my shoulders and marched toward the back door.

Inside I walked down the corridor to the entrance hall to discover Audrey's trunks sitting in the middle of the floor. My throat thickened. It was true. She had indeed returned. My ears tuned in to the raised voice coming down the corridor from the kitchen and staff dining room. I walked in that direction and stopped outside the kitchen doorway when I discovered Audrey had gathered the household staff. They stood gawking at her as she wandered the room, her pale flesh flushed and her eyes flashing. They silently tolerated her sling of insults and threats. I clenched my hands at my sides and gathered the courage to face her.

"Good afternoon. It appears we have company. Miss Boseman, to what reason does the Darlington household owe this visit?" I walked into the room with my head held high, feigning confidence while trembling inside. I hadn't used her maiden name since she had knocked the defiance out of me years ago for my refusal to call her mother. But never would I again breathe the endearment "mother" to her.

She spun to look at me. Her eyes bulged as though she stood possessed. "You! I know this is your doing."

I strolled to the long table used for meal preparation. A large black iron kettle sat steaming on top of the coal-burning stove. I looked down at the table where my hand gripped it to keep me steady.

"Answer me." Audrey stomped her foot like an unruly child taking a temper tantrum. But even in her outbursts, she had always maintained her authority.

My body thrummed with warning signals. Never looking up, I focused on the flour scattered across the table for the preparation of tea biscuits, the dough still resting in a bowl. I slowly trailed my finger across the flour. "To what do you refer? My father bringing his daughters to live with him in the city? Yes, I suppose that would put a damper on your life." I took a step and then another, touching the green tops of a bushel of carrots drooping over the edge of a wooden crate before looking at the nervous faces. "Please leave us," I said, and the staff scrambled to leave the room.

"Wait. I am the mistress of this home. I say who comes and who goes."

They halted and looked from her to me. I tilted my head and offered them a reassuring smile. "You are employed by Mr. Darlington. He will see to our unexpected guest when he gets home. Please, go about your duties."

They hesitated and muttered amongst themselves.

"Yes, Miss Katherine." Mrs. Dixon, the head housekeeper, stepped forward. "Come now, you heard Miss Darlington. Out with you all." At her command, they hurried from the room. She eyed me with concern, and I nodded, letting her know I could handle whatever came.

I rooted my feet and waited for Audrey's venom to spray over me. *I will not let her win,* I breathed. *Not this time.*

"You think you've outsmarted me?" Her rage simmered, but I did not let down my guard.

"It's not about outsmarting you. It's about doing what is right for my sisters and me. We wish to be with our father and not be subjected to your cruelty," I said.

She paced the small area in front of the fireplace and the table. "When I returned to Braxton Hall and found it closed and new staff to run the estate, I knew only one person could be responsible." Her lip curled with disgust when she paused to look at me. Her unconfined dislike for me and my sisters seeped from her very essence. How could one person maintain so much hatred and still exist?

"Why did you come back?" I eyed her unflinching. "For that matter, why do you ever bother coming back?"

"Your father is my husband."

"A marriage of convenience and nothing more. You said so yourself. The war is long over, and our father has returned. If you are so miserable, why don't you leave? We don't need you. We've never needed you."

"Is that so? When I arrived at Braxton Hall, I observed a house of brokenhearted little girls with no mother or woman to care for them."

"We had Dorotea."

"A governess isn't fit to run an estate. That fool was barely capable of keeping you all in line. She carries herself as though she was born to an affluent household with a title. I caught on to her scheme the first day I met her. She is in love with your father."

I dropped my head to hide my shock at her statement. Could it be true? Did Dorotea love Papa? A kernel of hope stirred in my chest before I pushed it away. No. The love between a man and a woman caused nothing but heartache. My parents' love deprived my sisters and me of our father.

As I recovered from the impact of Audrey's words, she continued with her tirade. I sensed she sought to rattle me.

"Your father appeared incapable of caring for his children. Moreover, our country was in the middle of a war. Someone needed to care for his estate and children—"

"So this is what this is…" I gestured from her to me. "Caring?"

"No, certainly not. I've not cared for much in life, and certainly not a household of spoiled girls."

"Perhaps you preferred your life as a chambermaid," I said before catching myself. I held my breath as she stiffened. Fear flitted in her eyes, and her mouth dropped open before she quickly snapped it shut. She had sought to rattle me, but I had unnerved her and myself. So the rumors were true. I willed myself to mask my astonishment.

She positioned a hand at her throat, grappling with how to react. I lifted my chin and regarded her unwavering. Then, as quickly as her uneasiness arrived, it vanished, and she stepped closer, her gaze boring through me.

"Indeed, I once was a domestic servant in a house of privileged daughters like you and your sisters. I washed their dirty linens and clothing. Scrubbed their floors and chamber pots. No gratitude or consideration ever came my way. I promised myself that one day I would run an estate of my own, not as a head housekeeper, but the mistress myself."

"So you punish my sisters and me for your hardships and others' deemed mistreatments?" I said. "Wrongs inflicted on you do not give you just cause to make others suffer for your pain."

"Don't they?" she said, bitterness running rancid in her. "You and your sisters have never known what it is like to go hungry or beg on the streets. To have people throw rotten food at you as though you are nothing more than a rat." Her eyes hazed as though her mind had walked her into the past. "You don't know what it is like to be beaten and raped or fight to stay warm at night under a blanket of snow." She shivered, and I saw a flash of vulnerability.

I swallowed hard, feeling a twinge of sympathy.

"Or to marry a man you think loves you only to have him die and leave all his wealth to his bastard child." She stood inches from my face, but I held my ground. She bared her teeth, convinced of the injustices she had endured and the world's need to pay. "He left me penniless after I endured years of his abuse and infidelity. But not this time. When your grieving father came to me, I saw my opportunity."

I gawked at her, and as though reading my thoughts, she said, "You are probably wondering how we came to meet." She moved away and strolled the room. "I met your parents a few times at social events when I was married to my belated husband. I tried to befriend Victoria Darlington, but she disliked me from the start. I see her smug face in the face of your sister Evelyn. Too proper for the rest of us."

I pressed my lips together to silence the retort on the tip of my tongue. I drew comfort from my mother's disapproval of Audrey. She must never have shared her distaste for her with Papa. If she had, why would he ever marry her? But Mama had never been one for gossip or idle chatter.

Audrey stood at the window overlooking the stable yard, her body rigid and hands fisted at her sides.

I pitied her for the hate seeded deep in her heart. While she was gone, I had gloried in the lightness that enveloped me until the mention of her name, or if I allowed myself to think of her. I wanted no part of the contempt that soiled my own heart, yet I had no idea how to rid myself of the poison.

"Why did Papa come to you?"

"I was recently widowed, and he had heard rumors of my situation," she said matter-of-factly before turning and flashing a cunning smile. "I saw an opportunity. By then it was believed the war would drag on for years, and it did. The Darlington wealth was no secret, and I sought to lay my claim."

"Why do you tell me all of this?"

"To make you see that I will stop at nothing to keep that claim."

I glanced at the door, regretting my decision to dismiss the staff. I lacked witnesses to what she said.

"Looking for your sisters? They aren't here. I'm told Evelyn and Adelaide have left for a day of shopping. Or don't you recall? As for your Papa, he is preoccupied with business. His one true love, besides your dead mother, of course."

Her coldness sliced through my determination not to let her see me falter.

"Grace is asleep in her chamber. The girl sleeps more than a dog." She shook her head in disgust. "And Alice…well, she raced off to warn you of my arrival, I suspect. I believe I saw your be-loved governess walking down the boardwalk as my carriage pulled up. She would have turned back if she'd seen me getting out. She is always interfering. So you see, my dear, there is no one but staff and you and me."

"The staff are loyal to my father and not handpicked by you," I said through clenched teeth. "I will see you removed from this house and our lives."

"Have you so easily forgotten what I promised to reveal to the fine people of New York after you were caught with that Negro man again?"

"I am not scared of your threats. I've told Papa about the vileness you spew. He will never allow it. In this house, we are under his protection. He will not leave us to your corruption."

"No?" She lifted a hand and eyed her fingernails. "I have other ways to handle the situation I find myself in. Accidents do happen."

My heart stopped.

"I mean, you and your older sisters are grown. So you could hardly be deemed orphans. But Alice and Grace—"

My vision blurred, and I lunged at her. She sidestepped, and I fought to keep my balance.

I whirled to face her. "You threaten Papa's life. I will see you jailed for this."

"A spoiled daughter's allegations against a widowed woman who took another woman's children and cared for them. I doubt you would have a case."

"Miss Katherine," a soft voice said, and I looked at Colleen, who crept hesitantly into the room. "Ye all right?" Her brow pleated, but I noticed the leeriness in her gaze. My heart swelled with her bravery in coming to my aid.

Audrey regarded Colleen. "I considered your release in recent months due to your incompetence and unbending temperament." She looked at me. "I see you have managed to turn her."

"I do not seek to turn or control anyone; that skill is best left to you." I strode to Colleen's side. "Colleen remains on as my chambermaid by her own choice. It appears you hired a woman with a mind of her own, who is not so easily exploited."

"You are the daughter of a whore, if I do recall. I believe my records show that you have a father who lives in the Points."

Colleen stiffened at her remark.

"Records?" I narrowed my eyes.

Audrey kept her gaze on Colleen, attempting to intimidate the girl. "I conduct a lengthy interview of those I hire to work in my home. One cannot have thieves and murderers roaming the corridors. I obtain information on their parentage, residence, and history, going as far as contacting previous employers, and hiring a detective if need be."

"Blackmail, you mean." I glared at her.

"Call it what you wish." She brushed her hands together as though to rid them of dust. "I am the mistress of this household and any other owned by the Darlington family." She strode toward us. "And I will stop anyone by any means necessary who tries to interfere." She pushed between us and walked to the doorway. "I've had a long journey. I must rest." Then, she was gone.

I stood trembling. I had been a fool to think I could rid myself of her by returning to the city. I considered her threat of harming Papa. I had to stop her and free my family from her clutches. But how?

Chapter 17

EVELYN AND ADELAIDE RETURNED FROM THEIR OUTING FOLLOWED by the coachman and a groomsman weighed down in packages. My sisters' faces were radiant with high spirits.

The Goddard ball was around the corner, and I relished the day it would be over, and they would stop cooing about the event. However, Christmas was upon us, and with our return to the city, our schedule overflowed with one social event after another.

Audrey had retired to her chamber shortly after her arrival and hadn't left it since. Her presence had upheaved our home. Staff raced to her every demand and the incessant chiming of her hand bell.

Papa had yet to return, and it was late when I walked into the study, searching for the key to my mother's chamber. The room had remained locked since my mother's death. I seated myself at the desk, searched the drawers for the key, and found it underneath a false panel.

I left the study and went upstairs, but hesitated outside my mother's chamber before inserting the key in the lock. It had been years since I had stepped inside the room, and I didn't know if I could handle the pain and loneliness it was sure to conjure, but my heart ached for the comfort of my mother. What I wouldn't do to sit in her presence again, to draw comfort from her wisdom and love. If I had just one more day, I wouldn't waste it. Instead, I would absorb everything she had to say and lock it inside my heart. I would tell her I loved her. I would have changed for her, and like Evelyn and Adelaide, I would have been a daughter she would've been proud of. But life hadn't granted me that privilege, and I struggled to understand it all.

I took a deep breath, unlocked the door, and stepped inside, closing the door behind me. A layer of dust coated a room frozen in time. My chest tightened. Papa hadn't touched an item in the room. Mama's shift and night-robe lay across the foot of the bed, and her embroidered slippers sat beside her side of the bed. I looked to my mother's vanity, and my feet inched forward. Her pewter horsehair brush lay on top, strands of her blond locks in the bristles. I touched a strand of hair, seeking to sense her essence before seating myself on the stool. I sought a glimpse of her in the mirror, but my reflection bore no resemblance to her. My chest rose and fell as a flood of emotions swept through me. I recalled how, as a child, I had come to her chamber as she prepared for bed, and she'd let me brush her hair until it shone. We talked about my sisters, my quarrels, and all that may have troubled me that day. I picked up one of the perfume bottles on the vanity and sprayed it into the air. I breathed in the scent, stale with age.

I blinked away tears and stood. I walked to the foot of the bed and knelt at the Spanish Renaissance carved trunk. Before opening the lid, I ran my fingers over the intricate details. I picked up items inside one at a time, savoring each.

I withdrew a fawn-colored silk evening gown and held it up. The off-the-shoulder dress had a low neckline and elbow-length puffed sleeves and was ornamented with ribbons. I recalled my mother wearing the gown and how Papa had gasped as she descended the stairs to the entrance hall where he waited, her golden hair parted in the center and neatly combed back into a chignon. I smiled, recollecting the evening. My sisters and I had knelt at the mezzanine rail, watching in awe and awaiting Papa's reaction when he saw her. His eyes had glittered with tears as he strode forward to embrace her. I thought about the love my parents had shared and how Evelyn and Adelaide sought to experience the same passion in a marriage. I held the gown to my chest and looked around the room, haunted by Mama's memory and how Papa had sought to keep the dead alive out of love. My heart grieved for him. The pain that came with loving someone so profoundly appeared debilitating, and I would never allow myself to experience that kind of pain.

I shook off the heaviness weighing on my heart and held out the gown, eyeing it with interest. I considered the upcoming ball and Evelyn and Adelaide's distress over my wearing a dress from last season. I could only imagine what they would say if I told them about my sudden inspiration. I set the gown aside and replaced the top items I had removed from the trunk. I gathered the dress and took it to my chamber before returning the key to the study.

Enthusiastic voices rose from the front of the house, and I exited the study in search of the excitement. I smiled as I viewed the hall entrance. Papa had returned and stood with Alice and Grace hugging his waist.

"My girls, how are you?"

Since reuniting with his family, he appeared less weary, and a softness had returned to his eyes. He didn't appear so haunted anymore, and I concluded that Papa hadn't known what was best for him. His daughters had been the medicine for his broken heart.

I stopped when Dorotea came into view. My thoughts returned to what Audrey had said about Dorotea being in love with Papa.

"Señor Darlington, welcome home," she said with a curtsy.

Papa's smile widened. "Thank you, Miss Ruiz."

Dorotea stood by, smiling as my little sisters jabbered and soaked up Papa's love and attention. I detected no jealousy over how he doted on them, only pure contentment and pleasure.

"Papa," Alice said, "Mother has returned."

He tensed at the news, and his happiness slipped. "Has she now?"

"She has been in her chamber all day," Grace said.

"She didn't like the food she asked Chef to send to her chamber and threw it into the corridor." Alice frowned. "She made a dreadful mess."

I grinned, finding amusement in my sisters' snitching on Audrey.

Papa and Dorotea shared a look before he clenched his jaw. "I need to speak to Miss Ruiz in my study. Why don't you girls join me later in the library, and we will catch up on your day."

They bobbed their heads and darted off.

"Miss Ruiz, if you don't mind." Papa gestured toward the corridor where I stood observing.

I ducked into a nearby room and waited for them to pass before tiptoeing after them to stand out of sight outside the open study door.

"So she has returned?"

"Yes, señor."

"I ask you to be candid with me. How is the morale since she returned? Is it as my daughters said?"

"I'm afraid so, and we all have been in a frenzy since."

"I should have listened to you." He rubbed his hands over his face.

"Señor?"

"The day you tried to talk me out of marrying her." He dropped his hands and regarded Dorotea, who stood before him with an obvious air of reverence and respect. His gaze softened. "The girls would have been better off if I had married you."

"Me, señor?" Dorotea buried her hands in the sides of her gold-striped sapphire dress.

"It is no secret, your dedication to this family. Your love for Victoria and my daughters. But one can hardly ask a servant to marry him," he said.

Dorotea's shoulders slumped ever so slightly. "No, señor."

I swallowed hard. Had Audrey been right? Did Dorotea love Papa? My heart raced, and exhilaration rushed over me.

He regarded her strangely. "Wouldn't you agree?"

"To what part, señor?"

"That it would be crossing boundaries for me to have asked you to marry me all those years ago."

"People would frown about the union between a domestic servant and a genteel man."

"I do not care what others think. I refer to making you feel obligated by your respect and love for my family." His expression softened as he regarded her.

Dorotea lifted her eyes to meet his. "I would not have felt obligated."

My eyes widened as Papa took her hand in his, and Dorotea moved closer, as though summoned by an invisible force. The same power lowered Papa's head, and their lips touched. Then an eagerness captured them as Papa moaned and drew her body closer. She lifted her hands to cradle the back of his head.

I stepped back, turning away from what was unfolding in the study. Guilt overwhelmed me for spying on them. I crept down the corridor toward the entrance hall and climbed the staircase to my chamber.

Inside, I sat on the edge of my bed, soaking in what I had witnessed. Audrey had been right for once, or at least partially correct. Dorotea cared for Papa, and it appeared he shared the same feelings. My skin prickled. What if Audrey had never been part of our lives? Envisioning Papa married to anyone but Mama had been something I never wanted to imagine. However, what if that someone had been Dorotea? The last years wouldn't have been so problematic. I felt lighter as I let my mind carry me away with the notion. Why couldn't Papa and Dorotea's union still happen? Not for the sake of my younger sisters needing a mother, but for Papa's happiness.

Audrey's face flashed in my mind. How could I get rid of her? To divorce her, Papa had to have just cause, and aside from the cruelty that ran through her veins, we didn't have any grounds or accusations against her that would hold up in court. Then an idea came to me. I could hire a private investigator to spy on my stepmother. He could follow her and see where and with whom she spent her time when she disappeared. But how could I come up with the money?

The following day I concocted a story to tell my father to explain my need of money, and I made sure to ask while he was busy, but I walked out of his study empty-handed.

Chapter 18

Dressed in Mama's gown, I perched on the window seat in my chamber with the window half open, welcoming the briskness of the evening air. Above, stars shone like grains of sugar against the dark velvet sky. Snow blanketed the courtyard, and the naked tree limbs sagged under its weight.

Contemplating the evening ahead, I ran a fingernail over the frosted web stretching across the windowpane. Preparation for the Goddard Banquet had filled the day, and with how Evelyn and Adelaide carried on, one would think we were hosting the event ourselves. Now that the event was upon us, I dreaded it no less. The evening promised to be a bore. hours spent with pretentious people talking about politics, social affairs, and other tortuous topics. At least if I had to attend the evening, I'd have Birdie's company.

Colleen returned to my chamber. "Yeer sisters and father are waitin' for ye. Miss Evelyn grows impatient."

"When is she not impatient?" I stood and closed the window. I strode to the bed where Colleen had laid out an ivory cashmere paletot, my hat, and elbow-length gloves. I sat and allowed her to pin my hat before slipping on the gloves and paletot. "Thank you for altering my mother's gown and seeing it readied for this evening."

She nodded. "Miss Evelyn will be displeased ye're not wearin' the one purchased for the evenin'."

"Let her," I said with a huff. "Wish me patience and perseverance for the evening ahead."

"I've always dreamed what it'd be like to attend a ball. After listenin' to your sisters' excitement, I am sure it will be an evenin' to remember."

I frowned and tilted my head to regard her. "I care little about such things. Yet such things mean everything to my sisters. I suppose it all comes down to what matters to a person, doesn't it?"

Her face grew dreamy. "I've imagined what it'd be like to dress up in a fancy dress, and waltz across a ballroom in the arms of yeer lover."

"You and every other lady I know. You may be a better fit for this family. My sisters see me as a misfit, as though I was created with missing parts or something, merely because what I see as important differs from what they see."

"Some of us are born to fit into molds," Dorotea said as she walked into the room. She came to a sudden, swaying stop. "That gown. It was your mother's."

I glanced down at the dress. "I found it in the trunk in her chamber."

Her face paled, and concern shone in her eyes. "I fear you may cause distress to your family. Your father will not be pleased that you went into your mother's chamber when he has kept it under lock and key."

My heart sank at her remark. I, too, had considered the reaction to my choice, but when I had seen the gown, I wanted more than anything to wear it. To feel close to my mother.

"What good does it do to keep her memory locked away in her chamber? I don't seek to cause them harm, but…"

"But what?" Dorotea pressed.

"I can't explain my need to wear this gown. I fear none of you will understand."

She whispered a prayer before gesturing for me. "Come now. Your family awaits."

I followed her to the mezzanine and paused to take a deep breath. The voices of my family echoed from the entrance hall below. I looked straight ahead, and my legs trembled as I walked out onto the mezzanine and into my family's view.

The chatter stopped, and someone gasped. I focused on each step as I descended. My heart pounded in my throat as I drew closer to my family.

"Kat!" Evelyn said. "What have you done?"

I lifted my gaze, but instead of focusing on her scowl, I looked at Papa. He stood with his mouth agape, appearing to fight an inner battle before he collected himself. He rubbed a hand over his face and pulled it down, his eyes flitting to me and away as I drew near.

My sisters peeked at him while Evelyn stepped closer to him, as though she were a mother bird seeking to draw him under her wing.

"Papa…" I swallowed the thickening in my throat. "I'm sorry if my need to wear Mama's gown causes you pain. It was not my intent."

He eyed me as though gutted, and remorse overwhelmed me. What had I done? Tears welled as I looked from him to the accusing looks on Adelaide and Evelyn's faces.

Papa shook his head and lifted a trembling hand to silence my plea for his blessing and understanding.

I pressed my lips together and peeked at Dorotea, who stood beside me. She slipped her hand in mine as I fought back the impulse to run.

"Señor—"

"Please, Miss Ruiz. Let me handle my daughter."

"Si, señor." Dorotea lowered her head.

Papa's eyes were moist as he regarded me. "You defied my orders to stay out of her chamber."

I opened my mouth to speak, but again, he lifted a hand to stop me.

A silent tear trailed down my cheek, and my lips quivered. Dorotea's arm encircled my waist, and I sensed her willing me the strength to persevere.

"You have unnerved me." His voice thickened with untamed emotions, and his words ceased for a brief moment before he continued. "But there is no wrong in what you've done."

He walked to stand in front of me, and my jaw trembled as I fought to control the vulnerability consuming me. He gently rested his strong hands on my shoulders. "You are a vision. Like your mother the day she wore this gown. I wish she was alive to see you." Tears escaped the corners of his eyes, and my heart swelled at the pride and love I saw on his face.

I had never felt more beautiful. "Thank you, Papa." I blinked off tears.

He placed his lips on my forehead, then stepped back. "You were right, that day in my study. I've considered your words often. It is time we honor your mother by letting her memory rest and moving on with our lives and whatever that entails. She would want us to go on." He glanced at Dorotea and then back at me. "She will always remain in our hearts."

I nodded and smiled.

Papa stepped away to slip into his overcoat, and Evelyn walked up to me as she put on her gloves.

"You can't possibly be thinking of showing up to the ball in that dress?" she said.

"Evelyn." Papa regarded her with a raised brow.

"But…"

Papa's face tightened, and Evelyn quelled her protest. Papa smiled at me and said, "Our carriage awaits. Audrey insisted on going ahead, but it's best not to keep her waiting."

The news of not having to suffer Audrey's company gladdened me. I turned my back on Evelyn and Adelaide's disapproving stares.

"I wish we could attend." Grace ambled up to Papa and hugged his middle before tipping back her head to look at him.

He smiled and dabbed her nose with a finger. "Your time will come when you attend all the social engagements you can handle. But this evening, you and Alice will remain in the company of Miss Ruiz."

Dorotea strode to Grace's side and took her hand. Dorotea's essence was like the warmth of a fire on a winter's night, and Grace leaned into the curve of her governess's side. "Chef Bernard has prepared various bonbons with chocolate creams and caramels, inspired by his recent return to Paris. He has requested that you ladies sample his creations in hopes of serving them this social season. I've planned for us to spend the evening in the games room, and what a splendid time we will have. Your papa and sisters will wish they had remained home." Her expression was tender as she looked at Papa. I recalled the kiss they had shared in the study and quickly regarded Evelyn and Adelaide, who seemed oblivious to the affection between our father and governess. Inwardly, I smirked at the irony. After all their cooing, pondering, and self-acclaimed expertise on matters of the heart, they had never sensed the secret love affair within our household. Perhaps they were the daft ones when it came to love, not me.

Alice and Grace's eyes grew large as they looked at each other and squealed with delight at the promise of an evening filled with bonbons and merriment. I envied them.

"It appears all will be fine in our absence," Papa said before kissing Alice and Grace's cheeks. "Farewell, my girls." His eyes rested on Dorotea, and she blushed under his gaze. He turned toward the door and held out an arm, and Evelyn and Adelaide rushed forward, taking up positions on either side of him.

I walked behind them, and we stepped outside. The evening's chill swirled under the layers of my gown, and I pulled the clasp of my paletot closer.

Chapter 19

OUR CARRIAGE ARRIVED AT THE GODDARD MANSION AND JOINED the queue of snow-dusted carriages pulling to the side and allowing guests to disembark. Adelaide and Evelyn leaned forward and pulled back the velvet drape to regard the whirl of activity outside. The mansion was aglow with every chandelier in the home illuminated. Flames flickered in exterior gas lamps adorned in garlands and holly, casting a glistening glow across the snow. The magic of the holiday season filled the evening, and murmurs of enthusiasm rose from those disembarking. Ladies, bedecked in jewel-toned silk, velvet, and taffeta gowns embellished with feathers and flounces under paletots and capes of cashmere and fur, mingled with gentlemen in dark three-piece suits and top hats.

Our carriage halted, and Mr. Kelly—healed and returned to his position—opened the door. "There we have it," he said with an endearing smile while holding out a gloved hand.

Evelyn, who had perched on the edge of her seat when the Goddard mansion came into view, eagerly took his hand and stepped out. Adelaide and I followed suit.

I searched the crowd on the boardwalk in front of the man-sion for Birdie. My gaze locked on a familiar face, and my heart thumped harder. Mr. Huntington stood on the boardwalk ahead, helping an older woman out of a carriage. She swiftly released his hand and said something to him before stepping to the side to wait with a pinched face, void of emotion. I studied her stiff posture and unapproachable demeanor. She eyed each guest as if she were a guard dog.

Mr. Huntington turned back to assist someone else. A younger woman stepped out, and I recognized her as the one I'd seen riding with him, the day Dorotea and I arrived at my family's home in the city. The petite woman smiled up at him adoringly, and I didn't miss the gentleness in the way he handled her. I turned away before they sensed me examining them and followed my family up the front steps and inside.

A staff member took our outerwear, and we moved from the entrance hall into the ballroom. The melody for a Spanish waltz played, and a line of couples moved about the dance floor. Adelaide and Evelyn inhaled, and their eyes grew round with wonderment as they sauntered into the room.

My pace slowed, and Papa leaned down and whispered, "Try and enjoy yourself, will you?"

I gulped and looked up at him. He winked and squeezed my hand, and I nodded. Someone called out his name and he left me to go and speak with them. My palms grew damp inside my gloves, but I continued into the room and took a position against the wall.

"Kat," Birdie's voice called, and I glanced to my left to see her sashaying toward me. She wore a seafoam green taffeta gown with a square neckline and short capped sleeves, ornamented with gold fringe, cording, and ribbons. Unlike my dress, hers followed the new trend of a slimmer skirt line and a rather large and unsightly bustle in the back. Her dark hair was piled high on top of her head with false hairpieces to add volume, and adorned with a sizable two-loop bow that matched her gown. Ringlets trailed down her slender neck. She was the epitome of grace and beauty.

"Why are you hiding back here?" she said in a low voice to

avoid drawing attention to me. She didn't wait for my reply. "I know you hate these events, but you can't press yourself against the wall all evening, attempting to fade into the background. Come." She held out a hand. I clasped it and permitted her to steer me from the safety of the wall. Once I was out in the open, she examined my gown, and her brow pleated but soon softened. "You look lovely."

I sensed her genuineness. "Thank you. It was Mama's dress."

"Your authenticity is what I admire most about you." She gave me a squeeze. "You follow your heart and don't subject yourself to the opinions of others. I wish I could be more like you." Her gaze drifted across the room, and sadness pulled at her face. I followed her gaze to where Zane Goddard stood conversing with two other gentlemen, one of whom I recognized as Mark Peyton, the Charleston gentleman who had stolen all common sense from Evelyn.

Birdie shivered before forcing a smile. "Doesn't Zane look dashing this evening?" she said, her voice laced with admiration.

Zane looked in our direction, his steel-blue eyes twinkling, his pomaded blond hair glistening under the glow of the enormous chandelier fixed with hundreds of various-sized crystals. I considered the man who had won my friend's affection. If one thought a man with a face beautiful enough to be a woman handsome, then he was undoubtedly that. But the smooth manner in which he conducted conversations and the way he interacted with people unsettled me. I had seen him mistreat staff, and turn his back on Birdie, withholding comfort when she was upset. No amount of convincing on her part would make me see anything amiable about him. He had disarmed Birdie with his charisma and good looks, but I believed it was only a matter of time before he turned on her and left her out in the cold. I wondered how Birdie, a woman with insight, piquancy, and a passion for life, could be so blinded by the love she held for him. Love was, indeed, an affliction.

"Look at her gown," a woman said, and my body stiffened, but I didn't turn to look.

"The fabric appears to be cotton and a decades-old style," another female persecutor said.

"Perhaps she had it shipped from the South," one of the culprits said with a cunning laugh. "Perhaps that mulatto man she likes to keep company with purchased it for her. If she was the marrying kind, she would probably marry him. Wouldn't that put a mark on the Darlington name?"

I bristled at the mention of my family and glanced at the women. I recognized them from previous events and deemed them rumormongers. They smirked with pleasure when they saw they'd captured my attention.

I thrust my chin out and looked away, but in my peripheral vision, I regarded the redhead as she said, "The Europeans think they are too good for us Americans. They consider themselves a progressive society and we, barbarians before they civilized us all."

"Indeed."

My hands tightened at my sides.

Birdie drew me away from the clucking hens and toward the refreshment table. "Don't pay them any mind. They take pleasure in trying to make others as miserable as them." She gestured at the young servant girl managing the punch. "Two, please."

Glasses in hand, we stood back to observe the guests. Evelyn's laugh drew my attention. She'd surrounded herself with friends, and they were engrossed in each other's gown and personal appearance. Soon their attention turned to studying eligible gentlemen around the room. They tucked their heads together, giggling and making a mockery of themselves. The saying "birds of a feather flock together" brilliantly defined Evelyn and her friends. Over the years, I had been subjected to their trivial conversations during luncheons at our home, leaving my brain dull and weighted.

Evelyn's gaze softened each time her wandering eye caught that of Mr. Peyton, who smiled, his expression dripping with affection. It was all quite nauseating.

My hands tightened on my glass, and I turned to look at

Adelaide, who stood with Mrs. Ainsworth, a woman forty years her senior. Her attraction to intelligent minds compelled her to surround herself with women several years older than her and those who had gleaned wisdom through their experiences. Adelaide never liked to waste her time with small talk and dove deeply into issues she was passionate about. Although Mrs. Ainsworth was wise for the most part, she could waver, becoming caught up in hearsay, an observation I had paid the price for telling her so when I was younger. My revelation resulted in a harsh scolding from Papa that broke my heart. Nevertheless, I also understood Mrs. Ainsworth was an influential woman with sincerity and empathy. No amount of wealth had brought her happiness; her first husband died within a year of marriage, her second five years later, followed by a third. She had outlived her children, burying two at birth, one at a few years old. Her one son who made it to adulthood had died in the war. She had led a harrowing life influenced by the desire to love and be loved, leaving her bereft. I lifted my glass to take a sip as a distinguished-looking gentleman with silver-threaded dark hair welcomed himself into the group. Mrs. Ainsworth said something and gestured at Adelaide. My sister offered a small curtsy and presented him with her hand. He placed his lips on her fingers and eyed her with interest. I braced myself, my glass still to my lips, as their interaction unfolded. Adelaide returned his look of appreciation. Jupiter! Thunder! They were hopeless, the whole lot of them.

"Kat, have you been listening to anything I've said?" Birdie tugged on my elbow, causing the punch to drip down my chin and neck. She reached for a linen napkin, and I took it and handed her my glass. I patted the dampness while keeping my gaze on the gentleman. "My apologies." I nudged my head at him. "Who is that man with Adelaide?"

She glanced in my sister's direction. "Oh, that is August Alexander. He is a professor at the College of the City of New York."

I studied Mr. Alexander with heightened interest. The college, formerly the Free Academy of the City of New York, had been renamed a few years prior. The goal of the founder of the institute had been to provide free education to the impoverished and descendants of immigrants. I decided Mr. Alexander was better than Evelyn's Mr. Peyton, and even he was far better than Zane Goddard.

"Love is in the air. You never know; you may find a gentleman this evening who will sweep you off your feet and fill your life with an abundance of happiness," Birdie said.

"I'd rather sail the seas, captaining a fleet. Or become one of those Buddhist monks in Tibet that Adelaide talks about, rather than being swept off my feet by a man. Or give one the responsibility for my happiness," I said with a snort.

"Again, positions unacceptable of a woman. Do not forget the skin you were born in."

"Haven't you?" I said before I could snatch it back.

She stumbled back, her face transformed with pain.

"Birdie, I'm sorry. I didn't—"

"Yes, you did. You meant every word. You can hold the whole world at bay, but it will never bring you fulfillment. You are no better than those ladies speaking about your gown. You inflict your pain on me with your words."

I dropped my head, unable to look at the hurt in her face. "You did not deserve the harshness of my judgment. I was wrong, and I am sorry."

We stood silent for several moments before I lifted my gaze. "Just as you are captivated by your writings and the creation of new recipes, I am moved by a sense of adventure and hope for a progressive world."

She crossed her arms and refused to look at me.

"Look, what I meant to say before is, am I to believe that a woman has never captained a ship during humanity's time on this earth? We have queens who have ruled countries; Queen Victoria holds such a position today. What of women like Hatshepsut, an ancient Egyptian pharaoh? She was considered one of the country's most victorious rulers. Her military crusades and notable building projects have outlived her. Or Cleopatra, who was said to have superior intellect and praised for significantly improving her country's economy. What about this Tubman woman who risked her life to free the enslaved and get them to freedom?"

"You play unfairly, acquiring Adelaide's knowledge and making it your own," she said, her posture easing.

"I may not bury my nose in books, but I've benefited from her studies. I am a quick study, shall we say."

She held up her hands in defeat. "You have made your point. You will remain unwed and happy alone."

I winced at her suggestion of a life of isolation and unhappiness.

"But may I remind you, dear friend, that life is not a fantasy? You can't just sail off to the end of the world because you don't like the current state of society. A life lived inside your head is no life at all."

"It is the safest place to exist," I said. "I'd rather earn my peace and a life of my making than end up alone and brokenhearted like Mrs. Ainsworth or Papa." I studied the people in the ballroom. "You see me as different or odd because my desires conflict with yours. I believe we humans are more alike than we care to admit. We create a divide in hopes of validating our vulnerabilities and fears."

"How so?" Her brow furrowed in her desire to understand what I was positing.

"I don't rightfully know. But perhaps we fear fading from view."

"Perhaps." She shrugged. "This evening is meant to be magical and festive. Let's leave deeper matters for another day, shall we?"

"All right," I said. "Again, I'm sorry."

"Yes, well, in time I may forgive you," she said bluntly.

"That is fair."

Then, heavy-hearted, I let her pull me toward Zane and the other gentlemen. Mr. Huntington had joined them and, maintaining his usual unreadable expression, he listened while Zane carried the conversation.

"And now we have these Black blue bloods, aiming to mingle with society and make a name for themselves. And since the passing of the Fifteenth Amendment, the bastards have the right to vote."

I leaned in and whispered to Birdie, "An amendment which focuses on color, race, and the male sex. Thereby neglecting the rights of women entirely."

"For my sake, please keep your forward thinking to yourself," she said. "I don't seek to make an enemy of Mrs. Goddard before I have married her son."

"Elizabeth," Zane said, eyeing her with appreciation as we drew close. She smiled and walked to stand at his side. I stood outside their circle, looking on awkwardly.

"Miss Katherine." Mr. Peyton opened the circle by shifting to bow at the waist. He had the elegance of a proper gentleman and all the poise Evelyn admired. To call him handsome would be untrue, yet to call him plain didn't quite suit.

"How do you do this evening, Mr. Peyton?" I offered a brief curtsy.

"I am well. I am pleased you and your family now reside in the city."

"I'm sure you are. It makes your courtship of my sister that much easier," I said more firmly than intended.

He eyed me hesitantly. "W-why, yes, it does indeed. I quite enjoy my time in your sister's company."

"Indeed." I eyed him intently, attempting to peel back the layers of the one who sought to break up my family. He shifted from one foot to another under my inspection, appearing unsure of what to say next. A bead of sweat trickled down his brow.

"Do you second Mr. Goddard's view on the Fifteenth Amendment, Mr. Peyton? You being from the South and all," I added a little too loudly.

He flinched, and I released him from my magnifying glass

inspection as I sensed the others regarding me. They had heard me, and I realized I couldn't back down. "Or are we to pretend the war changed deep-rooted beliefs overnight?"

Birdie clutched Zane's arm tighter, and her dark eyes flashed their warning for me not to cause a scene. Zane's boyish countenance hardened as he regarded me. The other gentlemen looked on with bewilderment at my bluntness and willingness to dabble in men's affairs. Mr. Huntington, however, eyed me with keen interest.

Birdie moved tighter against Zane, seeking refuge. I opened my mouth and closed it as I realized Birdie looked as if she wanted the floor to open up and swallow her. I'd done it again. I'd gone and harmed my friend in some way. Perhaps it was I who lacked common sense with my assertiveness.

"Go on, Miss Darlington," Zane said. "Do elaborate. Seeing as you have so much insight into the matter."

I regarded Birdie and swallowed hard.

"Come now; we are waiting." Zane narrowed his eyes.

I clasped my hands in front of me, sweat trailing down my spine.

"If we had women running this country, you would see women, Blacks, and Indians alike placed in seats of power. Then what would become of the world?" the man to his left said with a patronizing chuckle.

"Perhaps a female approach is what we require to bring about change," I said before I could stop myself.

"Oh?" He arched a sparse brow.

"For hundreds of centuries, society has bowed at the feet of those considered great men. Do not misinterpret what I say, because I see the quality we all bring. But history reveals how fear and the hunger for power have caused humans to commit unspeakable crimes against each other. We do not bring about change by force or by dividing humans as though they are herds of cattle, but by listening with an open mind and striving to do things differently than our ancestors have done before us, and theirs before them. How can we learn if we do not study the mistakes of the past?"

"Quite the insight for a young woman," Mr. Huntington said, and I sensed no challenge in his tone.

"Age is hardly a factor," I said matter-of-factly. "I see the world for what it is. The war freed the enslaved but are they truly free? They still fight for equality. And what of the Indians? People enslaved them long before ships arrived from Africa, claiming their hunting grounds and the land they had made their homes on, forcing them to reject their spiritual practices, and rejecting their way of life. Then, in the name of progress, the government sold the land or gave it away for free and forced the Indians onto reservations."

"And rightfully so," Zane said. "They are savages and practice witchery."

I cringed at his observation but avoided looking at Birdie. "You can't blame them for fighting to keep what was theirs long before the discovery of the New World. Again, power was abused to force everyone into a perceived ideal. Perhaps it is we who are the savages, Mr. Goddard," I said with an even stare before noticing Birdie's frozen expression. My heart bled for her, but I willed her to see the snake she sought to marry. "It says a lot about a person, the company we keep, doesn't it, Mr. Peyton?"

He shifted to regard me. "My apologies, but I do not follow."

"You are a Southerner and fought to uphold the system of slavery. Yet you befriend Mr. Goddard here. A Northerner who fought to end slavery, or so we are led to believe. Because he embraces an ideology not that far removed from a belief system practiced in the South, across America, and the world since the dawn of time."

"Belief system?"

Was the man daft? "Yes, Mr. Peyton. The outdated belief system has divided empires, countries, and humans for centuries. It is our ideology that makes us different. Our behaviors and actions make us different. Our heritage makes us different. But we are all still just humans. Society has abused, imprisoned, and enslaved people as though they are property, holding them captive with the justification that they are less, yet is it not we who are enslaved and prisoners of our fears and convoluted impressions?"

"You forget your place, Miss Darlington," Zane said, his face flushed, a cold glint in those steel-blue eyes Birdie found "irresistible."

"I know my place." I lifted my chin. "And it isn't in the shadow of a man."

"Kat," Evelyn hissed behind me.

I spun to discover her standing behind me with an ashen face. She grabbed my elbow and hauled me away.

I glanced over my shoulder as Zane laughed and said to the others, "Are we now to wage war on women with their opinions? A man will never find peace." The gentleman next to him shared in his ridicule.

I bristled at his conduct, but the embarrassment and shame on Evelyn's face when she released me made me shrink inward. My family had been everything in my life, and I wanted more than anything to secure their love. But more times than not, I felt they wanted to put me in a box of their creation.

Evelyn's eyes welled with tears. "Must you? You are making a spectacle of yourself."

I glanced back at the group. Birdie and Mr. Peyton had fled. Mr. Huntington remained, eyeing me from afar, while Zane laughed and engaged with two newcomers to the group.

She squeezed my arm. "Do not ruin this evening. Please, Kat. Do it for me."

"I am sorry." I pulled my arm away and rubbed the ache her grip left. "I promise to keep my opinions to myself for the remainder of the evening."

Evelyn lifted her gloved fingers and brushed away tears. "I promise I will never speak to you again if you have one more outburst."

Her threat tightened my throat.

"I must find Mr. Peyton and fix whatever mess you have created." She leveled a hard stare at me. "Perhaps you, too, can find some sort of enjoyment in the evening."

I opened my mouth to speak, but she put up a hand to stop me before turning on her heel and walking off. I glanced about the room for Birdie. The danger of an end to our friendship weighed on my mind. Not finding her, I turned and walked into the corridor. I had taken only a few steps when I saw Audrey slipping into a room nearby. She left the door ajar, and I peeked inside to witness her removing a flask from the folds of her gown and taking a big swig before concealing the flask. Her daytime drinking had been a known affair in our home, and she openly drowned her sorrows in a snifter of brandy in the evenings. I continued down the corridor, leaving Audrey to her eventual demise, and opened a door to the courtyard.

Stepping outside, I inhaled deeply as the chatter and laughter of guests faded to a distant hum. The frostiness of the evening air pricked my exposed flesh, and I hugged myself to ward off the chill. I blinked away tears of frustration, but they flowed freely. Misery engulfed me. Endeavoring to fit into the world and my family left me questioning where I belonged. My ideals and views of life differed from those around me, except for Jude. He was the one person who understood me. But where did he belong in my life? Society condemned our friendship. And Birdie—well, she was too preoccupied with trying to marry Zane Goddard to see a road of pain ahead of her. He had distinctly declared his perspective on her ancestors, and no amount of lust and proclaimed love for her would pluck the ignorance from him. Birdie deserved much better than the likes of him. I feared he'd break her heart and love would claim another victim.

Trussed up in my thoughts and sadness, I strolled the courtyard until I heard approaching footfalls. I patted my cheeks dry before turning to face the intruder and froze when I glimpsed his profile in the light streaming into the courtyard from the mansion.

"Mr. Huntington," I said, not in the mood for pleasantries. "What can I do for you?"

"I come seeking fresh air, like you, I suppose." I eyed him, and as though reading my thoughts, he said, "I assure you I am not a stalker seeking to throw you over my horse and ride away with you." His eyes sparkled with amusement as he tried to make light of our encounter. His lighthearted approach left me questioning the disappearance of his usual serious persona, but as I considered him, his expression sobered.

I shrugged. "I am not one for social events. I find them rather trying. I fear I've made a spectacle this evening." I looked back at the mansion. "Moreover, my directness has made Zane and his entourage uncomfortable and irate. I also earned my sister's rebuke, which has become a daily occurrence. And most devastating is that in my passion for making my friend understand my view on controversial issues, I said something that pained her. I wish I could take it back." I realized I'd said too much. "Forgive me. We are practically strangers, and I've unleashed all my burdens on you."

"No apologies needed. You held your own in there. There is no shame in that. If the friend you refer to is Miss Vello, she seems to be a compassionate woman and, in time, will forgive whatever transpired between you."

I studied him with the same imaginary magnifying glass I'd used on Evelyn's Mr. Peyton. I saw a hint of admiration on his face. Maybe exhaustion stifled my responses, because I stood silent, waiting on him to continue.

"We do not live in a woman's world," he said. "My mother is a woman like you, but in all respect, she doesn't come from a place of sincerity and devotion toward humanity."

After our encounters, I'd inquired about the Huntingtons and learned of Mrs. Huntington and the belated Mr. Huntington's influence in the city before his death in the war. But I also got the impression that Mrs. Huntington intimidated others, as her husband had done in his time. "I am not certain if that is a compliment or an insult."

"A compliment, I assure you. I admire a woman who stands firm in her convictions, despite how they came to be. However, I don't admire any person who uses such convictions to control outcomes in others. I do not consider you such a woman. On the contrary, I believe you see the others' plights derived from the passion of freedom coursing your veins. What perplexes me is why a woman of your status and wealth feels the need for freedom."

"It is hardly proper to speak of another's wealth," I said and quickly continued when his lips parted, and I assumed he'd attempt to issue an apology. "But I am not one to conform to what society dictates as proper. The Darlington wealth is my father's. One is a fool to think wealth provides freedom."

"Doesn't it? It brings comfort…"

"Yes, the comfort of a roof over one's head and food in one's belly, but it does not bring happiness."

"I know this to be true," he said quietly. "My mother has all the wealth a person can want, and it will never suffice."

"And you? You're the man of your household and the true heir of your father's inheritance."

"If we are to be frank with each other, Miss Darlington—"

"Kat will do," I said.

His face softened. "Kat." He rolled my name over his tongue. "The name suits you. You are short in stature and waste no time getting to the point. A hater of idle chatter, I suspect."

My cheeks heated at his perception. I couldn't fault him for speaking the truth. I nodded with a smile. "You're correct in your assumptions, Mr. Huntington."

"I will follow your lead and do away with formal addresses. Merritt will suit." He removed his outer coat, which he had been wise enough to collect before venturing outside. "May I?" He held out the coat for me, and I turned so he could drape it over my shoulders.

I welcomed the warmth of his coat and inhaled the familiar scent of bergamot and orange blossoms I had smelled when he sat next to me for breakfast at Rose Hill Manor. I turned back to face him, and he fixed the coat around me to keep out the cold.

He looked down at me with a slight grin. "You know, in the few times we have met, I have witnessed you standing in the rain wearing nothing but your undergarments, dressed in my sister's clothing, and now in my coat. If I didn't consider you a woman with grit, I might deem you a damsel in distress."

"That I will never be," I said with a scowl before it slipped into a smile. "You wouldn't be the first to sum a person up by first impressions, or we wouldn't be standing here now with me draped in your coat."

He laughed, a rich and exhilarating sound.

"Nor do you suffer much consideration about appropriate decorum between a woman and man. Because here we stand alone, in the dark, without a chaperone. How ghastly!" I said. "But then again, men do as they please, and society provides grace."

"I assume you care little for what others think, or you wouldn't have taken on Zane Goddard."

I waved a hand in dismissal. "Zane is a fool."

"Your friend, Miss Vello, doesn't see it so."

"She is blinded."

"How so?"

"Love. The curse of the human race."

His brow pleated. "I must say, I have never heard love described as a curse before."

"It's true. In my experience, the love between a man and a woman is detrimental to all. People who fall in love lose their head and identity."

"Is it identity you seek?"

"No…" My words faded as I considered his statement.

"You are a Darlington, after all. You have more identity than one could ever want." His eyes peered at me as though seeking to detect what made me tick. I didn't pose a threat to him.

He had not fled or insulted me for my views, and a flicker of respect that conjured inside me gave me the courage to speak candidly. "A rat in a cage, more like. To claim a spot in a highfalutin society created by people seeking wealth and position because they believe it brings them value in the eyes of the public is a philosophy I can't comprehend. It is a burden I do not wish to bear."

His brow furrowed. "You seek to reject your social status and live amongst the impoverished."

"No. I merely seek to be me. Nothing more, nothing less. Identity doesn't matter to me. Too much importance is put on such matters. This evening, I choose to wear this gown." I looked down and gripped the fabric of my gown. "My sister had ensured that I had a dress fashioned by one of New York's best designers, and to her dismay, I found this old gown of my mother's in her trunk. Earlier I overheard some ladies criticizing my choice because it is out of fashion. Their conditioned belief is that the dress makes me less than them. To think a garment defines one's worth in the eyes of another! That is a world I am in conflict with."

"Yet it is the world we must contend with," he said.

"Unfortunately, you are right." I tilted my head back and looked into his eyes. "I have told you more than I would say to most, and you have told me nothing about you."

He extended his hands. "What do you seek to know?"

"Who—" I stopped as a woman cried out.

"Remove your hands from me!"

Merritt stiffened and we looked in the direction of the fuss.

"You have avoided me all evening." A deep, raspy voice answered.

"Please excuse me," Merritt said before darting off as though Hell chased at his heels.

I followed to discover what the commotion was about and

observed the young woman Mr. Huntington had arrived with clutched in the unwelcomed embrace of a burly gentleman.

"Unhand her this minute," Merritt said.

My eyes narrowed as I recognized the mature gentleman as Mr. Flint. The poor excuse of a man had tried to wed Evelyn and Adelaide before they were barely fifteen. I had kicked him in the shin at a fall social two years back when he tried to manhandle me in the corridor.

Mr. Flint spun around and released the woman as Merritt lifted a fist and plowed him square in the face. I shrank back, and the woman looked at me wide-eyed.

"Merritt, no, please." She grabbed Merritt's arm, and he knocked her to the ground in his frenzy.

I watched in horror as he swung again at Mr. Flint, who ducked, and Merritt's fist missed its mark. Mr. Flint landed a punch and attempted another, but Merritt sidestepped, and Mr. Flint lost his balance on the icy ground and went down, barely missing the woman in the snow.

She scrambled to her feet as Merritt turned to continue his vendetta against the man. "Stop!" She put herself between Merritt and Mr. Flint.

As though coming to his senses, Merritt took a step back, breathing heavily. He shook his head and, noting my presence, glanced my way. Taken aback by the violence I had witnessed and his possessiveness of the woman, I whirled and walked back toward the mansion.

"Kat," he called after me, but I increased my pace, returning to the warmth and oppression of the party.

Chapter 20

Merritt

I STOOD NUMBLY WATCHING HER HURRIED DEPARTURE, STILL CLOAKED in my coat. She disappeared into the house, and I swiped a hand across my face but pushed my apprehension about what she thought of my conduct to the back of my mind as Mr. Flint pulled to his feet and brushed the snow from his clothing.

"I warned you what would happen if I caught you bothering my sister."

He flicked a tongue over the blood trickling over his lip and lifted fingers to touch the area. He regarded the blood on his fingers and delivered me a cold glare. "That will be the one and only time you will get the best of me," he said. "Bed your sister, if you haven't already. I will find another to share mine."

I bristled, and my hand curled into a fist, but Josie grabbed my arm and pulled close to my side, stopping me.

Mr. Flint regarded Josie's body so close to mine and shook his head before storming off.

My hands clenched at my sides, it took everything in me to keep from lunging at him from behind.

"You're bleeding," Josie said.

Her observation reminded me of the sting radiating over my cheek, and I wiped the blood trickling down my face. "It's nothing."

"Thank you for your aid," she said. "Mother will be most displeased when she finds out you were brawling like a street fighter."

"Let her be." I paced, trying to gather my composure before returning to the house.

"Who was that woman you were with?"

I halted and turned to stare at her blankly, my mind racing.

"The one wearing your coat," Josie said as though I needed reminding.

"That was Miss Darlington. Katherine Darlington."

"You called her Kat, and she was wearing your coat." She stood waiting for an explanation.

"In your predicament, you observed a lot." My annoyance simmered. "What were you doing out here?"

"I saw you leave and followed you. And it appears he did the same." She waved a hand at the door through which Mr. Flint had disappeared.

"Did he harm you?"

"He shook me up, is all. The lust in his eyes and the mishandling have left me rattled. But I do believe you quashed anymore interest from him."

"Let's hope. Or next I will take his hands," I said, meaning every word. "Then he won't be touching you or any other woman."

"I appreciate your devotion as my champion, but you can't be getting into quarrels at social events. It will bring reproach upon our household. Mother—"

"Spare me. I care not what Mother thinks." I took her arm and led her across the courtyard and inside out of the cold.

I paused at a mirror hung over a hallway stand and dabbed at the last evidence of blood, but I could do nothing to hide the reddened blemish on my face. "Go on now," I said to Josie. "I will see you in the ballroom. Be sure to be escorted for the rest of the evening. I don't trust the likes of Mr. Flint."

She nodded, unbuckling the clasp of her paletot, and walked down the corridor toward the entrance hall. I turned to the mirror, rested my hands on the stand, and observed the rage simmering in my face. I had witnessed the same unhinged look in my father's eyes as he had towered over me.

"Damn him to hell," I said.

Someone cleared their throat, and I jumped before spinning to discover Kat standing several feet away with my coat in hand.

"I'm sorry to disturb you, but I noticed the woman come in, and I wanted to return your coat." She held it out for me.

I walked over to her and stood peering down at her, but she avoided eye contact. "I'm sorry for what you saw out there."

"Your life is yours to do with as you see fit," she said with no hint of judgment. "My thoughts on the matter should not concern you. I shouldn't have been alone with you. If so, your lady friend wouldn't have found herself alone and at the mercy of Mr. Flint. The man has a reputation for roaming hands. I, too, have been subjected to his ardor."

I flinched, and my jaw tightened before I absorbed her statement in its entirety. "Lady friend?"

"Your companion."

"My sister," I said.

"Oh." She glanced at me, and my gaze dropped to her full mouth. "M-my apologies." She took a step back and thrust the coat at me.

Our hands touched as I reached for the coat, and I froze. She retracted her hand as though burned. Then, without another word, she turned and walked hastily down the corridor and vanished into the ballroom.

I stared after her, as I always seemed to do in our interactions. Not even Mira Densmore, the woman Mother worried would spoil my possibilities of acquiring a wife from a reputable family, had unnerved me like Katherine Darlington.

I left my coat with the butler in the entrance hall and returned to the ballroom. Kat stood talking to Miss Vello, the woman betrothed to Zane Goddard. The Vello woman possessed uncanny beauty and refinement, whereas Kat's attractiveness went deeper. She was like an unpolished diamond, and I had become mesmerized by the zeal and assurance with which she conducted herself. She was a woman with spirit and passion, defying all who stood in her way. She possessed courage and stood firm in her authenticity.

"Where have you been?" Mother's voice rose on my left, but I never broke my stare.

I sensed her peering in Kat's direction. "You can't be serious," she said with a huff. "I approve of your head being turned by one of the Darlingtons, but not that one. Besides, that girl resembles none of the Darlington sisters. There are questions regarding her parentage. Perhaps the late Mrs. Darlington wasn't so noble after all, and frolicked with a foreign lover who seeded the child. Can't you see she is the only one of the Darlington women with a darker complexion and brunette hair?"

I heaved a sigh and shifted to regard my mother. "Not tonight, Mother. It is none of your affairs, what happens between someone else's sheets."

"No son of mine will marry a bastard."

I gripped her wrist and leaned close to her ear. "Silence your tongue. I won't have you starting rumors about the family."

She yanked her wrist free, and her eyes spewed contempt before she nudged her head at someone behind me. I twisted to observe who she'd indicated and noticed Miss Evelyn Darlington. "It'd be best to redirect your desire toward that one over there. She will be more fitting for you. She likes the finer things in life and will make a good wife."

"You mean she will make a daughter-in-law who is easily manipulated," I retorted. "Do not concern yourself with a wife for me. Besides, Miss Evelyn has caught the eye of Mr. Peyton."

"The Southerner?"

"Yes, Mother. Although you pride yourself on meddling in everyone's affairs, it appears you missed that one."

"Surely Mr. Darlington disapproves. I bet it is the doing of that Boseman woman he married." She leaned closer and regarded an auburn-haired woman standing some feet away. "No one could believe it when he married a complete stranger and brought her into his home."

"A stranger to who, Mother? You?"

"There are far more suitable women he could have wed."

"Oh, I'm sure if Josie wasn't so young at the time, you'd have offered her up as a child bride," I said.

She hesitated as though considering the idea for the first time.

Bile burned my throat. "You would, wouldn't you?" I shook my head in disgust. "Good thing for my sister Mr. Darlington isn't Mr. Flint, but a decent man who puts his love for his daughters above all."

"Except when he married that woman," Mother said. "She is an opportunist. She was on the hunt for a vulnerable man with wealth."

I looked from Kat's stepmother to my mother. "Perhaps you and she are related in some way."

Mother bristled. "You watch your tongue, son. You aren't too old to get a well-earned whipping."

"Mother." Having my fill of her, I bowed and walked away.

I mingled, joining groups of gentlemen, drifting in and out of the conversation. My thoughts were captured by my interactions with Kat in the courtyard and hallway. I reflected on how the urge to kiss her had overtaken me. But her views on love and courtship would not be easily swayed. As the orchestra started another tune and a new dance commenced, I regarded her. Finally, I excused myself and crossed the room to where she still stood with Miss Vello.

I held out my hand when she looked up at me with a questioning look in her dark eyes. "Would you do me the honor of sharing this dance?"

"Go." Miss Vello nudged her with an elbow.

Kat shook her head. "I am not good at dancing. I'm afraid I would step all over you."

"Not to worry, I am a brilliant dancer and will guide you."

"I-I…" Kat's eyes flitted back and forth.

"What she means to say is, she likes to direct, and there can be only one leader. So you will have your work cut out for you, Mr. Huntington." Miss Vello gave her a gentle shove forward, and Kat flung her arm out to stop her. "Do try to stay upright." Mischievousness gleamed in Miss Vello's eyes, and I smiled at the camaraderie between the women.

I refused to take no for an answer and kept my hand extended.

"Oh, flummadiddle!" Kat said and slipped her small hand into mine. "I warn you, I will make fools of us both. I have not studied the dance manuals on etiquette like most women in this room."

"It is time we lightened this dreary evening up." I looked over her head at Miss Vello, who grinned from ear to ear.

"Make a lady out of her, will you, Mr. Huntington?" she said.

Kat blushed, glanced back at Miss Vello, and favored her with a scowl. Her face glowing with merriment, Miss Vello did not appear the least bit guilty in her attempt to embarrass her friend.

The distaste remaining from the conversation with my mother vanished as I led Kat onto the dance floor. I avoided the sour looks of envy from other ladies who'd eyed me all evening, hoping I would approach them and ask for a dance. Mother regarded us with pursed lips before turning her back and walking from the room.

I rested my hand along Kat's back, situated hers along mine, then took her other hand, clasped it, and positioned our extended hands. Once in form, we slipped into the other dancers and moved around the floor. The warmth of her hands sent a charge through me, and as I looked down into her upturned, heart-shaped face, my heart skipped a beat or two.

I smiled my encouragement as she stumbled then moved clumsily, compensating for her blunder. "We are characters in life's script, and that is all," I said. "All those who surround us are an illusion. Focus on my face alone."

She nodded, and I saw determination in her eyes as she concentrated on my steps. Soon she had the polka moves under control. Her eyes widened with delight, and she elongated her body and relaxed, letting me take the lead. The rest of the room faded as I became hypnotized by the confidence in the woman in my arms. Her skin glowed.

When the dance ended, I locked gazes with Mr. Darlington, who smiled and inclined his head, appearing pleased at my engaging with his daughter.

He strode toward us, and Kat caught sight of him. "Hello, Papa." Deep affection softened her voice, and I observed the tenderness in her face as she beheld him.

"My darling, you were a vision out there." He leaned in and kissed her cheek.

"Thank you, Papa. Mr. Huntington is a good teacher."

"It takes a willing student to learn," I said, winded.

"I wouldn't call my daughter a willing student. More of a leader," Mr. Darlington said with a wink at her. "But always a quick study when she wants to learn."

Kat straightened under his praise.

This relationship between parent and child hadn't been one I had experienced in my thirty years, but one I'd witnessed and yearned for as a boy. If I ever found a woman worth wedding, I aspired to be a parent my child looked up to, not one they feared.

"I hate to steal her away from you, but the hour draws late. I have an important meeting in the morning. I need to gather my daughters."

I inclined my head. "Always a pleasure, Mr. Darlington."

He clapped my shoulder and held out an elbow for Kat; she seized it and nodded at me before they left me to once again stare after the lovely Kat Darlington.

With her gone, the evening lost its appeal, and I gathered

Mother and Josie. Mother appeared in a foul mood, which only heightened when she noticed the blemish on my cheek.

"What happened?"

"A little mishap, is all." I placed Mother's paletot around her shoulders and guided my family out the front door and into our waiting carriage.

Later outside our home, I helped them out.

"I will be home late," I said.

"And where do you think you are going at this hour?" Mother leveled an accusatory look at me.

"None of your concern."

"Everything that happens in this family is of my concern." Her favorite statement.

I ignored her and gave the coachman our destination before returning to the open carriage door.

"You are going to see that woman!" Mother stomped her foot.

I climbed inside and slammed the door before hitting the roof with a closed hand. The carriage lurched forward, and I left the women on the boardwalk, feeling remorse for leaving my sister to suffer Mother's contempt alone.

The carriage moved through the darkened streets until it halted outside a brownstone apartment. I disembarked before the coachman could jump down from the driver's seat. "I won't be long," I said.

"Sir?" He sounded puzzled. I usually instructed him to return some hours later.

"As I said. Wait."

He nodded, pulled up his collar to keep out the chill, and settled in to wait.

I walked up the steps and rapped the door knocker before stepping back to wait.

The door opened, and she stood enrobed in a white satin night-robe, the lights inside revealing her curvy silhouette beneath the fabric. My chest tightened as my gaze trailed from her bare feet to her face.

"Merritt, darling," Mira Densmore cooed with a bat of her thick, dark lashes. "I wasn't expecting you, but do come in." She gripped my arm, pulled me inside, and closed the door behind us.

"I wasn't..." I stopped mid-sentence as she pressed her body against mine and her lips and tongue claimed my senses. Her hands tore hungrily at my clothing before I gripped her wrists to stop her. "Not tonight," I said, my voice thick with emotion.

She pouted and regarded me with beckoning, sapphire blue eyes. "Don't be a tease." She leaned forward and bit at my bottom lip.

"I come for your friendship."

"Friendship?" She took a step back.

I released her wrists, swerved by her, and removed my overcoat and hat. "Let's sit in the parlor, shall we?" I said as though she were a guest in my home.

"Have it your way." She gestured a hand in the direction of the parlor.

I strode to the room and sat in front of the fireplace. The flames burned low, and I watched her kneel to stoke the fire before adding another log.

"I can see you are troubled," she said without looking back at me. "What has captured your thoughts this evening? Am I to assume the blemish on your cheek holds weight?"

"A cut acquired while ridding myself of a nuisance."

She stood and seated herself next to me on the settee. The warmth of her thigh against mine would usually send my heart racing with desire, but the flames grasped my attention.

"I sense a change in you." She placed a hand on my thigh; it wasn't a touch of passion but one of concern. "We have always been honest with each other."

"Yes, and I've found great comfort in your companionship."

"Then do tell me, what has you rattled?"

"A woman," I said.

She inhaled, and I avoided meeting her gaze, but I sensed the ache in her tone. "A woman…"

"As you said, I've always been honest with you. You and I would never work."

"That is what you told me when I asked you to make me your wife. But I know I could make you happy."

I regarded the raw emotion in her face. "But I could never do so for you. I care about you, but not in the way you desire."

She looked down at her hands resting in her lap. "Our arrangement took a turn I never accepted. Although I didn't expect my lust to turn into something more, no matter how many times you reminded me, you didn't feel the same. I hoped in time, you would see me as something more."

I placed a hand over hers. "I'm sorry."

She shrugged and covered my hand with hers. "There's nothing to forgive. I was a fallen woman long before our paths crossed. We came to each other with our own demons." She stood and strode to the crystal whiskey decanter and filled two glasses.

I returned my gaze to the fire. I recalled the first time I had seen her on the Broadway stage after the war and how I'd returned each time she performed for a month and sat captive for the entirety of the five-and-a-half-hour performance. Then one evening, after the crowds had faded and performers exited the building, I stood waiting for her. Having experienced stalkers, she turned her body, ready to ward off an attacker, when I stepped from the shadows to speak with her. I convinced her to visit a nearby coffee house, and we sat conversing for hours until it closed. Lust turned into a friendship over the years, and I trusted her like no other. Trust had never come easy for me. At a tender age, I learned that safety was an illusion. My father's hand had been heavy, and his cruelty allowed no favors.

A memory surfaced from when I was around twelve and Josie, three or four. Father's business associate had double-crossed him, and he had returned home in a drunken rage. I understood how the night would unfold as his first blow sent my mother sailing across the entrance floor when she came to greet him.

"Leave her alone." I strode from the library.

"Ah, now he seeks to be a man." Father curled his lip in disgust.

I bent to help my mother up, but he gripped the collar of my shirt and reeled me backward. He slammed me into a wall and struck me with his fist until my vision blurred, and I slumped into his grip. Mother had never interceded, but stood by until he lost interest in the lack of fight in me and released his hold, and I slumped to the floor. Through blackened eyes, I saw him turn on Mother, who turned to flee, but he chased her.

"Merritt," a soft voice called from above before I heard her sobs. Fear snatched my breath. I blinked away the blood dripping into my eyes and scrambled to my feet at the sound of Josie's voice. Pain radiated through my head and upper body as I darted past staff members looking on as my father brutalized his family. I reached my sister, took her hand, and darted down the corridor, half dragging her behind me.

"Come." I dashed into a guest chamber and halted in front of a wardrobe. I opened the door, lifted her up, and put her inside.

"Are we playing the game again?" Her eyes rounded with concern as she regarded my face.

"Yes, and remember what happens if you stay quiet?"

She bobbed her head. "You will give me a prize."

"Good," I said.

She sat down and hugged her knees as I had taught her. I removed the cloth doll from one of the drawers and gave it to her. I had convinced her that the doll made her invisible to all happenings outside of the wardrobe. She clutched the doll to herself, and I noticed her tremble.

Weighted footfalls echoed in the hallway, and father called out, "Boy, where did you go?"

I tucked the clothes around her to hide her and whispered,

"Remember, don't come out until I come for you. No matter what happens." I closed the door.

"Where are you, boy?" Father yelled in his drunken voice, and a crash sounded like he had stumbled into something in his search for me.

I dashed to the bed and hid underneath. My heart drummed in my ears as I squeezed my eyes tight, further opening the gash over my eye. I willed myself to disappear. I prayed for a God. A hero. A protector. But no help came, only my father's hand as he pulled me from beneath the bed. The smell of the cigar he clenched between his teeth that evening had become a scent that still caused my knees to tremble. I kicked at him with my free leg, managed to get free, and dashed for the door, hoping to lead him away from Josie and keep her from witnessing his madness.

That night, I endured cigar burns over multiple places on my body—the scars a daily reminder of the monster who'd seeded me.

"Merritt." Mira waved a glass of whiskey in front of me and snapped me from the horrors of my childhood.

I shook my head to dislodge the past and took the glass. She sat beside me and took a sip of the amber liquid.

"They never seem to cease, do they," she said.

I regarded her, but the flames had captured her gaze.

"No."

"I know." Her shoulders slumped. The bond and commonality between us was rooted in fathers who should never have been called such. Hers had used her body in unthinkable ways, but unlike me, she never had a mother to step in. I don't know what was more painful, never knowing a mother or being given one who lacked the courage to save you. Mira had stabbed her abuser through the heart and kicked him into the street, leaving neighbors to believe he had been robbed, before she made her way to New York. I had envisioned my father's death many times in my younger years, before the war had done the job for me.

But he had created a monster almost his equal. Mother never

used her hands, but her words and manipulation brought the same pain. I had become numb to her harshness, but I couldn't say the same for my sister. I had spent all my life protecting myself and often felt I had failed her by not ridding us both of a mother incapable of love. I'd felt empathy for a woman who had endured unspeakable abuse at my father's hands, until I discovered a monster equally as dangerous had arisen after his death.

I took another swig of the whiskey. "We are quite the pair, you and I."

"Some may say fractured."

"Yes." I emptied the glass.

"Another?" she asked.

"No." I set the glass on a stand next to the couch. Although I partook in alcohol, I never drank any more than to take the edge off. I refused to become *him*. He had taught me all I never wanted to be.

"Tell me of this woman you mentioned."

I shifted to look at her, and she returned my gaze. Again, I witnessed sadness in her eyes. "What is it?" I asked.

"It was only a matter of time before someone took you from me. I know a man of your caliber could never remain infatuated with me forever."

"Infatuated? Is that what you consider this?"

She regarded me with raw honesty." Isn't it so?"

"At first, yes. But then it changed. We've been over this."

"Yes, I am not marriage quality. A woman like me could never be seen as a woman worthy of an affluent man. Tell me: this woman, does she come from a reputable family?"

I grimaced. "Yes. But she is not the marrying kind of woman."

"No?" She arched a perfectly shaped brow. "Then you've grown tired of me?"

"That isn't it. But I can't be bedding another if I seek to have her return my affections one day."

She stiffened. "She has bewitched you. You no longer seek a

woman to warm your bed, or my bed, as this is where you choose to visit me in secret. You care for this woman like you have never cared for me."

I swallowed hard, hating the pain I witnessed in her face.

Her lip trembled, and she dropped her head. "I've loved you from the night you stalked me in the street. I was foolish to believe I could make you fall in love with me. I know…" she lifted a hand. "Despite what you told me, I still hoped."

I took her hand in mine. "Mira, I wish…"

She lifted teary eyes. "Please don't. For my sake, don't explain why you couldn't allow yourself to love me." She cupped my cheek with her hand and stared deep into my eyes. "I will always love you, but I will keep our secret. So you never have to fear that I will betray you. If you convince the woman to wed you, she will never know about us."

"That isn't why I'm here."

"Oh, then why?"

"To tell you we can't do this anymore. Besides, our affair is hardly a secret, at least from Mother or the coachman. Staff talk, and they leave households. Is there truly anything kept secret in New York? The place is riddled with scandal." I squeezed her hand. "I can't change the past. Nor do I wish to. I speak of feelings beyond fleshly desires. You're a woman of worth, Mira."

She scoffed, not as one who had become bitter with life, but as a realist. "I doubt other gentlemen would deliver the same assessment with which you honor me. You succumbed to an illusion when you watched me on stage."

"Perhaps, but the woman I came to understand in the coffee house has held my attention. The world is filled with alluring women, but you have a substance unlike most."

"But that this new mystery woman possesses," she said with a sad smile.

I shrugged.

"Well, I hope she is worthy of a man like you. If I can't win your devotion, I hope she sees what I see in you. You deserve to be loved. You aren't him. You never will be."

"And you're more than your father's whore. The transgressions of our parents have claimed too much of our lives."

"Indeed, if one of us can find happiness, at least it is you." She stood and set her glass down before holding out a hand. "Come, I will show you out."

I stood and allowed her to lead me to the door. I slipped on my coat and hat. She leaned against me and softly touched my lips with hers.

"Goodbye, Merritt. I shall miss you greatly."

"If you ever need anything…"

She placed her fingers over my lips to silence me. "No, my love. Unless we pass each other in the street, this will be the last you will see of me."

My throat tightened, and my heart felt heavy at her words. She stepped back. I nodded and turned to grip the doorknob.

"Merritt…"

I glanced back at her.

"Thank you for everything."

"And you."

Tears slid down her cheeks. "I wish you much happiness."

Again, I nodded, then stepped out into the cold, closing the door behind me. I paused, squeezing my eyes closed. My heart grieved a loss.

"I hope I don't live to regret it," I murmured into the night.

Chapter 21

Kat—1870

MY FAMILY RETURNED HOME FROM THE GODDARD BALL, AND later, clad in my nightshift and robe, I sat on the edge of my bed so engrossed in my thoughts, I never heard Dorotea walk in until she stood before me.

"What occupies your mind?"

"This family," I said. "I was born into a large family, yet I feel so alone. I feel it would be easier to be anyone but me."

"What happened?" She settled on the edge of the bed beside me.

"The entire ride, Evelyn informed Papa of everything I did wrong, hoping he would set me straight."

"And did he?"

"No, he told Evelyn she should respect my stance and not seek to fit into a room. So we all had to endure her foul mood for the rest of the ride home." I stood and paced the room. "I am who I am. Why can't she accept that? I'm weary of knocking at the door of this family and begging to be let in. I see life and the world as I see it." I thrust my hands at the heavens. "Do they want me to cease breathing to change who I am? And if I could change to fit in, don't you think I would? Life would be a far cry easier. I have the love of my family, but their love often feels like it comes with conditions. It leaves me wondering if I belong here at all."

"Señorita Kat, you mustn't say such things. Your family loves you."

"I know they do, in their own way. But I'm tired of wondering where I belong. Or if I belong at all." I looked at Mama's gown, lying over the chair in the corner. "Tonight they laughed at me."

"Who?"

"Other ladies mocked me for my attire."

"Something you knew could happen before you wore it. But you still chose to."

"Because I am driven by a void within myself. I thought it was the void of my mother, but now I don't know. It's as though a piece of me is missing." I looked at her and saw that far-off look she often got. "Dorotea?"

"Hmm." She blinked. "What is it?"

"I am telling you my sorrows, and you aren't listening. Do I bore you?"

She flinched as though I had slapped her. "No, of course not." She stood and walked to stand in front of me. "You are loved. Very much so. I love you like my own child."

Her words rang true, and I noticed how she favored me. Of course, she loved my sisters, but often she had jumped to my defense when it came to Audrey, and suffered the consequences. Other times, I'd find her staring at me with a troubled gaze, and when she would catch me studying her, she feigned a smile. I recalled the tenderness between Papa and her, and a sudden notion caused my legs to tremble. I swallowed hard as I glanced down at my hands and then at Dorotea. We bore the same skin so easily browned by the sun. The same dark hair and eyes. Did scandal run deep within my family? Maybe Mama hadn't been my mother at all. Had I been a product of Dorotea and Papa's love affair?

"Señorita, are you ill?" Dorotea came forward and grasped my arm.

"I need to sit down."

She led me back to the bed. I knotted my hands in the quilt and chewed on the inner side of my cheek to hold back tears. It all made perfect sense. My sisters and I barely looked alike, or perhaps not at all. Had I forced myself to see similarities because of an inner truth I'd known all along.

"Señorita, you are frightening me. What has you so upset?"

"Shut the door," I said.

She hurried to do as instructed and returned to my side. "Speak to me."

"Sit." I patted the bed to my right.

After she had settled, I twisted to take her hands in mine. "I know."

A flicker of fear washed over her face before she smoothed it away. "Know what?"

"About you and Papa."

Her lips parted, but she quickly pressed them shut.

"I saw you in the study not long back. I saw the love between you."

She gulped and lifted slender fingers to brush back a stray tendril.

"Do you love him?" I said, but didn't wait for an answer. "How long has this been going on?"

She took my hands in hers and looked me straight in the eye. "Yes, I love him."

"And the affair, how long has it been going on?"

"There is no affair. We shared a moment of weakness. A kiss and tender embrace. That is all."

"So before, when Mama was alive, you and Papa—"

"No!" Pain reflected in her eyes. "Your mother was not only my mistress, but my friend. I would never betray her like that. My love for your father started after his return from the war."

Relief rushed through me, that what I believed about being a

Darlington remained untainted, but I pressed further on the issue. "But he was barely around."

"The heart knows what the heart knows. In the times I did see him, and knowing your stepmother would never love him, my feelings grew. It is wrong of me, I know. He is a married man."

"Scarcely," I said. "She is no more a wife than me."

"Still, she is his wife, and I must withhold my affection for him."

I studied the pain in her face and wondered, if Audrey had never come into our lives, if Dorotea would have become my stepmother. Life would have been more pleasant. But love caused nothing but pain, and the forbidden love between Dorotea and Papa confirmed my deep-rooted belief.

"For a fleeting moment, I thought maybe what I had witnessed in the study made more sense than what I have believed all my life," I said with a laugh, and shook my head.

"To what do you refer?"

"That Mama wasn't my mother. Or I was a bastard seeded by the love between Papa and my governess. I know it was foolish of me." She regarded me as though she'd seen a ghost, and I touched her arm. "I'm sorry. I don't mean to upset you. It was wrong of me to think you would betray my mother or that my family would be entangled in any type of scandal. Despite my awareness of mutterings about the difference between my sisters and me and that Mama had an affair with a foreigner, or I am Papa's bastard child that Mama took pity on, I've not given the rumors refuge. I suppose I'm feeling overwhelmed after the ball."

She nodded, but the wary look in her eyes never settled, and my heart plunged. I hadn't meant to hurt her, but I didn't know how to take away the pain in her eyes.

"All is well." She patted my hand and stood.

Her words should have offered comfort, but they rarely did. Whenever she made that statement, I'd come to know that all was not well and something grave simmered beneath the surface.

"Good night, señorita."

I returned her farewell and sat upright against my headboard long after she had gone, staring at the door. My thoughts turned from her and the love she held for my father to Audrey and the private investigator I sought to hire. If Papa wouldn't give me the funds, who could? Then his face came to mind, and I sat forward. My heartbeat sped up. Yes, he could very well be the one who could help me. I scrambled off my bed and walked to the desk. I opened the drawer, withdrew stationery, and dipped my pen. Then I began to script my plea.

Dear Mr. Huntington,

I understand you are in the business of investing and loaning money. I find myself in need of your services. I seek to hire a private investigator and can't obtain the funds from my father.

Rest assured, if you loan me the funds, I will see you are paid in full.
Sincerely,
Katherine Darlington

Later I crept downstairs to retrieve some chocolates Chef Bernard had prepared. On my way to the kitchen, hushed voices in the study drew me. I pressed my ear to the door and picked up the voices of Papa and Dorotea. I couldn't catch what they were saying, and when footsteps sounded nearby, I darted toward the kitchen.

Chapter 22

THE SUN PERCHED HIGH IN THE BRIGHT BLUE SKY, AND THE COLD of the afternoon nipped my cheeks and frosted my hair. The town square hummed with the spirit of Christmas as my sisters and I strolled hand in hand among the vendors and the festive street entertainment. Engrossed in conversation, Papa and Dorotea followed, and from time to time, I peeked over my shoulder, bearing witness to their admiration and esteem for each other. Despite the scandal Dorotea's love for a married man and his affection for her could bring, I relished the bliss on his face.

Grace and Alice skipped along beside me. Adelaide and Evelyn clasped each other's arms and squealed at every mediocre thing they saw. Happiness permeated the day in the absence of our stepmother, who had feigned a headache, no doubt, and stayed home in her chamber. Most likely causing a stir amongst the staff, as she had done since our arrival in the city. I had caught the disgruntled looks she gathered from the staff and overheard them lamenting about her. If Papa didn't intercede soon, we'd find ourselves in a staff shortage.

"Look, Kat, carolers." Grace pointed at a group gathering on a platform in the middle of the square. I glanced in that direction, then at her face, aglow with unabiding pleasure and happiness. My heart swelled as gratitude washed over me.

The carolers belted out "Up on the Housetop," and Grace, who'd come out of the womb singing, joined in. As we walked along, I relished the sound of her sweet voice and the perfume of freshly cut pine and cedar trees piled together for purchase.

"A candy cane for the ladies," a stout merchant said with a jolly, toothy grin. With the plunge in sugar prices after the war, candy making was on the rise.

Grace and Alice's eyes widened as they regarded the white candy shepherd's crooks. Grace's tongue flicked out over her lip. I recalled the delicious peppermint flavor and empathized with my youngest sister's sweet tooth.

Papa shuffled inside his coat for coins and placed them in the woman's meaty outstretched hand.

Disposing of the wrapper in Dorotea's outstretched hand, Grace popped the curved part of the candy cane into her mouth and let out a moan of pleasure before slipping her mittened hand back into mine.

We continued along until a tree vendor's collection pulled us to a stop. "Papa, look at this one," Alice said. "It would be splendid for the front parlor, don't you think?"

I regarded the sparsely needled tree with its hooked top, then considered more appealing choices.

"It is a lovely tree," Papa said. "A bit small for the parlor."

"I disagree," Evelyn said. "This one is more suitable." She pointed at a bushy tree rising over ten feet, and for once, I agreed with Evelyn; the tree was a better choice than Alice's pick.

"But this one looks sad, and no one will pick it." Alice's face fell as she fought to defend her choice. "Then this mister here will have cut it down for no reason." She gestured at the spindly man before us with a hooked nose and red tufts of hair poking out of his ears. I thought he resembled the tree.

"Why did you choose to cut this tree?" I asked the man.

He looked from us to consider the tree in question. "It has character," he said.

"A matter of opinion," Evelyn said in her pretentious way.

I craned my neck and studied the tree more intently.

"Patrons all seek the tall, full trees. A statement for any room, but this fellow stands out." He pulled the tree out for our inspection.

Evelyn wrinkled her nose. "That it does."

"I think it's perfect," I said.

Evelyn scowled. "You would."

"Ladies," Papa said firmly, "we will take the tree."

"But Papa," Evelyn said, "we must have a tree all the ladies will talk about for Christmases to come."

"They will," Adelaide said with a laugh, unable to contain her amusement.

I also found entertainment in Evelyn's distress.

"It simply won't do," Evelyn continued. "We will be the laughing stock of the holiday season. Please, Papa." Her grating whine drew the attention of passersby.

"Now who is causing a spectacle?" I leaned in and whispered to Adelaide. We exchanged a grin.

"Very well," Papa said, too soft to withstand his spoiled eldest daughter. "Pick a second tree. We will have one in the hall entrance and one in the front parlor."

Evelyn's behavior reversed, and a smile broke across her face before she squealed with delight. "Thank you, Papa." She leaned in, pulled his face down, and planted a kiss on his cheek. When she turned back to examine her prospects, I noticed an exchange of looks between Dorotea and Papa. Dorotea shook her head in disapproval, and Papa shrugged and offered a wry smile.

I rolled my eyes and continued on, leaving them behind.

At a vendor three stalls down, I paused to regard the beautiful arrangement of ornaments that as of late appeared on every street corner around Christmas. Gone were the days when we spent weeks creating garlands made of dried orange and lemon slices, nuts, and popcorn. The dusting of tree branches with diamond dust faded with the import of lavish spun glass and waxed ornaments.

The vendor's display held an arrangement of colorful glittered tin balls of various sizes and other creations. I picked up a spun glass set of angel wings and thought of my mother and how much she loved the holiday season. I recalled us flocking to the salon on Christmas Eve and sitting around Papa as he read the poem "A Visit from St. Nicholas" while Mama sat adding the finishing touches to the stockings she knitted for the staff. She'd look at us gathered around Papa, listening intently, and smile. After he finished the poem, we hung stockings and discretely filled them with the trinkets we collected for each other. Later I'd sprawl out on my belly before the fire with my sketchpad and charcoal pencils, sketching while my sisters played games and chatted until Mama ushered us off to bed.

My eyes teared up at the recollection of times past, and the sensation of someone touching my arm made me look at the area, but no hand rested on my flesh.

"I will take this," I said to the vendor, a woman with crystal blue eyes and full red cheeks. I reached into the burgundy velvet reticule dangling from my wrist and withdrew the coins Papa had given each of us before coming to the market.

The woman wrapped the ornament in brown parchment paper and handed it to me, and I dropped the coins into her hand. "Much obliged, missy," she said.

"You're—" A tug on my arm interrupted me. I gasped as a pickpocket ripped my reticule from my wrist. "You! Stop!" I yelled at the retreating back of a young boy of seven or eight. I darted after the scamp without considering the spectacle of a woman running in public.

"Kat!" Evelyn's voice rang out, but I ignored her and wove in and out of the crowd, trying to keep the rascal in sight.

Footfalls pounded close behind me, but I didn't look back. A man darted by me in pursuit of the thief, and nabbed the boy on the edge of the square.

"Hand it here," the man said, holding the boy by the collar.

I skidded to a stop and barreled into the gentleman and boy. "My apologies," I said as the man gripped my arm to keep me upright.

"That is quite all right. It is not you that needs to be extending an apology," the gentleman said, and I craned my neck to peer into the intense eyes of an unsmiling Merritt Huntington.

He freed me but did not release his hold on the thrashing thief still hanging in midair.

I gripped my side to ease a stitch while trying to catch my breath. Then, with my free hand, I snatched my reticule from the boy.

"Let me go." He clawed at Merritt's hand.

"You still yourself, and I will set you down."

The boy ceased his struggling, and Merritt set his feet on the ground but didn't release his hold on the boy's collar. "What do you say to the lady?" Merritt said firmly, but I glimpsed amusement at the dirty-cheeked boy.

"I've got nothing to say." He scowled up at us. "Rich folk got enough to spare."

"That may be so, but stealing isn't the way to go about it. You know, not long ago, you could lose a hand for thieving."

"That ain't the first time I've been told that." He used the back of his hand to wipe away the snot trickling to his upper lip.

"Perhaps you should listen."

"When the ache in my belly is gone, then I'll listen. Not that you would know anything about that." The boy settled his dark eyes on me. "Living in your fancy houses with servants waiting on ya. A warm fire and tables overflowing with food. No, I ain't feeling the least bit sorry for ya."

I regarded the fire in the boy's eyes and his dislike for two strangers. "What is your name?"

"Who's asking?" He craned his neck and peered up at me.

"My name is Katherine, but my friends call me Kat."

"Why you wanting to know?" He swiped a hand to move the flap of straight, raven hair away from his right eye. "We ain't friends."

"No, that we are not," I said. "But you tried to steal my reticule. I believe you owe me a moment of your time."

"I don't owe you nothing." He scowled. "And I ain't saying nothing 'til your friend here releases me."

I glanced at Merritt, and he nodded. He freed the boy, and although I expected him to make a run for it, he didn't.

He eyed Merritt suspiciously before looking at me. "Name's Ling."

"How old are you, Ling?"

He frowned as if pondering. "I don't know. I had my last birthday when my parents were alive. And that was four winters ago. I was eight then, so I guess that makes me twelve."

"Your parents are gone?"

He nodded, and his face pinched with longing. "Cholera took them. Been on the streets since."

My heart went out to the boy and the gravity of his loss. His eyes widened as he looked behind me, and when he looked ready to dash away, I gripped his arm. "Please wait."

"Kat, we've been looking for you everywhere," Evelyn said breathlessly.

I glanced behind me as she and the rest of my family dashed toward us, along with the young woman I recognized as Merritt's sister.

"Merritt, you gave me a fright, running off like that." She rushed to his side.

"My apologies, but I saw Miss Katherine chasing young Ling here, and I thought she may need my assistance."

"Why the chase?" Papa regarded my grip on Ling.

"Ling finds himself in need."

"What you mean is, he attempted to rob you." Evelyn narrowed her eyes at the boy.

"Let me go. I ain't gonna stand here and be insulted." Ling rolled back his shoulders and leveled an even glare at Evelyn.

"Yet you insult my sister and family by stealing from us," Evelyn said.

"Enough, Evelyn," I said, inserting myself between her and Ling. I rested my hands on his narrow shoulders. "I need to speak to my father, and I ask that you stay just a moment longer."

"Why should I? I see how she looks at me. Like I'm nothing but slop thrown out into the street. I am Ling Shen. Son of Hao and Min Shen. I come from a proud family—"

"Yes, yes, I can tell," I said with a smile. "Maybe I can help you."

His eyes widened, and hope shone in his face before he concealed it. "All right. I'll give you a minute, and that's all."

"Thank you," I said and turned back to my family. "Papa, please, may I have a word?"

He obligingly walked with me until we were out of earshot of the others.

"What is it?"

"I wonder if we may offer Ling a position in our household."

He opened his mouth to speak, and I held up a hand. "Hear me out. The boy lost his family some years back and has been forced to survive on the streets. He is a proud boy with heart and spunk. He deserves a chance at life."

"And you have had this epiphany in the mere minutes you've known him?"

"All paths cross for a reason. Mama taught me that. She also taught me that helping others is a noble thing to do."

Papa's eyes glittered. "She was too good for this world."

"There is good here if we but look. Why have we been blessed with plenty if we aren't to help those in need?"

"I've never considered you a good Samaritan, although you are good at heart."

"Yes, there is truth in your words. I've spent years trying to avoid my stepmother and trying to secure some sort of happiness. I grew weary of being angry and on guard. With our return to the city and walking into a time capsule of the past, I'm reminded of what Mama stood for: kindness and charity. I feel we can help Ling."

"What are you suggesting?"

"We give him a position in the kitchen or the stables. We see what skills best suit him and pay him a fair wage. Offer him an education."

He raised a brow.

"I will take full responsibility for him." When he didn't seem convinced, I continued to plead my case. "I know the pain of losing a mother, but I am not alone. Ling is. No child deserves that."

Papa used two fingers to rub the bridge of his nose. "All right, daughter. We will employ the boy, but you will take full responsibility for him."

I grinned and nodded. "Thank you, Papa." I leaned in and pulled his head down to kiss his cheek.

"God help me, but I am hopeless when it comes to you all."

We walked back to the others, and I took Ling's arm and pulled him aside. "I have a proposition for you."

"What's that?"

He looked past me as Evelyn blurted, "You can't possibly be considering having a thief in our home. I won't have it."

"Evelyn, silence yourself," Papa said.

"Ignore her." I kept my eyes trained on him. "She is unruly most times, but at the core of her is goodness. A bit spoiled, is all."

His face softened, and the mask of defiance and strength he feigned for the world vanished.

"I asked my father if we could give you a position in our

household. You would have a warm place to sleep, food in your belly, and we would pay you a fair wage."

He gawked at me before tears welled. "Why are you doing this?"

"Because I know what it is like to lose someone you love. I believe you have a purpose; if you had a choice, you wouldn't be thieving."

He dropped his head. "My mother said, no matter how poor we got, we weren't to take what didn't belong to us."

"Listen…" I gripped his chin, and he looked at me "…there's no dishonor in trying to survive. Your parents would be proud of you for surviving this long. I like to believe our loved ones are always watching over us."

A silent tear slid down his hollow, dirty cheek.

"What do you say to coming home with us?"

He gulped and nodded.

"There is one condition."

He stiffened. "What's that?"

"You will receive a proper education, and we will see to it. My sister is a lover of books, and we have a library bursting with books on subjects dating back centuries."

He brightened. "My father worked on the railroad, and my mother was a laundress, but in China, my mother's father was a *shi*—a scholar. My father's father was an artisan before the war and famine came, and they decided to come to America in hopes of finding wealth in the gold rush. M-my…" his voice clotted "…parents always dreamed of me having an education."

"And an education you shall have," I said with a smile. "Come, let's join the others."

We returned to my family and the Huntingtons. Thankfully, Evelyn had composed herself. I introduced my family to Ling, and all but my oldest sister welcomed him warmly. Evelyn nodded politely but didn't waste any words on the boy.

"I thank you for your aid in helping my family gain a new

friend," I said to Merritt, and encircled Ling's shoulders with an arm.

"It is an admirable deed you are doing."

"Everyone deserves a place to call home," I said. "With a proper education, perhaps Ling here will outsmart my sister Adelaide."

Ling offered a wary grin.

I regarded the woman standing next to Merritt. "I have yet to have the honor of making your acquaintance."

"I am Josie." She thrust out a small hand, and I took it.

"I'm Kat. And this is my family." I nodded in their direction. "And this is our beloved governess and friend, Miss Dorotea Ruiz."

"Señorita. S nor." Dorotea curtsied.

"How do you do?" Jose nodded in greeting.

A few more words were exchanged before we said our goodbyes.

"Kat," Merritt said, and I halted. "If you will give me but a moment more of your time."

"You go along with the family," I instructed Ling, and he obediently jogged after them. "What is it?"

"I received your request."

"Oh…" I said, surprised at my lapse in memory. "And what do you say?"

"I will loan you the money. I usually would ask what the money is for, but something tells me you wouldn't be forthcoming."

"Well, I am in the spirit of giving, and I will take a leap of faith in our developing acquaintance," I said, "and divulge why I requested your help. I seek to hire a private investigator to learn more about my stepmother and her comings and goings."

His brow rose.

"Before you judge me, she is a despicable woman, and the invasion of her privacy is not an honor you should defend."

"Am I to assume your father doesn't know?"

"I did ask, but didn't tell him what I needed the money for, and he declined."

He reached into his coat and withdrew his leather pocketbook. He extracted some banknotes and discreetly gave them to me.

"Outside of repayment, I am not committed to you in any form," I said.

"Understood and agreed." He held out a hand, and I clasped it. Our fingers lingered before I pulled my hand away. "I appreciate your service. I shall never forget this."

We strolled over to where Miss Josie waited for us, and she eyed me with curiosity. She seemed likable, with a gentle kindness.

"I am delighted we could meet again. And on terms not as dismal as the last," she said.

I nodded.

"Maybe we can have a luncheon one day? Any friend of my brother is a friend of mine." She patted his arm and regarded him with affection. I sensed their closeness. Alice and Grace shared a bond similar to that of the Huntington siblings.

"I'd best be going. I need to catch up with my family." I glanced their way; they had gathered around a vendor's stall, inspecting his goods.

"Merry Christmas, Kat." Merritt touched the brim of his hat.

"Merry Christmas," I said with a smile and nod.

Warmth rushed over me, and my heart rejoiced as I turned and hurried to catch up with my family.

Chapter 23

S NOW GATHERED IN THE CORNERS OF THE FROSTED WINDOWPANES on Christmas Eve. Outside, the storm howled and blanketed the boardwalks, steps, and landings in white. Tree limbs hung heavy with snow, and the spirit of Christmas infused the night.

Chef Bernard had spent months planning a decadent Parisian meal consisting of oysters served with lemon and a shallot mignonette, foie gras, cheeses, toasts au saumon, capon stuffed with water chestnuts, and a creamy chestnut soup with winter vegetables. After the meal, we retired to the music room with our bellies stuffed and satisfied.

The fire cracked and snapped as Papa stoked the smoldering coals and threw on another log. Alice and Grace lay on their tummies, alternating between playing marbles and spinning tops. Papa returned to his seat across from Adelaide, who had challenged him to a chess game. She eyed the board with satisfaction, her fingers steepled under her chin. Papa's eyes narrowed as he studied the board and then her, as though trying to figure out her strategy.

Audrey had arrived at the evening meal, her eyes hazed from laudanum, and she insulted the chef with every bite. She sat in a chair sipping brandy, her speech slurred, but her grumbles faded into the background, just as she had, with Papa's return to our lives.

I sat on the settee with Evelyn, cross-stitching, and added my own protests as my stitching turned out all wrong. "Ow!" I pricked my finger and quickly pressed it to my lips.

"Here, let me see," Evelyn said before delivering unwanted advice on stitching correctly.

I couldn't embroider like her and Adelaide; even Alice had picked up the knack more easily than I. Their impeccable workmanship would've made Mama beam with pride, but mine always turned out misshapen, leaving me frustrated. Evelyn blamed my lack of mastery on my left-handedness, but I silently believed my inability stemmed from my lack of interest in tedious women's pastimes.

"Checkmate," Adelaide said with an unsportsmanlike squeal.

"What? Where?" Papa leaned forward and rested his elbows on either side of the chessboard.

Adelaide pointed in all the directions she had cornered his king, and he slumped back in his chair and threw his hands into the air. "You reign as the undefeated champion."

Adelaide grinned at his praise, and Evelyn and I clapped.

"Bravo! Bravo!" Evelyn feigned a French accent.

"Oh, please, Evelyn." Audrey slumped in her chair and waved her glass around. "You are no more French than I. Drop the façade."

"Wife." Papa rose and walked to her side. "Why don't you go up to your chamber and rest? You look ready to collapse." He reached for the snifter, and she pulled it away and placed the glass to her lips. She drained the liquid and slammed the glass down on the side table.

"Enough," Papa said through gritted teeth. "Don't think I didn't smell the alcohol on your breath at the Goddard social. No wife of mine will be known as a tippling woman."

The domestic drinking of women was on the rise, and a grave topic with men. I had overheard a group of gentlemen commenting on Audrey's drunkenness at the Goddard ball.

"Wife?" she scoffed. "I am hardly a wife. You never visit my chamber or engage with me as a husband should a wife."

Papa hauled her up by the arm and guided her toward the door. "You will watch your tongue in front of the children."

"Phillip, darling, please." Audrey attempted to charm his fury. "I will do as you say, but won't you lie with me for but a moment?"

They left the room, and her pleas turned to weeping.

Stillness had blanketed the room, and no one dared breathe. I gawked at the empty doorway, and my heart thumped in my throat. Audrey's affliction had become more apparent with our return to the city. I often pitied her, but all empathy vanished when she became belligerent, and cruelty and malice streamed from her lips.

"Alice, Grace," Adelaide said. "Go back to playing your game. Everything will be all right."

"Yes." Evelyn feigned cheeriness with a clap of her hands. "It is Christmas. We will have no droopy faces. After Papa returns, he will read "A Visit from St. Nicholas" as he always used to do when Mama was alive. Then he will give us a special present."

Grace, too young to remember Mama, looked at Evelyn as though drawing on her memory.

"I scarcely remember Mama," Alice said.

I laid my hopeless stitching aside and stood. "Tonight we will honor all her favorite things. Remember, although she is gone, she remains in here." I pointed to my heart.

Evelyn smiled at me. "Yes, Kat is right."

"Gone but not forgotten," Papa said, entering the room.

Grace and Alice scrambled to their feet and raced to his side to wrap their arms around his middle. "Is everything all right, Papa?" Alice regarded him with a concerned expression.

"Do not fret, my sweet Alice."

"Will Mother be all right?" Grace asked.

"Nothing a good rest won't cure." He dabbed her nose. "Now, where is the book of Christmas tales?"

Grace darted across the room to get it.

Someone cleared their throat, and we all turned to regard Ling, cleaned up and looking dapper in the new clothes assigned to him. He held a platter of Christmas delicacies. Behind him stood Chef Bernard, eager to train his new pupil.

"Shoulders back, Monsieur Shen. Walk with dignity. Remember to take pride in what you have created. Food is love and an extension of our culture. We Parisians flatter ourselves by portraying passion through our food. It is a work of art."

"But I'm Chinese," Ling said over his shoulder, and I stifled a giggle.

"Go on, now. Don't hesitate." The chef placed a hand on the boy's shoulder.

Ling nodded and strode forward, the tray wobbling.

"Steady." Chef followed on his heels with a tray of steaming mugs.

Ling released a deep breath and rolled back his slender shoulders, and each step became certain. I smiled, my chest swelling with pride.

Ling set the platter down and straightened. He regarded Chef Bernard, who nodded for him to continue. Ling gestured at each item. "You have candied chestnuts, Yule log, and spiced bread."

Chef Bernard beamed, and Ling grinned and moved to stand out of the way. Chef Bernard's grandiose personality didn't allow for two chefs in the kitchen or in the same room. He stepped forward with assurance bordering on the whimsical, and placed the tray on the table beside the sweets. "Chocolat chaud for the ladies." He turned to Papa as we reached for the mugs of frothy cocoa. "And if you would like, monsieur, I can pour you some mulled wine."

"Much appreciated, Chef. But I will pass. You have outdone yourself, and my family offers our gratitude," Papa said.

We murmured thanks and giggled at the foamy mustaches lining Grace and Alice's mouths.

Chef Bernard grinned, revealing the wide gap between his front teeth, and bowed at the waist. "Your joy is the greatest compliment. Merci. Joyeux Noël." He spun to walk away, signaling Ling to follow.

I set my mug down. "Chef Bernard."

"Mademoiselle?"

"Could you bring one more mug of hot chocolate?"

"Oui, but for whom?"

"For Ling." I glanced at Papa, and he nodded. Then, I looked to Ling, who stood with his mouth agape. "My family would be honored if you would join us. What do you say?"

He glanced at Chef Bernard as though seeking permission.

"The Darlingtons are the ones you answer to when you are not in my kitchen. If the family requests your company, then you accept."

Ling looked back at me. "I accept."

"Splendid." I clapped my hands together.

"You can sit with us." Grace took his hand and led him to the floor in front of Papa's chair.

Papa settled in his chair, the young girls and Ling on the floor, and we three older sisters on the settee across from him. After the chef returned and everyone had a mug in hand, we waited with anticipation for Papa to begin.

He opened the book and cleared his throat before his rich, husky voice brought the author's imagination to life.

'Twas the night before Christmas, when all through the house
Not a creature was stirring, not even a mouse;
The stockings were hung by the chimney with care,
In hopes that St. Nicholas soon would be there;
The children were nestled all snug in their beds,
While visions of sugar-plums danced in their heads;
And mamma in her 'kerchief, and I in my cap,
Had just settled our brains for a long winter's nap,

When out on the lawn there arose such a clatter,
I sprang from the bed to see what was the matter.
Away to the window I flew like a flash,
Tore open the shutters and threw up the sash.
The moon on the breast of the new-fallen snow
Gave the luster of midday to objects below,
When, what to my wondering eyes should appear,
But a miniature sleigh, and eight tiny reindeer,
With a little old driver, so lively and quick,
I knew in a moment it must be St. Nick.
More rapid than eagles his coursers they came,
And he whistled, and shouted, and called them by name;
"Now, Dasher! now, Dancer! now, Prancer and Vixen!
On, Comet! on, Cupid! on, Donder and Blitzen!
To the top of the porch! To the top of the wall!
Now dash away! dash away! dash away all!"
As dry leaves that before the wild hurricane fly,
When they meet with an obstacle, mount to the sky;
So up to the house-top the coursers they flew,
With the sleigh full of Toys, and St. Nicholas too.
And then, in a twinkling, I heard on the roof
The prancing and pawing of each little hoof.
As I drew in my head, and was turning around,
Down the chimney St. Nicholas came with a bound.
He was dressed all in fur, from his head to his foot,
And his clothes were all tarnished with ashes and soot;
A bundle of toys he had flung on his back,
And he looked like a peddler just opening his pack.
His eyes—how they twinkled! His dimples how merry!
His cheeks were like roses, his nose like a cherry!
His droll little mouth was drawn up like a bow
And the beard of his chin was as white as the snow;
The stump of a pipe he held tight in his teeth,
And the smoke it encircled his head like a wreath;

He had a broad face and a little round belly,
That shook when he laughed, like a bowlful of jelly.
He was chubby and plump, a right jolly old elf,
And I laughed when I saw him, in spite of myself;
A wink of his eye and a twist of his head,
Soon gave me to know I had nothing to dread;
He spoke not a word, but went straight to his work,
And filled all the stockings; then turned with a jerk,
And laying his finger aside of his nose,
And giving a nod, up the chimney he rose;
He sprang to his sleigh, to his team gave a whistle,
And away they all flew like the down of a thistle,
But I heard him exclaim, ere he drove out of sight,
"Happy Christmas to all, and to all a good-night."

We broke from our trance as Papa finished the last word. Gloom rushed over me, for in those few precious moments, the turmoil in our home had evaporated, and enchantment had swept us away.

Papa closed the book and rested it on his lap. My sisters and I went to embrace him. Then he rose and regarded us with tear-filled eyes. "What a blessed Christmas this is. I've spent years missing your mother and failed to see she lives on inside of all of you. She may be gone, but she left me the most precious gift: daughters who embody all the good she offered the world. In each of you, a piece of her lives on."

My eyes blurred. He honored us with a statement that would live on in all our hearts.

I regarded Ling, who hung back, appearing awkward and uncertain.

"What did you and your parents do for Christmas, Ling?" Grace asked.

"The Chinese people don't celebrate Christmas. My parents said it is a European and American tradition."

"How dreadful," Evelyn said. "To never have Christmas is like never learning to walk."

"Hardly dreadful. Many cultures don't celebrate our traditions but have splendid ones of their own," Adelaide said. "The Chinese have many beautiful, meaningful festivals. The Lantern Festival, Winter Solstice, and Chinese moon festival, to name a few. Isn't that so, Ling?"

He stood regarding her in awe, as though she were a walking encyclopedia, and most days, I believed she was.

"Yes, Miss Darlington. My parents often spoke of their home country and its traditions. But I haven't experienced them myself, being born in America."

"If you don't run off on us, perhaps we can find books on your traditions, and you can be the orchestrator of bringing Chinese culture to life in America," Adelaide said.

Ling grinned and bobbed his head. "I'd like that very much."

"Then it is settled. We will learn together."

And just like that, Chef Bernard lost his hold on his pupil, and I lost my ward, because after that day, Ling became Adelaide's shadow. They pored over endless books until the midnight hour. How much knowledge could a brain retain, I wondered days later when I discovered them in the library, asleep and face down on the books splayed across the table.

Chapter 24

Jude

CHRISTMAS PASSED, AND NEW YEAR'S CELEBRATIONS CONSUMED the week leading up to the new year. At the end of the week I would return to school. Ironically, I would consider my return a reprieve.

Our neighbors, the Abrahams, were hosting their annual New Year celebration. As I descended the stairs garbed in white tie and black tailcoat for the event, the door knocker thudded, and I strode to the door and opened it, and my breath caught.

"What are you doing here?"

Bundled in furs and muffs, a rosy-cheeked Kat stood with Miss Ruiz on the landing. They were hunkered inside their outerwear to stay warm.

"Come in." I moved aside. They stepped inside, and I closed the door. "To what do I owe the pleasure?" My heart sang with pleasure at the sight of her. The dark tendrils framing her face had frozen in the frosty evening air. Melted snowflakes glistened on her furs and cheeks. Exhilaration charged through me. God help me, but she was a vision to behold.

"It appears you are going out." Kat gestured at my evening attire. "You look dashing."

"Well, thank you, Miss Darlington," I said with a grin, and executed a bow. "To catch your eye is an honor."

She giggled and swatted a hand in the air, pretending to quash my flirtation. Merriment danced in her eyes. The holiday season was complete with her presence; bliss washed over me.

Another rap sounded on the door, and I frowned.

"That is Mr. Kelly, my coachman." She walked to the door, opened it, and ushered him in, in her take-charge way.

He peeked around the stack of boxes wrapped in uniquely colorful paper, bright ribbons, and tinsel cords. More luxury stores were putting their mark on gift wrapping, reflecting material wealth and status.

"Go ahead and set them down right there." Kat pointed to a corner in the entrance hall. After he had followed her orders, she thanked him. "We shouldn't be but a few minutes."

"Yes, Miss Kat," he said. "Sir." He dipped his head at me on his way by.

"Happy New Year." I returned his nod.

"And to ye." The coachman opened the door, and a gust of wind sent a skimmer of powdered snow across the floor.

"This wasn't necessary." I turned back to Kat and Miss Ruiz after he left.

"Perhaps not, but it was an excuse to catch a glimpse of my best friend before he returns to school." She peered up at me through thick, dark lashes and offered a small, tentative smile. My throat tightened. "I had hoped we'd find time between busy social engagements to spend time in each other's company."

"Why are you not celebrating this New Year's Eve with your family?"

"Because they have gone to the Goddard's New Year celebration in New Port, and my invitation was recanted after my behavior at their Christmas ball."

My mouth dropped open.

She waved a hand. "I care not. The last one was a bore…" Her gaze drifted. "For the most part, anyway."

"They recanted your invitation, you say? How did they go about that?" I bristled at the audacity.

"In a roundabout way. They had Birdie deliver the message. But don't concern yourself on my behalf; I wasn't the least bit offended. On the contrary, I was relieved, in fact. And so was my dear older sister," she said smugly.

I laughed and shook my head. "You never cease to surprise me, Kat Darlington. You're one to always keep a person on their toes."

She grinned, amused at my delight in her shenanigans.

"I return to school in two days, but maybe tomorrow I could spare some time for a dear friend."

"You simply must make time. I won't take no for an answer," she said with a light stomp of her foot.

"When have you ever?" I said with a laugh, immensely enjoying the feisty lioness before me. She had always amused me with her fiery ways and uncaged tongue.

She shrugged, but a smile pulled at the corners of her mouth.

"Miss Darlington, Miss Ruiz, what a delight," Mother said from the landing above. Dressed in a peacock green satin gown, she descended the staircase.

"Good evening, Mrs. Williams." Kat shifted to examine her. "You look lovely."

"Thank you, my dear." Mother leaned in and kissed each of her cheeks.

"Señora Williams, it has been a long time." Miss Ruiz curtsied.

Mother embraced her. "Too long."

"How are you, my dear?" Mother gently gripped Kat's wrist.

"I am well."

"I had hoped we'd have seen you and your family this holiday season."

"Yes, I too wished, but with our late return to the city, we found little time for anything before the holiday season was upon us."

"Well, here you are. I reckon that will suffice." Mother regarded her with affection. "What brings you out here?"

Kat gestured at the gifts.

"Oh!" Mother touched her throat. "You shouldn't have."

"A small gesture of my affection," Kat said.

"Much appreciated," Mother said. "I'm afraid we are about to step out. We are to attend an event at the Abrahams' next door."

"How lovely. I noticed carriages arriving," Kat said. "A regal lady with a Southern drawl and her family appear to be guests. I couldn't help but notice her accent when she hurried her family inside. Not much for the cold, I presume." Her eyes twinkled with amusement at the Southerner's misery.

"The cold does take some getting used to," Mother said. "I longed for the mild winters of the South. It took Thomas and me years to acclimatize. I never thought I could get used to the bite that cuts right through your shoes and outerwear. That said, I will never get used to being a New Yorker. I do miss the South." Her expression grew nostalgic.

Kat hung on Mother's every word, giving Mother her undivided attention, as though what she had to say mattered beyond all else. Kat had a way of making others feel that they mattered. She never wavered and offered undying loyalty when you were lucky enough to win her trust and affection.

"I reckon I miss the hospitality and the warmth most of all." A smile transformed Mother's yearning gaze, and she touched Kat's arm. "Don't let me keep you. Please convey our good wishes to your father and sisters."

"I will." Kat turned and smiled at me before making her way to the door. "Ensure you come by before you leave."

I nodded and showed them out.

Kat spun back to look at me and said in a low voice, as though not wanting to let the guests arriving next door hear, "I forgot to tell you. I've decided to hire a private investigator."

Miss Ruiz gasped, and Kat glanced at her briefly before brushing off the woman's surprise.

"What for?" I said.

"Why, to spy on my stepmother, of course," she said with a smirk.

My eyes widened. "What are you plotting now?"

"Do tell us, señorita." Miss Ruiz stepped from Kat's shadow into the light, pressed her lips together, and waited for an explanation.

"I am at my wit's end with her disruption of my family and her threats. So I decided I would find out more about where she disappears, hoping to uncover something scathing that would give reasonable cause for Papa to divorce her."

"Am I to assume your father is fine with the plan?"

"He does not know." Mischievousness twinkled in her whiskey-brown eyes. "Without telling him what I needed funds for, I asked, and he declined, so I went elsewhere."

I folded my arms. "Do you care to enlighten me?"

"I asked Mr. Huntington."

Miss Ruiz gasped.

"Huntington? I do not know him," I said.

"No, I suppose not. Only in recent months did I meet him myself."

My chest tightened as her expression softened, and I suppressed a twinge of jealousy. "When I come by, I expect a full account of what you have been scheming."

"Hardly scheming. It's called gaining the upper hand. I will no longer be subjected to Audrey's threats, nor see her harm my family. Papa's happiness is at stake." She delivered Miss Ruiz a strange look, and the woman squirmed under her gaze. I never prided myself on women's secret language, but the pair's understanding was apparent. "Until then, good evening, my friend." She held out her gloved fingers.

I took her hand and kissed her fingers. "Until then," I said with a smile and released her.

She nodded before looping arms with Miss Ruiz. As they walked down the stairs, Kat said, "You mustn't tell Papa what I said about the investigator. It must remain our secret."

"But—"

"No buts. You must promise me."

"Very well, señorita. I know there's no use attempting to convince you otherwise once you have made up your mind."

Kat squared her shoulders and held her head higher. "I knew I could count on you." She released Miss Ruiz and strode past Mr. Kelly, who waited by the carriage's open door. Kat disappeared inside.

Miss Ruiz shook her head and mumbled something in Spanish, and Mr. Kelly chuckled.

I stood allowing the inside to heat the outdoors as I waited for their carriage to pull away. I glanced at the carriages congesting the street as drivers dropped off guests in front of the Abrahams'.

As the Darlington carriage lurched forward, Kat's face appeared in the window, and she waved.

I smiled and waved before closing the door and turning to discover Mother had remained behind me. "Your love for Miss Katherine is as apparent as that neck on your shoulders."

"I assure you it isn't."

"And I am a woman not easily convinced by the foolery of men. A blind man could sense the feelings you hold for the young lady."

"And this troubles you?"

She swept forward. "She is a lovely woman, with a spirit to match. I cherish the Darlington family. You know this. But others may not take kindly to a mulatto man with eyes for a white woman. For heaven's sake, even the census is broken down into how much Black blood is in a person."

Mother bore no prejudice for any human, but she craved a more just world. So, long before I'd read my first census, she'd educated me on the five categories of the census: white, Black, Chinese, Indian, and the focus on mulattos, right down to a person holding a mere drop of Black blood.

"Prejudice didn't stop you and Father," I said.

"No, it didn't." Father descended the stairs. "Nor should it, you." Pride for his family shone in his gentle eyes. "My darling." He pecked my mother's cheek before clapping my shoulder.

Mother gave him a half-smile, but her eyes reflected concern. "Forgive me, but I worry. I have only one child, and I want to save him from all hardship. However, I am sane enough to understand that it is impossible, and our love put the yoke upon your neck from the moment you were conceived."

"You carry unnecessary guilt." I wrapped my arm around her shoulders and kissed the top of her head. "I am grown. I can navigate this world with all its misguided hate and prejudices in all aspects. Times are changing, and fear of what was and the worry of returning to what was will only cause more tumult and malice. As a biracial man, I know how the world views me, but I seek to do my part to change that for all future generations."

"I know you will, darling. We need more people like you. I don't mean to put a damper on the evening. I just don't want any harm to befall you or the Darlington woman. People are disgruntled about white folks coming here, let alone living here." She pulled away. "I doubt I will ever see peace and unity between us in my lifetime. But, as outlandish as it may seem, like Mrs. Abraham, I too dream of a world for my grandchildren where we judge each other by acts of the heart and not by prestige, heritage, or the color of one's skin."

"I have faith in humanity." Father slipped on his overcoat.

"However, I don't have as much faith in our son finding a wife to give us grandchildren."

I laughed and went to retrieve my coat. "I will marry when the time is right."

"So you consider it?"

"Of course he does, dear husband. Your son and I have had several conversations about him finding a wife."

"A son who loves his mother and confides in her, not his father." He winked at me while regarding Mother. "Tell me, wife, is Miss Scott a contender?"

Miss Scott had assisted Father in his practice, and my parents had helped pay for her to go to New York Medical College and Hospital for Women. She had all the qualities a man would seek in a wife, but Kat had held my affection since we were children.

"She is a fine woman," Father added.

"You can't force love," Mother interceded. "If so, Pa would've made me wed our neighbor, who smelled as sour as a privy on a hot July day." She curled up her nose. "He was old enough to be my grandfather but had land and slaves, so Pa deemed him a suitable husband."

Father's cheerful disposition wavered at Mother mentioning my grandfather, whom I'd never met, nor cared to. "My father-in-law considered anyone a more worthy suitor over a poor Black man." He pulled Mother close and kissed her tenderly. "I'm happy his daughter dared to defy him."

"I second that," I said. "Now, enough from you two, or we will be late."

Papa released her and placed his hat on his head. "Miss Scott is invited tonight."

"And I will be cordial, as always," I said. "But I won't have you or Mother interfering. Arranged marriages are becoming a thing of the past in America, and rightfully so." I gave them a warning look before opening the door and offering Mother my arm.

The orchestra's melody and the mirth of guests greeted us

as the Abrahams' butler received us inside and took our outer-wear. Mrs. Abraham strode toward us with widespread arms. "Welcome." She embraced Mother. "You look lovely."

"As do you." Mother admired Mrs. Abraham's emerald green gown with black embroidery. "Is that dress from the Parisian designer Charles Frederick Worth's collection?"

"Yes." Mrs. Abraham beamed and spun for Mother's inspection.

"Magnificent. Truly a vision," Mother said with awe.

"Indeed," Father said.

Mrs. Abraham's eyes danced with pleasure. "Come. I want you all to meet some of my guests."

We followed her into the parlor, congested with people I recognized from our community. Miss Scott, in a garnet-colored silk gown, stood conversing with a younger, lighter-complected Black man, who appeared to be quite mesmerized by her. She glanced at me as my family and I entered, and I inclined my head in greeting. She smiled, and her body swayed ever so slightly.

Mrs. Abraham steered us toward the only White people in the room besides Mother. Mr. Abraham was conversing with the white man, who shook his head and regarded him with keen respect. The white woman touched the older Black man's arm and laughed, and he peered at her as a father would, with devotion and love.

The guests murmured amongst themselves and eyed them uncertainly.

"What was Ruby thinking, inviting them, of all people?" a woman leaned in and whispered to another gentleman. "We've got no place for Southerners here. It's bad enough we have to put up with the stain of that Williams woman. Before you know it, the whites will take over our community too. It shows that despite Ruby being one of us, her loyalty remains with the white parents who raised her."

The gentleman patted her arm. "Hush now, my dear. We don't want to insult our hosts."

I narrowed my eyes at them for the remark about my mother, and catching my awareness of their idle chatter, they shifted to regard Miss Scott and the young man.

Mrs. Abraham paused beside the Southern group, and they parted to make room for our arrival. "Everyone, I'd like you to meet my friends and neighbors. This is Dr. Williams, his wife Ellen Williams, and their son Jude." Mrs. Abraham glanced at us. "I would like you to meet my dearest friends, Willow and Bowden Armstrong. And this…" She stepped into the middle of the group and wrapped an arm around the weathered gentleman's waist, her face glowing with affection. "This is my father, James."

Her father shifted with apprehension when all eyes turned to him, but he held out his hand, and I clasped it. "Nice to meet you, sir," I said.

"My son-in-law tole me how you gwine to be a lawyer and what you aim to do after dey give ya dat dere piece of paper."

I smiled at the charm of the man's straightforwardness. "Did he, now?" I glanced at Mr. Abraham, and he grinned.

"Times sho' are changin', and et 'bout time." James beamed as though he had a stake in my future. "Young folkses lak you be de way of de future. Pittin' one man against de other ain't de way. Wid ambition and no fear, you can stand against de injustices. Bitterness only breeds more resentment, and in de end, we all lose."

Warmth surged in my chest at this man's wisdom, and I regarded him with great respect. I was aware from Mrs. Abraham's stories that her father had been born into slavery and remained so until emancipation. The deep crevices etching his face told of a life of hardship and sorrow, but his eyes blazed with a passion for life. He had survived what I could only imagine, yet he stood without malice and contempt, hopeful for change and unity. I recollected my mother's words in the coffee house some months back: *"For out of hardships, heroes are born."* My throat tightened as I absorbed the spirit of the man before me, and I felt a deep sense of honor. He had borne the brutality and iniquity meted out by the greedy and the powerful. Yet his words and actions revealed he did not live in the past. Therefore, no one could master him, and in every sense of the word, he was indeed…free.

"There is much truth in your words," I said. "People's actions and beliefs prove that, often unknowingly, we place shackles around our wrists regardless of our parentage and ancestors, and so we are mastered by our experiences and chained to the past. In doing so, we make our experiences our oppressors."

"Wisdom beyond your years. You are our promise of a better tomorrow," Mr. Armstrong said reverently before glancing at Ruby's father with the same respect. "James is indeed a wise man. I have sought his counsel many times in my life." He returned his attention to me and eyed me with all sincerity. "I urge you to use our mistakes as your compass and lead us into a future not stained by our transgressions. Men in places of influence with a vision like yours are our hope."

"Well said, my friend." Mr. Abraham clapped Mr. Armstrong on the back.

Mr. Armstrong regarded Father and nudged his head at the young man speaking with Miss Scott. "Saul mentioned his neighbor was a doctor. Our son, Sailor, will be attending medical school."

"You don't say." Father shifted to eye the man across the room.

I wondered how the couple had a biracial son, being previous slave owners and all. However, before I could pass judgment, Mrs. Armstrong leaned closer to my mother and said, "One of my dearest friends is his birth mother, but he won my heart from the day I discovered him on my doorstep. Miss Rita, the woman who raised me after my mother's death and in my father's absence, and Jimmy here taught me that love knows no bounds. Sadly, our beliefs put conditions on the heart's ability to love and how love should be given. We can't imagine life without our son, and I thank God every day for sending him to us. For he has been a blessing in our lives, and it grieves me to let him go off to school." I recognized the doting love of a mother in her expression.

"I understand all too well," Mother said, placing her hand in the crook of my arm. "Our Jude leaves again in a few days. I always count the days until his next visit."

"She'd keep me under her roof until I'm an old man if she could," I said with a chuckle.

Mrs. Armstrong's eyes glistened, and she said in a heavy Southern drawl, "I reckon I would do the same, but a bird can't fly if they can't discover their wings."

"This I know, but it is a struggle nonetheless," Mother said.

"Indeed." Mrs. Armstrong nodded.

"Would anyone care for champagne?" Miss Mercy, the Abrahams' young daughter, arrived with a pewter platter of flute glasses. I took a second gander at her, almost not recognizing her with her hair swept up in a grown woman's style and wearing an eye-catching mauve silk gown. She eyed me with interest, and I looked away, not wanting to give the impressionable girl a misguided interpretation of my lingering gaze.

My attention went to the corridor and the staircase where two white children, a girl and a younger boy, perched, peering through the balusters at the guests. The boy pointed at the refreshment table and said something to the girl. She swatted at his arm, pulled it back through the railing, and appeared to scold him. I smiled and excused myself before walking to the refreshment table and collecting an assortment of candies.

I strode into the corridor. "Well, hello there," I said, and they pulled back, the girl wrapping a protective arm around the boy's shoulder. "I come in peace." I held out my peace offering. "Why aren't you joining the other guests?"

"Because Mama says we are too young," the girl said softly.

"I see. Is your mama Mrs. Armstrong?"

"No. She is Mama." The blond-haired boy wriggled from the girl's grip and stood up. His chin barely reached the banister. "I am James. And that is Olive." He pointed a chubby finger at his sister while his blue-green eyes, identical to his father's, eyed the napkin full of sweets. "Are those for us?"

His sister held back but also regarded the napkin. I extended the offering, and the boy took a chocolate and quickly placed it in his mouth.

"James, mind your manners." Olive tapped him on the shoulder, never taking her eyes off me.

"T-thank you, mister," he said with his mouth full.

Olive frowned with displeasure, and I moved the treats closer for her. She timidly took one. "Thank you, sir," she said with a small smile. Her eyes widened with delight as she took a bite of the chocolate and swiped a string of caramel from her lip.

Young James's eyes asked permission to take another, and I nodded. He grinned, and his pearly whites chomped down on the chocolate. "Granny Rita makes good chocolate just like this. But Grandpa John and her took a boat to see her grandchildren this Christmas."

"We miss her." Miss Olive's shoulders slumped at the mention of her grandparents. "Mama says we have to share with Mary Grace and her family. But home isn't the same without Granny."

"Mama can't cook like Granny can," James said solemnly. "And Grandpa John tells good stories."

"No, Grandpa Jimmy is better," Olive said.

"No." James frowned up at her.

"Well, it seems like you have lots of storytelling to go around," I said with amusement at the sibling rivalry.

Olive glanced past me, and her face came alive. "Miss Scott!"

"Hello again, Miss Olive and Mr. James," Miss Scott said with a tender smile at the children as I shifted to regard her.

"This is our new friend. Mister…what is your name?" James looked up at me with a knitted brow.

"Jude Williams," I said.

"I know your friend." Miss Scott glanced at the napkin holding the last of the chocolates. "Does your new friend bribe his friends with candy?" Merriment danced in her large brown eyes. Miss Scott was a soft-spoken woman, but the torch of passion flickered in her, and I understood her to be a woman of purpose and commitment to matters that held her interest.

"No," I said with a grin. "But I couldn't allow my new friends to miss out on all the festivities."

"Miss Scott is going to be a doctor one day." Olive moved closer to the railing. "Grandpa Ben is a doctor."

I frowned and tilted my head to look at her. "How many grandfathers can two children have?"

"Grandpa Jimmy is in there." Olive pointed to Mrs. Abraham's father. "Grandpa John isn't brown like him. Granny said God made him extra special, like a velvet night sky that stands out against the stars. Grandpa Charles died, and Grandpa Ben is peach like us. Mama said our family knows what true love is."

I considered what Mrs. Armstrong had said moments ago but, curious about their understanding of love, I asked the children, "And what is true love?"

James jabbed a finger at his chest. "Love is born in here. Not in here." He moved his finger to his temple.

"Your mother is a wise woman," I said.

James bobbed his head.

"Well, it was a pleasure meeting you both." I held out the napkin with the last two chocolates, and they eagerly took them. I turned to Miss Scott and favored her with a half-bow. "Miss Scott, always a pleasure."

"Do you care to stroll with me in the garden?"

Her request took me off guard. "I-I…"

"Don't feel obligated." A flash of embarrassment crossed her face.

"Of course not. Why don't I gather our coats?" I gestured toward the front entrance.

Her face softened, and she nodded. As I strode down the corridor, she conversed with the children, and their laughter echoed after me. I grimaced. I acknowledged my parents' high esteem for Miss Scott and their desire for me to find a wife and have children. My mother's incessant chatter about grandchildren started before I barely reached fifteen. Yet, although I too admired the woman of quality I knew her to be, my heart belonged to another. The vision of Kat standing in the entrance hall of our home earlier crept into my mind, and yearning rose within me. I collected our outerwear and pushed Kat from my mind as I returned to Miss Scott's side.

She removed her elbow-length, white satin gloves and laid them on a nearby stand.

"Shall we?" I held out her white cashmere paletot and helped her slip it on before handing her the matching bonnet and woolen mitts.

Readied, we said our farewells to the children and continued down to the double glass doors leading to the gardens, alight with lanterns decorated with garland and holly berries. A few guests huddled in the small area and eyed us as we came out. Amongst themselves, they exchanged nods of approval.

Snowflakes brushed my cheeks and ears, and the magic of romance encompassed the garden. Again my thoughts diverted to Kat, and I envisioned holding her in my arms and kissing her under the light of the lanterns.

"Mr. Williams." Miss Scott paused, a vulnerability reflected in her upturned face. "Are you present?"

"Affirmative." I forced the daydream from my mind and broke into a humorless smile. I discovered at a young age that humor and charm served me well and got me out of problematic situations.

"The look on your face revealed otherwise," she said. Although void of judgment, her dark gaze probed for an explanation. "Do you care to share with me what or who placed that smile on your face?"

"An illusion and nothing more," I said, returning my gaze to what lay in front of me, and in my peripheral vision, I noticed her shoulders slump.

We strolled past a woman and her friend. One lifted her hand, attempting to cover the hearsay she spewed next. "Miss Scott is a better fit than that white woman I heard he has eyes for. But, I suppose the apple doesn't fall far from the tree. His daddy only had eyes for white women too."

Miss Scott and I tensed. I stewed at their contempt for my parents. "Some people shouldn't be granted tongues to utter such poison," I said.

Miss Scott looked straight ahead. "Let naysayers' words find no weight." Albeit firm in her stance, her mouth quivered. Perplexed, I wondered how the women managed to upset her.

The crust of snow crunched under our feet, and the faces and chatter around us faded as we narrowed our focus. We strolled to an unoccupied area at the corner of the house, seeking privacy from prying eyes.

"Are their ramblings true? Does someone hold your affections?"

I shifted to study the woman. Her countenance and searching gaze held sincerity and honesty, and my body tensed with increasing apprehension. The knowledge of my parents' sentiment that Miss Scott was someone they envisioned as a suitable wife put me on edge. Never had she given me a reason to believe she regarded me as anything other than the son of her employer.

"If we were to give wind to every gossip's presumptions, then we'd have no peace." I attempted to disarm the mutterings and my discomfort with a fetching smile.

"I concur," she said solemnly before her expression softened. "You have a way of disarming people with your charm."

Intrigued at her keen insight, I studied her. "An observation made after a mere few words."

The orchestra started to play again, and the melody drifted into the snow-blanketed garden. Lights from inside cast shadows from the dancers that elongated across the garden.

"But the truth, regardless," she said confidently.

I shrugged, unsure how to receive her frank view of me. Our

paths had often crossed in her time with my father, but we'd never had in-depth conversations.

"I don't wish to offend," she said, witnessing me grappling.

"None taken."

"Perhaps a change of subject is best," she said with a light smile, and a momentary quiet fell between us. Then she looked at me with a bashful expression. "I know it's very womanly of me, but I saw how strongly the Armstrong children took to you. Do you seek to have children one day?"

Uncertain where she intended to direct the conversation, I squirmed. My tongue felt thick and awkward as her openness pushed for me to be forthcoming. "One day." Sadness glinted in her eyes, and I considered the cause. A daunting disquiet settled in the pit of my stomach. "Why do you ask?"

"An observation and nothing more." She shuffled away whatever thought had momentarily saddened her, and her shoulders eased. "My father hoped for a son when my mother was with child. But Mother says he loved me nonetheless. I was an only child until my parents had my brother late in life. A surprise to us all, but he brings them much joy, and for that, I am glad."

She looked genuinely delighted, and the love and respect she held for her parents was plain. It endeared her to me because of my relationship with my parents.

She lowered her gaze and occupied herself with adjusting her mittens. "Despite my happiness at having my brother, my heart is heavy. I feel it is selfish of me to be happy that there is someone at home to care for my aging parents in my absence. Do not misread me. I am indebted to your family for what you have done for me, but I wrestle with my decision."

"We children do that to ourselves, don't we? Taking on the burden of our parents without regard to what makes us happy."

"Yes," she said.

"Rest your guilt when it comes to my family. There is no debt to be paid. My father took a liking to you and believes in your capabilities," I said. "Having Father's support will serve you well because, although midwives have delivered babies for centuries, the world is gradually awakening to the concept of female doctors. But Black female doctors is a hurdle we still have to overcome."

"I am honored, and I will forever be grateful to a man who saw something in me, enough to wager his money on my success. I can't let him down. And my parents are counting on me." Her face grew taut, and I considered the pressure on her shoulders.

"I believe you will awe them all," I said sincerely.

"My ambitions supersede delivering babies or bloodletting my patients. Instead, I wish to study diseases. I can't accept the rulings of my predecessors or colleagues that all diseases are the same, caused by the overestimation of the blood and nerves. Nor do I believe that bloodletting, purging, vomiting, and blistering will restore natural balance." She conversed with her hands like the choir conductor at Sunday services. "The human body is more complex than that. I intend to write a textbook of my studies and findings in hopes of aiding future doctors."

She charmed me with her passion for medicine and for bringing about change. "It isn't a wonder my father became smitten with you."

She smiled, and her smooth, flawless skin shimmered like gold dust in the glow from the lantern. "You flatter me by sharing with me your father's view. Beyond my initial reasons for wanting to practice medicine, your father's attention to cleanliness and antiseptic procedures urged me to pursue a deeper understanding of medicine outside the seemingly barbaric ways doctors have operated in the past. As a result, I question whether doctors have added more injury than help to the patient in certain conditions and procedures."

Mesmerized by her intellect and desires, I gawked at her, and she fidgeted under my gaze. "Forgive me for my intensity, but I believe in your quest. Your superiors and colleagues would be foolish not to see the importance of your convictions."

"Not all men would openly allow a woman to express her views, and for that, I thank you." Her eyes glimmered, and she gestured at me. "What about you? Everyone is talking about your accomplishments. What do you plan to do next?"

"I intend to return to New York and start my practice."

"Will you reside here in Brooklyn?"

"I know my mother would like that." I redirected my gaze, noticing the other guests had drifted back inside, and we stood alone in the garden.

She looked over her shoulder at the empty garden and then touched my hand. "I implore you to stay a moment longer."

My throat tightened at the tender searching in her gaze. I wondered what she was thinking. My qualms at remaining outside unchaperoned and the rapid shift in her demeanor unnerved me. I sought to end any preconceived notion she may have about my intentions. "Miss Scott, I-I must tell—"

"Do not worry, Mr. Williams. I am not a promiscuous woman who throws herself at gentlemen. My respect for your family outweighs the pondering of the heart."

"I never considered you anything but a lady." I swiped a hand over my mouth, and she winced as though the gesture had weakened her somehow. I frowned and dropped my hand. "I never knew…"

"I cared." She finished my sentence, not appearing the least bit awkward, whereas I wanted to retreat to the security of the house.

She gripped my hand tighter, and the warmth of her fingers through her mitten sent a shiver through me. The urge to put distance between us took precedence, but I feared humiliating her and remained still.

"I believe you're a gentleman in all regards. I envy this woman who has claimed your heart." She looked down at our clasped hands. "Our world doesn't make it easy for the love you seek."

"What kind of love do you refer to?"

"To love a white woman. Why would you choose such a life?"

"A question I ask myself each day. But like young James said in there, love is born in the heart. Society may frown on the union between a mulatto and a white, but I can't deny what I feel."

"Nor can I," she said, her expression holding no bitterness, but unmasked empathy. "In the end, someone always gets hurt."

Guilt made me avert my gaze. Did she care as deeply for me as I did for Kat? What if Kat could never reciprocate my love, as I could not return Miss Scott's affection for me?

The fire I witnessed in her eyes earlier flickered. "I do hope my revelation doesn't make affairs awkward between us," she said.

"Not at all," I said, the pitch of my voice exposing my deceit. "Apologies," I continued like a blubbering idiot before pressing my lips together to retain any dignity I had left. Did I have no skill at all concerning women? Kat had made falling in love with her effortless. I never had to guess what she thought because she spoke her mind with frankness.

She released my hand, and I glimpsed jealousy on her face before she gathered her composure. "I see the hold she has on you. I'm sure she is lovely and deserving of your affections."

"She does not know of the love I feel for her."

She ached a brow, and the glimmer of gold haloing her chocolate irises glowed even brighter. "Why not?"

"I haven't revealed how much she means to me because she does not see me. But it's not me," I added, more to still my mind.

"How can you be certain?"

"Because suitors, marriage, and children are the least of her concern. I've known her since we were children. I fear losing her altogether if she got a notion in her head that my feelings would change our friendship."

"Rewards are only earned when we take risks," she said. "As I did here tonight. I dreamed of this evening, but it turned out very different than I envisioned," she said sheepishly before sighing. "I enjoyed watching you with the Armstrong children. They're delightful children."

"Indeed."

"To see the world through their eyes, with their childlike innocence…they care not about matters adults can spend years agonizing over."

"There is truth in that." I shook my head with a light chuckle, thinking about Kat's and my exchange in the meadow several months back. I pushed the thought away as Miss Scott continued.

"Not long ago, I was consumed with self-pity and hostility and blamed God, the doctors, and the world for a disease that deprived me of something precious." She paused to clear her throat and lowered her gaze to adjust her mitten. After a moment, she lifted her head and looked past me, allowing an object in the courtyard to hold her attention before continuing. "Then I met your father in the Points, and that same day, I encountered a legless man sitting on the boardwalk, begging for a coin, and something told me to pause. I asked him what had happened to him, and he told me he had lost his legs in a coal mine explosion. He had two sons, one five and the other seven. They were breaker boys and worked ten hours a day, six days a week. Unfortunately, his sons died in that explosion. Consumed by the loss of her sons, his wife placed a gun to her head and took her own life."

My stomach plunged at the man's suffering. I remembered the day my father had told me about the anguish they'd endured with the loss of my brother. For weeks my mother never rose from the bed, and Father feared she never would, so deep was her heartbreak. With patients to attend to each day, he would leave and worry about what awaited him when he returned home. His passion for his patients and his love for Mother gave him a reason to rise each day.

"A tragedy so great, one wonders how a person can go on," I said.

"But somehow he picked himself up from the hell he had been thrust into and found a way to go on. The words he said to me that day have remained with me: 'We humans become so caught up in trivial matters and waste time complaining when there are many reasons to be grateful. It took losing all I loved and losing my legs to appreciate the ability to walk, my wife's arms, and the laughter of my boys, their fussing and mischievousness, and even my wife's nagging. If I could go back in time, I'd cherish every moment.' After our encounter, I decided to rid myself of the poison consuming me and search for enjoyment each day, whether big or small…to find purpose." Her voice thickened with emotion. "So many have faced far worse in life. People have endured sorrow most of us could never begin to grasp, but no matter how bleak life appears, they discover a reason to smile. Look at Mrs. Abraham's father and others like him who've spent years in bondage. If the enslaved could unravel a glimpse of pleasure in a miserable existence, then who am I to succumb to this devastation? I draw from people's courage and resilience."

"You're a remarkable woman, Miss Scott. A remarkable one, indeed." I tipped my head in acknowledgment. "You've managed to captivate me in ways few do. Who knows, if my heart hadn't already been lassoed, I'd be lamenting over you, not my friend."

She laughed. "Again, you flatter me. Come, Mr. Williams, take me back inside before people have us walking down the aisle." She cast me a wink, and I chuckled.

"I believe we have a well-founded friendship after this evening, don't you agree?"

She smiled at me and said, "I'd like that."

I took her hand, placed it in the crook of my arm, and navigated her back inside. My respect for her couldn't be tamed. She embraced the challenge of becoming a doctor in a man's world while conveying infinite pride and dignity to our people.

Chapter 25

Kat

FROM THE WINDOW IN THE SALON, I WATCHED FOR JUDE'S ARRIVAL, and when his carriage pulled up and he stepped out, I hastened to the entrance hall.

"You appear to be in high spirits today," Audrey said from the mezzanine.

I halted and looked up as she descended the stairs. "I won't let your misery ruin the day," I said as Mr. Holmes opened the door.

"Good day, sir. Miss Katherine is expecting you." He gestured for Jude to enter.

"Thank you, sir." Jude stepped inside and removed his hat. He glanced from me to Audrey as she joined us in the entrance hall. "Mrs. Darlington," he said with a bow.

She ignored him and leveled a hard glare on me. "I warned you what would happen if I saw him around here again."

"And I told you, your threats no longer have a hold on me," I said before turning my attention to Jude. I smiled and strode forward. "Come, keep your things. We will take a stroll in the court-yard, away from ill-mannered people." I placed my hand in the curve of his elbow and marched him toward the corridor. Audrey's face turned the shade of her hair, but I lifted my chin and strode by her.

"You have become brazen," Jude whispered as he allowed me to guide him away.

"Become?" I said with a laugh before lowering my voice. "I have always stood up to my stepmother, only now I do it confidently because Papa is here to keep the overlord at bay."

"Mr. Holmes," Audrey said. "Have a carriage prepared. I'm going out. There is a matter that requires immediate attention."

I put on my paletot, and we stepped outside into the warm sunshine.

"Jude!"

We spun back as Grace and Alice exited the house, their arms bare to the elements. They raced toward us, their faces aglow with pleasure.

Jude broke into a grin. "If it isn't my two deputies." He bent to embrace them, and they jumped into his arms, almost sending him sailing backward. He caught himself under their weight, and my heart danced at the exchange. Goodness was Jude's very essence, and to witness the affection my sisters and he held for each other endeared him to me that much more.

"We've missed you." Alice pulled back and regarded him with disapproval. "Where have you been? Christmas and New Year's have gone, and we didn't catch a glimpse of you."

He chuckled and rested a gentle hand on her shoulder. "Well, here I am now."

"Yes, but Kat will keep you all to herself," Grace said matter-of-factly. "She always steals your time."

"You two shouldn't be out here without appropriate attire. Go inside, or you will catch your death," I said.

Although I didn't want to share Jude's time with them, I didn't have the heart to send them away. I bent and scooped snow, formed a ball, and tossed a snowball at Jude. He jumped back and my attempt splattered on the ground.

He laughed and gathered his own and launched it at Alice. She squealed as it landed square in the middle of her chest. Grace giggled and swooped to form her own.

I collected another and readied it to throw, then I caught Ling standing next to the kitchen door, observing us, his arms weighed down with a load of wood. He smiled as he looked on, and I redirected my toss. I prided myself on the distance and accuracy of my aim as my snowball sailed through the air and hit him in the shoulder. His smile slipped, and he glanced in my direction before it reappeared. I sent him a cheeky grin. His rail-thin body and hollow cheeks had filled out in the weeks since he had come to our home. As promised, Papa had hired a professor to educate Ling three days a week, and on the other days, he earned his keep by helping Chef Bernard in the kitchen.

"Ling, come and join us," I said. "The snow is perfect for making a snowman."

"I can't," he called back. "Chef Bernard asked me to fetch more wood."

"You take the wood in and tell him I've requested your assistance."

He grinned, bobbed his head, and disappeared inside.

I turned to my sisters. "Now off with you two. Go get your warm clothes on and return. Make it swift!"

They hooted and darted back inside, returning minutes later bundled up, with only their faces exposed to the elements. They wobbled toward us under their many layers, and I giggled at their appearance. "Come, my little snow leprechauns. Let's make a snow family," I said.

Grace dropped to her knees and started forming a snowball. Together the girls worked on their snowballs, and by the time Ling returned, Grace had left hers to help Alice move hers into position.

"Come, Ling. Help us." Grace waved at him.

He darted across the snow and aided the girls, and together we constructed a snowman family. Jude helped the children dig through the snow to the stone path and retrieved pebbles from the courtyard for eyes and mouths while I broke branches and fashioned arms.

Alice stood back to examine our work. "They need noses."

"And buttons," Grace said.

Ling retrieved a small bundle of carrots from his coat and held them out with a wide grin. "These should work."

"You sneaky boy," Grace said with a giggle. "Is that what took you so long to return?"

He nodded, his eyes gleaming with naughtiness.

I laughed and clapped Ling's shoulder with a snow-crusted mitten, and he gasped at my thump. "Chef Bernard will be wondering where the carrots for the evening meal went, but one look in the courtyard will put him on the trail of the scoundrel." I smiled at the children's red cheeks and noses, and gleaming eyes. "We will worry about the buttons later. You all head inside and warm up. Perhaps if Chef isn't too irritated over us nabbing Ling, he will prepare you some hot cider to take off the chill."

The children wandered inside and left Jude and me to stroll the courtyard. His merriment disappeared, replaced with a solemn look.

"What troubles you?" I said.

"Earlier, regarding your stepmother…what threat did you refer to?"

"Oh, it's nothing to worry about." I waved a hand in dismissal.

"If she threatens you because of me, that doesn't rest easy with me."

"As I said, Papa has promised he will never leave us again, so her threats no longer frighten me. Since our arrival home, she has made herself scarce."

"Has she threatened to use me against you?"

I again tried to avoid answering him. "Honestly, you mustn't concern yourself."

Halting, he turned and gripped my forearms. His eyes searched mine, and I became swept up in the beauty of his hazel eyes and the tenderness in how he looked at me. "Please, Kat. When have we ever kept anything from each other?"

"I-I…well…" I tried to frame Audrey's insults in a way that would not hurt him, but grappled with the ugliness of what she had said.

"Tell me." His thumbs pressed into my arms.

"After your last visit to Braxton Hall, she said that if I were to see you again or defy her, she would spread lies about us. That Mrs. Cox caught you forcing yourself on me in the meadow and robbing me of my virtue." Pain flickered in his eyes before he stiffened. "And that she'd gather a mob and see you lynched."

He released me and ran a hand over his face before he started pacing. "The audacity of that woman." He had always been the calmer one of us, but his hands fisted as he kicked at a clump of snow.

I walked to him and touched his arm, forcing him to face me. "Please, don't allow her to get to you. Her threats are empty."

"It pains me to know she uses me to harm you."

"You needn't worry about me. And I'd die before I let her harm you. But if I have my way, she will be removed from our family by the time the snow melts. The private investigator I hired is hard at work," I said with a tender smile. "Come, let's sit over here." I took his elbow and led him to the pavilion. Inside I cleared away the dusting of snow, and we sat on the marble bench.

Jude looked at me in that uncanny way he often did before lifting a finger to brush back a tendril from my face, his fingers lingering on my cheek. "Kat…" he said in a ragged voice before clearing his throat. He fidgeted, and wiped his palms on his trousers.

"Are you well?" I asked.

"Yes. It's just…"

I frowned at the yearning I saw in his eyes before he dropped his gaze. "What?"

"There is something I must tell you, and I'm not sure how."

My chest tightened as panic took hold. "Are you sick?"

"No." He shook his head, and a small smile touched his lips.

"Then what is it?"

"I've wanted to tell you something for a long time."

"Now look who is keeping secrets," I said. "Out with it."

He swallowed hard, and my breathing halted. Good heavens! What was he about to tell me? I braced myself for impact.

"I am in love with you," he blurted.

"W-what?" I shifted to study his face, uncertain if I had heard him right. "What foolery do you speak?"

Pain reflected in his eyes. "It is so. I've known what is in my heart for years, but was too afraid to tell you."

"No," I said. "Don't say such things. I don't want anything to change between us."

"Change is not so frightening as you may think."

I shook my head and stood to put distance between us.

"No, Kat." He walked up behind me and turned me to face him. "You will hear me out."

I tilted my head back to look into his eyes. I frowned at what I discovered. The smitten look. My heart galloped and plunged, all within the same beat. How could I have been so blind? Birdie had been right. Jude had gone and gotten a foolish notion in his head. "Jude…no," I pleaded.

"I love you. I need you to hear me."

Tears pooled in my eyes.

"You don't have to say anything. And nothing has to change between us."

"Yes, it does. It changes everything," I said softly, remaining within his grip. The world spun around me, and I fought to keep from crying. Why did he have to ruin everything by falling in love with me? I loved him. God knows I did, but the love between a man and a woman was a threat. A path I would never choose willingly. "Why didn't you stop it?"

"One cannot stop love." His voice quavered.

"Yes, you can. I know you can. Take it back. Don't love me." I pounded at his chest.

He gathered me in his arms as my sobs burst forth. His breath was warm on my head, and the powerful drumming of his heart thumped against my ear.

"I can't lose you." I sobbed into the wool of his coat.

"You never will."

"Yes!" I pushed back. "You ruined everything."

He didn't release me, and his hands moved tenderly to grip my upper arms. "Please, Kat. Don't push me away. I had to tell you. I promised myself when I came home this time, I would tell you."

Agony ripped at my soul as I saw my misery mirrored in his eyes.

"Don't push me away as you often do with others."

An inner restlessness consumed me as his words resonated, but I didn't know how to shift the fear of loss and love that resided so deeply within me. Why did I feel with his revelation that I stood to lose him?

"You may loathe me for this, but I've dreamed of what it would be like to hold you like this…maybe without so much resistance." His eyes glittered with humor, and I narrowed my eyes. Leave it to him to bring humor into the tension between us. But he quickly grew solemn, even determined. "I must know what it would be like to kiss you."

I bristled. "Now I know you have gone mad."

"I assure you, I have not."

I scowled at him, aware of the gentle way his thumbs stroked my upper arms and the curve of his mouth. I considered his request and how I'd often imagined what it would be like to kiss a man, but I'd never acted upon the thought. Love came at too great a cost. But something in me made me pause. If I were to experience a kiss, there would be no safer person than him. Perhaps I could dip into the waters of passion between a man and woman and see what all the fuss was about. I'd reconfirm to myself that love was rubbish.

"Oh, flummadiddle!" I said. "If I allow you this kiss, you must promise me that nothing will change between us. And that I will not lose my friend."

He smiled and nodded, lowering his head.

"But…" I placed a mitten on his mouth and gave him a warning look. "This isn't only for you but for my own curiosity too."

He suppressed a laugh.

"Very well," I said with as much prudence as Evelyn, and I cringed at the resemblance.

I leaned in, and he lowered his head. Our lips brushed, and the motion felt strange and awkward at first. But as I relaxed into the foreignness, my body tingled at the warmth radiating from his lips, and I lingered. His hand touched my lower back, and I moved closer, allowing myself to forget everything around me as I became engrossed in the experience. His lips hungrily took hold of mine in my reluctance to part, and a jolt charged through me. Our bodies pressed together almost as though an invisible hand guided us, and I realized how much I wanted what was transpiring between us. I shivered within the enchantment. Then he released a soft moan before stepping back.

He stood regarding me with a passion so deep that I felt small and fragile under his gaze. Then the Jude I understood returned. "You appeared to enjoy that more than you expected," he said with a grin, the passion in his gaze never fading.

I touched my lips, still immersed in the intensity between us. Had he always looked at me so? I recalled the odd way he would stare at me sometimes. My stomach swirled with rising anxiety. Indeed. I had been blind to the truth.

I stepped from his grasp, coming to my senses. "Well, there you have it." I smoothed out my dress and coat. "Now you can stop with this foolish idea that you love me, and we can continue on as before."

He turned and walked toward the house and said over his shoulder as I dashed to keep up, "We can continue as before, but kissing you only confirmed my love for you."

"Fine, have it your way. But I won't let it happen again."

"We will see," he said with a laugh, as though he had the upper hand.

I scowled at his back and followed in silence, fuming over the smugness in his reply.

At the door, he opened it, stood back, and gestured for me to go ahead.

I pointed a finger at him. "You don't speak a word of this. Do you hear me?"

He inclined his head and smiled.

I glowered at him and marched inside, and his soft chuckle only agitated me all the more.

In the entrance hall, I set my wet mittens on a table and turned to face him. "Let me walk you out."

Again he dipped his head in agreement, and I spun and opened the door. He stepped out, and I took up a position at his side, clasping the elbow he offered, and took care not to slip on the ice glazing the steps.

"I look forward to completing my education and returning home," he said as though what had occurred between us had never happened. I seethed but didn't want our last moments together to be remembered as a dispute. I knew what had transpired between us in the pavilion could never be undone.

When we reached the boardwalk, Jude's driver stood by the open door of his carriage. My cheeks heated, as though he could read what had happened through the confusion between Jude and me, and I ushered Jude away from the carriage.

I released his arm and shifted to regard him, but I couldn't bring myself to look into his eyes. "Ensure you write to me." I fumbled with my hands, unsure how to act before concealing their trembling in the folds of my dress.

He lifted my chin with two fingers, forcing me to look at him. "Nothing will change. You have my promise."

I nodded, blinking back tears. "Good. Now you'd best be going."

He pivoted and ambled back to the carriage, and I stood back as he climbed inside.

"Take care." He lifted a hand in a wave.

"And you as well," I said with a small smile.

The driver closed the door, hoisted himself onto the carriage seat, and gathered the reins. Then, with a slap of the reins, the carriage lurched forward and moved into the street traffic.

My throat constricted as the fear that I'd never see him again rose. I wrapped my arms around myself to ward off the chill, then awareness hit me of the curiosity Jude and I had gathered from passersby. I held my head high, turned, climbed the stairs, and retreated inside.

Chapter 26

OUR CARRIAGE RODE ALONG THE WOODEN PAVEMENT STREETS of Manhattan, and the grating of Mother's voice in conversation had me knotted tight inside. Josie sat beside Mother across from me with her hands folded tightly in her lap. Subjected to Mother's nagging since our departure from home, she'd shrunken into her seat, her shoulders curled forward as though to ward off Mother's attack.

"Sit up, girl." Mother slapped Josie's arm. "You're too short as it is. You will resemble a hunchback before you are thirty. A woman must practice proper posture at all times."

Josie straightened and rolled back her shoulders, her grayish blue eyes blank.

"Leave her be," I said gruffly, placing a hand on my knee to cease its jitters. "You have been at her since we left home. There is not a moment of peace with your constant chastising."

Mother narrowed her emotionless eyes on me. "Watch your tongue, son. I am still your mother, no matter how old you get."

"So you keep telling me." I gave her an unwavering stare.

Momentarily, Mother redirected her scorn from Josie alone to the pair of us. She lamented how we were a disappointment and what an ungrateful lot we were, and wished she'd never had children. Then she moved on to other areas of turmoil she felt in her life.

I peered out the opening in the curtain to the boardwalk, seeking an object to claim my focus—a technique I'd utilized throughout my childhood when dealing with the onslaught of my parents' wrath and condemnation. I discovered concentrating on something outside of the turmoil maintained my sanity.

But today a scene unfolding outside captured my attention, and I struck the carriage roof with my hand, signaling the driver to stop. I leaned forward to get a better view from between the gap in the curtains. Kat and a dapper-looking mulatto man dressed in a dark three-piece suit stood on the boardwalk outside the Darlington townhome. Discreetly, I widened the gap in the curtain. My heart galloped at the subtle exchange between them and how the man lifted her chin, requesting she look at him. Jealousy gripped my chest as I considered the reserved demeanor of the young woman I had come to know. Did she hold affection for the man?

"Why have we stopped? What is it?" Mother said.

I released the edge of the drape and returned my attention to Mother and Josie.

Mother leaned forward and drew back the curtain for all to see who sat inside the carriage. I pressed myself back against the seat and gritted my teeth, waiting for her rebuke. "It's that Darlington woman. The one I warned you to stay away from." A *tsk-tsk* clucked from her tongue. "She is no better than the company she keeps. If I didn't know better, I would say the relations between her and that Black are questionable." She sat back in her seat, her back straight and lips pursed.

I drew the curtain closed.

"What is your infatuation with that woman? Beauty fades, son. And that Darlington sister lacks the elegance and poise of a woman who will give this family future heirs."

"She holds qualities beyond one's understanding. And what do you care about the Huntington name or the well-being of this family? You and Father barely tolerated each other. And it is no secret, what you suffered at his hand."

"W-We will not talk about the past." There was a tremor in her voice. "My husband is gone, and thankfully so. But at least I achieved something for my suffering."

I understood she spoke of the Huntington wealth and not her children. If Mother had any control over Father's will, she would've inherited the Huntington family's wealth. But Father left it to me, and I understood he chose me only because I was a male. Without me, Mother would be penniless.

I pounded the roof and signaled the driver on. The carriage lurched forward, and I inspected the woman across from me: the rigid set of her jaw; a face bearing no inkling of kindness; eyes that peered through you. She'd never said a kind word to my sister or me; if she had, it had gotten lost in the nightmare of our childhood. When we fell and hurt ourselves, or Father had beat us, we'd sought comfort from her, but she'd turned us away and told us to toughen up. The gentleness of a mother's hand, a mother's embrace, had been things I hungered for as a child. As an adult, I understood the woman who bore the title of 'mother' lacked the warmth and care of other mothers. She had learned that survival meant she had to shut out the world and focus on her existence. No bond existed between her and her children, and it was futile to hold onto the hope that she would come to love us. I tolerated her out of duty and nothing more.

As the carriage threaded through traffic, Mother continued to berate Josie, and I snapped. I leaned forward and gripped her arm. "I warn you, Mother, you will cease your contempt or I will remove you from this carriage myself."

She gasped and glanced from Josie to me as though I'd victimized her. "You wouldn't."

My grip tightened. "I would."

Her mouth stood agape before she snapped it shut. "You'd leave your own mother in the streets."

My tolerance for her had expired, and I wanted to be anywhere but in her company. Miss Densmore's face flashed before me, and I yearned for the warmth of her arms and affection. In our separation, I realized how I had clung to the womanly part of her that offered tenderness and devotion. I glowered at Mother. "Without a second thought."

She yanked her arm free, and I leaned back as her hand slipped to her throat. "You are no son of mine."

"I, too, wish it wasn't so. If you could, for one moment, consider someone else besides yourself, consider the difficulty your children have faced being born to parents who regard them as defective and a nuisance." Josie inhaled sharply at my remark, as though expecting hell unleashed with my refusal to let Mother have the upper hand. Mother's face never flinched; she stared at the wall behind my head, but conviction and weariness pushed me on. "To be born of a woman without a compassionate bone in her body. To know she detests the breath you breathe and your very sight. Many days I wish I'd been born a pauper rather than a child of Father and you." I wanted to cut her deep in my pain, but the hard glint in her eyes never faded.

Depleted, I glanced at Josie, noting the silent tears streaking her cheeks, and the need to protect her rose. I yearned to take away all her fear and pain and imprison it within me. I had failed her.

Mother followed my gaze, and jealousy and contempt transformed her face as she regarded Josie. "Wipe your tears, you fool girl. They are wasted. The world will chew you up and spit you out if you sit around weeping over everything. Your womanly ways and weakness cause your brother to forgo all sense in his quest to protect you from a cruel and unjust world. We are women. I never had anyone to protect me, and neither will you. Your brother abandoned his own mother. There was a time when it was me he sought to rescue. Believe me, he will abandon you too."

"I was a child. Father was too powerful for the both of us."

"And when you became a young man? What then?" Challenge flashed in her eyes.

"Like you, I tried to survive."

"And protect her." She nudged her head at Josie, bitterness contorting her face. The pain of abandonment manifested as anger and seeped from her very core.

"Your truth does not need to be Josie's. Father is dead. He can no longer harm us."

"Your weakness is repulsive. If you had been more of a man, you would've defended your family and stood up to him."

Her words pierced my soul, but I held back the emotions squeezing my chest. As a child and young man, I lived with guilt and shame over my physical inability to stand up to his blows. From a heap on the floor, I'd watch the demon inside Father beat Mother unconscious. "I did, and you know what I suffered for it. I defended until my body could no longer take the beating." I paused a moment before asking, "I've always wondered. Why did you stay and subject yourself to decades of mistreatment? I know it wasn't for Josie's and my sake."

"You are right. I wouldn't have taken two blubbering children with me if I had chosen to leave. I had my reasons for staying."

"Yes, the Huntington wealth appealed to you."

"It is the least of what I'm owed for what I have endured, but he left it all to you, didn't he? I had hoped the war would've taken care of the both of you. A disappointment, indeed." Her teeth flashed, and pure satisfaction pinched her face when I flinched.

"Mother!" Josie twisted to look at her. "Merritt is your son, and one any parent would be proud of. How can you spew such hatred?"

Mother turned eyes darkened with untamed emotions on Josie, who shrank back in her seat.

"Josie," I said.

She lifted her eyes to hold mine. Her face had lost all color, and her lips trembled.

"You need not defend me." I leaned forward and gripped her hand before turning my attention to Mother. "You are the tyrant created from Father's hatred. Bitterness has devoured any goodness you may have ever possessed. You are blind to the monster you've become. Even in death, he controls you. Father has won. You are him in the flesh."

Perhaps the numbness I felt absorbed the shock of Mother's powerful slap to my jaw because I was driven back by the force of it, but I felt no pain. "I am not him. I could never be him!" she shrieked.

"But you are. You are every bit the man you loathed, if not worse." I felt both satisfaction and remorse at the anxiety on her face.

Josie broke into tears. "Stop. Please stop."

Mother pressed her lips together, adjusted her clothing, and sat poker straight with her hands balled into fists on her lap. She had ceased her fight for the time being.

I closed my eyes, leaned against the seat, and heaved a sign. No matter how much I wanted her to be something different, she was incapable. Life experiences had left her unable to love or show empathy. I considered the peace that'd come with plucking her from our lives and sending her away. But I battled with how to remove one's mother from one's life. She would be alone, with no husband, no children, no extended family. To sentence her to such a cruel existence seemed unthinkable. The scandal would provide food for the gossipmongers of New York and taint me in the eyes of others. But I lacked the wherewithal to care. To live under the same roof with her felt like a death sentence to Josie and me. I had come to a crossroads in my relationship with my mother. I had to decide between the duty placed on children regarding their parents and Josie's and my sanity. The love I held for my sister outweighed the responsibility to a woman who considered herself first and her children as an afterthought.

I would bring the change to our household despite the disgrace it would bring upon me.

Chapter 27

Kat

DOROTEA STRODE INTO THE MUSIC ROOM WHERE I SAT PAINTING and regarded me. "What has your head in the clouds?"

"An artist's work, is all," I said, applying a stroke to the canvas before sitting back and tilting my head to examine my work. "Her face is all wrong."

Dorotea took up position behind me. "Do not fret, señorita. Inspiration will come. Perhaps when you clear whatever has occupied your mind these last days."

I laid my paintbrush and palette down and stood, avoiding eye contact with her. "Your imagination runs." I walked to the table under the window, lifted the pitcher of water, and poured a glass.

"Does it?" I heard amusement in her voice. "I saw you and Señor Williams."

I coughed on a mouthful of water, and the liquid poured over my chin. I gathered a napkin and patted at the dampness. "You were spying on me?" I still couldn't look at her.

"No, but from the upper window in the corridor, I saw you and Señor Williams alone in the pavilion."

"What else did you see?" My cheeks heated. I had fought to suppress what had transpired between Jude and me, yet each morning I woke, the memory returned. The lack of discretion in our conduct had plagued me. But when no whispers had reached me, and Evelyn never cornered me to ridicule me and fight for the honor and decorum of our family, I hoped I'd come out unscathed.

What had gotten into me? I'd lost all control. Each detail of the memory played out in my mind, and the accompanying sensations caused a shudder to race up my body.

My stomach knotted, and I set the glass down. "I think I'm coming down with something." I looked at Dorotea, misery churning within me. "I am fine, and then I'm not. I awake feeling elated, then sick to my stomach. I worry about the stability of my mind. I feel flushed and unnerved."

Dorotea regarded me with empathy before walking to the door and closing it. "Come, sit with me for a moment." She gestured at the settee.

I wiped my hands in the folds of my day frock and sat down, hands fidgeting in my lap. She settled beside me and placed a hand over mine.

"I assure you, you aren't coming down with anything. You've been bitten, is all."

"Bitten?" I shrank back. "By what? How do you know?"

She shrugged; tenderness radiated from her eyes. "Love."

I frowned before grasping what she referenced. I shook my head. "No, that isn't it. Maybe Jude was coming down with an illness, and when we—" I stopped, too afraid to reveal how wickedly I had behaved in broad daylight.

"Do you think you are the first young couple to show affection for each other and defy proper etiquette?"

"No, you have it all wrong. Jude and I are nothing more than friends. Although Birdie was right, Jude went and made a mess out of everything." I heaved a sigh, slumping into despair. "He dared to claim his love for me—and not the kind of love I hold from him." Tears clogged my throat. "And like a fool, I kissed him." I lowered my voice and gestured at the window providing a view of the courtyard. "Out there in the open, for all our household to see."

"Did you want to kiss him?"

"No…I mean, yes." I struggled with understanding what had happened. "Oh, flummadiddle!" I leaped to my feet and paced the floor. "This is all his fault. I told him this would happen."

"Calm yourself. It isn't so bad."

I halted and swung back to regard her with dismay. "It is. I will not fall in love, if that is what he thought the kiss would achieve. I've made up my mind. I will not correspond with him further if his letters speak of the matter. He promised our friendship would remain steadfast, but he lied because everything's changed. I can't stop thinking about what happened." I embraced myself to calm the trembling. "Love is for people like you, Birdie, Evelyn, and perhaps Adelaide, but not for women like my stepmother and me."

Dorotea stood and strode forward to grip my forearms. "Do not place yourself in the same class as Señora Darlington. You are young, and matters of the heart are foreign to you. However, your feelings may change over time, and you'll see the beauty in falling in love."

"No." I shook my head with determination. "I reject it, here and now."

"Very well, you see it your way," Dorotea said with a small smile. "Señor Alexander is coming to tutor Ling. Your father has requested I attend."

"Mr. Alexander? The professor from the Goddard ball?"

"Perhaps; I am not aware if he attended or not."

I crossed my arms over my chest. "Oh, he attended, all right. Adelaide was quite taken with him." I narrowed my eyes. "How did he wiggle his way into being Ling's tutor? Probably to get another gander at Adelaide. Or better yet, she has conspired to have him more readily available to her. First Evelyn falls for Mr. Peyton, and now Adelaide seeks to chase after the professor."

"You don't know that."

"I do. Our home will be empty before you know it. And it will be just Papa and I, sitting in rockers by the fire, talking about the days when life filled these halls."

"Even if Señorita Adelaide has eyes for Señor Alexander, Señoritas Grace and Alice are but children and won't leave home for many years yet."

"I won't have it," I said.

She threw her hands up in surrender. "You win. I won't argue with you." She spun, strode to the door, and walked out into the corridor with me at her heels.

The door knocker echoed, and Mr. Holmes, our butler, strode to open the door.

"Don't make a spectacle," Dorotea said.

"If I had a coin for every time someone said that to me, I'd purchase a ship and sail away to a faraway place where humans hadn't yet trudged."

Adelaide slipped from the library ahead of us and adjusted the skirt and bodice of her mauveine velvet day frock before tucking back tendrils of hair. She pinched her cheeks to add color and sashayed toward the hall entrance.

"What did I tell you?" I said. "I knew she was the culprit." I stalked after my sister.

A gust of wind swept across the floor as Mr. Holmes stood back to welcome the professor. "Good day, Mr. Alexander. We were expecting you."

My fingers bit into the flesh of Adelaide's arm, and she winced. "Kat, what are you doing?" She regarded me with confusion when I plucked her from view of the entrance hall.

"Why doesn't it surprise me that you'd fancy a professor?"

She stepped back and almost toppled over a fern in her desire to put space between us. She quickly grabbed the plant and kept it upright.

"Answer me." I took a step forward.

She pressed up against the wall. "Keep your voice down!"

She glanced toward the entrance hall, but the corner blocked us from view.

"Fine," I said. "Is it your doing, having him tutor Ling?"

"What is it to you?" she said with more sass than was usual for her.

"It has everything to do with me. This is my family and what happens to you all happens to me." I leaned close enough to catch every detail of the freckles peppering her nose. She gawked down at me, and I balled my hands on my hips, trying to make myself appear more perilous. "Well, don't just stand there gawking. What do you have to say for yourself?"

"Nothing." She lifted her chin and squared her shoulders. "And no amount of fuss from you will stop me."

"Stop you from what?" I swayed, losing any ground I may have gained on her.

She smoothed her clothing, and I took a step back. "From getting to know August more. He intrigues me."

My mouth dropped open before the hairs on my body stood at attention. Her intrigue for the professor had advanced to referring to him by his first name. "Oh, I can clearly see that, as can the rest of the household." I gestured at the staff going about their duties. "Don't come to me crying when you are bored stiff because I will most certainly tell you I told you so." I spun and marched back down the corridor to return to my painting.

I halted in the doorway when I found Audrey standing observing my painting. "Can I help you?" I strode into the room.

She never looked up but said, "You know you aren't that good. Terrible, in fact."

Weary and at my wit's end with my confusion over Jude and Adelaide's insistence on pursuing Mr. Alexander, I picked up a cloth and stepped in front of her. "I care not what you have to say." I covered the canvas before shifting to confront her. "What is it you want besides to criticize me?"

Her green eyes gleamed like those of the serpent she was.

"Oh, don't trouble yourself by believing I care what you need or want." She picked up the paintbrush, dabbed it in red paint, and regarded the tip intensely before marking an X on the bodice of my dress. She smirked, dropped the paintbrush, and strolled from the room.

Too numb to react or feel, I bent and retrieved the brush. I wiped the floor with a rag before seating myself in front of the canvas. I removed the linen and studied the face of the woman standing in the middle of an orchard, and suddenly inspiration bloomed. I dipped my paintbrush and began to paint with purpose.

Hours passed before I painted the last stroke and sat back to admire the masterpiece before me. "Very original indeed," I observed to myself

"Good afternoon, Miss Katherine." Colleen ambled into the room with a bucket, slopping water over the sides. "I've finished with yeer chamber, and Mrs. Dixon has sent me here to take over for the charwoman, Sara. She is under the weather today. Coughing up a lung, she is."

I considered my unusually talkative chambermaid, noting the gleam in her eyes. "Have you been day drinking?"

"What? Me?" She set the bucket down, her glow dissipating. "I don't drink. I ain't got use for the stuff. Spent most of my life walking over drunkards in the Points. My stomach roils at the thought."

"Forgive me, but there's something different about you."

She brightened. "Alfred be the cause of that, miss."

"How so?"

"He told me he loved me." She knelt beside the bucket, retrieved a rag, and wrung it out.

I reflected on what Birdie had told me about the relations between a man and a woman and how children came about. Once I had witnessed the ghastly deed between a stableboy and a chambermaid at Braxton Hall. The dreadful noises from the ordeal left me wondering how it could be pleasurable. "But we love each other," the pathetic girl had pleaded to Audrey when Mrs. Cox brought her before my stepmother, informing her the girl was with child. Again, the act of love had been incomprehensible and alarming. Audrey dismissed the weeping girl and the stableboy from our employment.

"You'd best mind you don't end up with child. My stepmother would see you out on your backside as quick as nothing."

She hunched over and began scrubbing the floor. "Just because ye love a feller doesn't mean ye will end up with child. Besides, me da wouldn't be none too happy."

I gathered my painting supplies and ambled toward the door. Beside her, I paused. "How does one know one is in love?"

"What happened to ye?" She sat back on her heels, wiping her palms on her pinafore before gesturing at the bodice of my dress.

I glanced down at the stain. In my inspiration to get the image in my head onto the canvas, I had forgotten Audrey's shenanigans. "It's *her* doing."

"Yeer stepmother's?"

I nodded.

"Why would she go and do a thing like that?"

"Why does she do most of the things she does?" I said with a shrug. "Do you love Alfred?"

She craned her neck to eye me. "I suppose so."

I bit the corner of my mouth, considering her answer a moment. "But how do you know?"

"It's a feeling ye get in yeer stomach. Like butterflies are swarming around down there. Then when yeer feller comes around, ye get all warm inside, and flushed. Sometimes ye can't think straight or catch yeer breath."

"Or act right, by the sounds of it." I mulled over the kiss in the pavilion but quickly shook my head to dismiss it.

She laughed and stood.

"I am going to my chamber. My painting should be dry by the time you are done here. Cover it, and bring it to my chamber when you are done."

"Yes, miss."

"Thank you," I said. "Mind what I said. Love can be your undoing."

She stood and moved her bucket closer to my painting. "And ye mind, ye stay out of Mrs. Darlington's snare."

I offered her a sad smile and turned to walk from the room. On the threshold, I halted at a gasp from Colleen. I turned to discover her standing before my painting with her mouth agape.

She lifted wide eyes to me. I grinned. All thoughts on the chaos of love vanished from my mind. I pivoted and paraded from the room.

Chapter 28

Kat

THE DEPARTMENT STORE'S INTERIOR EXTENDED AS FAR AS THE EYE could see, including a tea saloon and restaurant where women could dine without being ushered into the streets for indecency. Marble floors shone under the gaslights and the sun pouring through the floor-to-ceiling windows. In the center, under the dome ceiling, a woman enrobed in a flowing ivory gown sat playing the harp, evoking a relaxing atmosphere for shoppers. Trinkets, furs, dresses, jewelry, and other merchandise filled the space. Customers created a sea of vibrant, colorful dresses, and excited chatter rose and fell. Women sat in chairs strategically stationed throughout and cooed over their purchases.

I wondered who the brilliant men were who had come up with the idea of a shopping palace aimed at a female clientele. The rise of department stores allowed women the freedom in a male-dominated society to leave their homes and move freely throughout the stores without concern for acceptable social etiquette.

Through the full-length storefront windows, I regarded the carriages waiting with grooms prepared to load their mistresses' parcels. New carriages pulled up, and gentlemen stepped out and turned to help their lady companions out. At the boardwalk they parted ways, and the gentlemen detoured around the store to the private entrance to the smoking room while the ladies hurried to the main entrance of the store.

Empty-handed but mesmerized by the chaos and excitement, I trailed after Birdie. She walked with garments draped over her arm and trinkets dangling from her fingers. As another shiny item caught her eye, she suddenly stopped. I gasped as I collided with her and almost sent us both flying.

"Look at that reticule. I simply must have it." She stood gawking at an olive green satin bag gleaming with diamonds or crystals or something of the sort. "Here, hold this." She thrust a pair of side-button boots, a blouse, lace gloves, and furs at me, and I gathered them in my arms.

"Honestly, Birdie," I said with a huff as I tried to regard her beyond my load. "You can't possibly need all these items."

"Need? No. But I can't be stuck in the house a moment longer." She held the reticule up for inspection and proceeded to list every exquisite detail and express why she simply must have it, dulling my mind to no end. I wasn't sure who she sought to persuade, herself or me.

"I can think of several other ways to spend our time productively."

She raised a brow. "Like what?"

"There's a colonel by the name of Thomas Hoyer Monastery who recently opened a School of Arms to train fencing and self-defense here in New York. People say he has sailed the seas, is an adventurer at heart, has fought in several wars, and is a fencing master, amongst other things."

"You can't be serious." Birdie gawked at me in dismay. "And you think he would train you? A woman."

"No, but it's harmless to inquire." I shrugged.

"You'd be humiliated and thrown into the street." She shook her head, returning her gaze to the reticule. "You are bored, is all.

Perhaps you need to find more ways to fill your time, other than pastimes fashioned for men."

"What do you suggest?"

"Perhaps something more feminine," she said with a tender look of concern. "The Goddards seek to end our friendship, and I don't want to give them anymore fuel for their argument."

"You would allow it?" I swallowed hard.

"Of course not, but I don't seek to displease my husband."

My grip on her items tightened, and I glared at her, but she only had eyes for the reticule. "Your future husband seeks to end our friendship, yet you still want to marry him."

"And you still insist on remaining unwed." She kept the reticule and continued down the aisle. "So why do you have it in your head that you need to learn fencing and self-defense skills?"

"To quote a friend, 'Need? No. But I can't be stuck in the house a moment longer.'" Sarcasm hung heavy in my tone.

She spun to regard me. "Do you care to remind me why we are friends?"

"Because we complement each other," I said.

"How so?"

"If we were the same, our friendship would be a bore. You aspire to make me a proper woman, and I aspire to teach you to not take life so seriously."

The gravity in her expression faded, and her posture eased. "You know, you make it hard to be put out with you," she said over her shoulder as she continued to stroll the store. She paused in front of a hat adorned with a chaos of netting, ribbons, pearls, and blossoms.

My attention drifted to the windows and the people congesting the boardwalks. Businessmen, merchants, and workers mingled with scullery maids and laundresses who walked alone and unchaperoned on their way to and from work. Ladies of the upper class never ventured out alone, or we'd be deemed streetwalkers or public women.

I relished the sense of freedom this store and those like it offered. The independence of the women clerks and attendants alone spoke to a changing world. Hope stirred in me that one day our voices would be heard. I dreamed of a society where women had the privilege of leaving their homes unattended, and acquired jobs currently reserved for men. If granted the option to vote, I could only imagine the things we could achieve in a male-dominated society.

I regarded the women coming in and out of the private dressing rooms and the attendants who stood waiting to help and inspire them to purchase with exaggerated oohs and ahs. I watched the customers admire themselves in full-length mirrors, then, after an abundance of affirmations from their female companions and the attendants, confidently commit to purchasing the items. A farce, indeed. I shook my head and shuffled the bundle in my arms.

"Would you like me to take those for you?" An attendant appeared out of nowhere, reeking of perfume. I wondered if she'd dabbed herself with each of the perfume bottles elaborately arranged on glass stands to entice customers.

"Please." I gratefully unloaded the items into her outstretched arms, trying not to grimace at the overpowering blend of scents surrounding her.

"Find me when you are ready. I'll check back and see if you have other items."

"I'm confident she will have more. We scarcely got in here, and already it looks as though we've been here all morning," I said.

The attendant's eyes gleamed. "We are delighted you all have found items to your liking." Her shoes clicked on the marble as she bustled toward the front.

"What do you intend to wear to this gala your stepmother has planned for her birthday?" Birdie asked as she moved on from the hat.

"I never gave it much consideration."

"Why did I think any different?" She fell silent as she halted in front of a dress form displaying an exquisite off-the-shoulder emerald silk gown that made even me take a second glance. The rich color and how the layers fell provided enough glamour that the designer avoided extravagant embellishments. Instead they had nipped and tucked, pinching the gown's skirt and short capped sleeves to add interest. Black pearl buttons down the back corresponded with the black velvet trimming the bottom.

"Isn't it splendid?" Birdie held out a corner of the gown's skirt. Swept up in the details of the gown, I never responded. "Well, I'll be." She nudged me with an elbow, pulling my gaze away from the gown. "Finally, a gown has captured your interest."

I smiled and returned my attention to the dress. "It is quite lovely."

"Then you must purchase it."

I lifted the price tag and gasped at the price. "For a dress?" I stepped back.

"Oh, for heaven's sake, Kat. With what Evelyn spends on fashion, I'm sure your father can afford this one dress for you. You can wear it to the gala and shock your guests with your astute fashion sense."

"Why would I care about such trivial matters?"

"But think about it." Her eyes danced. "You will have to pick everyone's mouths up from the floor. Even Evelyn's."

Warming to the idea, I allowed my mind to run with the surprise I had planned for the evening. "You've convinced me. I will get the gown."

She clasped her hands together under her chin. "Splendid."

I allowed her to believe she had convinced me with what others would think of the gown, but she, too, would stand with her mouth agape.

Later, as Birdie and I stood on the boardwalk while her coachman loaded our purchases into the carriage, a woman's voice snatched my breath away, and cold panic rushed down my spine. I searched the people strolling the boardwalk, and my gaze froze on my stepmother as she exited a hat shop with another woman. I recognized her from luncheons at our home but had never made her acquaintance.

I seized Birdie's arm and pulled her behind the carriage and out of view.

"What has gotten into you now?" Birdie glowered and straightened her hat.

I pressed my body against the back of the carriage and eyed passersby regarding us with perplexed looks. "It's Audrey."

"That's the cause for all this—" she flailed her hand in the air "—acting as though we just dashed out with stolen goods?"

"Keep your voice down, or she will hear you." I swatted at her and ducked my head to peek around the edge of the carriage.

"Miss Vello, Miss Katherine, are you all right?" Birdie's coachman said in a low voice while keeping his back turned to us, as though not wanting to draw attention.

Gratitude for the coachman's common sense despite his mistress's lack rushed through me. "Yes," I whispered back.

He nodded, closed the door, and moved away. Birdie gripped my arm and pressed against me to take a look herself. Audrey and her companion laughed, and my stepmother appeared unusually cheerful. An attendant with an armful of boxes stood next to them, awaiting instructions.

"Have you ever seen her so chipper?" I whispered.

"Shopping has a way of putting one in good spirits."

As I studied the women, my attention went to a blond-haired man with a short-cropped beard who appeared around thirty years of age. He stood back, eyeing the women with interest.

"Do you see that man?"

"Where?" Her warm breath lifted the hairs on the nape of my neck.

"To the right. Behind them."

After a painstakingly long moment, she said, "He appears quite intrigued with your stepmother."

My stomach dropped, and I squinted to get a better look. Audrey glanced over her companion's shoulder and caught sight of the man. Her hand slipped to her throat, and her body went rigid. She spun on her heel and marched toward us, with the other woman hastening to keep up.

"Mr. Kelly," Audrey's voice called, and I craned my head out a little farther when she paused three carriages ahead of ours.

"Yes, Mrs. Darlington." Our groomsman stood at attention with his hat in his hands.

"Have my parcels delivered home, and see my friend home."

"And what about ye?" Mr. Kelly asked.

"Meet me back here in an hour."

"Straight away." Mr. Kelly assisted the attendant with the packages.

Her friend touched Audrey's arm. "Is everything all right?"

"You needn't concern yourself. A matter needs my attention. I will come for a visit soon."

"Very well." She took Mr. Kelly's outstretched hand and climbed into the carriage.

Audrey looked over her shoulder at the man, who had crept toward the boardwalk's edge, his brow puckered. She turned away and waited until Mr. Kelly pulled the carriage out into the street.

I glanced back at the stranger's retreating back as he dipped between the buildings and into the alley. "We need to follow that man," I said. "We can't lose him."

"No." Birdie gripped my arm. "I won't be racing through the streets like an unhinged woman. And certainly not after a strange man."

As Mr. Kelly's carriage joined traffic, Audrey looked around for prying eyes before ducking into the alley. My heart stuck in my throat. If Birdie refused, I'd go it alone.

I dashed from behind the carriage and onto the boardwalk.

"Kat," Birdie hissed.

I ignored her and hurried through the pedestrians to the

corner of the building. I pressed myself against the wall and peeked into the dark alley. I spotted the pair at the far end but couldn't get a good look. Someone snatched my arm, and I twisted to look at an unsmiling Birdie.

"If you insist on this fool idea, I won't allow you to go it alone."

I nodded my thanks and eyed all the unwanted glances directed our way. We needed to get closer and couldn't remain in the open. Several feet into the alley, crates were piled high against the building, and I stepped into the shadows, keeping close to the building as I approached them. Birdie followed, and we made it to the crates undetected.

"What are you doing here?" Audrey said.

"I haven't heard from you in a while. I grew concerned."

Through a gap in the crates, I watched them. The man casually leaned against the building with his knee bent and the sole of his shoe pressed against the wall. Audrey stood with her hands on her hips.

"Do you know what would happen if we were discovered together?"

"You've informed me," he said, his voice assertive.

"You risk everything." I heard panic in her voice.

A cold knot lodged in my stomach, and I gawked at Birdie, who looked back at me, her expression a mixture of disbelief and confusion. My heart hammered in my ears as I turned back to spy on the pair.

The man lowered his foot from the wall and stepped toward my stepmother. He gripped her waist, pulled her into a tight embrace, and pressed his lips to hers. She pounded at his chest with open palms and fought to free herself.

I stumbled back, sending the crates tumbling, and panicked; I grabbed Birdie's arm and raced back the way we'd come, never stopping until we reached the carriage.

The groomsman waited as though still perplexed over our

previous conduct. He threw open the door, helped us inside, and quickly closed the door. Through the gap in the curtain, I caught him looking around, preparing for an attacker.

Audrey stepped onto the boardwalk, her expression stony as she peered up and down the street.

"She saw us." I pressed my back against the carriage wall.

"How could she not? We created an avalanche of crates." Birdie gulped and regarded me with bewilderment.

I squeezed my eyes shut, trying to interpret what I'd over-heard and witnessed.

"By the looks of what happened in the alley, your stepmother is more than acquainted with him. Scandalous, her behavior. Downright scandalous. What will you do?"

"I don't know," I said as my heart slowed its pounding. I opened my eyes to regard her.

Audrey's secrecy had only amplified after her revelation in the kitchen, the day she'd arrived home from gallivanting only God knew where. I'd provided the investigator with the information she'd shared with me, but he'd failed to learn anymore, and the advance I'd paid for his services had run out.

"I'm not quite sure what happened back there." I recalled Audrey's struggle against the man's advances.

"You have to tell your father."

"Tell him what?" My insides roiled. "I witnessed an encounter between my stepmother and a man she appeared to know, and he pushed himself on her." I wondered why I wasn't bursting with elation at the discovery. Instead, I felt gravely disturbed.

"Yes, that is what I'm suggesting." Birdie's eyes flitted to the window. "He has to know."

"I agree, but first I need to know more. I need to find out who that man was."

She squirmed in her seat, appearing dismayed. "And how do you expect to do that?"

I chewed over her question before an idea hit me. "We will

wait until she leaves and instruct your driver to take us to the office of the investigator I hired to find out more about her. We will
give him details of the man in hopes of aiding him in discovering
more about their involvement."

"And if word gets back to Zane about my behavior in public,
I will have more than the honor of your family to worry about."

I lowered my gaze and picked at the cord trimming on my
reticule. "I'm sorry for any harm I've caused. I do appreciate you
not abandoning me."

"You are my friend. One helps a friend when they are in need."
She patted my hand, but I heard apprehension in her voice.

My heart swelled with love and gratitude for her willingness
to stand by me, but I worried her fears were well warranted, if
Zane found out about the spectacle we'd created in broad daylight
for all of New York to denounce.

Chapter 29

I OPENED THE DOOR TO THE FIVE-STORY BRICK OFFICE BUILDING, AND Birdie and I strode inside, climbed to the third floor, and entered the office I had visited twice since my hiring of Mr. Carson.

When we entered, a gangly man with flesh laid over mere bones rose from behind a desk. "Good afternoon. Can I help you?"

"Good afternoon. I am hoping to find Mr. Carson in."

"He is with a client, but if you want to wait…?" He regarded me from behind black-wired spectacles.

"We will. Thank you, sir." I gave him my name and sat in one of the empty chairs lining the dark green and mahogany-paneled walls.

Birdie settled next to me, gripping her reticule. She looked about the office and squirmed all the while. "I never thought I'd find myself waiting to speak with a private investigator. Leave it to you to drag me here."

We sat in silence, and she kept her eye on the door, seeking to escape at the first sign of someone she knew. Meanwhile I tried to recollect every detail of the man in the alley.

Sometime later, Mr. Carson's office door opened, and he walked out with a gentleman. As they moved toward the front,

Birdie lowered her head and shifted her body away as though hoping to fade into the background.

"As soon as I have any information, I will contact you," Mr. Carson said to the gentleman as they entered the lobby.

The gentleman glanced in our direction, pulled his hat down lower over his eyes, and avoided my gaze. He pressed his lips together and nodded at Mr. Carson before swiftly departing the office.

Mr. Carson never looked our way. He exchanged a few short words with the man behind the desk. Then he turned to look at us and moved smoothly forward. "Miss Darlington, I was fixing to contact you later today about some information I've gathered." He held out a well-manicured hand.

I stood and slipped a gloved hand in his. "Sorry to show up unexpectedly, but I have information of my own."

He raised a tapered brow before regarding Birdie, who remained in the same position with her body angled away from us. His eyes narrowed as he looked from her back to me. "Come with me, and we will discuss matters further." He turned and strode down the corridor.

I turned to regard Birdie and gave her a nudge. "Are you coming?"

She nodded and rose, appearing to have lost her voice in her desire to be anywhere but where she was.

Mr. Carson stood outside the open door to his office and waited for us. His black pomaded hair lay neatly combed with not a strand out of place. He wore a three-piece gray suit, and his skin possessed a sheen. Every aspect of the man was slick, which left me cautious the first time I met him. So far he hadn't given me anything useful, and I wondered if he sought to take advantage of a young woman without the wisdom and accompaniment of a man. But desperation kept me hopeful.

Inside, he gestured for us to sit in the two armchairs in front of an oversized rosewood desk that bore no speck of dust. All paper sat arranged neatly to the right. As we seated ourselves, he rounded the desk and rearranged his chair to an angle that suited him before he sat. His awkward mannerisms made me nervous, and I swallowed several times. He adjusted the inkwell and thumbed at an invisible dust particle on the desk before folding his hands and resting them precisely in front of him. Then, having achieved the comfort he required to engage with us, he leveled his gaze on Birdie, who looked as awkward as he had while performing the habits he required to function in the world. Her awkwardness, however, was born of the desire to escape. His brow furrowed, but he redirected his attention to me.

"What brings you to my office?" he said.

"Today, I ran into my stepmother in public. She exited a store with an acquaintance, and a man stood back as though waiting for her. After my stepmother dismissed the other woman, she slipped into an alley, and we followed. We witnessed them in an unbecoming position." His expression remained neutral and he waited for me to continue, but I noted a flicker of interest in his pewter-gray eyes. "I thought if we gave you details on the man, perhaps it would be of help."

He pulled open a drawer and retrieved charcoal and a sketch pad. "Please describe the man."

I gave him every detail I could remember, and his hand moved swiftly to capture my memory. Birdie, hesitantly at first, offered her insights, filling in details I'd missed. Her desire to help me transcended her wish to remain anonymous.

I held my breath in anticipation and knotted the fabric of my reticule as we waited for him to finish the sketch. I remembered what he'd said about contacting me with information he'd gathered.

Several moments ticked by before he lifted the pad and turned it for us to view. "Have I captured his likeness correctly?"

Birdie gasped and suppressed a small cry with her gloved fingers.

"Yes, that is him." I leaned forward, intrigued with his skill. I glanced at Birdie, and she nodded.

Mr. Carson gave away no insight into his thoughts on the man in the sketch as he set it aside, placing the charcoal next to the pad just so. Then he folded his hands and put them in the exact position they'd been in prior to his sketching. "Very well," he said.

I perched on the edge of my chair. "Do you believe this will aid you in finding out more about my stepmother?"

"Perhaps."

I frowned at his curtness and lack of information.

"Before we speak further, I must bring up the issue of payment. To proceed with your case, I require another retainer."

"But I don't have any more money to spend." My hopefulness faded, and I struggled to think of how I would come up with the money to advance further. The thought of asking Mr. Huntington again was out of the question.

"Then, I'm afraid I won't be able to proceed."

My heart raced, and sweat trickled down my back. I couldn't let the information he'd accumulated slip through my fingers. Given what we'd witnessed the man doing with Audrey, the demise of my stepmother felt closer than ever. And if she had seen us, life would only get worse for me, and her threats to harm Papa in the kitchen that day hung even heavier. Yet, what could she actually do? She was a woman without title or wealth and had no means to acquire aid in carrying out her threats. She had come to us with nothing, and if Papa divorced her on the grounds of adultery, she'd no longer be a peril to my family.

"How much more do you need?" I asked.

He stated a price, and my heart plunged. How could I come up with that much money? I considered the hefty price I'd paid for the gown, but I still wouldn't have enough if I returned it.

"If we pay the fee you're asking, what guarantee do you provide that you will give us information of any importance?" Birdie said with authority, and I turned my head to regard her. She squared her shoulders and leveled a stare at Mr. Carson. "You've used Miss Darlington's first payment but have provided no information. It leaves one concerned that you may not be the right investigator for the task."

Mr. Carson never flinched. "The little bird speaks." His tone held neither condemnation nor consideration, just matter-of-fact observation. "As I said earlier…" He looked back at me. "I have information about the so-called Miss Boseman before her marriage to your father."

I sat up straight, my heart pounding faster. Hope surged at the nearness of my freedom. I opened my reticule and fished for the remainder of my money.

Birdie placed a hand on mine. "We will pay your fee."

I gulped and regarded her.

She opened her reticule, removed a number of bills, and counted them before extending the money to him. "This should cover the fee."

Mr. Carson took the payment, flipped through the bills, then laid them on the sketch pad.

"Miss Audrey Boseman is an alias for Mrs. Winifred Cullivan, wife of the late Robert Cullivan. Upon his death, he left his wealth to his bastard son, Joseph Harrison, leaving his wife with a small inheritance but surely nothing to sustain her for longer than five years without supplemental income." He delivered the information in a detached monotone.

I recalled how Audrey, or rather Winifred, had come to us as Miss Boseman, and she'd always implied that she had been unwed. She'd found herself in a bind, and she and Papa formed an arrangement. Yet on her arrival in the city, she'd revealed details similar to what Mr. Carson had uncovered. Why had she felt the need for an alias?

Mr. Carson glanced at the sketch. "Joseph Harrison should be around thirty years old, and this man may very well be him."

"But their conduct was anything but that expected of a

stepmother and son," I said. "And when my stepmother spoke of him in the kitchen that day, she didn't refer to him with affection; quite the opposite, in fact."

"Which would leave one questioning what her motivation is. But if this man proves to be Mr. Harrison," he said, "I will get you the answers you seek."

"Please do it swiftly. I wish to remove her from my family once and for all. But I cannot do that without just cause."

"Understood." He stood and aligned his chair with his desk, taking an extra moment to confirm it satisfied his standards.

Birdie and I followed him to the door and said our goodbyes.

In the carriage, I slumped in my seat, overwhelmed with the day before I recalled Birdie's aid. "I will pay you back. I will return the gown on the way home, and the rest I will get to you."

She held up her hand. "Consider it a gift."

"I can't take your money," I said.

"It's done. We won't speak on the matter again. Besides, soon I will be a married woman, and one can only assume my husband will have more of a hold on my spending. I doubt the luxury of the hefty allowance my father gives me will find me in my husband's home," she said wryly. As the only child of her parents, she had acquired all she needed and then some. Although the Vellos hadn't accumulated the wealth of the most prominent families in New York, theirs was substantial.

"I can't thank you enough for what you have done for me today. I will never forget it."

She clasped my hand and presented an almost sad smile as her expression grew thoughtful. She turned her head to look out the window.

I wondered what troubled her so, before my own situation took precedence.

Chapter 30

I N THE FOLLOWING WEEKS, I KEPT THE INFORMATION I HAD OBTAINED to myself, awaiting Mr. Carson's investigation into the man in the alley. No mention of Birdie's and my conduct emerged, and when I invited her to join my family at the skating pond in Central Park, she eagerly accepted.

February brought milder temperatures, and the sun perched high in the vast blue sky as Papa and I helped secure Grace and Alice's skate blades to their boots. Ling bent over, strapping on his while eyeing the ice nervously. Evelyn and Mr. Peyton joined the other skaters while Adelaide stood wringing her hands, observing each new arrival, hoping to see the face of Mr. Alexander.

I sat on a bench with Alice's skate-fitted foot on my lap, fixing her leather straps. "Why couldn't Evelyn and Adelaide allow this one day without menfolk to spoil the day?"

Papa chuckled as he knelt before Grace, assisting her. "What category do Ling and I belong in?" Ling and Papa exchanged a grin before Papa said nonchalantly, "You won't keep your sisters together forever. It is the natural course of life for children to grow up and create their own lives."

"But why does everything have to change? Life has been good

since our return to the city. So why can't they enjoy having our family whole again?"

"Perhaps they are," Papa said. "Maybe you need to shift your views. In opening our circle, we welcome more people to our family and therefore more love and happiness."

"We opened our circle once, and look at the years of misery that followed."

"A mistake, no doubt," he said grimly. "But one to learn from. I did the best I could in an emotional situation. You can't punish me forever."

"And I don't seek to. I can't offer enough apologies for misdirected anger." I removed Alice's foot from my lap.

Papa stood and brushed off his trousers. "You all go along now." He gestured at the children. "Ling, you keep an eye on my women." Papa had developed a soft spot in his heart for the boy.

"I will, Mr. Darlington, sir." He squared his shoulders while balancing on wobbling legs. He offered an arm to each of my younger sisters. They beamed and stood on either side of him.

"Don't worry, Ling, you will be a wonderful skater before you know it. We will help you," Grace said as they led him toward the pond's edge.

After they glided out onto the pond, Papa turned to face me.

"I understand you only wanted the best for us," I said. "But I wonder, do you truly know the woman you married?"

Audrey had feigned another headache and retired to her room shortly after the morning meal, and I wondered if she intended to use our outing as an opportunity to meet up with the man again.

"Not like I did your mother, but they are two very different women. What brings on these questions today?"

I shrugged and held out a hand for him to help me up. Once on my feet, I leaned in and whispered, "You said you'd check into her comings and goings. I was wondering if you'd followed through. Secrets have a way of coming out, and I believe my dear stepmother has many."

His gaze flitted sideways, and an odd look crossed his face.

"Papa?" I touched his arm. "Do you know something about her?"

He swallowed hard and shook his head. "No, it's nothing. Come, let us go join your sisters."

I sensed he was withholding something, but I dropped my hand. "You go ahead. I'll wait for Birdie."

He nodded, leaned down, and kissed my cheek. "I love you, Kat. You must never forget that."

"I've never doubted your love," I said when he straightened.

A haunted look passed over his face, and my heart sped up, but before I could press further, he pivoted and glided onto the ice. I stood staring after him. What troubled him so? My heart grew heavy, but Birdie's cheerful voice made me turn to discover her, bundled up in furs, marching toward me with Merritt and his sister walking beside her.

"Look who I found," Birdie said, smiling and appearing to be in the best of spirits.

I gulped back my unrest about what I'd read in Papa's eyes and waved.

Merritt carried their blades slung over his shoulder. "Miss Vello's carriage and ours arrived at the same time." His face revealed no smile, as it rarely did, but his eyes glittered.

"I invited the Huntingtons to join us," Birdie added.

I bet you did. Why don't we invite the rest of New York as well? I bit my tongue, withholding the remark, and extended my hands in welcome. "What a lovely surprise." I looked at Josie, stationed at her brother's side, clasping the curve of his arm. Unlike her brother, she smiled with ease. There was something angelic about the young woman, as if she were too delicate or unique for our world. The sun's golden rays haloed her, giving substance to my observation. Merritt's rigid composure softened in her presence and spoke to his affection and admiration for his younger sister. I recalled his fury when he raced in to protect her, the night of the Goddard Banquet.

"It will allow us to get to know each other," Josie said.

"Indeed." I inclined my head.

I waited while they sat down to put on their blades. New Yorkers embraced winter's wonderland, and there were ponds and skating lakes throughout the city. Festivals and events took place all season long, and Central Park had no lack of visitors.

The band, a group of jolly-looking fellows with bushy beards and cheeks rosy from the cold, perched on wooden crates and belted out "Jeff In Petticoats." A small crowd gathered around them, clapping and singing the melody. Others escaped the ice and awkwardly walked toward a booth where a woman ladled out mugs of hot cider. On the pond, starry-eyed lovers clasped hands and moved about as though the rest of the world had faded. Children's excited voices and laughter echoed across the ice. Serenity embraced me.

"Good afternoon, everyone." Adelaide joined us with her hand tucked into the curve of Mr. Alexander's elbow.

My chest tightened at the sight of them together. However, I paused long enough to note the gleam in Adelaide's blue eyes and how she glanced up at him with esteem and absolute bliss. Mr. Alexander regarded everyone as though he wanted to retreat to the quiet of an empty classroom, rather than mingle with the bustling outside world. Adelaide loved to skate, and I wondered if he had come merely to please her. I remembered Papa's insight about opening our circle to allow room for more love and contentment. How could I deny her the happiness that radiated from her now? Did I not love her enough to set aside my own fears to grant her the right to be happy?

Everyone greeted the couple, but Adelaide regarded me hesitantly. I inclined my head and offered her a small smile. Her shoulders relaxed, and she thanked me with her eyes.

Birdie stood, and I gripped her hand, excitement thumping

in my chest. We stepped onto the ice, found a break in the crowd, and glided forward. Merritt and Josie took up a position behind us.

"Let's go." I pushed my legs faster, relishing the speed and freedom skating brought. Birdie giggled and allowed me to guide her. Exhilaration burned in my chest, and I continued at that pace until Birdie pulled her hand free and fell back to join Merritt and Josie and catch her breath.

I skated backward, grinning from ear to ear while keeping an eye out for other skaters.

Merritt's eyes twinkled. He released Josie and said something to her and Birdie, and they nodded. Then he leaned into his legs, pushed off, and moved his body side to side to gain speed until he drew closer to me.

"Care if I join you?"

"Of course not," I said with a devilish smile. "If you can keep up." I spun around, and swooshed off. His laughter rose behind me, and I sensed him close on my heels.

Two times I circled the pond, threading in and out of gliding skaters until a stitch formed in my side, and I stopped my speeding to allow him to catch up.

Powdered ice from his blades dusted the front of my long, Parisian blue woolen coat and the hem of my dress as he slowed his pace to match mine.

I gave him a smug look, and he shook his head with unmasked admiration and exaggerated a low bow. "My lady, your talents know no bounds." He straightened, and his smile remained on his lips.

"One may consider it showing off, but I don't believe the etiquette books state anything about a lady skating too fast."

"Literature you claim not to have read." His blue-green eyes flashed with amusement.

"True. So perhaps others have been too busy appreciating the moment to condemn me for the freedom skating brings," I said as he glided beside me.

"Well, I must say, you are better on the ice than on a dance floor."

I laughed at the memory of him compensating for my two left feet. However, my merriment vanished as the ache in my side persisted. "Do you mind if we sit a moment?" I gestured at a nearby bench.

He glanced over his shoulder at Josie and Birdie, who skated along engrossed in conversation, not paying us any mind. When he turned back, he gripped my elbow to aid me at the ice's edge. We seated ourselves on the bench, and I welcomed the moment to rest my legs and catch my breath. Passersby eyed us with interest and smiled with speculation of courtship, no doubt. But I brushed off their assumptions, unwilling to let anything ruin a perfect day.

"You amaze me," he said in a deep voice.

I glanced up to discover him regarding me and adjusted my focus to the frost glistening on his short-cropped beard. "How so?"

His eyes remained fixed on mine. "Your sense of adventure is enthralling. I haven't met a woman quite like you."

I blushed under his intense stare and lowered my gaze to my hands resting in my lap. "Not everyone sees my yearning for adventure and freedom as you do."

"I have a responsibility to my sister, but if I didn't, I might seek to leave New York behind and start anew."

I whipped my head up at the mention of life elsewhere. "Where would you go if you were gifted a different life?"

"On a ship far away from here…" His voice drifted, and he gazed over the pond as though a mysterious land summoned him. The wind tousled his wavy brown hair, and I sat quietly, allowing him time for reflection. Finally he turned ardent eyes on me. "I've had this heavy feeling of responsibility all my life. After meeting you, I dream of a life of adventure, free of responsibility. But sometimes I feel I would never be far enough away to get away from her—" He stopped, and shame immediately gripped his face. "I should not have spoken so candidly." He dropped his head, and

I yearned to touch his shoulder and reassure him that whatever troubled him would fade in time.

"To whom do you refer?" I said softly.

He looked at me, and tears pooled in his sorrowful eyes but never fell. He searched my face as though seeking refuge, and something within me wanted to provide the shelter he sought. I touched his arm and nodded for him to continue.

"Mother," he said in a thick voice.

I recalled the pinched face of his mother and the unapproachable way she conducted herself. "Oh, she does seem like the unapproachable sort." The opinion breathed life before I could recant it. I released a soft gasp and removed my hand from his arm. "Forgive me. Now who speaks too frankly?"

He straightened, and all unhappiness left him as he leaned back and placed an arm along the back of the bench. "I believe you have bewitched me, Katherine Darlington."

I shook my head. "Don't let foolery convince you I am anyone grander than I am."

He laughed, and my heart thumped at the lightness that swept over him. "What makes you think I'd aspire to spend time in the company of anyone other than you?"

I narrowed my eyes, trying to determine if he had conceived some futile sentiment about him and me. But as usual, men's ideals and emotions were foreign to me, so I gave up trying to decipher his intent and returned to the previous conversation. "Why does your mother grieve you so?"

He regarded me hesitantly.

"Pardon me if I have perceived wrongly, but I believe we are beyond the point of cordial acquaintance. I told you why I required your services and that all is not well within my own family," I said. "If I were born a man and the head of my household, I would've removed my stepmother the day she arrived at Braxton Hall. There's no doubt in my mind that she's a poison that seeks to destroy my family. But as women, we have little say in whose company we must keep."

"A child cannot choose their parents. Is it any different?"

"True, but as a man, you have the wherewithal to have her removed from under your roof."

His eyes widened at my remark, and he opened his mouth to speak but then busied himself with pulling off his gloves and resting them over his knee. He kept his voice low to keep his family's truth from passersby. "My mother's a heartless woman with no care for her children. With her in the same household, I worry about my sister's well-being and my sanity. She pushes us to the point of madness." He rested his elbows on his knees and clasped his hands in front of him. "My father was no different. He was no father and certainly didn't merit the title of a loving husband. Cruelty is indeed taught."

I mulled over his words, then said, "Is it? I am not so sure. You don't appear to me to be a hateful man. One can only assume that you have endured insufferable things with cruel parents, yet here you sit." I kept my gaze on his sister and Birdie as they exited the pond and sat to remove their blades. "Since we've sat down, you keep looking for your sister's whereabouts, as though to assure yourself of her safety. It leaves me to wonder for how long you have played the role of parent to your sister. I recognize the behavior because I, too, developed a need to protect my sisters from my stepmother's clutches."

His shoulders slumped. "Old habits are hard to break."

"Maybe some are not meant to be broken," I said.

He removed his blades and rose, turning to peer down at me. "I thank you for your words. It does the heart good to release the burden."

"I return the favor, is all," I said, and he caught my reference to the evening in the courtyard at the Goddard ball when I had dumped my troubles on him, a mere stranger.

He inclined his head in appreciation before his keen gaze searched mine.

"What is the cause of the serious faces?" Josie said lightly as she and Birdie joined us.

"Nothing to concern yourself with." Merritt replaced his gloves. "What do you ladies say to some hot cider?"

"It's a wonderful idea. Why don't I assist you?" Birdie set her blades down beside the bench, and they walked off to the cider vendor.

Josie settled beside me, and I sensed her gaze on me.

"He is quite taken with you."

I gulped. "Pardon?"

"You needn't look so dumbfounded." She patted my knee. "Despite the hardness that molds him, he has a good heart. Many ladies have sought his affections, but his head is not so easily turned."

Heat rushed over me, and needles pricked my body. I avoided her gaze and looked in the direction Birdie and he had gone as I pondered her meaning. Before my thoughts shifted to Merritt's claim that I'd bewitched him. A silly sentiment, of course, but I would heed all warnings. Never again would I be caught at a disadvantage when love swept up out of nowhere, waving its flag of absurdity. The heat of Jude's kiss hung like a phantom on my lips, and I had to stop my fingers from lifting to brush the memory away. "I believe your brother is a decent man, but I am not up for consideration," I said.

"Are you courting?" she asked.

I flinched before shifting to face her. "No. Of course not." There was an unintentional bite in my voice.

Her blue eyes grew round at my assertiveness, but she regained her composure and said, "I am not one to push a gentleman on a woman. I assure you, I mean well. I hope you won't fault a sister for wanting the best for her brother?"

I questioned her meaning of "the best" for her brother. "With all due respect, that is a bold statement when we are mere acquaintances," I said. "The times we've met, we've found ourselves in a bind—you at the mercy of Mr. Flint and myself at the mercy of a pickpocket."

She radiated genuineness. "A young boy you gave a position in your home, arranged for his education, and have now accepted into your family." She nodded toward Ling, who had mustered his skates and now moved around the ice as though it had become second nature to him.

I smiled as I observed him laughing as Grace and Alice chased after him. I softened at the kindness of her insight. But she wasn't done with her mission to tout the worthiness of a brother she held in high regard.

"And after spending time in Miss Vello's company, I believe her to be a wholesome woman with admirable values. The people we keep company with reveal a person's substance."

"I can appreciate a sister wanting the best for her sibling. However, regarding relationships and people, I'm learning that what I think is adequate for someone else is sometimes tainted by my fears and what is comfortable for me."

She accepted my words with a nod, and I adjusted my position as Birdie and Merritt returned with cups of cider. She laughed and chatted, and Merritt listened intently. I recalled the aloof way Zane conducted himself when his bride-to-be spoke. I wanted more for my friend, and with the wedding drawing near, I found myself lying awake at night, worrying about what awaited her.

"She is quite lovely, isn't she?" Josie said.

I observed Birdie as she smiled at something Merritt said, and their interactions seemed effortless. "In all regards," I said.

"She's very excited about her upcoming wedding. Finding the love she shares with Mr. Goddard is every woman's dream," she said reverently.

I compressed my lips to withhold my opinion. I loved Birdie too much to damn her marriage in the eyes of others before it had materialized. I hoped Zane would change for her sake, but I held no confidence in his capabilities.

Later, as the sun tucked behind the clouds and our legs ached with exertion, I removed my blades and readied to say my goodbyes.

"My stepmother is hosting a party for her birthday. I would like to invite you both. It promises to be one to remember," I said to Merritt and Josie.

"Do I detect a hint of mischievousness in your tone?" Merritt lifted a brow.

I stifled a grin.

"I don't like it when you get that look in your eyes," Birdie said. "I hope you aren't up to anything."

I jutted my chin and ignored her. "Do say you will come."

"Is this your method for a proper invitation?" Merritt said.

"Perhaps not appropriate, but done in true Kat fashion. Why waste time with a written invitation when you can just blurt out an invite?" Birdie said with a laugh, playfully nudging my shoulder with hers. My heart lifted at her decision not to ruin the day with pretentiousness. Besides, the outing had done her good. Her tense shoulders had relaxed, for the day at least.

We left the Huntingtons with an acceptance to my invitation to Audrey's gala and went in search of my family.

Chapter 31

I HEARD THE ORCHESTRA START TO PLAY AND THE MURMUR OF ARRIVING guests as Colleen put the last touches on my hair. The pins pricked at my scalp, and the addition of false hairpieces guaranteed I'd have a headache by the close of the evening. She styled my hair with a middle part, formed intricate knots, and pinned curls to cascade down my neck.

"That should suit." Colleen stepped back to admire her work before moving to lift the cage crinolette petticoat from the bed. She held it out for me. "We best get ye dressed."

I rose from the vanity, accepted the garment, and stepped into the waist hole. Colleen circled me to assist in pulling the ribbons tight and securing the petticoat. Next I endured the fitting of my corset as she huffed and grunted while yanking and tugging on the ties. Finally she released me when it felt like she'd pushed my insides into my breasts, and my ribs would crack from the pressure.

"Heaven help me," I said as she went to the bed to retrieve the emerald gown I'd purchased for the gala.

She ran a hand over the fabric. "Yeer sisters won't know what to think when ye parade downstairs looking like a proper lady. They will suspect something is up for sure."

I stepped into the dress, and the weight of the flounces only added to the torturing constriction of my attire. For one night, I'd endure the discomfort and all the additional fuss to guarantee I created a statement when I delivered my gift. I caught a glimpse of myself in the mirror and smiled, admiring my reflection and the seamstress's adjustments to the gown's fit.

Colleen placed the black velvet choker with a jet coral cameo pendant at my throat and secured the ribbon.

After she finished, I turned to face her and gripped her wrist. "Remember my instructions."

She pressed at the fabric of her white pinafore, and her concerned eyes met mine. "I'll do as ye request, but are ye sure ye want to do this? Ye won't escape unscathed this time, and I fear I may join ye."

"You will be fine. I will see to it."

I squared my shoulders and strode from the chamber. My shoes pinched, a hairpin seemed to be piercing my scalp, and my breathing felt constricted, but determination pushed me onward to the mezzanine. The music and the guests' voices grew louder as I drew closer. "Well, there is no turning back now," I said to the empty corridor before turning the corner and walking across the mezzanine.

I glanced down at the guests in the hall entrance below and noted the admiration of those observing me. My stomach clenched at the attention, and I turned to focus on the stairs. *Remain upright. Do not fall,* I repeated in my head as I descended.

"Kat," Evelyn exclaimed as I reached the last step. On the arm of Mr. Peyton, she swept toward me, shimmering in a peach taffeta off-the-shoulder gown, a string of pearls with an ivory cameo resting atop her small breasts. "You look radiant." Tears welled in her blue eyes.

"As do you," I said, offering Mr. Peyton a small curtsy. "Mr. Peyton, how do you fare?"

"I am well, Miss Katherine." He placed a hand to his middle

and returned a bow before offering me a broad smile, and the warmth in his eyes held no reservations after our last encounter.

"Splendid. I wanted to extend an apology for my ill manners at the Goddard ball," I said sincerely. "You're a gentleman in all regards and undeserving of my prodding. I tend to be protective when it comes to my family, but something tells me my sister doesn't need saving from you."

"That is benevolent of you. I accept your apology. But, I assure you, I've only the highest respect and admiration for Evelyn." He peered down at my sister, and I sensed the battle was lost even if I had objected.

Evelyn's mouth fixed in a stiff smile; I knew she was apprehensive about me venting my opinions. I kept my voice low, not wanting to generate a stir in the room of New Yorkers. "It appears the South still has a little fire left in them."

Evelyn and Mr. Peyton looked at me, perplexed.

I leaned closer and touched my sister's arm. "The South has indeed won the love of the North."

Evelyn's stiff stance melted, and she embraced me. "Thank you." Tears clotted in her voice, and my stomach twisted with guilt. Nevertheless, I clung to her a little tighter because what I had planned was sure to earn her disfavor.

She released me, and I made my way across the hall entrance, nodding at those who called out greetings.

Through the open double doors leading into the ballroom, I observed Audrey conversing with several ladies. When I entered the room, she glanced at me, and her eyes widened before her expression turned cold.

After Birdie and I'd caught Audrey and the gentleman in the alley, she'd never confronted me on my whereabouts that day. However, since then, she observed me from afar with a cautious and knowing expression. With Papa oblivious to the whole matter, I suspected she thought she'd instilled adequate fear in me over the years to ensure my silence.

In the past, passion had made me act impulsively but with no exoneration. Time had taught me how to guarantee Audrey never again had the upper hand. Waiting for information from Mr. Carson put me on edge for weeks, but I focused on maintaining an aloofness to the situation.

From my position just inside the door, I regarded Birdie and her parents speaking with Merritt. A quick glance around the room revealed no sign of his sister. The Goddards had declined Audrey's invite, and our household had suffered her outrage at their refusal to come to her birthday gala. Nevertheless, Birdie's casual demeanor in the Goddards' absence confirmed it was worth the battle. Mrs. Vello inclined her head and smiled at something Merritt said, and Birdie's laughter echoed. She stood a vision in a copper-colored taffeta gown with pleated layers, passementerie, and a high half-train.

"My darling." Papa strode toward me with widespread arms. I smiled and stepped into his embrace. "What have you done with my daughter?"

I laughed into the warmth of his shoulder, hugging him tightly. Again the guilt I had experienced with Evelyn in the entrance hall surfaced, but I shuffled it away.

Papa released me but gripped my hand and twirled me around. I saw pride in his expression, and I grappled with accepting happiness or reserving myself for fear the affection would vanish as the evening played out. Perhaps I should heed Colleen's concerns.

"Is everything all right?" Papa's forehead wrinkled.

I leaned in and pecked his cheek. "All is well."

When I pulled back, he nodded, but uncertainty shadowed his expression.

I left him as two other gentlemen paused to speak with him and crossed the room to join Merritt and the Vellos.

Birdie caught sight of me and stopped talking in mid-sentence to gasp. She raised her hands and clasped them under her chin before swooping forward to embrace me. "Kat, you have outdone yourself."

Over her shoulder, I smiled at Merritt and the Vellos. I noticed Merritt looked dapper himself in a three-piece dark suit with his light brown waves sleeked back. His gaze swept over me when Birdie released me, and his blue-green eyes glittered with appreciation. My heart skipped a beat as warmth raced over me. He offered a slight bow, and I curtsied. Then I exchanged greetings with the Vellos.

"The fiesta is lovely," Mrs. Vello said. "We were delighted to receive Mrs. Darlington's invitation."

I glanced at Birdie, and she shrugged with a knowing smile. I never had the heart to inform Mrs. Vello otherwise, so I let her believe my stepmother had graciously extended an invite.

"I'm delighted you could make it," I said.

Someone across the room captured Mrs. Vello's attention, and she said, "We will let you catch up. I see Mrs. Tinsel and need to speak to her about her upcoming spring charity bazaar. If you will excuse us?" She tucked her hand in the curve of Mr. Vello's arm, who inclined his head and smiled before allowing his wife to lead him away.

"I couldn't help but notice your sister isn't in attendance," I said to Merritt.

"Josie was feeling unwell, so she thought it best to rest."

"Please send our regards." My body stiffened as Audrey's laugh erupted, and I twisted to locate her amongst the guests. "Tonight is my stepmother's night, and celebrate her we will." I found her beside Papa, holding his arm, feigning for all that their devotion was as pure as my parents' love.

Papa never denounced or mistreated his wife in the privacy of our home or in public. On the contrary, although no love existed between them, he remained a gentleman. I felt inadequate in the presence of the man. Unlike him, I failed to look beyond my aversion for the woman he had brought into our family; in fact my revulsion had compelled me to great lengths to rid us of her. I mulled over my strategy for the evening. Maybe it was a mistake to present her with my gift in front of her guests. My mental arguments leading up to the gala returned. I glanced at Adelaide and Evelyn, smiling and chortling with their gentlemen callers, Mr. Peyton and Mr. Alexander. The evening was full of laughter and enjoyment, and I contrived to disrupt it all. I swayed on my feet, and the warmth of Merritt's hand on my back to steady me reconfirmed my conviction to terminate my plan.

"Are you all right?" he asked.

I never looked at him but mumbled a reply as I noticed a staff member standing at the hall entrance with my gift in hand. My heart galloped, and I excused myself. I hurriedly exited the room as the man turned toward the ballroom.

"Wait!" I gripped his arm.

The man's brow knitted. "Miss Colleen said you'd left strict instructions to have your gift delivered front and center for all the guests to enjoy."

"I've changed my mind. Have it returned to the safety of my chamber."

Above on the mezzanine, Colleen awaited the successful delivery I had assigned to her. I gestured for her to come down, and she darted down the stairs and scurried to my side. "The plan is off. Please see it is returned to my chamber."

"Yes, Miss Katherine." Colleen plucked my gift from the man's arms and hurried toward the staircase.

"Miss Katherine," Mr. Holmes, our butler, said, and I turned to discover him waiting to my left.

"Yes, what is it?"

"There's a gentleman here to see you. He says his name is Mr. Carson."

The room spun at the mention of his name, and my breath caught. What was he doing here? Had he come with information? "Where is he?"

Mr. Holmes nodded toward the front door. "I told him to wait outside, as he wasn't on the guest list."

"All right, I will see to him." I threaded through the guests gathering in the entrance hall, opened the door, and stepped out into the cool of the evening.

At the bottom of the stairs, a man stood in the shadows, away from the gas lamps lining the street. Although spring lay around the corner, my breath billowed in the evening air, and I grasped the marble banister as I descended, cautious of any trace of ice on the stairs.

"Good evening." Mr. Carson stepped from the shadows. "My apologies for showing up at this hour and unannounced, but I figured what I had to share with you wouldn't want to wait."

"It is quite all right." I crossed my arms as goose pimples erupted on my arms. "Let us not wait. What have you discovered?"

"The man you saw in the alley with Mrs. Cullivan is indeed her stepson and the bastard son of her late husband. I have followed your stepmother, and she has visited him at his home in Brooklyn on several occasions. Earlier today, I discovered them in each other's arms. This time it was your stepmother who initiated the kiss."

"On the cheek?"

"No, a kiss shared between passionate lovers. When I inquired with neighbors about the comings and goings of Mr. Harrison, they were suspicious of me, and no one would talk, but I found a reliable source."

"Who?" I took a step closer.

"A scullery maid."

"Disgruntled staff are common. How can you consider her a reliable source?"

"Hear me out." He lifted a hand to quell my doubt. "I cornered her coming up into the street from the kitchen. To my surprise, she bore a striking resemblance to Mrs. Cullivan."

"And?" My chest tightened with intrigue. "What else? Is it her sister?"

"No. After some convincing, the young girl revealed that Mrs. Cullivan was her mother."

I gasped and dropped my arms. "What do you mean, she's her mother?"

"Precisely what I said. Your stepmother is the girl's mother."

"How can this be? How old is the girl?"

"My guess…eight or nine."

"That would mean the girl would've been conceived before Audrey married my father. So why not bring the girl with her to Braxton Hall?"

He shrugged. "Perhaps a widow with no family is more convincing. One cannot understand every foolhardy ploy. In my years, I've witnessed many."

"What else did the girl say? Did you get a name? Or anything else of use?

"Her name is Gwyneth. I'm not certain, but one can assume, if my guess on the girl's age proves right, that Mr. Cullivan died before the girl's conception. Witnessing the relationship between Mrs. Cullivan and Mr. Harrison gives me cause to believe the son could very well be the father."

Could it be? Would she go to such great lengths to deceive a widower with five young daughters when our country was in the middle of a war? Many situations proceeded unnoticed while our country stood divided. Why would Winifred Cullivan's scheme be any different?

"It is all madness. How dare she humiliate my family like this!" I paced in a circle, grappling with digesting the information. "What did she seek by marrying my father if she had so many secrets?"

"In my experience, one who uses the tactic of aliases seeks to hide the truth. Your best bet at discovering the truth is the source." He nudged his head at our home. "Although our encounters have been brief, something tells me your resourcefulness is uncanny."

"I will find out the truth." I anchored my hands on my waist as indignation drummed in my chest. "I will take down Audrey…

Winifred, or whatever her true identity is. She will regret the day she messed with the Darlingtons. I won't rest until she is exposed." I ceased my rant as passersby slowed to listen.

Mr. Carson handed me a folded piece of paper and tipped his hat. "I will be in touch." He spun on his heel and vanished into the night.

I opened the paper and regarded the script. The first step to putting an end to Winifred Cullivan. I folded the paper and hugged myself as tears welled and my vision blurred. How dare she cause so much havoc in our lives…and for what? After a moment, determination took over, and I marched up the stairs. At the landing, I dabbed away any telltale sign of tears and opened the door.

Inside, I shivered from the cold while welcoming the warmth. Then, spotting the staff member I had spoken with moments ago, I signaled to him, and he hurried over to me.

"Miss Katherine?" he said.

"I've changed my mind. It's back on."

"Again."

"Yes." I scowled at him before catching myself and pressing my fingers to my temple. I held out the crumbled paper in my other hand. "Please give this to Miss Colleen and tell her to put it in a safe place. Then have my gift brought into the ballroom."

He hesitated.

"Make it swift," I said.

He jumped, and without any protest, scurried off.

"Kat, there you are." Birdie walked over from the ballroom. Her smile faded as she took one look at me. "What has happened?"

I gripped her arm and pulled her into the shadows of the corner. "Mr. Carson arrived with news."

Her eyes widened, and her hand went to her throat. "By the looks of your face, it is as we figured."

"Worse." I kept my voice slightly above a whisper. "Winifred Cullivan has a daughter."

Birdie shrank back. "What?"

I bobbed my head and quickly filled her in on what Mr. Carson had told me.

"Unbelievable. Why would she not tell your father? Or bring the girl to live with your family? None of it makes sense. Better yet, why not marry her late husband's son and leave your family out of her machinations."

"That, I intend to find out," I said through clenched teeth. "This will indeed be an evening she won't forget!"

I spun to leave, and she clutched my arm. "Whatever you're up to, you must rethink it. If all you state is true, she could be dangerous."

"I am not worried about her." I shook free and marched toward the ballroom, passion thumping untamed in my chest.

The staff member holding my gift strode ahead of me. In the center of the room, he positioned the painting I'd created the day my stepmother smeared the X across the bodice of my day dress. He pulled off the cloth, and I hung back as guests gathered around the painting and chattered amongst themselves. Adelaide and Mr. Alexander joined Evelyn and Mr. Peyton and tilted their heads to examine my work.

A lanky fellow with a few wisps of dark hair covering his head said to another gentleman, "Splendid work."

"The wit of the artist is remarkable."

The other gentleman laughed, and a course of snickers followed.

I drew closer and examined the painting. Three smiling ladies in lavish bonnets and silk gowns embellished with ribbons and lace strolled down the front steps of a grand English estate toward a waiting carriage. Behind them, an auburn-haired chambermaid with hazel eyes followed with a slopping chamber pot in hand. The middle of her bodice bore a bright red X, and spillage from the chamber pot smeared her dress and pinafore. The viewer's eye was drawn to the chambermaid's expression, which spoke of her displeasure and envy as she regarded her mistresses.

"Exquisite," a woman said to her husband. "The artist is unknown to me."

"Yet their artistry seems to have caused quite a stir." He nudged his head at the surrounding guests.

"I must get my hands on it before she does." She stared at a woman I recognized as her rival as she drew near to inspect my artwork.

Due to my distraction, I never noticed Adelaide and Evelyn approach me until someone tugged on my arm.

Evelyn leaned in and said, "You have done it for sure now." But I saw no evidence of the expected criticism in her expression. Instead, her blue eyes twinkled. "It appears the guests don't recognize the chambermaid. At first, neither did I, but after a second look, I realized who the artist intended her to be. I hope our dear stepmother doesn't put it together, for your sake. Or your attempt to humiliate her may switch directions."

Adelaide leaned in to listen in, and I tucked my head closer to theirs and whispered, "After I tell Papa what I've learned about her, none of you will care."

Adelaide's eyes widened. "What have you uncovered?"

"Not here. Later, when the guests leave."

My sisters gulped and nodded in unison. There was a soft outcry behind us. They pulled back, and we turned to regard our red-faced stepmother eyeing the painting with her mouth agape.

Guests turned to look her way, and she swiftly recovered her poise. "Lovely indeed," she said, followed by a fixed smile.

Satisfaction swelled in my chest. As the guests returned to studying the painting, Audrey's eyes met mine, and I saw the promise of death in her hazel eyes.

"Excuse me, Miss Darlington." I turned to face the woman who had appeared overly keen on claiming the painting before her adversary.

"Yes…" My senses whirled with all that was happening.

"The painting. Is it for sale?"

"W-well—"

"Indeed." Adelaide stepped forward.

"The artist. I am not familiar."

"He is a gentleman from Europe," Evelyn said, taking a position on my other side, and I gawked from Adelaide to her. "A family acquaintance from Britain. A fine artist whose works Europeans rush to buy without blinking at the lavish price tag."

A feverish yearning gleamed in her gray eyes. "How much does he want for this particular painting?"

Without so much as a blink, Evelyn rattled off an outlandish number.

"We will take it," her husband said without hesitation. "I will have payment delivered tomorrow."

"Very well," Adelaide said.

The wife appeared ready to burst with excitement as she spun to inform the room that her husband and she were now the proud owners of the painting. Her competitor glared at the couple. The purchaser puffed out her well-endowed bosom and smugly smiled at the other woman.

"I can't believe you two just did that," I said.

Evelyn and Adelaide smiled and turned their backs on the guests.

"We take pleasure in selling your first painting," Adelaide said.

"But the price?" I stood dumbfounded.

"So what? It will serve Mrs. Kennedy right for always trying to outshine Mrs. Mitchell." Evelyn referenced the woman's competition. "Besides, you can call this justice for enduring the brunt of our stepmother's abuse." She smiled at me and then grew serious. "Now, can we please continue to enjoy the rest of the evening? It only has the promise of more splendid revelations to come." She glanced at Mr. Peyton, and they exchanged a secretive look.

I frowned at the interaction and wondered what her words might suggest.

Papa's voice rang out. "May I have everyone's attention, please?"

Evelyn slipped by me and walked to Mr. Peyton's side.

A hush fell over the room. "Evelyn, darling." He extended a hand, and she walked to him, taking a position at his side. He smiled down at her before looking at Mr. Peyton and nodding at him. Mr. Peyton stationed himself next to Evelyn, and I noticed her take his hand in hers in the folds of her gown.

My heart thumped faster as she blushed and peeked up at Mr. Peyton. Papa draped an arm around her shoulder.

"I have an announcement. I am honored to tell you that I will be gaining a son. Mr. Peyton has asked for my daughter Evelyn's hand in marriage, and I wholeheartedly granted it. Their union will bring much joy to our family." He lifted his glass and turned to face Mr. Peyton. "Son, welcome to the family."

Mr. Peyton grinned and dipped his head in gratitude. Tears of joy streamed down Evelyn's cheeks while Audrey stood to the left of them, scowling and none too pleased that her birthday gala had become about Evelyn. Some gave the idea no currency and applauded while others scoffed and tucked their heads together to whisper their displeasure at the blending of Southern and Northern families. In the couple's bliss, they didn't seem to notice. I grimaced and returned my attention to my family.

"Don't tell me you don't approve of your sister's happiness." His breath warmed my ear, and I tilted my head to glance up into Merritt's eyes.

I swallowed back the fear gnawing at me and observed my sister. Bathed in the warmth of their tenderness toward each other, the anguish inside me lessened. "No," I said, suppressing the tears clotting in my throat. "Evelyn's exactly where fate intended."

"Have I misread you, Miss Darlington?" he whispered. "Have you fooled us all? Perhaps you are a utopian in more ways than your thirst for adventure."

I shrugged. In truth, I didn't know what I was anymore. I only knew that my defenses had begun to crumble. I'd grown depleted, warding off change. Observation told me Evelyn's engagement was the first of many to come to our family.

I pivoted and marched out of the room, seeking freedom from the swirl of well-wishers around my sister and her betrothed. Footsteps echoed in the corridor behind me, but I continued my retreat to the library.

Inside, I strode to the fireplace and stood near to warm my chilled limbs. Tears blurred my vision, and mixed emotions consumed me.

"Everything will be all right." His voice murmured behind me, and without consideration, I spun, abandoned all decorum, and threw my arms around him. I pressed my face into the fabric of his coat and wept until I noted the drumming of his heart and allowed the rhythmic sound to calm me. He held me with the tenderness I'd witnessed him bestow on Josie.

I released him and lifted my fingers to pat away tears before smoothing my hair and gown. "Apologies," I said, incapable of looking at him. "I am not one to express my anguish in such an unbecoming manner." I cleared my throat, trying to shuffle away the surge of defeat and loneliness that had plagued me all my life. My face heated at my display of frailty. What must he think of me, a capricious woman who comes unhinged at the slightest issue.

"Think nothing of it. Besides, tears are hardly a weakness but the way one cleanses the heart from suffering," he said tenderly.

His statement made me pause to reflect, and I looked up into eyes overflowing with compassion. "Thank you for your kindness."

He inclined his head. I noticed the dark spot on his chest where the fabric of his coat had absorbed my tears. He followed my gaze and placed his palm over the area. "Do not give it any thought."

I turned, strode to the settee, and sat. "Forgive me, but I can't return to the festivities." I kicked off my shoes.

His eyes widened before a smile took hold. "Ghastly! A woman who reveals her feet in the presence of a gentleman in hopes of enticing him to stay."

My soul grinned, but my face never changed. I gasped and clasped my hands over my heart, conveying a coy demeanor. "Not to mention the risk of scandal. Here we are alone and unchaperoned."

He seated himself next to me, and his knee touched mine, but neither of us moved apart.

"So your sister is to marry," he said.

I glanced down at my fingers and picked at my thumbnail as I mulled over what changes would come to our household. "It appears so. I wonder if Mr. Peyton will try to take her back to Charleston or if they will remain here in the North."

"I guess only time will reveal that."

I rested my hands on my lap and gazed into the fire. "I've spent most of the years after my mother died clinging to the desire to keep my family together. Governed by fear of losing another, I suppose. It was foolish of me to believe I could manipulate fate."

He stretched his legs out in front. "We've all been guilty of desiring to manipulate fate at one time or another."

"I suppose so."

We sat silently engrossed in the fire. I relished the peace between us. No words needed to be spoken.

Then I remembered, and I twisted on the settee to face him. A wave of exhilaration swept over me. "I almost forgot. I have splendid news."

He looked at me, and his brow furrowed. "Oh? What is that?"

"If you give me a few days, I will repay the loan I received from you. Despite the turn of tonight's events, the odds were in my favor. I can't thank you enough for assisting me in my time of need."

"Was the loan fruitful?"

I waved a hand. "I will spare you the details, but thanks to your help, I've acquired the necessary information."

"Splendid." His expression turned melancholy, and his head lowered.

I frowned and wondered at his response. Was he not pleased with the development? As one of New York's well-respected investors and businessmen, he sought to have the money returned, didn't he? What had gotten into him? He behaved as though I'd stolen something valuable from him. I quickly reviewed what had transpired moments before, trying to detect what I could have done to silence him, but I came up blank. I fixed my jaw to avoid shaking my head in dismay. Just when I thought I was starting to figure men out. My fingernails bit into my palms as I waited for him to shake off whatever had overtaken him.

After several painstaking moments, he inhaled deeply and covered my hand with his. I flinched at the gesture and looked into his eyes. What I witnessed there seized my heart. Oh, flummadiddle! Not again. What was it with men?

"Kat…" His voice was barely a whisper.

Just a few months ago, I would've leaped from my seat and thrown his hand away, but I stayed quiet. After all he'd done for me, I figured I owed him that much.

His eyes searched mine as though scouring for my thoughts, and my heartbeat gathered speed.

"I've come to care for you deeply. I don't believe I've cared for another as I do for you. Despite your transparency about never wanting to wed or indulge gentlemen's interest, I suppose I've failed to protect my heart." The vulnerability in his eyes snatched my heart, but I stood and ambled to the fireplace to create space and gather my thoughts. The desire to run never rose in me, which left me confused and questioning myself. Once before, I had allowed a man close enough to get in my head and confuse me. I placed my fingers to my lips, recalling the day in the pavilion.

He came to stand behind me, and I felt the warmth of his closeness. He placed hands on my forearms, and I permitted him to turn me to face him.

"I do not know what I feel. I've never given it much thought." I scrambled to explain myself at the pain in his eyes. "Not that you aren't a worthy opponent."

My attempt failed as he winced at my reference to us being in opposition. My shoulders slumped as the fight to preserve his dignity and whatever existed between us faded. A reckless idea entered my head, and I impulsively stood on tiptoe, leaned in, and brushed his lips with mine. He froze and didn't return the kiss, but then his strong arms encompassed me. I molded to his passion, my mind spinning with how the kiss I shared with him differed from the one between Jude and me. It was as though I went through the motions but lacked the euphoria.

Sensing my disconnect, he pulled back and released me. "I didn't expect that…"

"Nor did I. But I had to know," I said without a hint of regret.

"Know what?"

"If the world would disappear when we kissed."

"And?" Passion glinted in his blue-green eyes.

I shook my head. "I'm sorry. I don't want to—"

"Break my heart?" he said, then chuckled softly.

I nodded.

He lightly gripped my hand and regarded our entwined hands before looking deep into my eyes. Then, in a voice weighted with pent-up emotions, he said, "A heart can dream. But in the end, one can't change fate, can they?"

Again I shook my head, my soul heavy. I grappled with the right words to say to alleviate the defeat in his eyes.

He released my hand and stepped away, then walked to the door. He paused with his hand on the doorframe and looked back at me. He opened his mouth to speak, but then, thinking better of it, he offered me a smile and left.

I returned to sink down on the settee, numb with guilt and heartache. I stared into empty space until Birdie's voice drew me from my slump.

"There you are." Her shoes tapped across the floor, but I avoided turning to look at her for fear she'd detect my feelings. "You just disappeared. As Merritt put on his coat to leave, I stopped him, and he informed me he'd left you in the library. Do you care to tell me what you two were doing in here? And alone, by the looks of it. And why did he seem in a hurry to leave?"

I straightened and squeezed my eyes tight to ward off the sadness gripping me. "Enough with the questions." I pushed to my feet.

"Are you all right?" she asked but never waited for a reply. "I suppose what Mr. Carson revealed tonight is overwhelming."

I nodded, and although the news was important, what had occurred between Merritt and me took precedence. I wanted more than anything to share what had happened with Birdie, but I kept silent. What would she think of me? Like Winifred Cullivan, was I not also a fraud? I had vowed to ward off gentlemen suitors, but instead I threw myself at them and entered into lewd conduct. I'd kissed two men in a matter of months, not through their doing but mine. Maybe I ought to be tamed. The madness in my mind would become my undoing. I had yet to put my finger on how, but I'd concluded that Jude's confession of the love he held for me had fractured me somehow.

I turned to face Birdie, and her eyes dropped to my stocking toes peeking from beneath my gown and then to my abandoned shoes. Her brow pinched. "You've deserted your guests."

"Oh, for the love of New York!" I threw my hands in the air. "They aren't my guests. Or have you forgotten this is my stepmother's party? Besides, I have permanent grooves in my feet from those dreadful shoes. It is a crime, what women will subject themselves to in order to please others. I haven't taken a full breath all night. Colleen has this corset tied so tight, I'm sure I fractured ribs in the process." I bent to retrieve my shoes and marched toward the door.

"Where are you off to now?"

"To my chamber. Are you coming?" I said, never stopping.

"Do I have a choice if I want to visit with my friend?" Her reply dripped with sarcasm, and I smiled, finding entertainment in her rare moments of insolence. "Well, even if it was for a mere few hours, I enjoyed seeing you all dressed up." She fell into step beside me as we ducked into the corridor and made our way to the staff's back staircase. "Your painting caused quite the stir. It took me several moments to identify your stepmother as the chambermaid. Am I to assume that's why you splurged on the gown and arrived at her party looking like the queen herself?"

I laughed and shrugged. "Perhaps."

She gathered the sides of her gown to ascend the stairs, a grin on her lovely face, and shook her head. "Leave it to you. There is no taming you, is there?"

I thought of my predicament with Jude and Merritt. "Oh, I don't know," I said.

Later I changed into more comfortable attire and, free of the myriad of hairpins Colleen had arranged in my hair, I walked Birdie to the door as her parents prepared to leave. I hugged her and promised to visit soon.

After we bade the last of our guests good night and Mr. Holmes closed the door after them, Audrey abruptly turned, ascended the stairs, and disappeared without a word. Papa stared after her with a look of astonishment. Then, after a moment, he heaved a sigh, kissed Evelyn, Adelaide, and me, and headed down the corridor to his study.

"Come." I motioned for my sisters to follow me.

"What is it?" Adelaide said.

"That matter I told you I would tell you about later."

We entered the study as Papa seated himself behind the desk. "Ladies?" His brow furrowed. "What is it?"

Before closing the door, I peeked into the hallway for any sign of Audrey's return. Then I turned and said to my sisters, "You may want to sit down for this."

Their eyes flitted about, but they sat in the armchairs in front of the desk.

"Kat, you have me concerned," Papa said.

"I'm afraid you're about to become even more so." I rubbed my hands together in front of me and glanced back at the door, expecting Audrey to barge in at any moment and declare her innocence. I took a deep breath and focused on Papa. My stomach roiled with concern about what would happen after I informed my family of the truth about Audrey. Would Papa be cross? What if they didn't believe me? "Do you recall me asking for funds some months back?"

He tipped his head as though pondering before recollection glimmered in his brown eyes. "Yes, in fact, I do."

"Well, as you recall, you refused, so urgency pressed me to acquire funding elsewhere."

"From who?" he asked.

"That's neither here nor there. What matters is what the funds were for…" My heart suddenly took up residency in my throat.

"Well, go on." Papa leaned forward and clasped his hands in front of him on the desk.

I wavered a minute longer before I blurted out, "I asked for the funds to hire a private investigator." There. I had said it.

He straightened. "What in heaven's name for?"

My body quivered. What if he didn't understand my logic? I had ventured too far to retreat. "To find out more about your wife," I said, bracing for his rebuke as he tensed and his eyes narrowed.

Evelyn and Adelaide gasped. Yet, to my relief, they remained silent, and for that I was grateful, because their interference would only deprive me of the courage to proceed.

Papa waved a hand. "Go on."

I took a step closer, gripping the paper with the address tighter in my hand. "I hired a Mr. Carson, and over the last months, he has followed her to a home in Brooklyn. The home belongs to the bastard son of her belated husband."

"Wait!" Papa held up a hand, perplexed. "What husband do you reference? She wasn't married."

"So she led you to believe when you sought to make her our stepmother. Mr. Carson said her name isn't Audrey Boseman at all."

Papa's face turned ashen. "What madness do you speak?"

I hurried to continue. "Her real name is Winifred Cullivan. But I'm afraid her alias is the least of your concerns. It appears your wife may have a daughter working as a kitchen wench in the home of her stepson." My courage began to waver as Papa's hands turned to fists on the desk. "The son's name is Joseph Harrison, and I believe she is having an affair with him."

Papa wiped a hand down his face as he absorbed the shocking truth I had uncovered.

Evelyn rose. "How can you be sure?"

I gulped, and a shiver charged down my spine as I looked at her and back to Papa. "Because I saw her the day I purchased the gown I wore tonight. I followed her and a man into an alley. There I witnessed them exchange some words before he drew her into his arms and kissed her. In my dismay at what I saw, I caused a kerfuffle, and I believe she saw me. I got away but went straight to Mr. Carson to reveal what I had witnessed. He had information of his own to share and took a sketch of the man, which led him to reveal the information he came by to inform me of tonight. He has, on several occasions, seen the two entwined in a lover's embrace, as I believe he referred to it."

Papa scraped back his chair and stood to pace the floor.

My sisters and I exchanged nervous looks, and they came to my side.

"Leave me," he said. "I have much to digest."

As obedient daughters, Adelaide and Evelyn hurried toward the door. I paused and swallowed hard, eyeing him hesitantly. "I have an address for the home of Mr. Harrison." I withdrew the sweat dampened, crumbled paper from the folds of my dress and placed it on the desk.

He strode forward and retrieved it, looked at the address, and dropped with a thump into his chair. He shooed us with a hand. "Close the door after you."

We obeyed and had barely made it a few steps down the corridor when an object crashed against the closed door, followed by a string of curses.

We froze, and my sisters regarded me uncertainly. Evelyn wavered on her feet, and silent tears cascaded down her cheeks. "It is all so dreadful."

Adelaide stared numbly at the wall. "Poor Papa."

I embraced them both. "I'm sorry to cause you pain."

"To know is better than not to know," Adelaide said in a haunted voice.

Evelyn remained silent but nodded.

"The truth is in Papa's hands now," I said.

They mumbled their agreement.

Upstairs, I looked in on Grace and Alice and found them resting peacefully in their beds with their hands clasped together, as they had done to fall asleep since they were small. I perched on the edge of the bed and watched their chest rise and fall while considering the innocence on their faces. Had I done right by trying to free them from Audrey's clutches? Or would they suffer more when our stepmother found out she was exposed?

I stood, leaned down, and smoothed back a tendril of hair covering Grace's face, then placed a kiss on her cheek. Then circled the bed to regard Alice, and concern picked at me over how she worried so, because even in sleep, her brow was wrinkled. "Do not fear, little sister. All is well." I reiterated the words Dorotea had soothed us with since we were children. I caressed her cheek and pulled the quilt up under her chin.

I exited their bedchamber, leaving the door open the way Alice liked it, and walked down the corridor.

Voices drew me to the mezzanine, and I peeked around the corner.

"Mr. Holmes, have Mr. Kelly prepare a carriage."

"At this hour, sir?"

"Yes. I have a matter that needs attending. Please make it swift."

Mr. Holmes bowed his head. "Straightaway, Mr. Darlington."

After Mr. Holmes dashed off to do his bidding, Papa put on his frock coat and retrieved his hat. Then he paced the floor while he waited. I tiptoed down the corridor to my chamber.

After changing into my nightclothes, I climbed into bed and gazed at the ceiling until just before dawn, and when sleep finally came, my dreams were filled with Audrey's rage. "You will pay for this," she chanted.

The next day her words echoed in my head like a song that wouldn't cease.

Chapter 32

PAPA VISITED MR. HARRISON, AND AFTER SOME PERSUADING, THE man admitted to the years he'd blindly devoted himself to Winifred because he'd loved her. That love had produced their daughter, Gwyneth. Winifred abandoned the girl at birth, and as the girl got older and bore a striking resemblance to her mother, she demanded he place the girl in the kitchen and out of sight. He revealed he and his stepmother had been lovers before his father died and how as a young man of barely seventeen, he'd fallen victim to her manipulation. He'd never wanted her to marry Papa, but she'd left him with an infant daughter to pursue the Darlington money and counted on Papa never returning from war. Only days prior, she revealed what he'd always known in his heart: that she held no love for him but sought to obtain his inheritance. He had terminated all ties with Winifred and expressed shame for the depths he'd fallen to, all in the name of love.

Winifred's greed left us all reeling. My sisters and I grieved for her daughter and what she had suffered. What kind of mother would disown her own child? I gave thanks for Mama because we'd never questioned her love.

Papa had compiled all the information he needed to confront Winifred, and he set a plan in motion the following morning. He informed her he would file papers with the courts to divorce her on the terms of infidelity. He agreed not to put her out on the street; the family would remain in the city for the warmer months, and he'd permit her to return to Braxton Hall until the courts honored his request for a divorce. His decision to offer grace created a dispute between us. But he reasoned one does not tame malice with malice and that he wanted to bring the least amount of humiliation upon his family. He also wouldn't allow us to sway him to retract his proposal.

That day Winifred packed up her belongings, and as she stood in the entrance hall while Mr. Kelly loaded her trunks, she looked up at me where I stood on the mezzanine.

"You will regret the day you thought you could take on me. Mark my words." Venom blazed from her hazel eyes.

I gripped the railing tighter.

Papa marched forward. "Out now! Before I throw you into the streets and recant my offer to let you peacefully retire to the country."

She turned to regard him and cooed, "Very well, Philip darling. This won't be the last you hear of me." Then she whirled, marched out of the house, and down the stairs.

Mr. Holmes closed the door after her, and satisfaction crossed his face. Papa tilted his head to regard me and offered me a sad smile before turning and walking down the corridor toward his study.

In the following weeks, Papa's despondency at the mockery his wife had made of him lessened. Our gloom shifted to excitement, with Birdie's wedding days away. I half expected the Goddards to renege on my invitation, but they never did.

One afternoon, as I sat in the courtyard painting, basking in the warmth of the day and the perfume of cherry trees in full bloom, Mr. Holmes announced, "Miss Katherine, Mr. Williams is here to see you."

My heart jumped, and I looked over my canvas to discover

Mr. Holmes and Jude walking toward me. The wide grin on Jude's face sent a wave of warmth over me. He looked good.

"Thank you, Mr. Holmes," I said, pushing to my feet.

"Miss." He placed a hand to his middle and tipped his head before turning and ambling back toward the house.

"Look at you. A lawyer!" I said.

His hazel eyes gleamed. He extended his arms and took a deep bow. "At your service, miss."

"It's official. You're back for good."

"For now," he said. "I plan to set up my practice in Brooklyn."

"I am delighted. I have so much to tell you. Come, let us sit in the pavilion." I slipped my hand into the curve of his arm, and he covered my hand with his.

"It's good to see you, Kat. I've missed you."

"I had begun to wonder, as you didn't write."

"I wasn't sure what to say after how we left things last time."

"You mean how you left things. That was all your doing, not mine."

"If memory serves, it was you who kissed me," he said with a chuckle.

"Yes…well." My face heated with the recollection. "You mustn't speak about such matters so candidly." I released his arm as I stepped into the pavilion.

I seated myself and smoothed the fabric of my pink rose and cream satin day frock. He sat next to me, and my body warmed at his closeness. I snuck a peek at him and found him gazing over the courtyard. My heart beat faster as I took in his short-cropped hair and the healthy glow of his skin and the strength of his jaw. My gaze lingered on his lips, and the memory of our kiss sent a shiver through me.

Sensing my gaze, he looked at me, and I quickly lowered my eyes.

He took my hand in his where it lay on the bench between us and squeezed it gently. A million glowing fireflies swarmed in my stomach, and my eyes fell to our intertwined fingers. Something had changed between us, and I could not deny my love for him.

"A lot has transpired in your absence," I said.

"To what do you refer?" His eyes searched mine.

"Many things, but if I am honest with you, I've changed."

"How so?"

"It started with that day in here and what happened between us. I've had a lot of time to think."

He never moved, but I noted a hint of anticipation on his face.

I rubbed my thumb over the top of his hand, and my chest tightened. "There's something I must tell you, and I'm afraid you may not think too highly of me when I've finished."

"I doubt anything you've done can surprise me. I got over my surprise years ago. But do tell me what it is that appears to trouble you."

I shifted to face him and described every detail of the night in the library with Merritt. I saw every emotion one can imagine play across his face, and when I'd disclosed all there was to tell, I waited nervously for his reaction.

"You kissed him?" he said.

"You make it sound so terrible."

He released my hand and stood. "You've had fool-hearted ideals before, but this one beats them all."

A lump lodged in my stomach, and a quilt of shame encircled me. "Please don't let your pride make the kiss something more than it is."

"How would you like me to look at it?" He spun around and placed his hands on his waist.

I stood, and indignation erupted within me. "Don't act as though you lay any claim to me. I am not yours to condemn."

Hurt flickered in his eyes, and he lifted a hand to swipe it over his face. "That is fair, but it doesn't mean it bothers me any less that another man declares his love for you, and you see fit to kiss him in the process."

"He didn't declare his love for me," I said hotly before retracting an inch. "Well, not in the way you did. You got in my head. Maybe this is all your fault."

"So be it!" He thrust his hands into the air. "Blame me if that makes you feel any better. We aren't children anymore."

"Do you think I don't know that?" I folded my arms across my chest, trying to quell my trembling hands.

"This Huntington fellow aids you in hiring an investigator and seeks to take advantage of you."

"Do not blame him. He is a good man with admirable traits. Let's not forget I kissed him."

"But he never stopped you. What were you thinking? A lady shouldn't be flaunting herself around—"

"You didn't see a problem with a 'lady flaunting herself,' as you call it, in broad daylight. Or do you forget you openly welcomed my kiss, that day in the pavilion?" I thrust a hand at him.

His posture eased, and he lowered his gaze. "It is true."

"Your hurt runs untamed, and I'm sorry for my part in that. Truly I am." My hackles settled. "I don't want to fuss with you. You only recently returned. I don't want our first moments together to be filled with tension and rash judgment, spewing words we can't take back. We care for each other too much."

"You are right. Perhaps we should talk more about this matter another time," he said.

I nodded.

"But we will talk about it," he said firmly.

"Yes, yes, yes." I waved a hand of dismissal. I took his arm and led him toward the house. "I'll have Chef Bernard prepare us a luncheon. Grace and Alice will be delighted to see you."

"And Mrs. Darlington?"

"You needn't worry about her. Papa has filed with the courts to divorce her."

"That is quite the development," he said. "What forced his hand?"

"I will tell you everything later. But I knew she would hang herself one day, and so she did. And the private investigator only hurried the process along." I rolled my shoulders back and smiled.

"Well, I suppose I have Mr. Huntington's money to thank for relieving you of her, and the privilege to enter your home without being thrown into the streets," he said with a grin.

I laughed as he opened the door, and we strode inside.

Chapter 33

FOR HOURS I STARED AT THE DOCUMENTS IN FRONT OF ME. THE words faded in and out as the day ahead summoned my thoughts. Weeks had passed since the day Kat arrived with the repayment for the loan. During the visit, my mother greeted her with hostility, but I'd interceded. The bruise on my heart from Kat's rejection of my affection for her burrowed deep within me, but my respect for her remained steadfast.

"Your carriage is ready, sir." Mr. Murphy, our butler, stood at the study door.

"Thank you." I gathered the documents I had spent the morning reviewing and placed them in the drawer.

Josie floated into the room, looking charming in a China blue silk gown. Her hat already pinned on, she held a closed umbrella in her lace-gloved hand. "I simply can't wait to see what Birdie looks like. I lay awake last night dreaming of what today would be like."

I chuckled and pushed to my feet. "I'm sure you did. I saw you checking the clock all morning."

She blushed, and her gray-blue eyes gleamed a deep blue, reflecting the hue of her gown. "A wedding is a romantic affair."

"Let's go and get it over with," I said, not in the mood to

witness Elizabeth Vello and Zane Goddard declare their love before God and all of New York. In our encounters, I'd deemed her not only a rare beauty but a decent woman unlike the pretentious Goddards.

"Are you two coming?" Mother said from the entrance hall.

"Yes, Mother." Josie's body tensed, and her bliss diminished. She hurried to join Mother while I followed at a pace more to my liking. I had yet to figure out what to do about the difficulties Mother added to our lives.

The carriage ride to the cathedral was no different from any other day in the Huntington family. Mother ranted and numbed her children's minds with criticism and contempt. The wound in my soul reflected on Josie's face, and again I grappled with how to cut out the rot within our household.

When we arrived, Josie's excitement about the wedding had evaporated under Mother's onslaught. Mechanically, I helped the women disembark. My body thrummed, ready to snap at any moment. My head and jaw throbbed from clenching my teeth to avoid lashing out at Mother. I pushed through the protocol and obligation demanded by society, although rage simmered within me.

Wedding guests emerged from carriages and stood in groups conversing while others moved toward the cathedral. I walked my family to the door. "You two go on and take a seat. I will be in shortly."

Mother scowled and clucked her tongue. "Where are you going at a moment like this? Surely there is nothing more pressing than escorting your family to their seats."

The peaceful sound of the harp drifting from inside and the joy that usually occurred on a wedding day couldn't lessen the affliction of her irritation. I turned my back to Mother and touched Josie's arm. "I will be back."

Her eyes flitted from Mother to me, and she nodded.

"Disgraceful. A complete embarrassment." Mother gripped Josie's arm and hauled her through the open doors.

I stared after them before dropping my gaze to regard my trembling hand hanging at my side. Then, with the urgent need to breathe and dislodge Mother's nagging from my head, I hurried down the stairs and ducked behind the cathedral, putting distance between myself, the cathedral, and the murmurs of guests. The thrashing of my heart confirmed my existence, but my world grew darker each day. I feared how long I could survive before I did something I'd regret. My nights had become restless, consumed with dreams of my father standing over my mother's bloodied body; then, as an observer, I realized it wasn't my father but me. The horror would pull me from the dream, and I'd sit upright, my body drenched in sweat. Maybe it was Mother's plan to drive us mad? Without us, she would hold our family's money.

I straightened my shoulders and squeezed my eyes tight to shut out the noise and the whispers in my head. I gasped as someone collided with me, and I opened my eyes and instinctively reached out to steady them. I sensed the delicacy of the one in my arms and glanced down into panic-filled eyes.

"Miss Vello?" Her hair hung in disarray, and her face was swollen from crying and a blemish that marred her cheek. "Are you all right?"

She never stepped from my grip but placed her hands on my chest. "Please, I beg of you, take me away from here."

My throat tightened, and I looked behind her for her pursuers or whoever had caused her so much anguish. "What has happened?" I eyed her cheek.

"He struck me. Kat was right. I told him the truth, and this is the result. If I wed him this day, I will suffer unthinkable cruelty at his hands." Her dark eyes were drowning in sorrow, and the affliction I witnessed mirrored the vast ache in my soul.

"This is his doing?" I lifted her chin to inspect the mark.

She nodded, and my jaw tightened.

"Do you want me to accompany you home to your parents?"

"No, I can't face my parents. I am dishonored. He coerced me to give myself to him with the rationale that we were to wed and no one would ever find out. If I do not marry him, I am ruined. No man will ever want me. He will see to it." She pressed her forehead against my chest and wept.

I glanced around, unsure what to do, but desiring to offer the woman comfort, I wrapped her in my arms. A fool idea conjured in my head out of nowhere.

"I will marry you," I blurted.

She pulled away and searched my eyes. "What…Why would you want to marry a disgraced woman? And not only that, I bear Indian blood."

I frowned, taken aback by her bold confession. I had thought the Vello ancestors were Spaniards, but her family's origins were no concern to me.

"One may consider it a fool idea," I said of the recklessness I proposed, "but you find yourself in need of a man who will honor you. And I find myself consumed with misery, seeking to bring happiness to my life. Perhaps in time we could give that to each other."

"But what of Kat?" she said. "I know you hold affection for her."

"I do, but she told me she couldn't return my sentiments."

Her brow knitted. "She never informed me that you two discussed the matter, but that's Kat." A small smile parted her lips, and she dabbed at her cheeks.

"Could you marry a man who held feelings for your friend?"

"Perhaps in time, those feelings will dissipate." She echoed my words of moments ago while staring at my shirt collar as though considering the idea more seriously. Then indignation flickered in eyes as dark as two pebbles, and she tilted her head back to examine my face. "If you're certain, I will take you up on the offer to become your wife. I will forever be indebted to you."

"No, I will not enter into a contract in that manner. I am no more certain than you, but I, too, want to forget everything. But we'd best not wait, or rational thoughts may set in, and we might both change our minds," I said with a smile.

A flicker of uncertainty gleamed in her eyes before she suppressed it and returned my smile.

"I will get the carriage. You stay out of sight, or someone may talk us out of this reckless idea."

She nodded, gripped the sides of her wedding gown, and ducked between two buildings to wait. I turned and jogged back to the cathedral and breathed a sigh of relief to find our private carriage hadn't moved. Our coachman stood conversing with another driver.

"Merritt," Josie called. I spun to discover her walking toward me. "Where have you been? Are you all right? The wedding is delayed because no one has seen the bride."

"I am fine. Perhaps better than I've ever been." I gripped her narrow shoulders. "Do you trust me?"

Her brow pleated. "You know I do."

"I will be gone for a few days. Can you manage Mother until I return?"

"Yes, but won't you tell me what has you looking like a little boy about to set out on an adventure?"

I pulled her to me and kissed her forehead. "Trust me. Now go back inside before Mother comes out and tries to stop me."

She turned back to the cathedral steps, and I swung to instruct the coachman. I ducked into the carriage and shut the door. Exhilaration warmed my body, and nerves knotted in my gut when the carriage lurched forward. I was mad, all right. Only a fool would steal another man's betrothed and wed her on their wedding day.

Chapter 34

Kat

WHISPERS AND SUSPICIONS RIPPLED THROUGH THE WEDDING guests when Birdie never showed up for her own wedding. My worry over her disappearance negated any pleasure I may have felt over Zane's humiliation. He'd stood at the altar with his eye on the doorway, pearls of sweat beading his brow, and as time ticked by, his hands balled at his side, and his face turned scarlet. Finally, after almost an hour had passed and there was still no sign of the bride, Zane stormed down the aisle and out the door. The Goddards ducked out of the cathedral after him.

A few days passed before Mrs. Vello sent word that Birdie had contacted her and told her she was safe. She said she couldn't go through with the marriage when she saw how Zane had reacted when she revealed her heritage. She said she needed time to collect herself but would return soon, and she was sorry for any grief she may have caused them.

The Goddards quickly worked to tarnish Birdie's reputation, and as rumors spread, I ached for my friend and her family. Mrs. Vello's true heritage was revealed. Those with the shallowest of hearts disparaged and shunned the Vellos. However, those who truly cared for the Vellos remained steadfast.

One afternoon after Birdie had been gone almost a week, I walked down the corridor and ducked my head in to check on my young sisters in the music room. Alice marched around the room dressed in knight's armor while Grace pretended to be a distressed princess. I paused to watch them a moment before smiling and walking on. Adelaide and Evelyn had gone out but were expected back soon. Papa had met a client at a coffee house to negotiate a partnership.

The door knocker rapped, and Mr. Holmes hurried to answer it. When he opened the door, I halted, and my heart leaped into my throat when I saw her standing on the landing with a smug look. Never pausing for Mr. Holmes to speak, she barreled by him and marched into the entrance hall. "Where is the Indian lover?" she said loud enough for the household and those on the street to hear. "Find her and get her out here." In her gloved hand, she held an envelope.

Mr. Holmes glanced nervously into the street, where passersby paused to eavesdrop. He swiftly closed the door to protect our family from whatever had caused her to become unhinged. "Mr. Darlington left strict orders that you're never allowed in this home again. Leave now, or I'll have you removed." He rolled back his shoulders and thrust out his chest, endeavoring to stand up to Winifred's height.

She spun and jabbed a finger in his face. "I am not leaving until I tell her it's all a fraud, this family she sought so hard to defend and have me removed from. I will be the one who has the last laugh."

Mr. Holmes nodded to another male staff member who had emerged from a nearby room at the onset of the noise. Mr. Holmes snatched her arm, and I drew closer as the other man took her other arm and hauled her toward the door. She dug in her heels and fought them all the way. When she caught sight of me, her protest turned to feverous glee. She craned her neck to regard me, her eyes flashing as the men dragged her. "I always knew it. I thought your parentage was a scandal your family tried to keep hidden.

You aren't a Darlington! You are but a discarded child whose own mother never wanted her."

Her dagger landed in the middle of my heart, but I strode forward, uncertain of the madness she spewed. Mr. Holmes struggled to open the door and maintain a grip on his prisoner.

"What lies do you spout?" I scowled.

Before they shoved her out the door, she tossed the envelope onto the floor. "It's all in there."

When they released her, she straightened her hat and walking dress and sent me a gleaming smile that spoke to the poison racing through her veins. The door closed, and I walked over to retrieve the envelope. Her words screamed in my head as I looked at the name scripted on the front: Dorotea Ruiz. I looked around for Dorotea, but my need to understand Winifred's accusations pressed me forward. I opened the envelope with trembling fingers.

Over the years, I had gathered enough understanding of Spanish to translate the words.

My dearest friend,

My mistress is dead, and the threat of her finding out the girl still lives is over.

"Mr. Holmes, I heard commotion…" Dorotea called from the mezzanine.

I glanced up from the letter as her words ceased.

"Señorita? Is everything all right?" She hurried down the stairs, glancing at the rattling letter in my hand.

"Is it true?" I said, my voice but a whisper.

"Is what true?"

"Winifred said I'm not a Darlington. This letter is addressed to you and—" I glanced at the signature "—Marta says that the girl's mother is dead. Am I the girl she is referring to?"

Her eyes widened, and she placed a hand on her chest. A

chasm opened in my gut. I had trusted her to always be honest with me.

"Let us send word to your father. We will discuss everything."

"No, you will tell me everything now." I shook away the hand she placed on my arm as heat trailed up and down my body, and numbness took hold.

Dorotea's face was filled with anguish as she appeared to grapple with what to say.

"Just tell me the truth," I pleaded.

"I think we should wait for your father—"

"Tell me now!" I clutched her arm and pressed my fingers into her flesh.

Dorotea shooed the staff who had gathered around, led me into the salon, and closed the door before turning to face me.

I stood trembling before her, and she gripped my shoulders to steady me. "It is true." Tears clotted in her voice. "You were not born a Darlington, but you are one in all senses."

I stumbled back. "What do you mean? Be frank."

"Please, I beg of you, wait until your father's return. Let him tell you everything." She stepped forward in an attempt to embrace me.

"No!" I took several steps back until my knees knocked against a table. "I knew." I shook my head. "Deep down somewhere, I always knew I didn't belong." Tears blurred my vision, and I lifted my hand to look at the flesh I believed was kissed by the sun and my love for the outdoors and adventure. I brushed away my tears with my hand and regarded Dorotea's skin. "We are the same. You and I."

She nodded with tears cascading down her cheeks. "Your parents never wanted to hurt you."

"They aren't my parents," I said. "Everything is a lie."

"No, señorita." She walked toward me, but I put up a hand to stop her.

"Tell me who I am, or I promise to flee this house and never return." My hands balled at my sides, and I leveled a hard stare at her.

She gulped, appearing not to know what to do with herself. "You were born in a country estate outside of Barcelona. Your mother was a duchess. After she had failed to provide your father with a son, he threatened to seed one with her younger sister. Your father was away on a crusade when your mother found out she was pregnant, and she told no one of her pregnancy. But when she could no longer hide it, she retired to the countryside to wait to give birth. My friend, Marta, was her handmaid. When you were born and not a boy, your mother…" Her voice faded, and pain and worry pinched her face.

"My mother what?" I strode forward and gripped her hands. "Please, Dorotea, tell me every detail. I must know."

She pulled me into her arms and pressed my head to her shoulder, smoothing my hair as she had as a child. "S-she ordered your death upon the rocks of the cliffs," she whispered.

Pain stabbed my heart, and I crumpled into her. She gripped me tight to hold me upright, until I pushed away. "Why did Mama and Papa never tell me?"

She extended her hands for understanding. "How does one tell a child their mother could be so heartless? Also, if your mother found out you still drew breath, they feared she'd send someone to finish the job."

I gasped for air as the shock of it all became too much. Then I burst into tears and fled the room.

The butler stood in front of the front door, which was still open. "Mr. Holmes, prepare a carriage," I told him.

"Good afternoon, Mr. Holmes," Evelyn said, gleefully walking into the entrance hall with Adelaide at her heels and a groomsman following with their packages.

"Never mind." I bolted by my sisters, who gawked at me.

I gathered the sides of my day dress and raced down the stairs. "Mr. Kelly, wait," I called out as he prepared to slap the reins and take the carriage around back. I darted to the front of the carriage. "Get me out of here, and make it swift."

"Send for Señor Darlington. Tell him he must return at once. It's urgent," Dorotea called, fear in her voice.

"Kat!" Evelyn and Adelaide hurried down the stairs.

I opened the carriage door, climbed inside, and had hardly closed the door before I pounded on the roof to signal Mr. Kelly.

"No, wait," Evelyn called out as the carriage lurched forward.

Misery burrowed up from my soul, and I placed my face in my hands and wept. When I had no more tears, I hiccupped and heaved a sigh. How could a mother be so cruel? How could she not want me? Why…why did no one ever tell me? Endless questions raced through my mind before a face interrupted my thoughts, and the need for comfort took hold. I struck the roof, and Mr. Kelly slowed the team and steered the carriage to the side of the street. I opened the door and gave him an address.

I closed my eyes to absorb the truth of what Dorotea had told me as the team took off. I considered the tenderness Mama had bestowed on me and how she would draw me onto her lap. I'd look up into blue eyes so full of love and devotion. She loved me. Papa…believed in me and accepted my views and candor without judgment. I wasn't easy to love, but he loved me nonetheless. He had never picked favorites between my sisters and me and appreciated us for our differences.

When the carriage stopped, I leaned forward and waited for Mr. Kelly to open the door.

"Here ye are, Miss Katherine." His thick, unruly gray brows lowered. "Will ye be all right, miss?"

"Yes. Please wait for me." I took his extended gloved hand.

He tipped his hat.

I walked by him and up the steps to the home and rapped the door knocker. The door swung open. "Hello, Mr. Washington. Is Jude home?"

"Why yes, Miss Darlington. He's in the courtyard. Do come

in." He placed a gloved hand to his middle and stepped back to permit me entrance.

I stepped inside and waited for him to guide me down the corridor and out the double doors to the courtyard. The fragrance of peonies wafted down the corridor, accompanied by the melody of a robin. But my grief denied any appreciation of such beauty. I walked after the butler on leaden legs as he shuffled across the stone path at a pace slowed by age.

Jude sat at a black wrought iron table in the center of the courtyard with a newspaper spread before him. The sun made his skin glow, and my heart jumped at the sight of him. Unaware of our approach, he lifted the silver coffee pot to fill his cup before looking in our direction. He halted in mid-motion, and his hazel eyes widened in concern when he spotted me.

"Mr. Williams. Miss Darlington is here to see you."

"Thank you, Mr. Washington." He pulled to his feet and quickly dismissed him. Then he strode forward, frowning. "What is it, Kat? Are you all right?"

My words hung on my tongue as I tried to formulate how to speak aloud the truth I had discovered.

He cupped my shoulders with his hands and gazed into my eyes, seeking an answer. "Your family, has something happened to one of them?"

I shook my head, and again the pain of the truth became too much, and I flung my arms around him, clinging to the one solid thing in my life. "It's horrible," I said into the fabric of his white shirt. The fresh scent of his spicy-woody cologne sang to my senses. "Everything is wrong."

He wrapped me in his arms, and I welcomed the strength and protection I found there. I took what felt like the first full breath since Audrey's revelation.

He rested his chin on my head. "Tell me what troubles you so."

I hesitated a moment, feeling that if I spoke the words, it'd make it real. "I-I am not a Darlington."

His breath caught.

"Winifred arrived with a letter from Barcelona. She sought revenge, and she got it." I pulled back and peered up into his eyes. "I don't know all the details because Papa wasn't home when I ran out. I know my birth mother was a duchess in Spain. And..." Tears snatched my words.

Tenderness and love radiated from his eyes, and he lifted a hand to cup my cheek. "It is all right."

I placed my hand over his as tears freely cascaded down my cheeks. "Because I was not a boy, she ordered my death upon the rocks."

He winced when the words fell from my lips, and the ache in his heart blazed in his eyes. "Oh, Kat." His thumb caressed my cheek.

"I am such a fool." Hopelessness overwhelmed me. "I believed in a fantasy of our family. I took pride in being a Darlington. I loved my parents and sisters with all my heart. I'd die for them. But now—"

"It changes nothing," he said, releasing my cheek. "It does not matter what the truth is. The Darlingtons loved you enough to take you in and to love you like their own." He tipped my chin up with a finger, forcing me to look at him. He used his thumb to dry my tears—to no avail, as they continued to silently flow. "How can one not love every part of you?"

Something inside of me melted. "What would I ever do without you?"

He inhaled deeply. "You shall never find out." His promise soothed my aching soul. His gaze shifted to my lips, and then he looked deep into my eyes. An invisible force drew me closer, and his eyes asked for permission. I nodded, and he dipped his head, and his warm lips met mine. The world and pain gave way, and I kissed him hungrily. I wrapped my arms around him, and my fingers pressed his back. I needed him. To be without him felt like dying at that moment. My mind raced as my body spasmed with desire. Whatever was happening between us, I wanted more.

When our lips parted, I rested my head against his chest, and he held me with so much tenderness that I felt my heart would fracture more from the love and gratitude teeming inside me than the pain of learning the truth of my parentage.

"You got in my head, you know," I said with a small laugh. "I couldn't sleep. I couldn't concentrate. All I could think of was that day between us in the pavilion. It's all your fault, you know. All the distress you've put me through."

He chuckled, then said, "It has happened, hasn't it? You've fallen in love with me."

"No," I said gently, baffled at how my fervent rejection of the love between a man and woman had evaporated. "Well…I don't know, really. I know everything feels right when I kiss you and you hold me in your arms."

His arms tightened around me. I felt safe and loved beyond measure. I never wanted the moment to end. I frowned into the warmth of his chest as I mulled through the thoughts and emotions rushing through me. What if this was love?

"Jude?"

"Umm," he whispered, his throat thick with contentment.

"What if I have?"

"Then we take one day at a time," he said, kissing the top of my hair.

The security in his words, and his understanding of how change terrified me, tugged at my heart. I wanted to discover what loving Jude entailed, and I would fight for whatever was happening between us.

Too soon, he released me and entwined his fingers with mine. "Come, your family will be worried about you. I will see you safely home."

Chapter 35

I ARRIVED HOME AND OPENED THE DOOR TO ENCOUNTER PAPA PACING the entrance hall floor, and Dorotea and my two older sisters huddled together, comforting each other. Papa halted, and they all turned to face Jude and me as we stepped inside.

"Kat!" Evelyn and Adelaide dashed forward, their cheeks and eyes red from crying. They embraced me and squeezed me until I couldn't breathe.

"We were so worried you wouldn't return," Adelaide said when we parted.

"We never knew," Evelyn said and burst into tears again.

"But it changes nothing." Adelaide gripped my hand and gave it an extra tug. "You hear me?"

I nodded and glanced at Papa as he and Dorotea walked forward. He never spoke but reached out, pulled me into his arms, and held me fiercely. His heart hammered against my ear and I heard him gasp. "I am sorry, my darling. So very sorry."

"I know, Papa." I held him tight.

"Thank you for bringing my daughter home," Papa said to Jude when he released me.

I tilted my chin to look at Jude. He peered down at me, and I smiled at the love I encountered in his eyes.

"Of course, sir." Jude inclined his head at Papa.

"Kat! Kat!" Alice and Grace bounded down the stairs, their faces grave with concern, but no tears stained their cheeks. I suspected the truth had been withheld from them, probably for the best, until I comprehended it myself.

"I've been dreadfully worried," Alice said. "What happened?"

"We are glad you didn't run away for good." Grace took my hand in hers. "I wanted to when Mother lived with us. I snuck food from the kitchen and packed a suitcase, but I was too scared of the dark to go on my own."

I smiled through my tears and caressed her face with a hand.

"Girls, your sister is home now. Why don't you go to the courtyard? It's a beautiful day. I need to speak to your older sisters," Papa said.

"Is everything all right?" Alice bit at the corner of her mouth, her eyes flitting to each of our faces.

Papa offered them a sad smile and nodded.

"I will take my leave," Jude said.

"Can't you stay for a little while?" Grace peered up at him with large, dark, pleading eyes. It was a look I recognized all too well because I'd fallen victim to my youngest sister's charm far too often. "You could come with us to the courtyard." She never intended to give up easily.

The turmoil of disappointing her pulled at his expression. "Your family has matters to attend—"

"It appears, Mr. Williams, you've managed to enchant the Darlington women," Papa said before winking at me. My cheeks heated, and Evelyn and Adelaide exchanged a smirk. "Perhaps you would be so kind as to oblige my younger daughters for a while."

Jude nodded, and Grace and Alice squealed. He draped his arms around their shoulders and led them away. "Why don't you tell me what mischievousness you've all been up to."

I heard the girls' chatter until the door clicked closed.

"All of you come. There is much to discuss." Papa directed

his gaze at me. Then he walked down the corridor to the library, with us following behind.

I tried to ease the hammering of my heart. Was I prepared for any more disclosures? Surely the truth couldn't be any more sinister than what had already been exposed.

Inside the library, Papa gestured for us to sit and closed the door behind him.

I seated myself on the settee, and Adelaide and Evelyn sat on either side of me. They each took one of my hands in theirs while Dorotea took a position behind me, resting a hand on my shoulder. Surrounded by support and love, I regarded Papa as he came to stand in front of us.

After a brief moment, he cleared his throat and centered glistening eyes on me. "Kat, the truth about your parentage was revealed in part today, and I may regret how it was delivered for the rest of my life." He lifted a finger to his lip, attempting to quell its quivering, and again cleared his throat. "S-so often, your mother and I grappled with how we would tell you, but she left us while you were still too young to burden you with an ugly reality."

Tears pooled in my eyes again as I observed his struggle to say the right words.

"Then, drowning in my own despair over the loss of your mother, I failed to meet my daughters' needs. Once you confronted me that day and forced me to remove myself from the past, I fought to compensate for the lost time." He extended his hands in a plea for understanding. "Miss Ruiz and I discussed that we needed to tell you the truth, but I feared the pain you would suffer. It's a parent's duty to spare their children from any unnecessary heartache…"

"I understand, Papa," I said, my heart melting at his pained expression.

His shoulders slumped. "I fear I have caused you more hurt by not dealing with the matter sooner. I wanted to choke the life from Winifred when Miss. Ruiz told me what she'd done, but my contempt was prompted by guilt over my lack of courage to tell you. But know this, Katherine Darlington." He tilted up his chin and looked me square in the eyes. "Darlington blood may not run in your veins, but you were loved from the moment the servant girl, Marta, arrived at our villa and placed you, but hours old, in your mother's arms."

I gulped and gripped my sisters' hands a little tighter. Evelyn removed a lace handkerchief from the cuff of her afternoon frock and dabbed the corners of her eyes.

"Later that night," Papa continued, "we placed you in a cradle next to our bed and watched you peacefully sleeping. Your mother took your little hand in hers, and instinctively you wrapped your finger tightly around hers and wouldn't let go. We made a promise to you that night that you would never know what it was like to not be loved, and you would be a Darlington in all ways that matter."

"And you have kept that promise, Papa," I said. "Forgive me for running off."

"There is no forgiveness needed. Winifred's ruthlessness is in-comprehensible, and I regret the day I brought her into our home and what this household has suffered at her hand—and you most of all," he said. "I ask that you find forgiveness for a father too afraid to lose those most precious to him."

I stood and went to him. He embraced me as though never intending to let go and kissed the top of my head.

"I love you, Papa."

"And I you, my daughter."

I released him and returned to my sisters, who hugged me.

"Nothing changes between us." Adelaide, attempting to con-vince us all, reiterated what she'd said in the entrance hall.

"Yes, it does," Evelyn said.

My heart skipped, and Adelaide and I gawked at her.

She smiled and said, "I will see my sister as a woman of strength and conviction and not as someone I need to change. You're the force who kept our family together through times when we didn't know how to go on."

"Thank you." I brushed away tears as my heart overflowed with happiness. "You Darlingtons are making me weak."

Everyone laughed, and Dorotea favored me with a look of deep affection and wiped away tears of her own.

Papa headed for the door. "I'll be right back," he said, returning moments later with my younger sisters and Jude. The younger girls raced to my sisters and me.

"Jude, perhaps you should stay," Papa said. "Any man capable of taming the heart of a lioness has won my respect."

Jude bowed his head in acknowledgment and stood quietly inside the closed door with his gaze on me. I smiled at him before turning my attention to Papa as he spoke.

"Miss Ruiz." Papa motioned for Dorotea to join him, and she swept forward to take a position at his side. He took her hand and regarded her the way he had Mama. My heart expanded with warmth. Papa had fallen in love with our governess, a woman worthy of taking a place at his side. Although no one could ever fill Mama's shoes, Dorotea Ruiz was the next best choice, and our love for her was unwavering. I envisioned Mama smiling from heaven at the union. She'd want Papa to find happiness with a woman who possessed the compassion and devotion to treasure her daughters as she had.

My sisters and I exchanged looks of excitement, and we huddled together in anticipation.

"It pleases me to inform you that the courts have honored my request to divorce Winifred, and tomorrow I'll see she is removed from Braxton Hall. Miss Ruiz and I cannot remain living in this house together unwed. I made a mistake once before and married a woman without consideration of how you all would welcome a new stepmother." He smiled at Dorotea and then returned his attention to us. "Miss Ruiz and I desire to marry, and we seek your permission."

"Yes!" we squealed in unison. Alice and Grace jumped up and down, clapping their hands.

Papa laughed, and Dorotea's eyes pooled with tears. My sisters and I raced forward to embrace them.

When we parted, Papa said, "We will marry in private as we do not want to take away from Evelyn's upcoming wedding. Also, if it is all right with you, afterward we seek to take a honeymoon. Do you think you can manage affairs here while we are away?"

"Of course, Papa," Evelyn said. "You needn't worry about a thing. Us Darlington women are a strong breed."

As my family chattered about the excitement unfolding in our lives, I took a step back, and Jude joined me, encircling my waist with his arm. I leaned my head against his shoulder and observed the beauty and healing power of empathy and kindness filling the room. Life hadn't granted me a birth mother who was capable of loving me, but it had provided me with a family and a man who loved me unconditionally. Winifred's news had gutted me, but I believed the abundance of love in my life was strong enough to heal the gaping mother wound inside me. For love was, indeed, the compass that had guided me home.

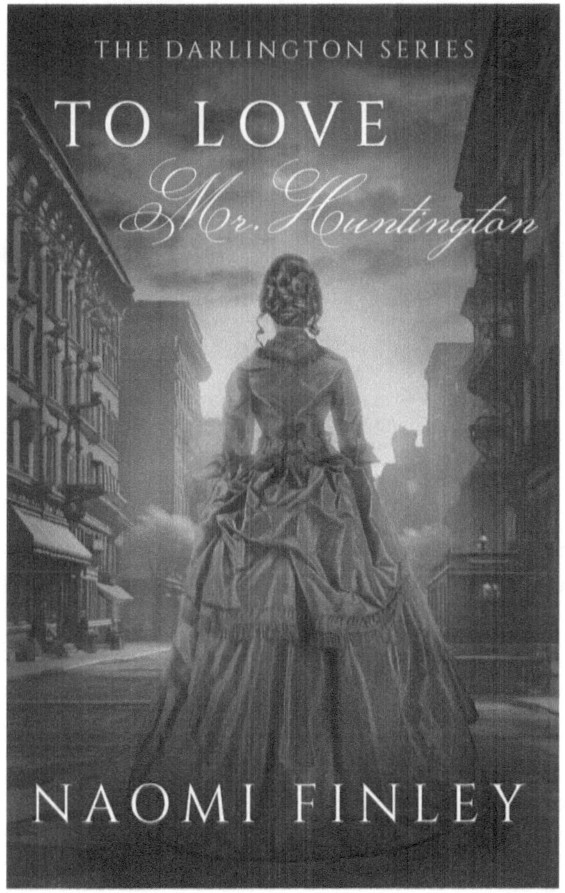
THE DARLINGTON SERIES
TO LOVE
Mr. Huntington
NAOMI FINLEY

Chapter 1

Birdie—Manhattan, New York, 1871

SWEAT TRICKLED DOWN MY BACK AND DAMPENED MY FOREHEAD AS I sat fidgeting in my family's carriage on the way to the cathedral. The anticipation over my wedding gown, designed by the highly sought-after Madame DeRose, had been at the forefront of conversations amongst the ladies of New York since the Goddards announced my engagement to their son. The ivory dress was constructed of the finest silk and embellished with hundreds of tiny pleats and intricate details. And like most brides, I fantasized about my soon-to-be husband's reaction when he saw me walking down the aisle. However, as we drew closer, the gown's weight restricted my breathing more than usual.

The union between myself and Zane Goddard, the son of an influential Manhattan family, had been an event people looked forward to with great excitement. But my enthusiasm had waned, replaced by anxiety and confusion.

"Madame DeRose did a splendid job on your gown," Mama said, snapping me from my musing.

Across from me, Mama's dark eyes gleamed with pride and excitement for the day ahead and the promise of a good life for me.

For her sake, I forced a smile, but my heart pounded faster, and my throat tightened at the pressure to please my parents and avoid bringing reproach upon them. I looked away to peer out the gap in the curtain, grateful that the side of my veil shielded my welling eyes from her. I considered my future husband and the love I held for him. The previous night, I'd lain awake for hours, mulling over my best friend Kat Darlington's advice for me to tell Zane the truth about my heritage before we wed. Then, when exhaustion overtook me, I drifted into a restless sleep filled with nightmares.

Mama's enthusiasm about my wedding was at odds with the emotions swelling in my chest. My inner lip was tender and raw from my constantly gnawing at it all morning. Nausea roiled in my stomach. What was I doing? To enter into a marriage founded on secrets would eventually lead to failure. I had become more convinced of it in the weeks leading up to today.

"Are you all right, darling?" Papa said in his usual soft voice.

I regarded him and fought to keep my tears at bay. "Yes, Papa." I nodded and smiled tenderly.

He frowned. "Perhaps it's wedding jitters that have caused the look of distress I've noted since you came down this morning." He nodded at my hands knotting the yards of veil piled around me.

Mama's eyes narrowed as she studied me. Then she brightened. "I'm sure that's all it is. All brides are nervous on their wedding day." She leaned forward and gripped my hand, lowering her voice as though Papa couldn't hear her. "You aren't concerned about your wedding night, are you?"

I felt my face flush, and a twinge of shame rippled through me. My parents would be disappointed if they knew I'd given myself to Zane. "No, Mama," I said, and she released my hand.

The carriage slowed and pulled to the right, and my heart thumped in my ears. Mama lifted a gloved hand and brushed back the curtain to peek outside. The murmur of guests arriving filled the sunny afternoon, and the driver moved the carriage down the street and stopped some distance from the guests.

"I need to speak with Zane," I blurted, and Mama and Papa gawked at me.

Mama, a superstitious woman, gasped before collecting herself. "No one must see the bride before she walks down the aisle, especially the groom."

"Please, go and fetch him," I said urgently. "I wish to speak to him alone. And ask the driver to pull the carriage around back."

"We will do as you ask." Papa moved to open the door.

"Very well, but I don't like this. Not one bit." Mama shook her head.

Papa stepped out and turned to offer Mama a hand. She pressed her lips together and disembarked but shifted to say something to me. Papa intervened and closed the door.

"Nicolas, you are too soft with our daughter. She has had you wrapped around her finger since she was born." The carriage muffled Mama's voice, but not enough that I couldn't make out my parents' conversation.

"And you care too much what society thinks. If our daughter wishes to speak to Zane, I will do what it takes to calm her mind," Papa said before instructing the driver.

Through the gap in the curtain, I observed them walking back toward the cathedral. The carriage lurched forward. I released the breath I had been holding and pressed my head back against the carriage wall. I squeezed my eyes shut to cut off the threatening tears. I remained so until the carriage pulled to a stop some moments later. Opening my eyes, I folded my hands in my lap and composed myself before the carriage door was yanked open.

"Elizabeth, for heaven's sake, what is the urgency?" Zane's voice was deep with agitation.

The anxiety I often felt when he became agitated churned inside me. "Don't cause a scene. Please come inside." I waved a hand at him.

He grumbled under his breath but climbed in and settled on the seat across from me. His eyes ran over me with appreciation;

however, no compliments fell from his lips. I had become accustomed to his lack of affirmation of appearance or good deeds. Any words of tenderness faded once I'd yielded to his coercion to lie with him some months after our betrothal. After our lovemaking, something changed in him, and he no longer felt the need. I regarded the man I loved with all my heart, the man I was moments away from walking down the aisle to wed. His wavy blond hair lay slicked back and glistening, and his unsmiling, steel-blue eyes stared at me, waiting for an explanation.

"I-I…" I swallowed hard, my words catching in my throat. My courage began to wither as his jaw tightened, and my insides quivered. "There is something I must tell you before we wed."

He arched a brow. "Then out with it." The bluntness and cold way he regarded me gave me pause. Perhaps the nerves of the day had gotten to him too.

"There is something that has been troubling me, and I can't marry you without telling you the truth," I blurted before I could change my mind.

His eyes flashed with a hint of concern before he gave me a blank stare.

"I haven't been honest with you. Well, I never lied, but I withheld something from you."

He straightened, and his eyes narrowed. "What is it you've kept from me?"

"I've wanted to tell you. Honestly, I did."

"Elizabeth, be frank," he said as though I was a child.

My fingernails bit into the palm of my hand. I locked gazes with him. "It is about my heritage."

"What about it?" For a moment, I saw a hint of vulnerability on his face.

"My father's ancestors are from Spain, and so was my mother's father, but my grandmother was Mohican."

His mouth dropped open, and he paled before regaining his

composure and running a hand over his face. He leveled a hard look at me. "So you are telling me I am about to marry a savage?"

"Zane, please," I pleaded, leaning forward to reach for his hand. But he jerked it back as though my very touch repulsed him. Tears clotted in my throat. "What does it matter? We love each other and have committed to a life together."

"The shame you bring to my family. People will mock them and me," he said through clenched teeth. He lunged forward and gripped me by the throat.

I gasped and cried out, but his fingers tightened. His hot breath stung like a hot iron on my cheek. I gawked at him while clawing at his hand to free myself.

"You've ruined me." His face turned crimson, and his eyes looked deep into mine.

"Please." My cry came out as a hoarse whisper. "You're hurting me." I felt the pressure of restricted blood flow to my brain, and frantic tears trickled down my face.

Murder shone in his eyes. Black spots clouded my vision, and my surroundings spun. Then he released me with a shove. I slumped against the seat, gasping for air and rubbing my throat.

His jaw taut, he straightened his double-breasted frock coat.

"I am sorry," I said. "I will have my parents tell our guests the wedding is off."

He snapped his head back to look at me, and before I could block it, he reached out and stuck me across the face. I cried out, shrinking back into the corner and cradling my cheek.

"You will do no such thing." He kept his voice low. "You will go through with this wedding, and you will tell no one what you have revealed to me today. Do you understand me?"

I nodded.

"You will pay dearly for this. I promise you one thing—your life will not know comfort."

The devil himself shone in his eyes, and Kat's warnings rang in my head. She had been right about marrying him. How could I have been so blind? I hung my head, never looking up when he exited the carriage, and the door shook on its hinges as he slammed it behind him.

I glanced around the empty carriage as panic took hold. I plucked the veil from my head, ripping out strands of hair in my haste. I threw it on the seat, opened the carriage door, and stepped out. My surroundings remained blurred. Not knowing where I intended to go, I gathered the sides of my gown, turned away from the cathedral, and broke into a run.

Blinded by tears, I sprinted aimlessly until I collided with a solid form. The impact knocked the wind from me. Hands gripped me to keep me upright, and I glanced up into the face of Merritt Huntington.

"Miss Vello?" His blue-green eyes gleamed with concern. "Are you all right?"

I never stepped from his grasp, instead placing my hands on his chest. My legs threatened to give way at any moment, and my brain whirled with the madness that had transpired in the carriage. *"You will never know comfort,"* Zane's words echoed in my head, and fear like I'd never known before clutched my chest. "Please, I beg of you, take me away from here."

He looked over my head as though searching for pursuers. "What has happened?" He observed my cheek, and grimaced.

More than ever, I needed a friend. I couldn't go through with the marriage or face my parents. The truth was, I was a coward, and the shame of it all shrouded me. "He struck me," I said. "Kat was right. I told him the truth, and this is the result. If I wed him this day, I will suffer unthinkable cruelty at his hands." I scoured his eyes, seeking an ally, and glimpsed the ache ripping through me reflected in his eyes. But, consumed by hysteria, I lacked the capacity to reflect on what plagued him.

"This is his doing?" He tenderly lifted my chin to inspect the welt.

I nodded, and his jaw tightened.

"Do you want me to accompany you home to your parents?"

"No, I can't face my parents. I am dishonored. He coerced me to give myself to him with the rationale that we were to wed and no one would ever find out. If I do not marry him, I am ruined. No man will ever want me. He will see to it." I pressed my forehead against his chest and wept until his following words silenced me.

"I will marry you."

I pulled back and again searched his eyes. "What… Why would you want to marry a disgraced woman? And not only that, I bear Indian blood."

Taken aback by my candid confession, he frowned. Desperation and fear drove me to reveal all my secrets to a man I barely knew, but one who had radiated kindness in his dark, brooding way.

"One may consider it a fool idea," he said. "but you find yourself in need of a man who will honor you. And I find myself consumed with misery, seeking to bring happiness to my life. Perhaps in time we could give that to each other."

"But what of Kat?" I said. "I know you hold affection for her."

"I do, but she told me she couldn't return my sentiments." His expression softened—a softness I'd never witnessed in Zane's face. He was in love with Kat.

I frowned. "She never informed me, you two discussed the matter, but that's Kat."

He loved my best friend, and I was a fallen woman. The Goddards would surely make both our lives challenging. And what of Kat? Would she be angry with us? But she loved Jude. She just didn't know it yet. My mind focused elsewhere. The protection of a husband, one that came with the influence Merritt Huntington would provide, felt like my only option to build a barrier between the Goddards, my family, and myself. I had witnessed the tenderness in how Mr. Huntington interacted with his younger sister Josie. Indeed, goodness existed within him. Yes, perhaps he was right. I offered him a nervous smile and blotted at the tears staining my cheeks.

"Could you marry a man who holds feelings for your friend?" he said.

"Perhaps in time, those feelings will dissipate." I focused on the collar of his shirt and mimicked his earlier words. What madness had we conjured up? I tipped my head up to study his face. "If you're certain, I will take you up on the offer to become your wife. I will forever be indebted to you."

"No, I will not enter into a contract in that manner. I am no more certain than you, but I, too, want to forget everything. But we'd best not wait, or rational thoughts may set in, and we might both change our minds," he said with a mild smile.

I quelled all common sense and returned his smile.

"I will get the carriage. You stay out of sight, or someone may talk us out of this reckless idea."

I nodded, gripped the sides of my wedding gown, and ducked between two buildings. I peeked back at Mr. Huntington as he turned and dashed toward the cathedral. Then I pulled back and rested my head against the building, my heart hammering in my ears. I had started the morning as the soon-to-be Mrs. Zane Goddard, and if everything worked in my favor, I would become Mrs. Merritt Huntington. Fear strummed through me but simultaneously, a twinge of excitement.

Several moments passed before a carriage rolled down the alley and stopped. The door opened, and Mr. Huntington stepped out and waved for me to hurry. I dashed forward and slipped my hand into the warmth of his.

"Are you sure about this?" I asked him.

"No surer than you, I'm certain." Mischievousness flashed in his eyes. "Now let's get you inside before I'm witnessed stealing the bride."

I smiled, ducked into the carriage, and arranged my flounces of fabric around myself. He entered and sat across from me before striking the carriage roof with a hand, signaling the driver onward.

"What is the plan?" I eyed him with anticipation.

"I've instructed the driver to stop so we can purchase you a dress that won't make us so conspicuous. We can hardly blend in while you're wearing the gown of the century. Afterward, we will head to the train station and purchase tickets to Connecticut."

I frowned. "Why Connecticut?"

"It's far enough away that the influence of the Goddards won't bear weight. I doubt the registry can provide us with a marriage license today, but we will apply first thing in the morning."

In the brief time since we'd formulated our outrageous plan, he'd put significant consideration into the outcome. Perhaps I was naive, but his thoughtfulness concerning the predicament I found myself in comforted me.

I pushed away the nagging of logic and clasped my hands in my lap. "I hope you don't come to regret this choice."

"That makes two of us," he said calmly, but the dark, mysterious demeanor I had come to associate with him remained. "I must warn you, I am not an easy man. I will make you no promises except one."

I swallowed hard and stared deep into his emotionless eyes, trying to read his soul. "Which is?"

"My mother will have much to say about this arrangement. You won't find a friend in her. Her agenda is self-serving and never for the good of the family. Furthermore, I've been told I am complicated. But I promise you, you will never feel the blow of my hand."

My nerves thrummed.

"Not so wonderful an arrangement, is it?" He regarded me with inquisitive eyes.

I shrugged, but perspiration dampened my neck. Was I bartering one miserable existence for another?

"Do tell me, Miss Vello: are you willing to marry a man who can promise you nothing but this one thing?"

I considered my options and the scorn I'd face from the Goddards and society. I recalled Zane's wrath in the carriage and unconsciously raised a hand to cradle my throat, again sensing his fingers as he sought to crush my trachea. "It's a risk worth taking," I said with a heavy sigh.

About the Author

Naomi is an award-winning author living in beautiful British Columbia. She loves to travel and her suitcase is always on standby awaiting her next adventure. Her fascination with history and the resiliency of the human spirit to overcome obstacles are major inspirations for her writing and she is passionately devoted to creativity. Naomi is married to her high school sweetheart and she has two adult children and two dogs named Egypt and Persia.

Sign up for my newsletter: authornaomifinley.com/contact